Mais ⟨...⟩ ⟨...⟩or
of over one ⟨...⟩ she's
writing strong, ⟨...⟩working cowboys, dissolute princes
or multigenerational family stories, she loves getting
lost in fictional worlds. An avid knitter with a dangerous
yarn addiction and an ave⟨...⟩ Maisey
lives with her husband and three ki⟨...⟩on.
Check out her website, maiseyyate⟨...⟩d her on
Facebook.

Susan Stephens is passionate about writing books set
in fabulous locations where an outstanding man comes
to grips with a cool, feisty woman. Susan's hobbies
include travel, reading, theatre, long walks, playing the
piano, and she loves hearing from readers at her website
susanstephens.com

USA Today bestselling, award-winning author **Lisa
Childs** has written more than eighty-five novels.
Published in twenty countries, she's also appeared on
the Publisher's Weekly, Barnes & Nobles and Nielsen
Top 100 bestseller lists. Lisa writes contemporary
romance, romantic suspense, paranormal and women's
fiction. She's a wife, mum, bonus mum, an avid reader
and a less avid runner. Readers can reach her through
Facebook or her website lisachilds.com

One Night...

One Night...
to Scandal

MAISEY YATES

SUSAN STEPHENS

LISA CHILDS

MILLS & BOON

First Published in Great Britain 2022
By Mills & Boon, an imprint of HarperCollins*Publishers,* Ltd
1 London Bridge Street, London, SE1 9GF

www.harpercollins.co.uk

HarperCollins*Publishers*
1st Floor, Watermarque Building,
Ringsend Road, Dublin 4, Ireland

ISBN 978-0-263-30559-3

MIX
Paper from
responsible sources
FSC™ C007454

This book is produced from independently certified FSC™ paper to ensure responsible forest management.

For more information visit: www.harpercollins.co.uk/green

Printed and Bound in Spain using 100% Renewable electricity at
CPI Black Print, Barcelona

THE QUEEN'S BABY SCANDAL

MAISEY YATES

To Jackie, Megan, Nicole and Rusty.

Finding true friends who understand you, relate to you, make you laugh and even try to politely respond to the 100 raccoon pictures you send them a day is a rare thing. I think it might even be magic.

Thank you for being my friends.

CHAPTER ONE

QUEEN ASTRID VON BJORNLAND had never been to a club before. But she was reasonably familiar with the layout of the Ice Palace, nestled in the Italian Alps, hidden away from commoners and social riffraff—as defined by Mauro Bianchi, the billionaire owner of the establishment—in spite of the fact that it was a place she'd never before visited.

She and Latika had done an intense amount of research on the subject prior to hatching their plan, and image searches of the facility itself had been involved. Though, the findings had been sparse.

Mauro was intensely protective of the image of the club as exclusive. And the only photographs that existed were photographs that had been officially sanctioned by Mauro himself, and included only the main areas, and none of the VIP locations that the many articles Astrid had read stated were stationed throughout the club.

Her palms were sweaty, but she knew that the invitation that she held in her hand was good enough.

Latika had assured her of that. And Latika was never wrong.

When Astrid had been looking to hire an assistant the year before her father had passed, she'd made discreet inquiries among the circle of dignitaries and royalty she knew, and Latika had appeared the next day. Polished, sleek and just a bit too good to be true.

It hadn't taken long for Astrid to realize Latika was hiding something.

"I had to get away from my father. He's a very rich man, and looking to consolidate that wealth by marrying me off to a man who is... He's not a good man. I will need to stay out of the spotlight completely. So all of my work will be done quietly, efficiently and with me out of the picture."

That was all Astrid had needed to hear. She knew all about the looming specter of potential arranged marriages and overly controlling fathers.

And so, she had hired Latika on the spot.

She was a whiz of an assistant—and had become an even better friend, and ally—and able to conjure up near magic with the snap of her fingers. In this case, magic had included: an excuse for Astrid to go to Italy, a car rented on the sly, an extravagant and extravagantly skimpy designer dress, jewels and shoes, and a near impossible invitation to the party.

And now Astrid was standing and waiting behind the thick velvet rope, in line, for entry.

Astrid had never waited in a line before. Not once in her life.

Astrid had never waited full stop.

She had been born five minutes before her twin brother, Prince Gunnar, much to the dismay of her father and the entire house of nobility. And that had essentially set the tone for her entire life.

A tone that had led to this particular plan, as dangerous, unlikely and foolhardy as it was.

All of those adjectives had belonged to Latika. Who had scolded Astrid the entire time she had aided her in putting the plan together.

Latika had *many* opinions, but none of them really mattered. Both in terms of what she would help Astrid accomplish, and in terms of what Astrid would choose to do. She would make happen whatever Astrid asked her to make happen. And that was the simple truth of it.

Astrid tugged at the hem of her impossibly short white dress. It was daring, and nothing like she would wear in her real life, but that had been part of the plan.

She could not look like Queen Astrid. If her brother found out, he would come down to the club and physically drag her out. Not to mention if any of the various government officials found out, they would do the same.

But she was doing what had to be done to wrest control of her kingdom into her own hands. Control of her future.

She would find other ways if need be, but this plan had come together with so much expert timing that Astrid was willing to chance it for several reasons.

And, she had been willing to wear a gown that was essentially a suit jacket with nothing beneath it. The neckline gaped, showing curves and angles of her body she normally kept well hidden.

Her red hair was loose, cascading over her shoulders, and she was wearing a single, long emerald on a chain, which swayed perilously between her cleavage and made her feel like she was drawing attention.

Of course, if she wasn't drawing attention to her cleavage, then she was calling attention to her legs, with that abbreviated hemline in the sky-high heels. And perhaps her rear, where she knew the white dress clung with a kind of saucy cheekiness. At least, that was what Latika had told her.

But the final thing that Latika had said to her as she had dropped her in front of the queue for the club was that she absolutely had to be back out at the curb by two in the morning.

The timing was essential, and if she missed the timing at all, not only could the plan be in jeopardy, but Latika's job *certainly* would be. And by extension possibly Latika herself, given that her position at the palace had been insulation for her for the past three years.

Astrid was the figurehead for her country. And she had power, it was true. But her father's antiquated board, along with the elected government, had authority and if something was ever put to a vote, whether it be a member of staff or law, then Astrid would be outweighed. It would be thus, she had been assured, even if Gunnar had been made king. Even if he were not born five minutes *after* his sister.

Though, Astrid was not convinced of this.

And she had found a loophole. And that loophole was why she was here.

It certainly had nothing to do with Mauro Bianchi. Not in the personal sense. She didn't even know the man, after all. But she knew about him. Everyone did. A self-made billionaire who had risen up from abject poverty thanks to his grit and determination.

In Astrid's opinion, had this been the Middle Ages, he would have been a marauding conqueror. And as she was dealing with arcane laws more firmly in the Middle Ages than in the modern era, that had only made him all the more attractive to her as she set about hatching her plan.

She took a step forward in line as all of the people

shuffled upward, and she found herself facing a large, grim-looking bouncer with a pronounced scar running across the length of his face.

She squared her shoulders, and then, changed tactics. She arched her breasts outward instead, and rather than affecting her typical severe glance, she went with a pout, just as she and Latika had been practicing in her hotel room tonight before they had gone out.

"Here is my invitation," she said, somehow feeling like she hadn't quite gotten down the simper that the other women in the line had thrown out when they had presented their invitations to the bouncer.

But it didn't matter. The invitation—while for a person who didn't exist—was for the person she was playing, and it was legitimate.

"Of course," he said, looking her over, something he did in his gaze that Astrid had never had directed at her before. "Enjoy the party, Ms. Steele."

He kept the card firmly in his hand, and ushered her inside.

It was a strange and wondrous place, some rooms carved entirely of ice, and requiring coats for entry, others fashioned of steel and glittering lights, everything fading into each other like a twisting, glittering paradise.

Astrid had grown up surrounded by luxury. But it was not a modern luxury. Not in the least. It was velvet and drapes, gold and ornate wrought iron. Cold marble and granite.

This was color, twisted metal and light. Fire and ice all melded together in an escape for the senses that verged on decadent.

There was a dance floor that was suspended up above a carved icy chamber. It glittered and twisted, casting refracted light all around. Railings around the outside of the platform prevented the revelers from falling below. She had never seen anything quite like it.

It was like something from a dream. Or a fairy tale.

If fairy tales contained house music.

And for the first time, a slight thrill went through her.

She had come about this entire plan with the grimness of a general going to war.

At least, that was what she had told herself. She had told herself that it had nothing to do with the fact that she wanted one night of freedom.

Had told herself that Mauro Bianchi had not been her target because he was attractive. Because he had a reputation for showing women the kinds of pleasure that was normally found only in books. No.

She had told herself that he was a *strategic* target.

A man with no royal connection or blood, which would make the claiming of her position even more unquestionable. Had told herself that a known playboy was sensible because as an unpracticed seductress, she would need a target that would have very low resistance.

Because she knew where to find him.

She had told herself all of those things, and the more she had read articles about him, the more she had seen images of him, his face, his body, the dark tattoos that covered his skin...

She had told herself that none of that mattered. That his beauty was secondary, and indeed only a perk in that it was a genetic point of desirability.

But now that she was here... Now that she was here in this club with dance music wrapping itself around her skin, and the thrill of her deceit rocketing through her like adrenaline, a smile spread across her lips.

Freedom.

This was a moment of freedom. A moment to last a lifetime.

Yes, she was doing this to claim the maximum amount of freedom a woman in her position ever could. But even so, she would go back to her life of service when all this was said and done. But this… This was a moment out of time.

Not a moment to think about the future. Of what it would be like to finally have the power over her country she deserved. To finally get out of her father's stranglehold. Not a moment to ponder how the ache of loneliness she felt inside might finally be assuaged by holding a child of her own. A child she would love no matter what.

She was Alice, through a looking glass. Not Astrid.

And she was going to seduce a man for the first time in her life. Possibly the last.

All she had to do was find him. And then she saw him, there could be no mistaking him. He was up on a platform above the dance floor, surveying the party below. It could be only him. That dark, enigmatic gaze rolling over the crowd with an air of unquestionable authority.

Astrid was royalty in Bjornland. She was the queen.

But there was no mistaking that here in this club, Mauro Bianchi was king.

The king of sin, of vice, of pleasure.

The kind of king who would never be welcome in a state and steady nation such as hers. But the perfect king for tonight.

She took a breath and made her way over to the stairs, thanking a lifetime of deportment for her ability to climb them with ease even in those spiked, crystal heels she had on her feet. She let her fingers drift along the rail in a seductive manner, the kind that she had been warned against as a girl. She had been taught to convey herself as cool. Sexless, really.

She was the first female monarch in Bjornland since the 1500s. The weight of the crown for her could never have been anything but heavy.

Her father had ever been resentful of the fact that it was the daughter who had been born first. Resentful. Distrustful. Doubtful.

But her mother… It was her mother who had made absolutely certain that there would be no creative shifting of birth orders.

Astrid had been born first. And her mother had had the announcement issued with speed and finality.

Her mother had also made sure that Astrid's education had been complete. That she had been trained in the art of war. Not just the kind found on the battlefield, but the kind she would face in any and all political arenas.

There was a ruthlessness, her mother had told her, to all rulers. And a queen would need to hone her ruthlessness to a razor-sharp point, and wield it with more exacting brutality than any king.

And so she had been instructed on how to hold herself, how to be beautiful, without being sexual.

She was throwing all of it away right in that moment. Allowing her hips to sway, allowing her fingertips to caress the railing like she might a lover.

She had never had a lover.

But it was the aim of tonight.

And so, she could forget everything she had learned, or rather, could turn it upside down in this place that was like a mirror of her normal life.

That was how she felt. As if she'd stepped through the

looking glass. As if she was on the other side of wealth and beauty. Not the weighted, austere version, but this frivolous palace made of ice. Transient and decadent. For no purpose other than pleasure.

She tossed her hair over her shoulder, and the moment she stepped onto the dance floor, she looked up.

Her eyes collided with his.

He saw her. He more than saw her.

It was as if there was an electric current in the air.

And so she did something she would have never done on any other day when her eyes connected with a strange man's from across the room.

She licked her lips. Slowly. Deliberately.

And then she smiled.

She tossed her hair over her shoulder and continued onto the dance floor.

There were many women, and men, dancing by themselves and so she threw herself into the middle of them, and she allowed the rhythm to guide her movements.

She knew the steps to any number of formal dances. Music composed to complement a dance, not music created to lead it.

But she let the beat determine the shift of her hips, the arch in her spine. And for one, wonderful moment she felt like she was simply part of the crowd. Exhilarating. Freeing.

And then she felt the crowd move. But it was more than that. There was a change in the air. In everything around her.

And she knew already what it meant.

The king was on the dance floor.

She turned, and she nearly ran into a broad chest, her face coming just to his collarbone.

He was wearing a black jacket, black shirt with the top two buttons undone, exposing a wedge of skin and dark hair, tantalizing and forbidden—in her estimation—as no dignitary she had ever encountered would approach her without his tie done up tight.

She looked up, and her heart nearly stopped. And then when a smile tipped his lips upward, it accelerated again.

Photographs had not prepared her.

She'd first seen him in a gossip magazine a year ago when Astrid had brought in a copy of a particularly vile rag that had featured a scandal about Astrid's brother—who had not spent life on his best behavior in the slightest.

But it wasn't Gunnar and his naked exploits with a French model that had held Astrid's attention. First of all, it was a terribly *common* thing. Even for Gunnar. It wasn't even interesting.

But second of all…

Oh, there had been Mauro. A dissolute, salacious, scandalous playboy in a tux, with one woman clinging to each arm as he walked through one of his clubs.

Her heart had stopped. The world had stopped.

That was just a photograph.

In person…

He was beautiful, but not in the way the word was typically used. He was far too masculine a thing for simple beauty. Hard and angular like a rock, his jaw square and sculpted, his lips perfectly shaped and firm looking. His dark eyes were like chips of obsidian, the lights on the dance floor swallowed up in those fathomless depths.

He said nothing, and she wouldn't have been able to hear him anyway. But he extended his hand, and she took his, the spark of fire that ignited at that point of contact spreading over her body like a ripple in the water. Sharp and shocking at its core, rolling over her wider and broader as it expanded.

He caught her and held her against his body.

She had danced with men before, but they had not held her like this. So close that her breasts were crushed to hard, muscular midsections, a large commanding hand low on her back.

And then his lips touched her ear, his whisper husky. "I've never seen you before."

She moved back, tipping her chin upward so that she could see him, so that she could look him full in the face. Except, she could hardly sustain it. She looked down.

And he captured her chin, forcing her to meet his gaze again. If she hadn't been wearing those heels she would have been so incredibly dwarfed by him there would have been no responding. But he lowered his head, and she leaned in.

"Because I've never been here before."

"It's always nice to see an unfamiliar face," he said, this time brushing her hair back from her face as he whispered.

"Dance with me," she said, not bothering to whisper this time.

The way that the rather predatory grin slid over his mouth told her that he understood.

That she wanted to do more than dance.

His eyes burned into hers as he gripped her hips, dragging her toward him as they moved in time with the music. She felt his touch everywhere, not just where he had his hands, but all the points in between, down deep, in the most intimate parts of her. She had danced with men before, but it had never been like this. Of course, the perfectly polished aristocrats who had always attended the balls she'd been at had never been anything like this.

There was an element of danger to this man. And she found herself drawn to it.

In fact, she found she wanted to fling herself against it. Against him. She had always been asked to be strong, but she had also been sheltered in many ways. Her take on the world was theoretical. And now, she was being tasked with ruling an entire country, while still suffering from that same fate.

Power, but with chains around it.

She wanted to test herself. To test those bonds.

It was what she was here to do.

"Maybe you could show me your club."

His grip tightened on her, and he looked at her for a long moment, before taking her hand and leading her from the dance floor. He held on to her as he took her down the stairs, away from the pulsing music. But they didn't go back to the entry, where people had crowded in. Instead, he moved her down a slim corridor with black flooring that had gold light shooting through the spaces in the tile. He pushed open a door that simply looked like another obsidian panel. "You will want a coat," he said, not taking one for himself, but offering her a snow-white one from a rack by the door.

"Thank you," she said, taking the coat from him and putting it on.

She quite wondered if covering her body might put her out of this advantage, but he was the one leading her, so she supposed she had better follow instruction.

Another thing she had never been very good at. But unlike waiting, it was something she had been asked to do quite a bit.

Something she now wished to avoid.

The room he led her into was made entirely of ice, the walls carved in intricate designs, crystalline, nearly see-through. By a deep navy blue couch was a wall that allowed a mirror view, however rippling and obscured, of revelers next door.

"You are quite bold," he said. "Asking me to show you my club."

"And yet, you seem to be showing me."

"I don't know that you realize just how rare it is for me to take a woman up on such an offer."

"And here I thought you took women up on such offers on a nightly basis. I've read about you."

His lips twisted upward in a cynical impersonation of a smile. "Of course you have."

"I'm sorry," she said. "Should I pretend I don't know who you are? Should I pretend that this is simply a chance encounter, and I came to your club with no prior knowledge of who you were?"

He affected a casual shrug. "Many women would."

"Perhaps those women have the luxury of time. I don't."

"You don't have a bomb strapped to your chest, do you?"

She swallowed hard, letting the edges of her coat fall open, revealing the only thing she had against her chest, that emerald, which immediately felt cold in the icy room. "You're welcome to look for yourself."

His gaze flickered over her body, and it didn't stay cool. "I see. Someone waiting for you at home, then?"

That was close enough to the truth. "Yes," she said.

"Can I have your name?"

"Alice," she said.

"Alice," he repeated. "From?"

She knew her English was quite good, but that it would also be colored by an accent. His was too, though different from hers. She liked the way it sounded. She wanted to hear his voice speak his native tongue. And hers. What sort of accent would it give to her own language? And what sorts of words might he say...?

"England," she said. "Not originally. But for most of my life."

"What brings you to Italy?"

"Your party," she said.

"I see. Are you an enthusiast when it comes to clubs, or are you a sex tourist?"

The words were bold, and she knew that she was playing a bold game and she needed to be able to return in kind.

"In this instance, I suppose it's sex tourism."

"Am I to understand that you saw my picture in the news and decided to make a trip all the way to my club for sex?"

Nothing he'd said was a lie. There might be more in her reasoning, but she had seen his photo. And she had wanted him on sight.

"Chemistry is a fairly powerful thing."

"Can you feel chemistry with a photograph?"

"I didn't even have to go looking for you," she said. "You came to me. So that makes me wonder if it's possible."

And that was the honest truth.

She had never expected Mauro Bianchi to approach her. No, she had expected that she would have to chase him down. That she would be the one pursuing him. And yet, he had simply appeared. And now, he had taken her to a VIP room. So it all rather did beg the question if chemistry could be that obvious.

The expression on his hard face did something then, and she couldn't quite put into words what that was. He looked quite irritated, but at the same time perhaps a bit impressed with her boldness and her reasoning. And he couldn't argue. Because here they were, sitting in this private suite, strangers who had never met until only a moment ago.

"I think the only thing to do then is perhaps test your theory," he said, his voice lowering to a silky purr.

"That is what I'm here for," she said, fighting to keep her voice smooth.

"Perhaps you would like to see my private suite."

"I would like that very much," she said.

This was moving much quicker than she had anticipated. But it was also going exactly according to plan.

She had expected…obstacles. Resistance.

Perhaps because the last year of her life had been marked by such things. Endless resistance from her father's officials. Endless proclamations being made. Demands that she be married. The concern over her producing an heir, as for her, there would be a time limit, unlike with men.

But they had not counted on one thing. Because they had not educated themselves, not to the extent that she had.

Men. With their arrogance. Their certainty that they were right. That they could not be bested, least of all by her.

She had read the laws. She had studied. She had made sure, above all else, that she was prepared for her position, and that she would not be taken by surprise.

Because for the protection of the queen, for the protection of the throne, if she claimed that her issue had no father, that it was the queen's alone.

And there were no questions of legitimacy. A law set into motion to protect the queen from marauders, Vikings and barbarians, anyone who might seek to use her to claim power.

And at this point in history, in time, used to protect the queen from forced marriages, and politicians who overexerted their power, and sought to keep a nation in the dark ages.

All she needed was her marauder.

And she had found him.

"Yes," she said. "Let's go to your room."

CHAPTER TWO

BY THE TIME they had gone through a maze of high-gloss marble corridors and arrived at Mauro's suite, Astrid was trembling. She did her best to try to disguise it, and hope that he would perhaps assume it was because they were surrounded by ice. But the fact of the matter was, the pieces of the structure that were not made of ice were quite comfortable, and she imagined he assumed no such thing.

She was so good at pretending to be confident, serene and as if she were in possession of every secret in all the world, that sometimes she even convinced herself such things were true.

Sometimes she forgot what she really was.

She was a queen, that much was true. A queen with quite a lot of power, education and confidence that was rightly earned.

She was also a woman who had been kept separate from peers for most of her life while she focused on her education. A woman who had danced with a man, but never, ever kissed one.

She was a virgin queen, above reproach as her mother had always instructed her to be.

But matters had become desperate, and so had she.

And she was waging war in a sense, and that meant she could not afford nerves. Even as they rolled over her in a wave, the reality of the utter disparity between the two of them a strange and intense sort of drug.

An aphrodisiac and a bit of a terror.

She was used to having a mantle of power over her, but he didn't know who she was. And here, in this private room he had just ushered her into, he was the experienced one. He was physically so much more powerful than she could ever hope to be, and her guards were well and truly dismissed. She had no one to snap her fingers for and call for rescue. She didn't even have her phone, as she and Latika had agreed that her being traceable to the club in any manner wasn't acceptable.

It was why the timing of everything was so crucial.

His suite was warm, wonderfully appointed with furs in a dark ebony, and bright white cotton spread over a massive mattress.

She looked over at him, and his lips curved as he closed the door behind them.

"Second thoughts?"

"No," she said, squaring her shoulders. "Not at all."

"I did not take a woman who would freely admit to being a sex tourist as one who would be overcome by the nerves of an innocent."

She laughed, so very grateful for all the years she had spent at various political events dodging barbs of every sort, allowing her an easy smile and confident stare even while verbal daggers were being thrown her way. "Naturally not. It's only that… We haven't even kissed yet. And I do want a bit of certainty regarding chemistry."

"A woman of high standards."

"Exceptionally," she said. "I should have mentioned

to you that I am—as far as sex tourists go—not a backpacker. I only go first-class. And if things are not to my liking, I don't stay."

A dark flame burned yet higher in his eyes, a clear response to what he obviously took as a challenge.

"I was going to offer you a drink," he said.

"Why? Because you think you should fare better if my senses are dulled?"

He chuckled and moved to her, wrapping his arm around her waist and pulling her against his body. He took hold of her chin, keeping her face steady as he stared down into her eyes.

"Let us test the chemistry, then," he said, his voice rough.

He bent down, closing the distance between them, and it was like a flame had ignited across her skin.

His kiss was rough, commanding and intense in ways she had not imagined a kiss could ever be. And this was why she had chosen him. It was why he was the only one she could fathom being with.

She had known, somehow, that he would be the one who could make her forget, for just a moment, what she was. That he could be the one who made her exult in feeling delicate. Fragile.

His masculinity was so rough. So exciting. His kiss that of a conqueror. And how she reveled in it. Gloried in his touch. His hands, large and impossibly rough, held her face steady as he angled his head and took the kiss deeper, deeper still, his tongue invading her, making her tremble, making her knees weak.

When they parted, he stared down at her, those eyes shot through with intensity. "Is that quite enough chemistry for you?" he asked.

"Yes," she whispered. "I think that is exactly the chemistry I was looking for."

He stood back and shrugged his jacket off, tossing it carelessly toward the couch on the opposite side of the room, and then he began to unbutton his shirt.

Astrid's mouth went dry as she watched him expose his body. His chest was hard looking and muscular, his abs clearly defined, with just the right amount of dark hair dusted over those sculpted ridges. And he had tattoos. Dark, swirling ink that covered his shoulder, part of his chest geometric patterns that she couldn't quite divine the meaning of.

But the beauty of tonight was that it didn't matter.

It didn't matter what any of this meant to him. All that mattered was what it meant to her.

Freedom. Wildness.

A night with her very own barbarian.

The kind of man she would scarcely have been allowed to speak to if her handlers were present. Much less be alone in a room with.

Much less be on the verge of…

"Pictures don't do you justice," she said.

"I have a feeling that dress doesn't do *you* justice," he returned. "But I would like to see for a fact if this is true."

With shaking fingers, she reached around behind her back and slowly lowered the zip to her dress, letting the soft white fabric release itself from her body and fall to the ground, a pale, silken pool at her feet.

She was still wearing those impossibly high heels and a pair of white panties. Nothing more. He seemed to approve.

Her breasts grew heavy, her nipples tight, her body overcome with restless anticipation.

Then he sprung into action, his muscles all languid grace and lethal precision as he took her in his arms and swept her up off the floor, carrying her over to that large bed and setting her down on the soft, black fur that was spread over the top.

He said something in Italian, something completely unfamiliar to her, something she assumed was something like a curse, or just something so filthy no one would have ever seen fit to teach her. Anticipation shimmered deep and low inside her.

He drew away from the bed, his eyes never leaving hers as he slowly undid his belt, drawing the zipper on his pants down as he divested himself of the rest of his clothing, leaving him completely naked in front of her.

Astrid was one for research. For being prepared when going to war. And as such, she had done a fair share of figuring out just what happened between men and women in bed, not simply in the perfunctory sense. She had done a bit of pictorial research.

But it had not prepared her for this. For him. All of him.

He was quite a bit more of a man than she had ever seen, and she had certainly never been in the same room as a naked man before. So deliciously, impossibly male.

"You are stunning," he said, advancing on her, moving toward the bed. Her stomach twisted, fear and excitement twining together and becoming something so exciting, so unbearably potent she could scarcely breathe, let alone think. She licked her lips, grabbing hold of the waistband of her panties and pushing them down her legs as she arched her bottom up off the mattress, managing to pull them only down to her knees, then uncertain how to continue. He clearly took her uncertainty as an intentional coquettishness, and she was happy to have him think so. He growled, moving down to the bed and grabbing hold of the scrap of lace and wrenching it from her body. Leaving her bare and exposed to him.

His eyes roamed over her hungrily, and there was something so incredibly close and raw about the moment that Astrid had to close her eyes.

Because there was no title here to protect her. No designer clothing, no guards. Nothing between her and this man. This man who seemed to want her, though he'd had many other women.

Astrid was used to being special. Singular. But she had none of the hallmarks here that made her any of that. She was simply a woman. She was not a queen.

And yet.

And yet he still wanted her.

She began to push the shoes off she was wearing, and he moved over her, gripping her wrists and drawing them up over her head. "Leave them," he said, pressing a kiss to her mouth before skimming his hand over her curves, his thumb moving over her nipple, an arrow of pleasure hitting her down low, making her feel aching and hollow. And then he kissed her neck, her collarbone, down to the plump curve of her breast, his tongue tracing a line around the tightened bud there.

She squirmed, arching against him, but he held her wrists fast with one hand while he continued his exploration with his mouth, and his other hand, which had moved to her hip, and was now drifting between her thighs.

Her hips bowed up off the bed when he touched her there. His fingers delving expertly into her silken folds, finding her embarrassingly wet for him.

But then, there was no point to embarrassment. Not now. Not with him.

This was her one night of freedom.

Her one night to claim a lifetime of greater freedom.

And she would not do it with a whimper. But with a roar.

She moved her hips sinuously, in time with his strokes, with the soft suction of his mouth on her breast.

He moved his thumb over the most sensitive place between her legs, stroking back and forth, and she cried out, caught off guard by the intensity of the sensations he created there. When her release broke over her, it was a shock, shattering her like a fragile glass pane, the sharp, jagged edges of her pleasure making her feel weak and vulnerable.

She clung to his shoulders, kissing his mouth, moving her hands over his finely muscled back as she did. She shifted beneath him, feeling the hard, heavy weight of his erection against her thigh. He began to move away.

"It's okay," she said in a rush, while she still had her wits about her.

And she knew what he would interpret it to mean.

She also knew, from much of her reading, that he was a very careful man when it came to these matters.

But she was counting on him being lost in the moment. She was counting on him being mortal.

This was her killing blow, so to speak, and she had to deliver it and not falter.

"Please," she whispered against his mouth and she rolled her hips upward, so that his erection was settled against her wet heat, and she arched back and forth, the pleasure making her see stars.

She could see, mirrored in his own eyes, no small

amount of that same pleasure. Of that desire. That need. He was no stronger than she, and she had been counting on that.

He growled, wrapping his hand around his arousal and positioning himself firmly against her before he slammed inside.

His savage kiss swallowed her cry of pain, and she knew that he misinterpreted it as pleasure as he lost control and pulled out slowly before thrusting back home again.

Astrid closed her eyes tight, willing herself to make it through this without crying, without embarrassing herself.

She simply hadn't anticipated it would hurt quite so badly.

He was lost to it, and she needed him to be. She only wished that she could join him.

She held his shoulders, burying her face in his neck.

And then he seemed to grasp some kind of hold on himself, his movement slowing, his pelvis rocking forward, hitting her just so, and creating a spark inside her she had been convinced would be lost in this encounter.

But it wasn't. Oh, it wasn't.

Suddenly she felt it. Deep and pleasurable and building inside her. Overcoming the pain. Overcoming everything else. It was wonderful. Beautiful and real.

He kissed her as he held her hips and drove home, hard and relentless, and welcome now. It was like she couldn't get enough. As if he couldn't go deep enough, hard enough.

There was something mystical in this joining that she couldn't figure out, but it had something to do with that instant spark that had happened when they laid eyes on each other.

Maybe even with the spark she felt when she had first seen his picture.

And when her release broke over her, it was different from before. Her body gripped his, drawing him deeper, pulsing around him as light exploded behind her eyes. And she didn't feel shattered. She felt renewed. Reinforced as he broke apart, as he trembled in her arms, this large, muscular, experienced man, reduced to shaking as he spent himself inside her.

They lay there, not for long. Only a few moments. While Astrid tried to catch her breath.

And then she heard the sound of a clock strike two chimes.

"What time is it?"

"Two?" he asked, his words muffled, sleepy.

"I have to go," she said. She scrambled out of bed in a panic, hunting around for clothing, getting dressed as quickly as possible while Mauro looked on.

"You're not going to just leave."

"I have to," she said, desperation clawing at her.

"Give me your name."

"Alice," she said.

"Your full name. I wish to find you again."

"Alice Steele," she said, the lie tripping off her tongue.

"That's wrong," he said.

"No," she said, panic like a wild thing inside her. "It's on the invitation."

"That isn't your name," he said, his dark eyes seeing straight into her.

She straightened and looked at him for one last, lingering moment, before she fled. She made her way down the halls, thankful that he was naked, and therefore wouldn't be able to move as quickly as she.

By the time she made it out to the main part of the club, Mauro was right behind her. She kept on running, one of her shoes flying off as she did, as she made an uneven escape down the stairs and tumbled straight into the limo that Latika was driving.

"Go," she said.

"Were you successful?"

She looked back at the doorway and saw him standing there, holding her shoe in his hand.

"Just go," she said, panic and emotion rising up in her throat.

And Queen Astrid escaped into the night, without her virginity, but very hopefully, carrying her heir.

CHAPTER THREE

"FORGIVE ME FOR saying so, sir, but you do not seem your-self."

Mauro Bianchi, dissolute playboy and renowned bil-lionaire, looked over at his assistant Carlo, and treated him to a fearsome scowl. "You are *not* forgiven."

Not because his assistant was not wrong in his ob-servation. No. Mauro was not himself, and had not been for the past three months. He could not pretend he didn't know why. He did.

He was held utterly captive by memories of a bewitch-ing redhead, and a stolen hour in his private suite of rooms.

By the way she had run from him, leaving him hold-ing her shoe.

And by the discovery he'd made when he had gone back to his bedroom.

The blood left on the sheets.

It was entirely possible the woman had started her period, he supposed.

Also… Also a possibility that she had been a virgin. Though he could not fathom a virgin speaking as boldly as she had.

A virgin going back to a man's room for sex, and only sex.

And she had said there was someone waiting for her at home.

He was captivated by the mystery of her, by the erotic memory of her, and nothing he did allowed him to shake it.

Apparently his staff was beginning to notice.

Certainly, the paparazzi had.

Wondering why he'd yet to turn up anywhere with a new woman on his arm, and there was endless speculation about that.

Some even suggesting that he might be in a real relationship, rather than just engaging in one of his usual transient sexual dalliances.

Of course, the press could not be more wrong.

His bed was cold and empty. And Mauro Bianchi could not remember a time in his life when that had been true before.

As soon as he reached sexual maturity, he'd not been alone unless by his own choosing. As a homeless boy, he'd found quite handily that if he were to seduce a woman who did have a bed, he could get not only sex but a nice place to stay.

He had never been shy about using his body. It was one of his many tools. Something that could bring him profit and pleasure, and why not?

He behaved thus even still.

But since his encounter with Alice. Alice Steele, who he knew was not real. He had searched high and low for women bearing that name who resembled her even slightly. Women who resided in England, and then indeed anywhere, and none fit her description.

As he suspected, her name was not real.

She was like a ghost. And the only thing he had to assure himself that she had been real at all was the shoe.

The shoe that sat on his nightstand. Not the act of a man who was in his right mind. Not at all. But knowing that did not entice him to change it.

He didn't feel in the mood to be in his right mind. That was the problem.

He was in the mood for *her*. Hungry for *her*.

He'd told himself he'd never be hungry again. Never want without having.

She'd forced him into that position and it made him feel...

Powerless.

Which was a foolish thing. He was a man at the top of the world. At the top of his field. She was... She was nothing. Just a woman in a club. He was a man who'd risen from the slums of Italy in defiance of his father, a man who had been rich and titled and had wanted nothing to do with his son.

On the far wall, between the windows that overlooked a view of Rome below, news was playing on the TV. He always had news on. It was imperative that he keep up with world events, and he was well able to absorb information without giving it his full attention. His ability to multitask another part of his storied rise to success. His aptitude for numbers, and investments, and indeed for picking places that would become the hottest locations in terms of real estate and trends, had made him incredibly wealthy.

That required him to work constantly, and to pay attention to a great many details at once.

Of course, he could pay people to do much of the day-to-day things now, but still, if he didn't have a lot of input he was bored easily.

Without a female in his bed for the past three months he was growing intensely bored and incredibly bad tempered.

But no one appealed to him. None at all. None save…

Suddenly, a flash of red hair caught his attention and he gave his full focus to the TV, where a woman was sitting in a private-looking room, pale legs crossed at the ankles, hands folded in her lap. She was dressed incredibly demurely. Her red hair was pinned into an elegant bun, her butter-yellow skirt falling below her knees, her high heels sensible and sedate.

She looked so very like the woman—*his* woman—from three months ago, and yet like a different creature entirely.

She was regal in her posture, her every movement elegant, each slight turn of her head intentional.

"Sir," Carlo said.

"Shut up," Mauro said, grabbing the remote and turning the TV up.

She was speaking, but it was in a different language, something like Norwegian, but slightly different, and he didn't speak it either way. They were not putting up subtitles on the screen, but the news commentators were going over the top in his native Italian.

"Queen Astrid von Bjornland issued a statement today to her people, that she is about to embark on an unusual path for a woman in her position. The queen is pregnant, it seems, and is determined to raise the child alone. Invoking an old rule native to the country, the queen is able to claim herself as the sole parent of the heir to the throne."

The camera panned away from the woman, shrinking the video down to a small square, where two news anchors were sitting at a desk now, a man and a woman.

"And only women can do this?" the man asked, looking somewhat incredulous.

"Yes." The female news anchor nodded gravely. "An old, protective law that ensured a queen would not be bound to one of the country's invaders, should she be forced against her will."

Against her will? She had…

That lying bitch.

She was pregnant with his child.

More than that, she was denying him his right as a father.

It took him back in an instant. To what it had been like to be a boy. Knowing his father was there in the city, an omnipresent being in his mind who had been potentially around any corner. Who had, to him, been possibly any well-dressed man walking by.

He'd known his father was a rich man. A powerful man.

A man who didn't want him.

And he had done his best to be careful—with every woman except this one—but he'd always known that with sex there was a chance birth control would fail. And he'd always known that should that ever happen he would not be like the man who'd fathered him.

He would never let a child of his wonder like that. Would never leave him abandoned, unanchored to what he was.

Would never deny him anything he had.

Yes, Astrid von Bjornland had money, had a title. But

their child was more than her. That child deserved *all*, not half.

And yet there she was. Claiming his child as hers and solely hers, when both of them knew he was well involved.

He remembered the way she had looked up at him, the way she had trembled just before he'd entered her body.

"It's fine," she had whispered.

It had bloody well not been fine. He hadn't realized he'd stood up until he looked over and saw Carlo's shocked expression.

"Sir?"

"Ready my plane," Mauro said, his tone hard. "I'm leaving."

"Where are you going?"

"Bjornland. I hear it's lovely in summer, and a bit harsh in winter. However, I hear their queen is a lying snake all year round. And that is something that needs addressing."

"Mr. Bianchi…"

"Don't worry," he said. "I'm not going to make an international incident. Provided she falls in line."

CHAPTER FOUR

"WHAT THE HELL were you thinking?"

The voice boomed.

"Excellent," Latika said, her tone dripping with disdain. "His Majesty King Gunnar has arrived. Oh, wait. But he is not king, is he?"

"I still outrank *you*," Astrid's brother said, sweeping into the room, each one of his thirty-three years evident on his face thanks to years of hard living. "And lest you become confused, darling Latika, I don't covet my sister's position. In fact, I would rather die. However, I do have some opinions on how she might conduct her business."

"That's *very* fascinating," Astrid said. "Except it is not."

"Why didn't you tell me?" he asked, his tone turning fierce, and she felt momentarily bad for her anger. Momentarily.

"Because. Telling you defeats the purpose. This is no one's business but mine. And that's the entire point of it. My heir. No one else's."

"Except, there is someone, isn't there?" Gunnar asked. "I know how these things work."

"Science is a wonderful thing," Astrid said drily. "Perhaps that was the method I employed to find myself with child."

"I don't suppose you're going to tell me," Gunnar said.

"No," she responded. "But you didn't have to return to Bjornland on my account."

"I fear *very much* that I did. You have created an incident."

"You create incidents nightly, brother dear."

"I am not the heir, Astrid. And I am a man. You know that unfair as it is… It is different."

"There is no incident," Astrid insisted. "I am well within my rights to do this. I have done all of the research required to discern that."

"Father's council will oppose you. That is their function. To keep control and power, to keep traditions. To curb your power, because father believed that men were best left in charge and not women at all."

"They can try," Astrid said. "But they won't succeed. They will not, and they cannot. Don't you think, Gunnar, that I made absolutely sure I could not legally fail in this before committing?"

Gunnar shook his head. "You underestimate the power of old men who feel their traditions are being threatened."

"This is a very old law," Astrid said, looking square at her brother. They could not be more opposite in temperament. Gunnar was a risk taker. The rebel prince who spent his life skydiving out of planes, serving in the military and piloting helicopters. Who would have been perfectly at home at a club party like the one Astrid had attended only three months ago. When she had turned her world upside down, and made a choice to wrest control of her life away from the hands of those men he was talking about now.

He was like a Viking. His eyes the color of ice, his hair

blond. His beard a darker gold that gave him a roguish appearance the press waxed poetic about.

The Viking Prince.

He was also her very best friend in the entire world, in spite of the fact that he was a massive pain. Latika saw him *only* as a pain, that much was clear. The feeling, it often seemed, was mutual.

"I have not underestimated anything. And I'm prepared for a fight. But there is a reason that I could let no one know before I made my announcement public. I also made sure that every media outlet was aware of the law in Bjornland. The one that protects the queen should she need to claim an heir as solely hers. Well, Latika ensured that made its way out to everyone."

"Did you?" Gunnar asked. "Just how involved with all of this were you?"

"Latika does what I ask her to," Astrid said.

Latika held up a hand and arched her dark brow. "It's all right. I don't need you to protect me from him. I have done my duty by my queen. And by this country. I may not be a citizen by birth, but I swear my allegiance, and you well know it."

"For now. Until you go back to America. And then, all of these problems will be ours and ours alone."

"Problems that I willingly took on," she said, her tone firm. "I am a queen, I am not a child."

"Your Majesty." One of her guards rushed into the room, his expression harried. "It seems that we have an uninvited guest at the palace, and while we had thought to shoot him on sight, he is quite famous."

Astrid blinked. "I'm not sure I understand."

"A man has walked into the palace without permission," the guard clarified.

"Then why didn't you shoot him?" Gunnar asked.

"The fame," the other man said. "We would be liable to create an international incident."

"Who is it?" Astrid asked.

"Mauro Bianchi."

Astrid's stomach clenched, the blood in her veins turning to ice. There was no way. No possible way that he could know. She just didn't give him that much credit. That he would recognize her. That he would care.

"What does he want?"

"He wishes to see you."

"Now I really don't like this," Gunnar said. "Please tell me that this man was not involved in the creation of your child."

"Define *involved*," Astrid said.

"You know exactly what I mean. Don't play coy, particularly if you don't want to be treated like a child."

"The child is mine," Astrid repeated. "And mine alone."

"Please speak to him?"

"Yes," Astrid said. "I will speak to him."

"And I shall accompany you," Gunnar said.

"No," Astrid said. "I will speak to him alone."

"You're not *my* queen," Gunnar pointed out.

"I was unaware that you had become an expat of our beloved country, my dear brother."

"You are my sister," he said. "And that takes precedence over any title."

"Then as my brother I ask you to respect my wishes. The fact that men would not respect my wishes is the reason this is happening."

"I understand," he said. "I understand full well why

you feel you had to do this, Astrid. But you're not alone. You have my support, and you will have my protection."

"I don't need it," Astrid said. "I possess the power to command that he be shot on sight. Frankly, I could ask the same of you."

"Were you... Issuing an order?" her guard asked.

"Not yet." Astrid flicked a glance between her brother and Latika. "Will you please keep an eye on him?"

"I don't get paid to babysit," Latika pointed out.

"And I receive no compensation for spending time in the company of a snarling American," Gunnar bit out. "But here we are."

Astrid left, muttering about how she wouldn't have to have him shot on sight, as he and Latika were just as likely to kill each other during her absence.

She made her way out into the antechamber of the Royal Palace, her heels clicking on the marble floor. When she saw him, her stomach dropped. His impact had not been diminished by their time apart. Not in the least. In fact, if anything, her response to him was even deeper. More visceral. Possibly because she knew exactly what he could make her feel now.

"May I help you?" she asked.

He stopped and reached into his jacket, and all of the guards in the room put their hands on their weapons.

"Stand down," Astrid said. "He isn't going to shoot me."

"Not at all," he responded. Instead, when he pulled his hand out, he was holding a shoe. *Her* shoe.

"I had thought that you might possess its partner."

"I'm not sure I know what you're talking about."

"Is that so? *Alice*."

She stiffened, straightening her shoulders. "I am

Queen Astrid von Bjornland. And I do not know anyone by that name. You are mistaken, sir."

"And I am not blind. Your hair down, a bit more makeup and a bit more skin is hardly a convincing disguise, my Queen. If you wished to truly fool me you will have to try much harder than that."

Irritation crept up her spine, irritation that he was not minding what he said in front of her guards. Irritation that he was here at all.

"Leave us," she said, gesturing toward the guards.

The room cleared, every man leaving at her behest. At least she commanded authority over her own guards. There was that.

"Does every man in your life defer to you in such a manner?"

She met him full on, making her expression as imperious as possible. "Not just the men."

"I am no one's puppet," he said.

"I did not need you to be a puppet."

There was no point in lying to him. He wasn't stupid. It was entirely too clear that they had met before. And there was something... Something between them, an electricity that arced across the space. There was no pretending anymore. She simply had to find out what he wanted and provide him with that, and try to end this encounter as quickly as possible.

"I need my freedom," she said. "I am queen, and there are a great many people who don't respect my position. I did what had to be done."

"You tricked me into getting you pregnant."

"I *seduced* you. I didn't trick you. You went along with everything happily."

"You said everything was all right. You said it was fine to have sex without a condom."

"I said it was fine. And for my purposes it was. I sincerely hope that you don't treat every hookup in such a casual manner when it comes to protection."

"I don't," he said, the words gritted out through his teeth.

"Just with me, then. But still. I did not trick you. The fact that you assumed *fine* meant what you wanted it to mean and went along with it speaks to how foolish men are where sex is concerned."

As if she would have been capable of making a more rational decision in the moment.

"I want my child," he said.

"It's *my* child." Hers. Her child to love and to raise as she saw fit. To support and protect. And give all the things her parents never had. "By law. I can declare my child fatherless, and I have done so."

"That might be a law, Queen Astrid, but it is not reality. I am the father of your child whether you speak it or not. And I am not one of your citizens."

"No. But you are in my country. Which is where my child will be born. And my child is one of my citizens."

"You underestimate me. You are so arrogant because of your position. You have no idea who you are dealing with. You feel that you face opposition? Do you truly understand what opposition is? It is not a disgruntled cough during a meeting that makes you feel as if someone might be challenging you. No. I will give you so much more than that. If you would like to learn about opposition, I will give you a study in it."

"You should know that I don't respond well to threats,"

she said, her tone like ice. "Indeed, I don't respond to them at all."

"You don't respond to *empty* threats. Because that is all the red-faced, posturing men that you've dealt with in the past have ever issued. But I will tell you, my Queen, my threats are never idle. They are very real. I might be a bastard of ignoble birth, but the power that I possess is very real indeed. What will the public think if I were to claim my child?"

"Why?" she asked. "It is my understanding that a man in your position will want nothing to do with the child. And that is one reason I selected you, lest you think that I meant you any harm or wanted anything from you."

"You assumed you knew what manner of man I was based on the press and what they had written about me, and that was your first mistake. Tell me, Astrid, what does the press say about you? How true is it?"

"The press has never had occasion to write about a scandal of mine. And I knew full well going into this that I was inviting that. You cannot scare me."

"You have imagined the wrong sorts of headlines, I think. I doubt what you want is a long-term custody battle looming over your head. The problem here is that you imagined me as a prop. A means to an end, but what you failed to see as you read all of those headlines, as you examine all those photos of me in the articles and imagine me touching you. Imagine me claiming that body of yours, and we both know you imagined it. That you got wet thinking of it late at night in your bed. You forgot what I am."

Astrid drew back, her heart thundering. Because he was so close to the truth, it cut her close to the heart. He wasn't wrong. She had imagined him as a chess piece.

Capable of strategy, certainly, but she had also imagined that she could see ahead to every move he might make. That she understood what sort of man he was, and what he might want. But his standing here had proved already that he was not anything like she had anticipated.

She had thought of him as a barbarian, as a conqueror so many times. But in a vague, fantastical sense. In a sexual one. She had not thought in concrete terms about what it would mean to go up against this man.

Because she had not imagined he would oppose her. On that score, he was correct. She had imagined nothing like this.

She had underestimated him. And it galled her to admit it.

"What else could you want?" she said. "Anything else. I know you don't need money, and I will not insult you with such an offer. There are business opportunities to be had in Bjornland, and I am more than willing to facilitate easing the way for you. Whatever it is you want, I will give it. Only don't ask me to sacrifice this. This is what I need to claim the throne, and I will not…"

"I will not be managed. I want nothing less than what I have demanded. I want my child."

"Why?"

"Because as a boy I sat back and watched my father live in excess while my mother earned her meager pay in ways that cost. A man with money who does not care for his own is not a man at all. He is weak. Vile. The lowest form of being to ever walk the earth. If indeed you can call what he does walking. He would be better suited to crawling on his belly. I am not that man. And I will be damned if I will allow you to manipulate me. To think that I can be bought."

"What do you suggest?"

"I suggest shared custody, my Queen. But I imagine that's going to damage the optics of your little kingdom."

She blinked, not entirely certain how that would work. "There is no way that I can do that. You have to either be out of the picture entirely, the secret to the world, or you must…" Her stomach rolled. "You would have to marry me."

"Why not?" He shrugged a shoulder. "You had no intention of marrying, clearly."

"I had no intention of being maneuvered into a political marriage that wasn't of my choosing. That isn't quite the same thing."

"And yet I find in this moment the end result could likely be the same. There would be no downside to a marriage between the two of us. You can consolidate the power as you see fit, you will not be forced to marry a man chosen by this council that you're so opposed to, and I certainly have no interest in meddling in the affairs of your country."

"And you are a prime candidate for marriage?"

"Not at all. But aren't games of infidelity stock standard for royals?"

"It would require a bit more discretion than you seem capable of exhibiting."

"I can be very discreet when I choose. Tell me, my Queen. Have you seen a single headline about my sexual exploits with a virginal redhead in my private suites? No, I don't think you have. Had I wanted a headline there would have been one." He stepped forward, and tossed her shoe on the ground in front of her, the crystalline material glimmering in the light. "It seems I was able to find you without resorting to such tactics. Or trying this on any of the feet of all the eligible maidens in the country."

She thought suddenly so clearly. The queen was in check. The king had her cornered.

She could not see a way out.

"What is a queen without a king, after all?"

"According to the history of the world, more powerful."

"Not if the queen has been shamed and disgraced in the media."

Panic tightened around her throat, and as he advanced on her, shamefully, something other than panic took hold of her. A sense of shameful, heated desire that she despised.

"I have no designs on your kingdom. What I want is to give my son or daughter validity. To ensure that they have all that is rightfully theirs. And if I benefit from having my name attached to Bjornland, and to royalty, then so be it."

"Is that what this is to you? A game?"

"That's what it was to you. The fact that you don't like the outcome of that game is not my concern. You played with me."

"Whether you think so or not, I wasn't playing with you. I was helping myself."

His expression shifted, a deadly light in those dark eyes. "Do you know what a child who was born in the gutter dreams of? What it must look like from the very top. When you are born looking up, it concerns you greatly. How it must feel to look down. I know the answer to that now. And yet, any real sense of belonging in high society escapes me. I am looked upon as a trinket often, to women who wish to slum it. A bit of rough on the side. And surely, you must know that, as you did not see me any differently. In fact, I would suggest that you thought I wasn't smart enough to find out what you had done."

He began to circle her, a wolf, a predator now, looking at her as if she was a sheep. "Did you think that somehow my impoverished, low-born eyes would not be able to recognize you when you went from common club slut to queen? What you, and all of your kind, would do well to remember is that the odds are greatly stacked against someone born in my position, and if I make it to where I am, the chances are I am much smarter than you've ever had to be. Much more determined. My patience undoubtedly greatly exceeds yours. And that means that on this score I will win. My ruthlessness exceeds yours too. Yours is all theoretical. You have no idea the things I've done to get where I am. And I don't regret a single one."

Her heart was thundering. A sick feeling invading her body. Because what could she do? He was correct. He could flay her in the media.

Expose what they had done as something seedy. Call it a one-night stand, expose the parentage of her child, and the origins of it. Or, she could take hold of it now. Say the two of them had fallen in love. Yes. A love match. She could control the narrative. She could find a way to spin it.

"You must pretend to be in love with me," she commanded.

"You've already suggested to the entire world that your child had no father. How do you profess to shift that now?"

"I will say that we had a whirlwind romance. But that I was not brave. And I was afraid that you might be rejected by the council, by my people. But in the end, you came after me, and my heart won. I will say that I trust that my people will honor what I want in my heart. We will live separate lives. We will be married only in the eyes of the law. You may conduct your affairs as you see fit as long as you do it quietly. And as long as you wait."

"Wait?"

"You will remain celibate for the first two years of our marriage. If anyone were to get wind of the fact that you are having affairs so soon after our child was born, and so soon after I professed that the two of us had fallen in love, it would cast everything into doubt. Already having you as my husband will be an incredibly difficult thing for the nation to accept."

"More difficult than you staking your claim as an unwed mother?"

"Possibly not. But I was prepared for that fight. Because this position is one that I was born to be in. And I must fight for it daily because of my sex. And you tell me what you would have done in my situation."

"Likely exactly what you did. Though, I would have chosen someone with transparency, and paid for their silence."

She could have done that. She had thought about it. But the fact of the matter was she had seen him and become captivated. It was something that she had a difficult time admitting, because it made it clear that there was a personal element to what had occurred. That was something she didn't really wish for him to know.

That when he'd said she had thought of him at night, thought of him and become aroused, he wasn't wrong.

No. He wasn't wrong at all.

What she had done had been clouded by desire. And

it was easy for her to try to pretend it had been a clinical maneuver on her part. But the inclusion of Mauro Bianchi had always been suspect. She had tried to tell herself there were many reasons apart from the fact that she wanted to touch his body. To kiss him. To have him.

Well, now she'd had him. But not in the way that she had once wished.

She was queen, and he had come into her palace. Her country. She should feel a sense of power, regardless of his threats. This was her house. Not his. And yet, all she felt was the sense that she had let a tiger inside. One that didn't care about hierarchy or blood.

One that cared only for what he might possess and how. He might exploit the weaknesses of those around him.

"You have a deal," he said. "An engagement, more accurately."

"Good," Astrid said. "That means we have a lot to do. A lot of training to prepare you for your role as consort."

"I thought you would have known by now," he said, a dangerous smile curling that wicked mouth of his. "I am not one to be trained. I am not the one who will be receiving instruction. What you will have to learn is how to be a woman who would stand at my side. A woman who would compromise her kingdom for me. At the moment, you're not believable in such a role."

She narrowed her eyes. "I don't understand the need for a farce."

"You're the one who demanded it. It isn't my fault if you didn't think about what that might mean."

He took his phone out of his pocket and pressed a number, holding it to his ear. "Carlo," he barked. "For the time being I will be relocating to Bjornland. You will have my things sent here until further notice."

Astrid bristled, trying to regain control of the situation. "Of course you will move into the palace."

"No," he said. "I will not. When we are married, we can perhaps share the same residence for part of the year. Until then, I am more than comfortable procuring my own lodgings."

"There's no point," she said. "There's no point, everyone already knows that I'm pregnant."

"Yes, but what must be made clear, to you and everyone else, is that I am not a pet. I will have nothing to do with the day-to-day running of your country. I am not a man who needs to rent a space in a woman's bed to have a roof over his head. I am not a man you can control. You would do well to remember that."

He then turned and walked from the throne room, leaving Astrid standing there wondering how all of this had spun out of her control. It had started out as the perfect plan, and now it wasn't even her plan anymore.

Mauro Bianchi had given her many firsts.

Her first time waiting in line.

Her first time having sex.

Her first time feeling utterly and completely at the mercy of another person.

She was trapped. And she could see absolutely no way out.

CHAPTER FIVE

IT TOOK MAURO less than twenty-four hours to acquire a penthouse in the small business district of Bjornland's capital city, only three miles from the palace.

It was a simple thing to figure out a temporary work setup, where he could call in to any meeting he might be needed at over the next few weeks.

He wasn't leaving Astrid unattended. Not now. Not until everything was settled between them. Legally.

He also wasn't a dog that could be brought to heel, which was why he was refusing to move into the palace.

It took less time than that for him to acquire an engagement ring for his royal bride.

He had no doubt that she would be expecting to use a piece of jewelry belonging to the royal family, but he would not have it be so. He was not a house cat, and he would be damned if he were treated like one. That meant consolidating as much of his own power in the moment as he could. And what he had found was that there really wasn't much that couldn't be solved with money. Money was the universal way of gaining power and control. He might not have a title, and he might be theoretically beneath Astrid in this country, but he had no doubt he could buy the government of this country many times over.

And he found that as long as he made it clear that was the case, people rushed to accommodate him.

He also managed to procure a reservation at what he had been assured was the queen's favorite restaurant. It was the most highly coveted in the entire country.

The next step had been ensuring that he could get the queen to the restaurant. He'd thought about kidnap, but, with as many guards as she had, it would be needlessly complicated.

He had discovered through his research that the queen had an assistant. And he intended to use her if necessary.

He picked up the phone and waited while it rang. "Yes?"

"Is this Latika Bakshmi?"

"How did you get this number?" He could hear her lips go tight, could sense that her gaze had gone narrow and cold.

"I have connections," he said easily. "This is Mauro Bianchi. I hear that you are the minder of my new fiancée."

"She is not your fiancée. At least, not yet. As it is not printed in any papers anywhere."

"Is that the standard by which engagements are measured?"

"In this world."

"We have a verbal agreement. More than that, she is carrying my child."

"I would kill you myself to protect her," Latika said. "I hope you understand that."

He was impressed. It took real leadership to inspire that kind of loyalty. Real friendship. He had not been able to get a read on his betrothed, not in a meaningful sense, since meeting her outside of that initial encounter, when she had been pretending to be someone else entirely. She seemed frosty. Distant, and completely unlike the beautiful, witty woman he had met that night. But the fact that Latika seemed quite so dedicated to her indicated that there was something more than she had shown him. Not that it mattered either way.

None of this had anything to do with her.

Not in a personal sense. It was all about his child.

He would no sooner touch her again then he would allow a snake in his bed.

"I admire that," he said. "But I would also like to remain unmurdered. I do not want to hurt your princess. I simply want to ask her to dinner."

"You *are* hurting her," Latika said. "By pushing this marriage the way that you are."

"What do you suggest? That I allow my child to grow up without my name? Without me?"

He would not let his child grow up alone.

There was a long pause. "She didn't think you would care."

"I do," he returned. "I don't know the relationship you had with your own father, but surely you must understand that it is a loss to me to think I might not know my child."

The pause on the other end of the line was longer this time. "What exactly did you need to know?"

"I would like to take her out to dinner tonight. I was hoping you could facilitate that."

"I think that I can."

By the time Mauro pulled up to the palace that night in his newly acquired car, he had every puzzle piece in place. What he had said to her about the way that he maneuvered the press was true. If he wanted to be seen by the press, then he was. Likewise, he knew how to avoid them. He was more than happy to cultivate a certain image in the media as it suited him. And more than happy to be left alone when it suited him, as well.

Tonight he needed an audience. And he had made sure that there would be one.

The restaurant itself was built into the side of a mountain. The views it offered of the valley below, a broad swath of mist and green, made him understand why Bjornland was listed as one of the world's most pristine undiscovered gems.

Staff in the kitchen had ensured that the photographs he wished to have taken tonight would be taken. A bit of money in the right palms, and the paparazzi would be let in the back doors at the appropriate time. He was bound and determined that he would secure this union and bind Astrid to him as quickly as possible.

He did not get to where he was in life by waiting. Or by leaving anything to chance. The palace doors opened, and she appeared.

Dressed in an immaculate emerald green dress with a wide, square neck that showcased her delicious breasts. The dress skimmed her curves, falling down below her knee, hugging each line and swell of her body like a lover.

It was a shame she was so beautiful. Considering he knew exactly what she was. Even knowing, his body responded to her. That connection that he had felt from the moment he had first seen her defied any kind of logic, and it continued to do so.

A valet came to the car and opened the passenger side, and she paused before getting in.

"It is you."

"Did your faithful sidekick not tell you?"

"She did not. She was rather intentionally vague." Astrid sank down into the car with a great deal of overly dignified posture. She looked like an arched hen, stiff and tall, but visibly ruffled. "She may in fact find herself looking for a job."

"I would only hire her in my company," he said, treating her to a grin he knew was wicked. And it had the desired result. Her color mounted, her indignation increasing.

"Why would you do that?"

"She helped me. And I am loyal to those that help me. Make no mistake."

"That's interesting," she said as he put his car in Drive and roared away from the palace. "It's interesting because you have rather a reputation for treating people as if they're disposable."

"You mean women," he said, pointedly.

"Yes," she said.

"I have many women that work at my company, and they will tell you differently."

"I mean *lovers*," she clarified.

"And yet, here you are."

"That's different," she said.

"If you say so. The media makes much about my reputation, and a good portion of it is deserved. I am a man with a healthy sexual appetite, and I have never seen the point in pretending otherwise. However, I am a man from a particular background. And I learned long ago that only people with a disposable income could afford to treat others as if they were disposable. I was dependent upon the kindness of others for a great many years, and I have not forgotten it."

"But to hear the press tell it…"

"I'm ruthless," he said. "Relentless in my pursuit of the almighty dollar. And that might be true. I have thought nothing of buying property out from under the rich and titled. But I have not—and will not—send anyone to the poorhouse. I have scruples. Isn't that an inconvenient thing for you to learn?"

She said nothing.

"Does it bother you?" he pressed. "The idea that I might not be a caricature that you can easily pin down? You wanted me to be a villain, did you not? Someone that you could easily say deserved to have his child hidden from him. After all, if I am everything you seem to think, I should not have a child in my presence, should I?"

She was frozen now, that stiff posture adding to her silence.

"I am not a nice man," he continued. "On that score you are correct. I like excess. There you are correct, as well. But there are certain things that I cannot endure. That I will not abide by. I do not treat human beings like trash. Not the poor. And certainly not children. Least of all my own."

"How kind of you," she said, archly, making it clear she still found his standards of humanity beneath her.

"Do you actually want this child?" he asked as they continued up the winding mountain road that he knew would lead them to the palatial restaurant.

"Yes," she said, her tone fierce. "I want this child very much. My life has been incredibly lonely. Filled mostly with tutors and sycophants. My brother has been my primary companion for most of that time, but he had a very different life than I did. He had a lot more freedom."

"You are the queen," he pointed out. "You have more power than he does."

"More power in this case is not more freedom. I'm five minutes older than my brother," she said. "*Five min-*

utes. My brother is everything the old men of my father's council could possibly want in a leader. A tall, strapping man. An alpha male with the kind of immediate presence that gives a sense of confidence and intimidation. And me?" She shrugged. "I'm a woman. But, if not for a little bit of acrobatics in the womb, they would have the leader they wanted, and not the one they're stuck with. Do you have any idea how much that galls them? How much they resent it? I can feel it every time I'm in their presence. And make no mistake, a great many citizens of this country feel the same way. When my father passed away, I think they all hoped that there would be some secret switch. That I would abdicate. That I would do the right thing. That is what some people think. That it would be right for me to abdicate because of my gender. I have been above reproach all this time. And I have been opposed every step of the way for no other reason than that I was born a woman. It was my mother's deepest wish that I would not allow them to take what was rightfully mine. And I have not. I will not."

"And the child… The child helps you accomplish this."

"The issue of me needing a husband was being pushed. And there was a possibility that they would have the right to select a husband for me. There is also a great deal of responsibility placed on the production of an heir. Once I have produced one, some of the council's oversight is removed. This is a protective method that has been in place in the country for generations. To ensure that a royal is doing their duty by the country, and if not, then decisions may have to be made."

"And there is some arcane law that says the queen can be considered solely responsible for her own issue."

"Yes." She sighed heavily. "It seemed the smartest thing to do."

"It might've been," he said. "Had you chosen any other man."

"Do you know what I liked about you?" she asked. He heard a slight smile in her voice.

"No," he returned. It was true, he didn't. Based on his interactions with her he would have assumed she liked nothing about him at all.

"You reminded me of a warrior. I liked that about you. I thought… That is the kind of genetic material I need for my child. And you might judge that, I understand. But it made sense to me at the time. I was feeling a bit desperate."

He let silence lapse around them for a moment. The only sound that of the tires on the road, the engine a low hum running beneath. "The problem with warriors," he said finally, "is that you cannot control all that they might do."

She laughed. A small, humorless sound. "Understood. Understood all too well at this point."

It was then that they reached the summit of the mountain, the restaurant glittering against the stone.

"Oh," she breathed. "This is my favorite."

"Good," he said; and he fought against the strange curl of pleasure in his stomach that he had pleased her in some way.

There were glittering Christmas lights around the perimeter of the restaurant, green boughs hanging heavily over the doors and windows.

"It's a bit early for all of this," he commented.

"Perhaps," she agreed. "But it's nice all the same."

She softened a bit, talking about Christmas. It confounded him. He didn't much understand the joy of Christmas.

He'd never had a Christmas, not really.

They left the car with the valet, and he looped his arm through hers as he led her into the restaurant. She was like ice beside him, but he didn't pay attention to that. Instead, he leaned in, his lips brushing against her ear. "You will have to look as if you enjoy touching me."

"I didn't realize this was an exhibition."

"You are Queen Astrid von Bjornland, and I am Mauro Bianchi, the most famous self-made billionaire in all the world. Everything we do is an exhibition."

"Most famous?" she asked drily. "You think very highly of yourself."

"I didn't realize that ego and honesty were considered the same thing in your world."

"I consider ego very important. Never think that I'm insulting you for pointing out that you have a healthy one. After all, I'm the queen that millions think should not have a crown. How do you think I walk with my head held so high?"

"Well, now," he said. "That I can respect."

"Whatever you think about me," she continued. "I guarantee that you don't have the first idea of what it means to operate in my world. You might be rich. But you don't understand the expectations that have been placed on me. No one does. My brother… He tries. It cannot be said he doesn't. He is my twin, and the closest person to me in the entire world. But he can't fully understand. I don't know that a man ever could."

"Is that so?"

"Yes. Now, I imagine that being of low birth, as you are—"

"Low birth," he said. "What a delicate way to phrase it."

She shrugged. "I wasn't trying to be delicate in particular. But being from the kind of station you are, I imagine that you reached some opposition when you were trying to ascend. I also imagine that once you proved yourself capable, then it was assumed you were capable."

"I confess, my prowess has never been called into question. In any arena."

"I was born to this," she said. "My blood runs blue. My education, my upbringing… It was all geared toward me finding success in this career that I was born for. And yet whether or not I am capable of handling it… My marital status, whether or not I'm carrying an heir, all of those things, seem to matter more. I am a pass-through ruler. And believe me when I tell you they will all pray this child is a boy."

"England seems to have done all right for itself," he pointed out.

"It isn't the same. Our country is smaller, the government is run differently. We don't have parliament."

"Let us go inside," he said.

They were standing out in the chilly air, Astrid looking up at him, and he had a feeling that she was putting off the moment that they would have to go in and face the public. But then, she had no idea the level of public that would be in attendance.

"All right," she said slowly.

She allowed him to lead her into the restaurant, and he knew that he was being allowed. After all, this woman did not seem to cow under any threat or circumstance. Whether or not the council respected all that she was, he did. He could see what she was. It oozed from her every pore. From the very way in which she carried herself.

He moved his hand to her lower back as they walked into the warm restaurant. It was very Scandinavian, with a sparse design aesthetic, the windows looking out over the impressive mountain view, the trees inky and black against the backdrop of the rich velvet sky, the stars glittering like diamonds.

"This is a beautiful place," he commented, keenly aware of the fact that all of the eyes in the room had turned to them.

"Yes," she said, somewhat absently. "It truly is."

He leaned in, conscious of the fact that they would be being photographed now. "And what is your favorite thing on the menu?"

"I always get the special," she said. "Whatever is seasonal. Oh, and if there's an appetizer with one of the Bjornish aged cheddars, I always get that."

"You have a fondness for cheese?"

"I would distrust anyone who doesn't."

"I see. So that is how you arrive at conclusions regarding who you can trust and who you can't? Which foods they have an affinity for?"

"I've yet to surmise a more adequate way of parsing a person's character.

"Well," he said, "I like cheese. What does that say about your metric?"

She looked at him, those lovely, green eyes appraising. "I chose you, didn't I?"

The words were cool and unsettling. They made him feel much more like she might be in the driver's seat than he was comfortable with.

The maître d' appeared and quickly ushered them to a semiprivate table, which Mauro liked because it gave the appearance that they were attempting to stay out of the way, while still allowing for the paparazzi to be able to get discreet photos.

In his experience, the quality of the publicity was all in how you courted it. Or how you appeared not to.

And just like that, he was reminded of who was in control.

At least tonight.

She was a fascinating woman in some ways. He was not accustomed to dealing with women—with anyone—who had even a comparable amount of power to his own. Astrid was a queen, and the idea that she could snap her fingers and have him executed infused him with a particular kind of fascination he had not dealt with before.

He hadn't anticipated a powerful woman being quite such an aphrodisiac, and yet it made sense. What good was strength and power if it went untested? What good was strength and power when pitted against someone weaker?

Far more interesting to spar with an equal.

When a waiter appeared, Mauro spoke quickly to him, procuring the specials, and requesting a special appetizer with local cheese for the queen.

"You did not have to order for me," she said.

"Perhaps not," he said. "But I thought it might make an interesting challenge." He looked at her. "You did not have to let me order for you. I imagine you could have stopped me at any point."

"It's true," she bit out.

"I imagine that you could call the waiter back now and reverse my order if you find it unsatisfactory."

She sniffed. "Well, you got what I would have ordered anyway."

He smiled. "That isn't true."

"Oh, yes?"

"Yes. It isn't true because you would never have asked for a special entrée to be made for you."

She sniffed again. "I told you, I was raised to be a queen. Why do you think that is beyond my scope?"

"Because you were raised to be very careful. That is something else I know."

"It's true. My mother always stressed that I would be scrutinized much more closely than a potential king would be. It's impossible for me to know if it would have been different for Gunnar if he were the heir. But he gets much more leeway in the press, and his behavior is considered something of a national pastime. Of course, he is not in immediate line to the throne. So perhaps that's the reason why. But it really is impossible to know."

"I imagine you could never risk looking overly commanding."

"No," she said. "Neither could I… Neither could I ever risk dancing too close to a man."

"And so you disguised yourself in something unsuitable and went to my club?"

"The truly amazing thing," she said, "is that people don't look closely at other people. We never search for the unexpected. I've never put a foot out of line, and so no one would ever think that they might spot me at your club. Least of all wearing the dress I had chosen. It was the perfect moment to engage in a small rebellion."

"It was coup in many ways, it could be argued."

"I suppose. To claim the power that should've been mine all along."

The two of them began to eat in silence and Mauro became aware of the sound of a camera. It was subtle, but it was evident, and he made sure to reach out and brush his fingertips across Astrid's knuckles. She startled, drawing her hand back.

"Your Majesty," he said. "Never make the mistake of thinking that we might not be in the presence of an audience."

"An audience?"

"I made sure the press knew that we were here."

She went still, as if she'd transformed into a pillar of salt, the stony expression on her face one of biblical proportions. "What are you up to?"

"Did you honestly think that I called you here without a plan?"

"I suspected that we would discuss these things together." She said the words through tight lips, her expression serene, even as the waves emanating from her were not.

"Smile," he said.

As if on cue, she did so, and to anyone observing them it would seem that they were having a friendly exchange.

"This is not your show," he continued. "That is one thing you need to learn about me. I am subject to no one and nothing. Least of all you. You made a choice. You stepped into my world. And now, you have ensured that you'll never fully be free of me. This was your decision, not mine. And now, here I am. I am the thing you must contend with. You assume that your consequence would be carrying my child. No, my Queen. *I* am your consequence."

"Damn," she said, keeping that smile stretched wide. "A consequence I had not foreseen. How unusual."

"Indeed."

And he knew that his next move was one she had not seen coming either. It would be cliché to wait for dessert.

The move of a man who was calculating the entire event. But he was determined to make it look as if theirs was a spontaneous proposal. If this was what she wanted, the look of love, the look of a real couple, then he would give it to her. But he would give it to her on his terms. If she thought that she could be in charge of creating their narrative, she was about to be sadly disappointed.

He reached into his jacket pocket, and he produced a small ring box.

The shock on her face was not manufactured. Not in the least. It was clear to him that she had not been expecting this. Not at all. And it gave him an illicit rush, a thrill, to have her at his mercy. Because that night when he had first met her, he had felt a connection between the two of them that he had never felt with another woman before. And she had been using him.

That that bothered him at all was laughable. It shouldn't. And yet, it did. His every emotion tangled up in this thing that he had neither anticipated, nor ever thought to protect himself from.

And then it had turned out the connection was a creation. All a part of a tactical war she was waging, unbeknownst to him. He did not handle such things well.

And now, it was her turn. Her turn to be caught off guard.

He dropped to one knee in front of her, a position that she probably saw men in often, but this was not a pose of submission. Not a gesture of deference on his part.

He opened up the ring box, the piece that he was presenting her a true marvel of design. Clean and simple, like this restaurant that she favored so much. Something that reminded him of what she had worn the night they had met. A creation designed to complement who she was, rather than adding unnecessary adornment.

A large, square cut diamond, clear and bright, in a platinum setting.

Something that worked with the lines of her elegant hand, rather than overwhelming them.

"Queen Astrid," he said. "Would you do me the honor of becoming my wife."

It was not a question. And she seemed to know it.

He could sense the electricity around them, the entire restaurant now rapt at the scene in front of them. Shutters were going off, cameras raised, while people snapped completely obvious cell phone photographs of the moment. And now he had her. Now he truly had her.

"Yes," she said, her answer wooden, stiff. "Of course I'll marry you."

Her smile was effortless, the result of years of practice and breeding, he could only assume. And to anyone else she would look positively joyful.

But he could feel her rage.

Her desire to make him pay.

And it only fueled that damnable fire in his veins.

"You've made me the happiest man in the world," he said.

Then he grabbed her hand and tugged them both to their feet, drawing her up against his chest and gripping her chin between his thumb and forefinger.

The look in her eyes, that glinted there, threatened to cut him. But her actions remained agreeable.

For a woman for whom reputation was everything, this was a hostage situation. And as a man who didn't care at all what anyone thought, it was a victory.

Then, he lowered his head, and claimed her mouth with his own.

And that was the moment he had not planned for.

He hated this woman. Despised the way that she had deceived him, used him. The way that she had been intent upon hiding his child from him.

But this remained. This spark.

The electricity of the room wasn't simply coming from the excitement of the spectators around them. No. The electricity was in them. Arcing between them with uncontrollable sparks.

He wanted to devour her. Part her lips and slide his tongue against hers. Luxuriate in this until it consumed them both.

And it was that feeling. The sense of being out of control. Of wanting…

That was what pulled him back. Because he would be damned if he would crave a thing that was out of his reach ever again.

He pulled himself away from her, staring down in triumph at her swollen mouth, her stunned expression.

"I believe this makes you my fiancée."

And just like that, he had the queen in check.

CHAPTER SIX

"How dare you make a move like this without consulting the council."

"Which move?" Astrid asked as she faced down the long board table of very angry men. Men her father had appointed to their positions over the course of his rule. It was traditional for the monarch of Bjornland to have consult of a council. With more freedom being handed over to the ruler after marriage, or after an heir was produced.

But the way this particular council had been established, without her approval, even as her reign was approaching, and with life terms given to those who sat in their positions, was unheard of. And allowed only, she imagined, because she was a woman.

Her father had installed babysitters for her.

He'd never cared that she'd done nothing but demonstrate her ability. He couldn't see past what he considered her fundamental flaw. She was female, and would therefore be a weaker ruler. Inclined to lead with her emotions. To be swayed by her hormones in a way a man was never led about by the member of his body.

The very idea sent Astrid into a small internal rage.

Men were always so concerned with what women might do during a certain time of the month, and yet they were slaves to the whims of the lower halves of their bodies at all times of every month.

That her father had considered her weak and fallible because of her sex was, in her mind, a sign of the weakness in him.

But with her upcoming marriage, and the baby coming, they were on the way to becoming less powerful, and they were certainly sitting there looking as though they knew it.

"The one where I decided that I would be taking control of the child that I carry, or the one where I got engaged?"

"Either," Lars, the lead councilman, replied.

"Both are done," she said causally. "There's nothing to discuss."

She had whiled away her time letting these men occupy their seats. Not making waves. So that when she had the moment to consolidate her power they would be blindsided. And that was clearly what had occurred.

She would remain calm even now. Better to have them unable to anticipate her next moves.

To the outside world it might appear as if she was taking orders. As if she was allowing herself to be walked on.

But she had the trump card. And she refused to waste energy flailing when she was in the process of succeeding in a tactical strike.

The ring on her left hand felt heavy. And her lips still felt tingly from the kiss she had shared with Mauro at the restaurant. Perhaps *share* was too strong of a word. That kiss had been a conquering. Truly, the barbarian had reached the gates, and no amount of planning on her part had been sufficient to keep it from being so.

She had handed him the keys to her kingdom. She might as well tilt her head back and let him slit her throat.

And if it were ancient times, perhaps that's what would have been done. At least, after she had produced his issue.

But he claimed that he wanted nothing to do with the kingdom specifically, and right now, looking at all of the faces staring back at her, feeling the rage emanating from them, she could only take comfort in the fact that the only people more upset about this development than she, were them.

As much as she could feel her plan spinning out of control, she imagined that they could feel their control on the kingdom slipping out of their grasp.

And as long as that was the case, she would be happy enough.

"He is the father of your child?" Lars pressed.

"That is the question on the lips of everyone in the world at the moment, it seems," she said, keeping her expression serene and her shoulders straight.

"You claimed there was no father," another of the men said from the other end of the table.

"Well, I think we all know that's a lie. Even men such as yourselves don't spring from holes in the ground. They are made the typical way." She received raised eyebrows in return for that statement. "Do not all of you go looking so shocked that I am a woman. After all, if I were not, you would not be here, with the layers of additional power my father bestowed upon you. To protect myself I was willing to invoke that particular law written in our books. But it turns out, I didn't have to. The issues that Mauro and I were having—personal issues—have been resolved. And now we will be able to present a united front for the kingdom. I fail to see how this is not a winning proposition for the entire nation."

"A playboy," a dissenting voice said. "And one from the gutter at that. He is well beneath you, and beneath this kingdom."

"Is he?" she asked, with no small amount of ice in her voice. "Have I not lowered the kingdom sufficiently to reach his level? I should think that by mere virtue of the fact that I am a woman, I would have slipped us down several ranks in your estimation. Not to mention my very nonsecretive pregnancy, which the whole world knows occurred out of wedlock."

"My Queen," Lars said. "You know that you have nothing but support from the council. That is why your father solidified our position before his death. To make sure that we could support you."

"Support. Undermine. In the grand scheme of things is there any difference? I knew that in order to claim my independence I had to either marry or produce an heir. Handily, I will be able to do both very soon."

"How soon shall the marriage take place?"

"Two weeks," she said, the words, the commitment, sending a stab of terror through her body. She had not discussed this with Mauro. But she imagined that the sooner the better as far as he was concerned. After all, he had taken control of the timeline by making their engagement so visible, and thrusting it upon her without giving her any time to be coordinated. He could hardly get angry at her for keeping up with that push forward.

Well, maybe he could. But maybe it would do him some good to be angry.

She had the terrible feeling that she was going from

one battle of wills straight into another. She also had the terrible feeling that the council wasn't going to go quietly.

She suddenly had the distinct vision of being pulled between Mauro and the table full of councilmen.

She also had the clear vision of Mauro being able to pull her away from all of them.

She disliked that.

She had intended to rescue herself. The idea of needing his help was galling indeed.

"That is impossible," her largest dissenter said, rubbing his hand over his face. "You know we cannot coordinate a wedding in that time."

"Then don't coordinate it. I assume you don't want a heavily pregnant queen wandering down the aisle, which means expedience should be welcome. And if that's too difficult for you, I will arrange it myself. It will coincide with the tree lighting, and other Christmas festivities Bjornland will be celebrating, and I can think of nothing better."

"You will add unnecessary duties to the staff at this time of year?" Lars sneered.

"Not at all. I will boost the economy and provide with it extra money for the season. And I am well able to ensure it all goes to plan without involvement of anyone in this room."

"How?"

"I have an assistant for a reason. And believe me, she is more efficient than this group of people all on her own. If the idea of helping to coordinate this wedding intimidates you, then I'm certain that Latika will happily take up the banner."

"This is *unprecedented*."

"That's fine. I don't mind being unprecedented in this

manner, as I am unprecedented in every other way. You were the only ones that seem to have an issue with that. You are beginning to drag down the entire country."

"Mark my words," one of the men in the back said. "If the country is to fall, it will be on your head."

She firmed her jaw, calling on all the strength she'd spent her life culminating. "Then so be it. But it will not be my head alone, but my new husband's, as well. You will find he is nothing but a staunch supporter of me. You might be able to oppose me, but when I am joined with him I will only be stronger. Two are better than one. And the two of us will be vastly better than twelve," she said, looking at them all meaningfully. "I will send you an invitation to the wedding if you wish. Otherwise, you may take a backseat. You will have to get used to that."

On that she turned on her heel and walked out of the room, listening with satisfaction as each step echoed loudly around her.

She had been angry at Mauro last night about what he had done. She had been uncertain with how to proceed. But she knew now. Everything had a purpose now.

Suddenly, this marriage actually seemed like the best idea.

It might never be a real marriage. She didn't need it to be a real marriage.

He would be a figurehead, and she… She would finally be able to be the queen that she was always meant to be.

Dinner that night was at the palace, and it was filled with pronouncements. Mostly made *at* him. Mauro wasn't used to such things, and he found he had limited patience for it.

Though there was something exceptionally alluring about Astrid, even when she was being a pain in his ass.

Sometimes, especially when she was being a pain in his ass, and he didn't fully understand that.

"We are to be married in time for the tree lighting in the palace. It will be integrated into the ceremony in point of fact."

"Is that so?"

"How pregnant did you expect I should look on the day of our wedding, for all the papers to see?"

For some strange, inexplicable reason the idea of her looking pregnant—her stomach round with his child—did something to him that he could not explain. Something he didn't want to explain, even to himself.

"How pregnant you are or aren't when you walk down the aisle doesn't matter to me," he said. "The only reputation I have to maintain is one of total debauchery and general disdain for social niceties. For me, this is on brand."

"How nice for you," she said, drily. "We will marry in a month."

"When do you suppose you will learn I don't respond well to commands?"

"I don't know. I suspect we have a lifetime to discover that."

"Surely not a whole lifetime," he said. "Only while the child is…a child, I'd assume. Do we really need to be so pedantic that we stay together for eighteen years?"

"I hadn't considered it," she said, her expression bland. "Marriage, to me, is forever, but it certainly doesn't have to mean together."

"Elaborate," he said. "I am not from a household that contained a marriage. My view of it is limited to sitcoms and crime dramas. Both give a very different idea of what it means to be married. I imagine the truth lies some-where between happy hijinks and murder."

Astrid chuckled softly, pushing food around on her plate. "Yes, something like that. I think that middle ground is called 'quiet disdain.'"

"Speaking of your parents' marriage?" he asked.

"Yes. You know, my father never wanted me to be queen. My mother was stubborn about it from the be-ginning. From making sure the announcement that the press received was unambiguous about which child was born first."

"But he was the king. Couldn't he override her deci-sion?"

"Yes," she said. "He could have. There were many reasons he didn't. That he would suffer in the eyes of his people, and the world, being a large part of that. Also... He knew I wasn't incompetent. If I had been I think he wouldn't have hesitated to have Gunnar named the of-ficial successor to the throne. My father wasn't an easy man, but he had a strong sense of duty. I don't know that he... I don't know that he loved anyone. But he loved the country. As for my mother..."

"Did she love him?"

"I don't think she did. Mostly they spent their marriage sleeping with other people, once Gunnar and I were born. Heir and spare in one go. Exceedingly handy."

"Before your idea to circumvent the council, what was your thought on who you might marry?" He didn't know why he was curious. He shouldn't be. Not about this minx who had upended his whole life, forcing him into a situation he didn't want to be in.

No, he didn't want to want this child. But he did.

His mother was dead now, gone. Years of hard living

having taken their toll on her. Installing her in a luxury penthouse for the last six months of her life had probably extended her time on earth, but not by as much as he'd hoped.

His father still lived, but he'd vowed he'd never speak to the man again.

The child, his child, would be a real flesh-and-blood connection he could have here on this earth. This child was something real to care about. To want to care for.

He didn't…want to need those things, and yet he found he did. It was more than just a feeling of responsibility. It was something that called to a deeper place inside him.

One he'd done a great job pretending wasn't there for the past thirty-five years of his life.

Just another reason to find Astrid enraging.

But he found he was still curious.

"I didn't think about it," she said. "I imagined my parents would be involved in helping curate a selection of acceptable suitors. But they never did. My father died when I was twenty-nine. I still don't know why he didn't try to marry me off before then. A year ago, I thought of this plan. Oh, I hadn't chosen you specifically but I had decided I would have a baby alone."

"You never wanted love?"

She lowered her head, shaking it slightly. Then she laughed. "All I ever wanted was for the people around me to see that I was competent. Not in spite of being a woman. Not barely acceptable when they could have had a man. But qualified. A passionate leader, a good leader. One who loves her country and all of its people. Fantasies of romantic love have never factored into my life. I can't even get respect, why would I hinge any great thing on love?"

He could relate to that feeling, though his was not a sense he did not deserve love, but the deep, abiding belief it did not truly exist.

Love, in his mind, was an illusion. When life became bleak, love was always the first thing to crumble. In the end, people would always choose themselves. They would not choose another person. Not really.

It didn't make him sad anymore to know that. As a boy, it had. He'd been convinced if only his father could love his mother, they would be a family and be happy. He'd been convinced that if only his father would meet him, he would love him and he would want to give him and his mother the money they needed to live.

But his father loved himself. He loved the life he had in the palazzo on the hill with his wife and their real children. The children he'd made intentionally, with the aristocrat woman he'd chosen. Not the gutter trash he'd knocked up during a dalliance.

His mother had made it very clear where she'd stood in his father's eyes. Never to make him feel sorry for her. Never to cry about injustice.

Only to make it known why any reconciliation was impossible.

Still, he'd always thought it could be so as a boy.

He'd found out as a young man he'd been wrong.

"What about you?" she asked. "Am I interrupting any marital plans?"

"No," he said. "I intended to whore my way around the world. I intend to continue doing so when our need for total discretion is resolved."

"Excellent," she said, though her tone sounded quite crisp.

"Does it bother you?"

She shook her head. "Not at all. You recall I intended to walk away from you and never see you again. I hardly intended to own your sexuality for the rest of your life. I intended to forget your name."

He smiled. "And now, here we are."

"What *the hell* is happening?"

He turned to look, at the same time Astrid nearly gave herself whiplash twisting around when a large man, who had slightly different coloring, with blond hair and a beard, but was identical to her in the stubborn set of his jaw, came striding into the formal dining room.

"It's five in the evening, Gunnar," Astrid said, as she recovered herself. "I hope you didn't get out of bed so long before your typical wake-up time just to question my life decisions."

"I'm questioning *his*," Gunnar said, the anger in his expression making abundant sense now that he knew for sure this was Astrid's brother.

"Your sister is having my baby," Mauro said. "What precisely should I have done to treat her in a more respectful manner? I have proposed marriage to her."

"And you'll get your hands on the kingdom?" Astrid's brother was like a very large, angry Viking barreling down on him, and if he weren't an accomplished street fighter, he might have been concerned for his safety.

"Whatever your plan is… It is not going to succeed," the other man continued. "Astrid is much stronger than that."

"I'm aware of that. It's one reason I'm so fond of her."

"Your stories are conflicting," Gunnar said. "My sister made it very clear there was no father of her child. Then suddenly, you appeared."

"We had a disagreement. That disagreement has been resolved."

"It's a political marriage," Astrid said, sounding tired. "There's no point lying to him. Neither of us can get away with lying to each other ever. It's one of the worst things about having a twin."

"You don't have to do this," Gunnar said.

"I do," she insisted. "I overplayed my hand and I lost. But now we have a scenario that helps me in the end."

"In what sense?" Gunnar asked.

"The council is madder at me than you are," she said, her mouth lifting up into a small smirk.

"That is something," Mauro said.

"I assume," Gunnar said, turning his focus to Mauro, "there are official documents that can be drawn up and kept secreted away in your personal vaults well away from Bjornland?"

"Of course," Mauro said. "Discretion is key in my line of work."

"I didn't know *discretion* was part of your vocabulary," Gunnar said.

"Because you've never gotten wind of a single thing that I appeared to be obscuring. I find hiding in plain sight is often the best plan."

Astrid's brother regarded him with what appeared to be grudging respect.

"Now that you're through treating me like a child…" Astrid said.

"Yes, I'm sure that if I appeared with a random fiancée you'd take it in your stride."

"Of course not," Astrid said. "I'd renounce her as a gold digger."

"Then don't expect me to sit back and allow you to make choices I find…deeply suspicious."

Mauro leaned back in his chair. "You should find it deeply suspicious. Though, as I said, I have no designs on your country."

"What do you have designs on?"

Mauro leveled a gaze at the other man. "Is it so difficult to believe it's your sister?"

Gunnar shook his head once. "Not at all. But there are easier women in the world to be with. My sister has an obligation first to her country. My sister will never be able to take her husband's name, or be his housewife."

"What a happy thing, then, that my name means less than nothing to me. I am a bastard son of a whore. My name is dirt in civilized circles. But I do have money. And money allows me to go where I like, to get what I like. Better still, I have no house. A series of penthouses, yes. Private apartments nestled in exclusive clubs. But nowhere one would expect a wife to put on a twinset and pearls and…bake. My lodgings are reserved for more exotic uses."

"You may have to childproof them soon enough."

Astrid's response to that was to treat her brother to an evil glare. But she said nothing. She was a strong woman and certainly more than capable of speaking up in a situation like this and yet now she chose to remain silent.

He could only assume there was a reason. One that had nothing to do with being intimidated.

"My clubs are no place for children. But then, that is another issue. I want my child. Is that so hard to believe?"

"Most men of your sort do not."

"Then they are not men," he said. Simple. Hard.

And that seemed to earn him the most respect of all.

Eyes that were like chips of ice appraised with a coldness that would have sent a lesser man running from the room. Then finally, Gunnar turned his focus back to his sister. "Proceed with planning your wedding, Astrid, by all means. I won't stop you."

"You *couldn't*," Astrid pointed out. "I command an army."

The corner of her brother's mouth tipped up in defiance, and at that moment he could truly see that they were twins. "I said I *won't* stop you. Not that I can't. My choice of words was no accident."

"Then we're all on the same page," Mauro said. "Including those of us who had no choice in the matter."

After that Mauro had the feeling that whatever other obstacles might rise up in the future, his brother-in-law wouldn't be one of them.

"It's actually a good thing you're getting married so quickly," Latika said, staring appraisingly at Astrid in her close-fitting lace gown.

"And why is that?" Astrid asked.

"Because this dress would no longer fit you if you waited even another week. It's getting snug as it is."

"I'm pregnant," Astrid sniffed.

The word sent a sudden jolt through her.

Words like *heir* made it all detached. But the fact remained she was going to be a mother and no matter how much she wanted to be, the reality of it felt weighty, and infused with the weight of the unknown.

But then, everything in her world felt inverted right now and there was no finding normal. Mauro was… He was a presence even when he wasn't in the palace. He had committed to working mostly in Bjornland until the wedding, leaving only a couple of times, and even then never staying overnight. He had a residence in town but she swore she could feel him.

And the feeling was…

It was electric and it was unsettling.

She wanted him. And there was no room in this situation for want. Especially when he was a brick wall she couldn't read.

He didn't seem to want her at all.

The night of the engagement he'd kissed her, and then he'd pulled away like nothing had happened while her entire body had continued to burn like a wildfire had been set off in her belly, spreading out over everything.

They could talk, and it felt cordial, but even that seemed…calculated.

She'd come closest to knowing the man the night she'd met him in his club, of that she was certain.

With no names, and no truth, she'd seen pieces of the real Mauro somehow.

He wasn't giving her any of that now.

He asked her questions. He shared his own information with an easy defiance. As if he enjoyed his disreputable history, and lived to shock people with it.

But none of it was real.

None of it was what existed on the other side of a wall she shouldn't even want to scale.

He had been a means to an end. He continued to be.

The world was agog over their union, but they'd quickly recovered from her declaration that her child had no father becoming a shock engagement. Mostly because, more than anything, the world wanted a love story.

Even if it was improbable and unbelievable.

Maybe most especially then.

"I wasn't insulting you," Latika said.

Astrid looked at the wall, refusing to look at her assistant. "It sounded like it."

"Well, I wasn't." She tilted her head to the side, her glossy black hair sliding over her shoulder. "You truly will make a magnificent bride."

"I don't care about that. I want to be a magnificent *queen*."

Latika sighed. "You're already that. You don't need a husband to make it true. Even if you need one to help insulate you."

"Somehow this is starting to feel a little bit like the forced marriage I was avoiding."

"Except..." Latika trailed off, as if she thought better of what she'd been about to say.

"What?"

"You've already slept with him," she pointed out. "You *are* attracted to him."

"It isn't a factor now," Astrid said, her cheeks getting warm.

"Isn't it?"

"No," she scoffed. "He's no longer interested in me anyway."

"Why do you think that?"

"He's... Well, he's completely cold toward me, and anyway..." She sighed. "I don't know. I don't know what I want from this. What I want to do. What would you do?"

Latika blinked. "Do you mean in this exact situation? Because I don't think I can answer that."

"Okay," Astrid said slowly. "I grant you that my current situation is a little bit unorthodox."

Latika snorted. "A little bit?"

Astrid turned around, facing her assistant instead of

the mirror. "What do you do with men? I don't have any experience with them. Except for that one night. And I hardly think that counts."

Latika sighed heavily. "I can't say as I have any brilliant suggestions on how to handle a man like Mauro."

"But surely you must have some idea how to handle men?"

Astrid could see Latika decide to dodge the question. While she valued that skill in Latika when it came to her acting as a shield between Astrid and the rest of the world, it was deeply annoying at the moment.

"Latika, we don't speak overly much of your past because I can see that it hurts you, but if you could offer me some insight…"

"I can't. I always knew I would be married off to a man I didn't love, and I was sheltered from men to…preserve me. When the man my father chose turned out to be an ancient European with a reputation for treating women ill… Well, now I am here. I know how to plan and organize any event, how to make casual conversation with people from all walks of life. I might have been roped off from having my own social life, but I was forced to participate in the social lives of my parents. I've planned your wedding, but I can't help you here, I'm afraid."

"If nothing else, it's very helpful to have you. To have a friend."

Latika treated her to a small smile. "What is it you want from him? Because it seems to me that while you might have failed in the first iteration of your plan, this one is going to work just fine."

"That's the problem," Astrid said. "I'm really not sure what I want. I should want to keep things compartmentalized. We have a good agreement. We really do."

"But…"

"There's no *but*," she said quickly. "Not really."

Latika sighed. "You have a crush on him. You have ever since you saw his picture in that magazine."

Astrid sputtered. "One cannot have something so… benign as a crush on a man like Mauro Bianchi. Anyway. I'm a queen. Queens don't have crushes."

"You're human. A human woman. You would have to be blind not to notice his appeal."

"So you've noticed it, then."

Latika laughed. "International playboys aren't really my thing."

"No. If they were you might not want to pinch my brother's head off every time you were in the same room with him."

Latika shifted. "Maybe."

"I need to stay strong with him," Astrid said. "I need to make sure that I don't blur lines between us."

"If you think so," Latika returned.

"You think I should do differently?"

"I wouldn't dare question you. But mostly… I had a high-handed…unorthodox upbringing, you could say. I was very cloistered, and protected. Something I know you understand. Even now sometimes I feel like I'm hiding. If I had the ability to claim freedom the way that you did, I would take it. And I know that I was a little bit disapproving of your entire plan, but it was only because I worried for you."

"So you think that I should continue on with a physical relationship with him?"

Latika shrugged. "If not him then with someone. But it seems to me that you have feelings for him. Also, you're pregnant with his baby and marrying him, so it seems that he's the most convenient target around."

"He hates me," she said. She was suddenly very aware of exactly what that strange emotion she could feel vibrating beneath the surface of the man was. "He really does. And he wants the child, and I don't understand why. I mean, he says it's because it's a man's responsibility to be a father…"

"And you don't believe him?"

"I just think there's more." She shook her head. "It's the strangest thing. It isn't that I think he's lying. Just that I can sense there's something else. And he's never going to tell me."

"Have you asked him?"

"Why would I ask him? I just said I'm fairly certain he hates me."

"You should ask him about that too. About whether or not he actually hates you. It seems to me that he could have taken a much more extreme tactic with you than he has."

"Oh, than forcing me into marriage?"

"You have to admit, as things go… His version of forcing you into marriage is fairly kind."

"*Kind* is not the word I would use for it."

"Okay. Maybe that was an overstatement. But he isn't after your country. He isn't after any of your power. And you have to admit that when compared to basically every other man in your life—except for Gunnar—that's fairly significant."

"That might be the first nice thing I've ever heard you say about my brother."

Latika rolled her eyes. "Well, it's not going to happen again. Don't get used to it."

"I'm getting married." A sick feeling settled in the pit of her stomach. She couldn't even blame morning sickness. "I wonder what my mother would think of all this."

"She would be proud of you," Latika said. "I didn't know her, but from everything you've told me I think she would approve greatly. Think of all she did, the way she put her marriage in jeopardy to ensure your position on the throne. She would understand why you were doing all of this."

Astrid had nothing else to anchor her. Nothing that made her feel particularly assured, or like she even knew which way was up. But if she could just imagine her mother being proud. It was the one thing she'd worked for all these years, really. And even if she'd never get the words of approval she'd always longed for, she knew that she was doing what her mother had always wanted her to do.

That she was becoming what her mother had wanted her to be.

For now, that would be enough.

And the mystery of Mauro, and the problem of what she was going to do about him, would have to wait to be solved.

However, the countdown to the wedding night was ticking down... And she imagined she would have to make a decision before then.

CHAPTER SEVEN

MAURO HAD NEVER given much thought to the Christmas season. As a child it had meant next to nothing. Something for other children to celebrate, for other people to enjoy. As for his life, it had always been a reminder of the ways in which he had very little in comparison with those. Not in a monetary sense. He hadn't cared about that so much, at least apart from being fed.

But in the sense of family.

While he'd had a long succession of uncles throughout the course of his childhood, it certainly wasn't the same as the sorts of families—whatever shape they took—who gathered around Christmas trees and dinner tables during that most festive season.

As an adult, it had meant little more to him than an excuse to throw themed parties at his clubs across the world. Everyone enjoyed the excuse to engage in revelry. All the better it was an excuse to cover up past pain and breakaway issues with family, and lovers new and old.

He was under no illusion that many of the people who patronized his clubs were doing just that. But, it wasn't his job to worry about the emotional well-being of the people who danced their way to oblivion in his establishments on a nightly basis. He envied them their oblivion, in point of fact.

Typically, he felt nothing.

That sense of blurry freedom that came with alcohol and other substances didn't resonate with him. Not anymore. It violated his sense of control, and that was an unpleasant place for a man like himself to be in. He could not have what he wanted.

But then, that was true of a great many things lately. Astrid dominated his dreams, and now here it was, attending a Christmas tree lighting, on his wedding day. As the holiday held such little significance for him in general, this would be the marker for it for the rest of his life, whether he wanted it to be or not.

A marriage that wasn't a marriage. For a child who was no larger than an avocado at the moment.

But the child wouldn't stay the size of an avocado. Indeed, that child would grow. A son or daughter. One that he… He would have to hold it. Care for it. Granted, both he and Astrid could hire enough people to make sure that neither of them ever had to interact with their progeny if they chose. But he failed to see the point of that. It would make him barely a shade better than his father. And that just wasn't… It was a strange thing to him to discover he had standards, but it turned out he did.

A fact that was in ample evidence as he stood there in his bespoke tux, custom made for this day.

His wedding.

And tonight would be his wedding night. A wedding night that would herald the beginning of two years without sex. That was something he had not yet fought his bride on. There would be no way he would fall in line in such a way for that long. It simply wasn't reasonable, not for a man like him.

If nothing else, it was the principle of the thing. And he would not be dictated to.

"Two minutes."

The order from Astrid's petite, efficient little assistant came almost in defiance to that thought.

She was a pretty woman. With jet-black hair and golden-brown skin. Her glittering eyes and sharp features gave the impression of an astute field mouse, always in motion, and never missing even the faintest twitch of movement around her.

"Don't worry," he said, "I'm not going to leave your princess at the altar."

"I didn't think you were. Considering you were the one who pushed for this in the first place."

"I get the feeling you don't trust me."

She squared her shoulders. "I don't trust anyone. Not in the least."

"Interesting."

"Why?"

"You don't seem like the type of person who would be that hard."

"Very few of us are exactly what we seem. Astrid might be. Utterly and completely who she seems to be. And if you hurt her, I will have you executed."

"I have no plans to hurt your queen."

"Good. Then we have no problem."

She turned and left, and Mauro lingered for a moment, waiting until it was time for him to walk out of the holding room, as he thought of it, and toward the chapel. He was ushered to a back door that took him to the front of the sanctuary. All eyes were on them, and he knew that only approved photos were allowed. There were no cell phones present in the sanctuary. Only official photographers.

Thus was the royal protocol demanded by the very angry council that had been hands-off in every way in regards to the wedding, except for things like that. Things that made it all feel like a circus performance, more than anything else.

Not that he was opposed to a circus.

He was quite an accomplished ringmaster. But he preferred to have greater control of the show. And not the kind being exerted here.

He took his position, and music began to play, a hush falling over the room. Neither of them had attendants. It was not a tradition in Bjornland, and anyway, it made no sense for him or for her. So it quickly became a bridal march, and the guests rose, turning toward the doors, which opened slowly, as if building anticipation for what they would reveal.

And what they did reveal was as a punch to his stomach.

She was exquisite. The first time he'd seen her she'd been in white, but she had been draped in fabric designed obviously to seduce. And he was a man who enjoyed the obvious. This was something more.

The lace gown clung to her curves, lovingly shaping to her beautiful body. The neckline was scalloped, the rounded curves drawing attention to breasts that he knew were soft and plump, and just the right size to fit in his hand.

She was like a goddess, her red hair cascading around her shoulders like a copper-gold halo, the light from behind seeming to ignite it. She did not have a veil, but rather a simple, jeweled circle that draped across her forehead.

She did not carry flowers. Her elegant hands were empty, her engagement ring glittering on her finger as she moved toward him, slowly, with purpose.

And suddenly, inspiration for just how he would handle his wife hit him, like a falling anvil.

She had used her body to bring them to this moment. She had used him.

And he had absolutely no qualms now about using her. Until his desire for her was spent. Until his lust for her had been quenched. How long had she tormented him?

Months.

Months before he had found her again, and in the months since returning to Bjornland. Since their engagement. He had wanted her, and not allowed himself to have her. He had desired her, and not allowed himself to stake a claim.

Celibacy for two years? Why? When the most beautiful, intoxicating woman he'd ever had in his bed would be with him. Bound to him. When he would be living part-time in the palace of a necessity. He had easy access to her, and there was no reason he shouldn't make free use. At least, not in his estimation. There was terror in her eyes when she approached him, her hands trembling as she clasped his.

He wanted her to tremble before him. But for a different reason.

He wanted her out of her mind with need, as he had been. So incredibly naive. And he had not been naive.

He had never considered himself naive. But that was what she had done to him. And why shouldn't he reclaim himself?

He felt a slow smile cross his lips. And as the priest led them in their vows, he allowed himself to skim over the words. They didn't matter. Neither of them were forsaking all others for as long as they lived. There was no point to such a thing. Death would not be what parted them. But rather a calculated move on both their ends.

Love was not what had brought them together, so it did not matter what tore it asunder.

What mattered was tonight. Tonight, he would make his queen beg. Tonight, he would stake his claim in the marital bed.

She might not be his for life, but she was his for now. And he would make sure that the time they did have was spent naked.

That was what was wrong. Of course it was. Those moments when he felt compelled to understand her... They had never been about that. They had been replacement for what he truly desired. Her body, pressed against his. Her body, pliant and willing. His inside hers.

That thought got him through the ceremony, and then on to the reception.

And there was a moment, where the dance floor was cleared, and he and his bride were meant to dance together.

"Quite an elaborate party for a farce," he said the moment they were joined together, his voice nothing more than a husky whisper.

"What's the point of engaging in a farce if you don't go all the way?" Her spring-green eyes met his, and his gut tightened.

Indeed. There was no point engaging in a farce if it didn't go as far as it could. And that was what he intended to claim for himself tonight. All of it. Everything.

"The food is good," he said. "At least."

"What an odd detail to focus on."

"I also like your dress," he said, lowering his voice. "Or rather, I suspect that I like the body beneath it."

Her cheeks immediately turned pink. "Really? I mean… I don't know…why you would say that either. I would rather talk about the food."

"I like food a great deal," he said, very intentionally moving his hand so that it rested lower on her spine, hovering just above the curve of her ass. "You see, I spent a good deal of my childhood starving. And when you have experienced something like that… You become very protective of your next meal. And you appreciate it when you get it."

"That's terrible," she said, clearly uncomfortable. With the change in subject being so sudden, with everything.

"There's nothing to be sorry about. But you see, this is why I enjoy the many vices I do. Because there were very few in my life as a child. Very little I could depend on. As I got older I learned to depend on myself. To make my own way. I have not been hungry since. It is a powerful thing, realizing you can change your own world."

Astrid nodded slowly. "I know. I know because that was what I had to learn. That I could change my world. That I could change my world and not violate my duty. Not the part of it that counted."

Something turned over inside him, and he felt a sense of grudging respect for her. And more than that… Understanding.

"We should be making our departure soon," he said.

"Should we?"

"A married couple very much in love is eager to escape on their wedding night. At least, that is my sense for it."

She looked away from him for a moment, and then back. "Right. I hadn't thought of that."

"Of course not," he said. "I did. In fact, I've thought of little else beyond the fact that it's our wedding night since you stepped out in that dress."

Her eyes met his, wide and full of uncertainty. A strange thing with Astrid, who made it her business to at least appear certain at all times. "We have an agreement."

"Cannot agreements be amended?"

"You didn't give any indication that you wanted ours to be amended."

He was tired of talking. He was tired of being civil. This was the problem with business negotiations. It was the problem with needing to be civilized. At least when he had lived on the street there had been an honesty about it. About the transactions he'd engaged in with women who wanted his body, and would allow him to share their beds. In honesty and all motivation. It was clear. In the upper echelons of society, things like tact were required, and in Mauro's world those things were overrated.

He was done with words. He was done with verbal sparring.

He tightened his hold on her and she gasped, her head falling back, her eyes wide as she looked up at him. And he smiled. Because this reminded him of that night in the club. This reminded him why even if he could go back and undo what had happened between them knowing what he did now, he probably wouldn't.

He lowered his head, claiming her mouth with his. He parted her lips ruthlessly, sweeping his tongue in deep so that he could taste her. Taste this one thing between them that was utterly, completely honest.

They had an audience still. A captive one. They were

out on the dance floor, and he was kissing her as if she were air and he was a man deprived of it. She clung to him, shaking, and that was when he knew he was going to get exactly what he wanted. Her, trembling beneath him. Begging for him.

He pulled away from her. "We should make our way to our room, don't you think?"

"Is that what this was about?" she said in a hushed whisper.

"No. You will find out exactly what this is about. When we go to your room." He thought for a moment that she might protest. But instead, she lowered her eyes, and then when she met his gaze again, they were blazing. "Then let's go to bed."

Her heart was racing, threatening to thunder out of her chest.

Yet, she had gone with him.

She had allowed him to lead her from the room. She was... She didn't know what was happening. He flew in the face of everything they had agreed, everything she had decided was appropriate. But he had kissed her, and then she didn't care. And then the idea of being married to him and not sharing his bed had seemed like an impossibility.

Because from the moment she had seen his picture for the first time in the papers, the idea of *not* being in his bed had been torture. She had been contending with that part of herself for the past few months.

Badly.

Because what did it say about her? That she was merely another groupie of his? One who had dressed up her motivations for being with him into something a bit more noble, when her reasoning was as base as anyone else's.

Right now, she felt base. Utterly and completely. Was reduced to a grasping creature made entirely of need and desire. That was all she was, it was all she could remember being. This woman who needed his touch more than she needed anything else.

That kiss the night they'd gotten engaged had been kerosene. And the kiss tonight had been a lit match against it. She was not strong. Not with him. Not with this.

She had stood tall and steady, with a will of iron since she had started to rule the country two years earlier. Before that she had been a model citizen. Studying, completing vast amounts of charity work. She had been strong. She had been for so very long.

She wanted something else now. She wanted to be held in someone else's strong arms. To let him hold on to her, and in so doing, take some of the weight of the crown, of her duty, off her. Even if it was just for a night.

How twisted was it that even her one and only time being with a man was rooted in a lie she told herself about it being all for her country?

When what it was had been… She had done it for her country. For herself. The baby part. But there had been other ways. But she had been willing to use him first. Before she resorted to science. Because at the end of the day she had wanted him. And it was all fine and good to try to make excuses, to try to tell herself she'd been selecting the finest specimen genetically.

She had told herself a lot of pretty lies.

What she had been was a girl with a crush. Latika had been right about that.

A girl who had a crush and no understanding of how to handle it.

She had spent a life dealing with people who catered to her too much, counterbalanced by constantly feeling opposed and undermined. Great authority, but with a very short leash. It made it difficult for her to figure out how to actually know people. How to relate to them.

The fact of the matter was she didn't know. And she never had. Her brother was her friend, but he was also a royal.

Latika was someone she also considered a friend, but Latika worked for her, and that created a strange sort of dynamic. She was isolated. And a bit spoiled. And she had behaved that way with him. Like a child entitled to something, one who had seen a shiny toy that she wanted, and had come up with all sorts of reasons why she deserved it.

But he wanted her now. And she wanted him. Even as remorse for her behavior flooded her, she still wanted him. Their rooms were next to each other. As was custom. He had not spent the night in the palace yet, and she wondered if he ever really would. But for appearances, they had readied the standard royal bedchambers. She wondered which room this would happen in. And what would happen after.

What would happen during.

The very thought made her shiver.

He dragged her down the empty corridor, and then suddenly pushed her up against the wall. His dark eyes blazed into hers, fearsome and filled with the dark emotion she couldn't name. It was like rage but hotter, desire but with a knife's edge.

He had not looked at her like this the night of the club.

This was something more. Something deeper. Something that carried the layers that their relationship contained. A relationship she had forced him into.

Because he was here out of a sense of duty, she understood that all of a sudden. Not because he wanted to be her husband. Not because he was drawn to the idea of being married to a queen.

Not because he hungered for power or lusted for money.

Because of his own integrity.

She had convinced herself that she was acting with some kind of integrity when she had fooled him. But it had been self-serving.

Guilt lashed her like a whip. And for the first time she wondered if she was much more her father than she had ever previously imagined.

She had always thought of herself like her mother. And Latika had said, just tonight, that her mother would have approved of what she done.

But her mother had never harmed anyone. Would have never lied.

Her mother had told the truth when Gunnar and Astrid had been born. At great cost to herself in terms of her marriage.

Her mother believed in honesty, if not in showing love. It was her father who would have stooped to subterfuge to do what he had imagined he might have to do to save the kingdom.

Her actions were the same.

Right because she had found a loophole, because she imagined her own sense of justice to be the one true version of it.

And this was her penance. This man. This large, muscular angry man who was paying it right along with her.

She didn't know what he might do next. But he didn't make her wait long to find out.

He cupped her cheek, his touch gentle, and almost all the more terrifying for it. All that leashed strength. She could feel it. The force of his rage, and the way that he held it in check so that he could softly move his thumb over her cheekbone.

He lowered his hand then, gripping her hips tightly and surging forward, letting her feel the evidence of his desire. And then he lowered his head, kissing her, harder, deeper than he had back in the ballroom.

She was drowning in it. Drowning in him.

There was no more time for thought or self-flagellation. If this was her punishment she would submit to it. Because it was also her salvation.

Her moment.

Because he was strong. And he could hold her.

Because he was angry, and he could feel it in a thousand ways she had never really allowed herself to feel it.

Because he wanted her. It opened the door to allow her to feel her own want.

"Your room or mine?" he asked, his teeth scraping along the side of her neck. "Where shall I take you, out here in the hallway?"

The idea made her shiver with need, but she couldn't allow something like that. No.

"The bedroom," she said softly.

"As you wish."

He hauled her to him, lifting her off the ground and carrying her a few steps toward the bedroom, opening the door and propelling them both inside before he slammed it behind them. The room was familiar to her. She had inhabited it for the past couple of years. And yet, somehow with this man inside it, it felt completely different. He should look civilized in that custom-made tuxedo of his, the dark, elegant lines conforming gracefully to his body. But he didn't.

Instead, it seemed to provide a greater contrast to that strength, to his feral nature.

He tugged at his bow tie, letting it drape over his shoulders, and then he advanced on her, his movements quick and decisive as he grabbed hold of the zipper on the back of her dress and dragged it down, letting it fall to the floor, that custom creation that was worth thousands of dollars. He stepped over it as if it didn't matter and picked her up, carrying her to the large, ornate bed and placing her at the center of it, where she was surrounded by lush, velvet pillows, the cool, soft texture such a contrast to that hot, hard man above her.

"I would say that the night you approached me in Italy was your show. Tonight it is mine, *cara mia*. And I will enjoy every moment of it."

He grabbed hold of his bow tie, tugging it from his shoulders, and then he took hold of her wrists, encircling them easily with one hand and drawing them up over her head. He smiled, then in one fluid motion took the strip of black fabric and tied it securely around her wrists, leaving her bound.

Desire and fear raced through her in equal measure, electricity shooting down between her thighs, the sensation of being hollow almost unbearable.

"Just making sure you stay where I want you."

"Mauro…"

"How badly do you want this?" he asked, tracing the edge of her lace bra cup with his fingertip. "How badly?"

"I need you," she whimpered.

"Well, let's see how long you can withstand this." He let his fingertips drip beneath the edge of the fabric, one calloused pad skimming her nipple, and she cried out.

"So sensitive," he said, chuckling darkly as he pressed a kiss to that vulnerable place between her rib cage, down to her belly button, down farther. He pressed his mouth over her lace-covered mound, his breath hot against her skin as he scraped his teeth over the delicate fabric. She shivered, arching into him.

"That's the thing about going into a lion's den, *cara*," he said. "Sooner or later he's going to eat you."

He hooked his finger through the fabric on her panties and tugged it to the side, revealing her to his gaze. And then he moved in, laughing at her with bold, intense strokes. He curved his arms around her thighs, locking his fingers together and dragging her toward his face, holding her firmly against him as he continued to lavish attention on her with his lips, his tongue, his teeth.

He drove her to insane heights, and then brought her back from the edge. Over and over again until she was sobbing, crying with her need for release.

He traced circles around that sensitized bundle of nerves with his tongue, before lapping her in one slow lick, her climax pouring over her, leaving her spent and shaking and breathless.

But he wasn't finished. He began to toy with her, using his fingers, stroking her and teasing her until she found her release again. And again, this time with his mouth at her breast and his fingers buried deep inside her.

He brought her up to her knees, turned her away from him, where he lowered his head and laughed at her from a different angle, until she was trembling, begging for him to stop.

"Please," she said. "Finish."

"We are finished," he said, his voice rough. "I think you've had enough."

"You didn't… We didn't…"

"I said that was enough. It was a very long day."

He moved away from her, and she rolled onto her back, her hands still bound. He took hold of one end of the knot, freeing her in one easy tug that seemed to make a mockery of the way she had felt at his mercy.

Had she wanted to escape, she could have. The whole time.

The captivity had been only an illusion, and she had been so willing to sink into it because of what she wanted from him.

Because she had wanted him to hold her captive, to force her to feel those things, so that none of it was her responsibility.

He had proved that he could. But now… Now he was leaving.

"I'll see you tomorrow."

She was about to ask if he wanted her, if he had ever wanted her, but she could see the thick, hard outline of his erection pressed against the front of his black pants.

She could see that he wanted her, and he was still walking away.

"Good night," she said, the words thin and shaking.

"Good night."

And he didn't even have to get dressed to leave, because he was still fully clothed, and she was… Destroyed. Her bra was wrenched up over her breasts, but still clasped, her underwear shifted and torn in places.

She was humiliated. She had a feeling that he had intended to leave her humiliated.

She couldn't even feel angry, because she kept remembering the things that had occurred to her out in the hall. What she had done to him.

The humiliation he must've felt when she was on TV saying their child had no father.

Tonight he had demanded submission from her. He had exerted his control.

And now he was finished.

But she was not.

It took only a moment for Astrid to come to a decision.

She couldn't exist in this. In this world where he took his anger out on her body in such a way. She would give him an apology.

And she would make it one he would never forget.

Apologizing was another thing that Astrid had never done. But she was sure that she would do it well.

CHAPTER EIGHT

MAURO STRIPPED HIMSELF NAKED. He needed a cold shower. Something. Anything to deal with the desire that was still riding through his body. He had intended to make her feel out of control. To give her a taste of what she had done to him that night at the club.

When she had pushed him past the point of thinking clearly. Past the point of being sensible at all. And he had. He had, but in the end, she had somehow still done something to him. Overridden anything sensible. Destroyed every barrier that he had placed between the two of them.

The fact that he had been able to walk away had been a damned miracle. And now...

He was shaking. He was. He had wanted to make her tremble, had wanted to make her boneless, mindless, and he had done it. But at what cost?

What cost to himself?

He did not know the man he was when he touched her.

He went up in flames.

The connecting door between their bedrooms suddenly opened, and he turned.

It was his wife.

And he was completely naked, so there was no hiding the fact that he was aroused, that his cock was hard, and ready for her. That he was in no way in control of his needs or desires.

"What are you doing here?"

She was still naked, her entire body bare and exposed to him, her pale curves temptation he was not sure he could fight. Was not certain he could overcome.

"I came because I owe you an apology."

She began to walk toward him, her hips swaying gently, her lush curves and wild, glorious hair, tumbled around her shoulders, making him think of an ancient goddess.

"You owe me an apology?" he asked, the words sounding stilted.

"Yes. I owe you a great many things. And one evening will not be sufficient in making amends. But I would like to try."

"What are you doing?"

She moved nearer to him, pressing her palm against his chest, her touch soft, bewitching. "If you have to ask, then I'm not doing a very good job."

She walked a circle around him, slowly, appraising his body, her fingertips grazing lightly over his skin as she did. She stopped in front of him, those green eyes intent on his, blazing.

"I am a queen," she said. "I have been, my entire life, even before I bore the title. That's how it works. When you are the heir, you must behave as if you are from the beginning. There is no other option. There will be no quarter given. And I have… I have lived my life that way. Above reproach in many ways, as we discussed. But also without nuance. Without subtlety. There is no humility in me. I didn't learn it. I like to think there's compassion. Caring. And that mostly in my life I have acted in a way that would not do harm to others. But I have always been set apart, and I have always lived that way. My connections with those around me... I'm incapable of separating them from my status. I am not like you."

"Indeed," he said, grabbing hold of her wrist and holding her fast. "Because I'm not blue-blooded like you?"

"Yes," she whispered. "Yes."

Rage fired through him, but it wasn't because of that. It was because of all of the feelings inside him. The deep, roaring desire that he had to take her now, in spite of the fact that he had told himself he would not.

"You've lived more than one life," she continued. "And because of that I think you understand more. I think you see more. I have my struggles. Things that I have had to overcome. But they are in this world. My battlefield has been an ivory tower. I see my country from an elevated stance. My people. It is a necessity in many ways so that I can have an overview. So that I can know as much, and have time to look at it all. I fear sometimes that leads me to see people in general as statistics. Or chess pieces. I saw you as a chess piece. And I used you and for that I owe you an apology." She looked up at him again, and desire made his gut tighten.

"I am a queen," she repeated. "And I bow to no man. I never have. But for you... For you I will get on my knees."

And without warning she did just that, her red hair sliding over her shoulders as she went down. And then, she looked back up at him as she raised her hand, wrapping it around his hardened length.

And he knew he was lost. Knew that there was no way he could fight this. Not now.

He was finished. His control was at an end. And when

that slick, pink tongue darted out over his arousal, when she closed her lips over him and took him in deep, there was no more thought.

She clung to him as she lavished attention on his body with that imperious mouth.

He had heard it issued demands, had heard it whisper lies. And now that same, traitorous tongue slid effortlessly over him and stoked the flame of desire in his stomach.

Women had done this for him many times. It was not an unusual act, but there was something in the way she did it that made it something entirely new. Because she was queen. Because she was Astrid.

Because she made him feel the way no woman ever had before.

Because. Because many things he didn't want to think about. Didn't want to acknowledge.

He was at the verge of being able to hold back no more. And he didn't want that. Didn't want it to end that way. Not now.

"Enough," he growled, pulling her away from him.

"I haven't finished," she said, a small smile tilting her lips upward.

"If you wish to truly bow before me, my Queen, if you truly wish to make amends, and allow me use of your royal body, then I have a decidedly better way for you to kneel."

He swept her up off the floor and into his arms, carrying her over to the bed and positioning her there, on her hands and knees, her deliciously shaped ass on full display for his enjoyment.

He stroked himself, looking at her, at the image that she created there.

He was a fool. An absolute fool. He should have turned away from this long ago, but now it was too late. Now, he had to have her. Now, there was no going back.

If she wanted to apologize for her treachery, then he would take it out on her body. It would be no hardship. She was giving herself to him freely, and it was because of the ruthless seduction he had subjected her to only moments before.

This was control.

He still had control.

He pressed his fingers between her legs, pushing inside her tight, wet body as he tested her readiness.

She was ready. So very ready, and so desirous of him that it nearly made him lose his control then and there.

He joined her on the bed, positioning himself at her entrance and pushing inside slowly. She was so tight, so impossibly perfect.

She moaned, slow and long as he withdrew and thrust back home. And as he pounded inside her, he watched. The way that her elegant spine arched as she felt her pleasure build, the way she curled her fingers around the bedspread.

He couldn't see her face, but there was no denying it was her. His queen.

On her knees for him.

He held on to her hips, showing no mercy as he pushed them both toward a release he knew would consume them both.

And as his pleasure roared through his blood, screamed through his system like a freight train, there was one last thought before his release burned each and every one away like stubble and hay beneath the flame.

She was on her knees for him.

But he was on his knees too.

And then there was nothing. Oblivion. Sweet, desperate need being satisfied as he poured himself inside her.

His queen. His wife.

When it was through, she collapsed onto her stomach on the bed, then rolled to her side, curling up into a ball, her expression sleepy and satisfied.

And he remembered the way she had run out on him the first night.

How he had tried to run out on her not long ago.

It would be better to keep her with him. To keep her here.

He had tried it the other way, and he didn't like it.

If this was to be about him staking his claim and finding his place, then he was free to make that decision.

And so he wrapped his arm around her waist and drew her up against him, holding her tight.

He was on the verge of deciding on an entirely new plan.

One where Astrid being his wife meant her spending her nights in his bed. And only his.

For there was no way he would ever allow another man to touch her, he realized that now.

She was his woman. And she was carrying his child.

And the decision to hold her all night seemed to make everything clear.

His.

Only his.

CHAPTER NINE

OF ALL THE things Astrid expected to wake to the morning after her wedding, a scandal wasn't one of them.

After all, there had been ample opportunity for a scandal to break over the past couple of weeks, and yet none had.

But then, Bjornland being isolated as it was, it was often cloistered from the rest of the world, with news filtering out slowly. But, given that Mauro was arguably more famous than she the world over, she would have expected something like this to break sooner.

The breakfast table was covered in newspapers. And she didn't have to be terribly insightful to figure out that someone from her father's council was responsible for the delivery of the day's tidings.

"What is this?" Mauro asked, taking his seat at the table with utter confidence.

He did everything with supreme confidence. As he had shown her last night. Repeatedly. Until he had made her shake. Made her scream. Until she could no longer tell where her body ended and his began.

Something had changed between them last night. What had started in anger had ended with something else. It wasn't absent anger. It was imbued with an intensity that spoke of nearly every emotion.

All she knew was that by the time it was all over, the most natural thing in the world had been to curl up against him.

In many ways, she felt like a lamb choosing to sleep nestled up against the side of a lion. Mostly, she just had to trust that he wasn't going to eat her.

She had the feeling that Mauro was undecided as yet.

"Our reckoning," Astrid said, lifting one of the papers up. "At least, that's what it appears to be."

"I see my past has caught up with me."

Astrid began to read past the inflammatory headline.

The brand-new consort to the queen of Bjornland used to work as a rent boy.

There was no real escaping from the truth inherent in the headline. There were some seedy details included. Though, it didn't sound as if Mauro had been working the street so much as being passed around among bored older women.

"Why didn't you tell me?" she asked. "More interestingly, why has this not been in the press before?"

"Because, one of the women would have had to be willing to admit the fact that they paid me for sex. And apparently Lady Catherine is just close enough to death's door to do such a thing now." Astrid continued to stare at him, trying to figure out what he was feeling. He didn't look upset, nor did he look ashamed.

Being connected to such a scandal was the stuff of nightmares for her, and it made her skin feel like it was too tight for her body. Mauro was simply… He didn't seem to feel a thing at all.

"Also," he continued. "I make my living from scandal, Astrid. My clubs are all about debauchery. At what point do you suppose this would have been an interesting headline for a man famous for immoral acts? No, it's only interesting now."

She pressed her fingers to the center of her forehead. "This is a fantastic look to show the world," she said.

"You chose me as the father of your child."

"And now these are things our child will see. It's printed in black-and-white…"

"Do you have regrets, my Queen?"

The words were so cold and hard, and they hit her square in the chest. "No. Not in the way that you mean. But there are consequences for this. For our son or daughter. That's what I care about."

"Not about your own pristine reputation?"

She took in a labored breath. "I would be lying to you if I said I didn't care at all for the reputation of my country, and myself. But I can't deny my own involvement in bringing myself here. Is there anything else that you need to tell me?"

"I came from the gutter, Astrid. You do not ascend to success in the amount of time I did without crossing a few barriers between one side of the law and the other. Without making bargains with morality. You simply don't. I regret nothing of what I did, because it brought me to where I am. Once I figured out that I could control my fate, I took every opportunity to do so. At a certain age I discovered that women quite enjoyed me. And if it was something I was going to go out and do anyway for recreation, why not get a place to stay for the night, a hot meal. And some cash in my pocket. I have no moral qualms about what I did."

For the first time, she saw a spark in his face. In his

eyes. "The rest of the world does," he continued, stabbing a headline with his forefinger. "The rest of the world that leaves people behind, blames them for accidents of birth that see them thrust into a guaranteed lifetime of poverty. And believe me, we will be able to overcome this. Were I a woman in the same position... I fear my reputation would be beyond salvation. Fortunately, I'm a man, and one that now has money."

"Is that what you think?"

"It's what I know. My mother was nothing but a whore in the eyes of the world until the day she died. No one ever admitted her to their parties. Not even with me as her son. Of course, by the time of her death I wasn't quite as well-known as I am now. I imagine at a certain point any amount of money can erase a life of harlotry. My mother did what she had to. For us. Because my father, though he possessed the ability to support us, decided to pretend we didn't exist. No, don't ask me to apologize for selling what I had. Anymore than she should apologize for it. People with money are willing to buy it, and they're willing to pay quite a bit. They would rather buy sex than buy dinner for anyone in the slums, so you tell me what's to be done."

"I didn't say I was judging you," she said, but at the same time, she felt like something had shifted. Because what had happened between them last night was not a simple transaction. Then she wondered if it was for him.

It was deep and elemental and intimate. Had been from the first time. She couldn't imagine simply handing her body over for a few dollars and a place to sleep.

Because you've never been asked to do it. You've never had to. You were protected and you were insulated, and

the most despicable thing you ever had to put up with
was your father not believing in you.

She gritted her teeth. "How long did you do that?"

"Truthfully? Not even quite a year. Just something I did to save up money and move myself on to the next thing. I did that. I also worked as a bouncer at a club. That's where I got familiar with that sort of environment."

"Did you… Did it bother you? To be with women you didn't want?"

"I could make myself want them all. And if I didn't want them specifically, I could make myself do it for the money. A soft bed is quite arousing when the alternative is the streets."

She blinked, ignoring the scratchy feeling behind her eyes. "What did your mother think?"

"We never discussed it," he said, chuckling darkly. "Clearly. But then, she always behaved as if I might not know what she did with men coming through the house at all hours."

"So, you had a house?"

"Yes. For a time. I left when I was sixteen, because I couldn't bear it anymore. To watch her submit herself to that. Neither could I tolerate the ones who came to my room after, seeing if I would give for free what my mother had charged for. Don't worry. No one ever did anything to me. I was lucky. And that's the other thing, in the grand scheme of things, given my background, I was quite lucky. What I did, I did with a certain amount of choice involved. It's more than I can say for many like me. Don't waste any sympathy on me."

"I have sympathy for the headlines."

"They don't bother me. Though, I wonder if I should be concerned about you."

"There need be no concern," she said, pushing herself into a standing position.

She despised the weakness that had settled into her limbs. Hated that the press had been able to make her feel this way. That her father's councilmen were succeeding in trying to sabotage them so soon after the wedding.

This idea that bad press should be avoided at all cost, that being scandal free was an essential, was old thinking. Old thinking that was part of the Astrid she'd been before. Before she'd decided to take control of her own life by having her own child.

That Astrid could not care so much for scandal.

That Astrid would do things differently.

She took a breath. "I will be damned if anyone is allowed to write the story but us. We have done our best to control it from the beginning, and I don't see why we can't continue on as we began. We should go. We should go to Italy, visit your clubs. Show that I am in absolute support of you and all that you are."

He arched a brow. "Are you sure you don't just want to have a press release where you stand behind me looking regretful while I confess my many sins?"

She waved a hand. "No. I have no interest in that. None at all."

"Reputation is of no concern to me," he said.

"Well, it is of a concern to me," she said. "And I will not allow the press to decide what that reputation is. I'm clearing my schedule."

"Shall we take your private plane or mine?" he asked.

"We both have private planes?"

"Yes indeed," he said.

"Well, that just borders on absurd."

"It might, but I think it would be difficult for us to consolidate, given our busy schedules."

"I suppose."

"Mine, then," he said. "It has the whiskey I like on board."

"That isn't fair. I can't drink any."

"I never said any of this was going to be fair."

Astrid frowned. "I don't suppose you did."

The doors to the dining room burst open, and in charged one of the men from the council, his face red. "Do you see the censure you have opened us up to?" he railed against Astrid. "If your father were alive to see the disgrace that you have brought on his country…"

Mauro stood, slowly and decisively, his manner intimidating, his body radiating with a dark energy. "If your father were alive, he would see a woman standing strong in the face of embarrassingly tiny adversaries. And that is what you will continue to see in the coming days. I never met the old king, so I cannot speak confidently of what would give him pride. But he would at least not be able to deny the strength and sense of honor that Queen Astrid exudes."

Astrid said nothing, she simply watched as the councilman turned and walked out of the room, clearly not at all mollified by Mauro's interference, but likely gone off to lick his wounds, as he clearly didn't possess the wherewithal to stand against a man of Mauro's presence.

She could have defended herself. She had done it for years now. This was hardly going to be the straw that broke the camel's back. But she was tired, and she was reeling from the revelations in the paper in front of her.

And for all that Mauro was tangled up in the challenges she was dealing with now, she was grateful to have had him there to stand with her. It wasn't always about needing to be rescued or defended. But sometimes it was good to know that someone was there to stand with you. To be the first to speak in defense.

To know that someone else was on your side.

She didn't know when that switch had occurred. Mauro had felt like yet another in a line of adversaries, and suddenly now she felt as if they had melded into a team. If nothing else, Mauro would want a stable environment for their child.

She took a breath. "I think we have a plane to catch."

By the time the plane touched down in Italy, yet another scandal had broken.

Mauro was ready to track down journalists and cockroaches from his past and present alike and create some real scandal.

He minded the rumors about his life as a prostitute less than the stories that greeted them the moment they touched down in his homeland.

His father had come forward.

Dominic Farenzi, titled old duke and part of one of Italy's oldest aristocratic families, had finally claimed his son.

Oh, not for a happy reunion, no, the duke would never do such a thing. He wanted his name in the press. To attach himself to the scandal by dragging Mauro's name down further.

And, of course, it made perfect sense. Mauro had taken a different last name as he had ascended the ranks, partly because he didn't want every old relative of his mother's coming out of the woodwork to demand endless paydays. He had wanted to avoid situations that involved blackmail.

His former clients—the women he slept with—would have most certainly recognized him, but Dominic would have no reason to recognize him on sight. They had met only once, and Mauro had been young.

He had looked up at the old man with all of the hope only a boy could still possess after such a miserable upbringing—and the old man had gazed back with a sneer. And told Mauro exactly what he was. Not a part of that lineage, but a mistake. A mistake that should have been nothing more than a stain on his sheets.

But now... Now that his profile had been raised, and now that he was royalty by marriage, his father had made the connection, and more than that, had seen his opportunity to use the connection. Money... The old man had that. This was something more, and obviously he wished to use it.

"So, you're not a commoner," Astrid said when they were settled into his awaiting sports car and driving through the winding streets.

"I might as well be. I'm a bastard. Dukes and bastards are a time-honored tradition, in every culture, I should think. I am not royalty. Not by any real standard. But there are any number of people clearly willing to use this connection, and I would have told you he would be the last person to do it, out of a sense of self-preservation. But I suppose this is the problem with aging enemies. They figure perhaps they only have a certain number of years to even concern themselves with answering for the consequences of their actions. Why not see what happens?"

"All fine for him. But he's playing with your life."

"Though, in this case there is nothing for me to be ashamed of. Though I would suppose that vicious commentary about my mother will follow. Thankfully, she's dead. And none of this will be her problem."

"I'm sorry," she said. "I had no idea… When I chose you I miscalculated in more ways than I realized."

"I imagine you didn't wish to choose the bastard son of a twisted old man who also moonlighted as a gigolo to be the father of your baby."

"That's not what I meant," she said quickly. "I only meant that I didn't know how much the media would be able to discover. And how much they would use against you. They can be brutal and vicious, my mother instructed me on that early on."

"It doesn't affect me much," he said. "I have been brutal and vicious to myself in the public sphere for years. I found self-deprecation to be the best defense. But, it's not exactly a good look for the queen of a nation I don't suppose."

"Possibly not," she said.

"Did you always know who your father was?"

"I can't remember exactly when I truly became aware of who he was and what that meant. Yes. It was never a secret. Not for me. I think my mother wanted me to be aware. I think she wanted me to know that there was a certain amount of injustice at play. She wanted me to understand. Something that I appreciate greatly. Because it helped to shape me into what I was. It helped me understand where power came from. There are titles. And then there is money. And both bring their own kind of power. It's certainly better to have them together. One can be earned, and one cannot be. I decided never to waste my time caring about something that I could never go out and earn for myself. And so, I simply decided to work at getting money. Because I would be damned if the last word on who I was came from a man who didn't care whether or not I lived or died."

"I understand," she said. "I mean, I really understand now why you won't abandon your child. Why it means something to you. I'm sorry. It was so… I was only thinking of myself and my goals. Sometimes I get so focused on this idea of the greater good, and I remove the humanity from it. In this case, I decided that the greater good was something that I wanted. And I truly didn't think of you."

"It doesn't matter. What matters is that I won't be like my father. Ever."

"I believe it." She looked out the window, at the buildings that closed in around them, tall and brick, rebelling against the age that was beginning to crack at the foundation.

The farther on they went, the more faded the glory of the buildings around them. It did not appear that they were headed in a direction where Mauro would live, or have a club.

"Where are we going?"

He was questioning that himself. Questioning it because he had decided that he would take her to see, so that she had the whole story, but it was one thing to think it, and quite another to do it. He imagined that Astrid had never been near a slum in her life.

"It's the whole story. So that there are no more surprises. I think that is important to see."

Astrid was quiet after that, and he maneuvered the sleek car around the corner, until they reached a sparse, wasteland of an area that contained a crumbling apartment building, and tarp set up as tents around the property.

"If you're lucky, you live in there," he said.

"Oh," she said, her eyes wide as she took in the sprawl of humanity around them. "This is where you're from?"

"Yes." He cleared his throat. "I imagine you have not had an exposure to such things."

"No, I have. I've been involved in quite a few outreaches worldwide where I went and distributed medical supplies and food. But… It's not the same as living in it. It's not the same as… Growing up this way."

"This is what I am. I have no shame in it, and I never have. The press is going to attempt to make it a shameful thing, and I'm sure that there are only more lurid details of my sexual exploits to come. There will likely be women who spent wild nights with me in my club eager to tell their story. For all I know, more of my… Clients from my early years. These things will continue to happen. As long as there is money or fame to be extorted, it will occur. It was one thing when I was selling sin. It's quite another in this position."

"It's all right," she said. "I… I did this to escape from the hold that the men on my father's council had over me. I did this to gain independence. What good is independence if I'm still held hostage by a desperate need to make myself look better than I actually am? My desperate need to be something I'm not. Whatever the true nature of our relationship is… We are having a baby."

There was one last place. His house, if it still stood.

"Just a little bit farther," he said.

Their home was at the wall of a dead end, beneath an office building that he had never imagined housed businesses that were terribly legitimate. The place looked abandoned now, the windows boarded up, a notice posted on the side.

"This is where we lived," he said.

"This is your house?"

"Yes."

"Where does your father live?"

He turned toward the vast mountain that rose up above the buildings around them.

"There. He lives there. And he has a view of the whole city, down to the slums. While we had a view of those mansions up on the hill. And I knew that the man who fathered me was there. Somewhere. That he was there looking down on that very house, this very spot, and feeling nothing. It was motivating. And I…"

He parked the car suddenly and got out, looking around to make sure there was no one loitering nearby.

He had no doubt that he was well able to handle any attacker who might come out from behind the shadows. He had learned to defend himself against grown men when he was just a boy. Maturity, and years of hard labor in the gym, had only honed his physique further.

Plus, he was ruthless. He had learned to fight, not in arenas, but in situations that could very well have turned into life or death. That meant when he was under threat, he gave no quarter.

And should anyone step forward to threaten Astrid— to threaten his child—he would not hesitate to do what needed to be done. He took a breath of the air, stale down here, and warmer, boxed in by these tall, narrow buildings. And it reminded him of what it meant to be a boy. To be trapped here.

To be helpless.

He loosened his tie, feeling as if he was choking on the air around them.

He felt a hand on his shoulder and turned to see Astrid standing there. "Are you all right?"

"I'm fine. I haven't been back here, not since I left my mother's home. After that I went off to find my way, and once I had acquired enough, I sent for her. I bought her a house. One up there on the hill. So that she could look down on everything here, the same as he had done all those years. So much hard living. She did not last long after. I blame him. I always will."

"I don't blame you."

"I met him once. My mother told me which house was his, and I climbed the hill. I walked right up to that house, and I stood there on the front porch, full of the bravado of a young boy, just barely more than thirteen. Convinced I was a man. I knocked on the door, and I asked to see him. I thought they were going to send me away, but he heard me. He heard me and he came to the door. I thought that if I explained to him what our situation was... What my mother was forced to do..." That moment, that sick humiliation and shame, that deep, unmet need all seemed close to the surface now, rolling through his stomach like an angry ball of fire.

"He knew. And what's more, he made it very clear to me that my mother had not turned to prostitution as a desperate single mother. But rather, that was how she had found him."

"How vile," Astrid said. "How could he speak to you like that?"

"Oh, he took great joy in it. In making sure that I

knew that I was never going to be seen the way that he saw my half brothers and sisters. That my mother's blood made me unsuitable. But you know... It's his. It's his blood that I regret the most, not the blood of the woman who did what she had to, to allow us both to survive. Who cared for me, even when it was hard. No, I don't feel shame over carrying her blood. But when I think too deeply of his, I can feel my skin crawl. After that, I decided I would never covet what I could not have, not again. I took great pains to make sure that I could have whatever it was I pleased. I started making plans. I thought about all the places people went when they had money, and I figured that what I would want was a way to take the money of those people. Which is what I've done. Hotels. Clubs. Resorts and destination vacation spots. I appeal to those who have money to invest in fantasy. And with that I've built something real. With that, I will make a life for my child far and away what my mother was able to do for me, in spite of how hard she tried."

"Your father is a disgusting, opportunistic animal. We will give him no satisfaction with what he's trying to do."

"Oh, the press will give him plenty, I have no concerns about that."

"How unfair," she said. "How unfair that they all want to give you attention now."

"Let them," he said. "It makes no difference to me. It only proves that suddenly I have something that they want. Now my father can use me. How novel. All those years I could have used him. Well, fortunes of change."

He stepped away from the old house. From the tightness in his chest.

"I shall take you to my offices."

"Oh, really?"

"Yes," he said decisively. "I have spent a great deal of time in your domain, my Queen. It's time you came to mine."

CHAPTER TEN

MAURO'S OFFICES WERE impressive indeed. The contrast of the brilliant, steel-and-glass-framed building when juxtaposed against the slums they had just visited struck Astrid particularly hard as he ushered her into his office, paneless glass windows making up the entirety of the walls, overlooking Rome. Overlooking even the houses on the hills.

And she understood it. What it meant. Why it mattered. She understood what had shaped him.

And she felt…

It was a strange thing, to have this man let her in that way. She couldn't say that she knew very many people in such a deep way that she did him.

She knew no one in such an intimate fashion.

But his showing her the slums… The house. Talking about his father.

It was all new. This feeling for another person. This feeling like she knew him. Like she could feel the things he felt.

He pressed his hand to her lower back as he led her deeper into his office, and somehow as he did that, she felt as if he had wrapped his hand around her heart and squeezed it tight.

"These are the corporate offices. As you can see, I have a few."

"Yes. You do." It wasn't just a stark contrast to the slums, but to the palace and Bjornland, which was gilded and old-fashioned in every way. "The clutter of the palace must drive you crazy," she observed.

"I was thinking the same about you," he said. "You enjoy that restaurant we went to the night we got engaged. And it's quite spare. You also seem particularly fond of the ring I bought you."

She squeezed her hand into a fist, feeling embarrassed that he had seen through her so easily. "It is very pretty. Yes, I suppose the rooms in the palace are not necessarily to my taste."

"You should have them redone."

"That's simple?"

"Why not?"

"Because of tradition, and things. It's hardly... It's hardly appropriate to go changing everything right when you're crowned."

"Is it not?" he asked.

"I wouldn't think."

"You've been queen for two years."

"Yes," she agreed. "I have been."

"If you're not afraid to take control of your own destiny, you should be able to take control of your bedroom decor."

"Fair enough," she replied. "Perhaps I will do a bit of a redesign when we get back." She frowned. "If we... Are you coming back with me?"

It was such a vulnerable statement. So very silly. She didn't know why she was exposing herself to potential rejection like that. Especially considering he wasn't supposed to matter. But then, he wasn't supposed to have revealed such intimate and crushing things about himself either. He wasn't supposed to be human. That was the crux of the problem. The longer she was around this beautiful, god of a man, the more she saw his humanity. And that was dangerous in a particular way nothing else had ever been.

"I will be back intermittently," he said.

"I see."

"Though, I should make one thing very clear," he said.

"What is that?"

"That the idea that you might spend time in other men's beds is now off the table."

"Is it?" She tried to sound surprised, or maybe even mildly annoyed about his heavy-handed proclamation, but instead, she was certain that some of her hopefulness had broken through.

"After what happened on our wedding night… I should think that was quite obvious."

"What happened?"

"The explosion between us."

"It is as it ever was," she said, trying to sound casual. "Is it different than the first time? Is it different than it normally is?"

Of course, that last question revealed just how much she didn't know.

"It is never like that. Not with anyone else. And if you cannot feel how it was different than our first time…"

"I do," she said.

"Then surely you must know that this is a fact. There will be no one else."

"What about for you?"

"I don't want anyone else."

"And if you did?"

"I suspect we would have a discussion about it before anything occurred. I am nothing if not honest."

"So, should I wish to sleep with another man, we will have a discussion?"

"There will be no discussion. I would separate the man's head from his body."

"Well, that doesn't seem equitable."

"I didn't say that it was."

"I'm a queen," she said. "The rightful queen of Bjornland. You marrying me does not make you a king."

"But we are in my kingdom now," he said, a smile spreading slowly across his chiseled face. "And that is one reason I took you to see the slums that I grew up in. So you would understand. You think that you know because you have read articles. You think that you know because you have spent time in my bed. But unless you have seen where I was. You will not understand what it means that I am here."

So, he hadn't been showing her out of any desire to connect with her emotionally. She didn't know why, but that made her feel... She didn't like it. She wanted something more from him, and she hated that she did. She wanted something more from him, and the very idea of it made her feel uncomfortable. And also needy and vulnerable in ways that she didn't want to confront.

"I'm very impressed," she returned.

"I don't require that you be impressed. But you should understand. I am a man who sees no obstacle that he cannot overcome. If you think that you might win with me, *cara*, you are sadly mistaken."

The feelings that rolled through her body were tumultuous. She had no idea how to parse them all. On the one hand, his stubbornness, the fact that he was not intimidated at all by who she was, made her feel like she was adrift. She was accustomed to subtle challenges, not open ones. It also made her feel alive. Alive and particularly invigorated. That she could step into this place that was his, only his, as she had done that first night, and to be consumed by his world. By him. Even if only for a moment.

She wished that she could spend more time with him here. And maybe she would. There was no reason she couldn't split her time between Bjornland and Italy. Her ability to govern was not impacted by whether or not she was directly in residence in the palace.

But he hadn't said that he wanted her to. Instead, he had simply said that he would be staying here.

"There is a gala tonight," he said suddenly.

"Oh?"

"Not the sort of thing I usually bother myself with. In fact, I usually take great joy in turning down the invitations."

"All right."

"But we are in a different position now, are we not?"

"You are," she said. "I attend galas the world over, as a representative of my country."

"And I tend to sink deeper into debauchery at my clubs."

"We make choices."

"Well, now I'm going to make a different one. As we are making a show of solidarity, I figure there will be no better way of doing that than appearing so grandly upon the world stage."

"I suppose so," she returned.

"You are mine," he said. "And the world has only understood thus far, I think, that I might be yours. But they will understand after tonight."

She was his? But how did he mean that? And why did she want it to mean...? Why did she want it to have meaning?

The way he made her feel when they were alone in the dark was a heady, sensual rush that affected not just her body but also her soul.

It had nothing to do with performance and everything to do with... She didn't know.

She didn't know, and she hated not knowing. "That sounds ominous," she said, instead of any of the things she'd been thinking.

His dark eyes caught and held hers, and didn't let go. "You will understand too. After tonight. You will understand."

Mauro was not one to question his own decision-making. He never had been. There had never been time for any such things. He was a man of action, by necessity. He had never been one to Monday morning quarterback the decisions he'd made to propel his life in the direction that he wanted it. He was questioning himself now. If only a bit.

He was a headline the world over at the moment, and while in many ways he didn't mind at all, in others...

But he was set to beard the lion tonight.

His father would be at this event. That was one of the many reasons he had avoided things like this in the past, as much as he tried to pretend otherwise. He had allowed his father's presence to deter him from joining society in Italy for a number of years.

He had always told himself it was because there was no point.

He was not a man who dealt in galas, after all.

He liked to appeal to the darker, more sensual side of the moneyed set in the world. Liked to gather in the blackness, carrying out sultry, libidinous acts in the shadows.

He was going to have to work at changing the headlines. Not for himself, not even for Astrid, but for his child.

He did not deserve to see his father only as a horror, who was also the son of one.

He might not feel shame over what he was, but his child invariably would. And that would have to change.

He straightened the cuffs on his jacket and looked toward the room in his penthouse that Astrid had secreted herself in earlier. He had forced the issue of being the one to choose her gown, and she had been put out with him, as she had a stylist who was in charge of selecting all of the dresses she wore for public appearance.

Mauro had made the point—the excellent point, if he said so himself—that Astrid appearing in something a bit different would only support the narrative about their relationship being a defining one.

The gown he had chosen, with the help of his assistant, was exactly what he wished to see his beautiful, curvy wife in, but now she seemed to be hiding out.

"Astrid," he said. "We are about to pass the point of being fashionably late."

The door cracked slightly. "Do you care?"

"No. I like being fashionably late, because it makes people talk. But I thought you might care."

"I don't think I can possibly go out in this."

"It is nothing compared to that white dress you wore the night you first seduced me."

"That was different," she said archly. "I was not being photographed, and I was trying to seduce you."

"And tonight you are my wife. And we are in my part of the world, and I expect for you to present yourself in such a manner. I will wear any ceremonial dress that you require in your country. But you must indulge me here."

"Okay. So that is how it will work when we are in Italy, or when we are in Bjornland. But what about when we're in… Holland?"

"We will both wear wooden shoes. Now, show me the dress."

She opened the door all the way, and the tiger that he was barely keeping leashed inside him leaped forward.

He no longer wanted to go out. Rather, he wanted to spend the entire evening exploring the ways in which that gown clung to her body.

It was a burnished gold that set off a fire in her glossy red hair, the color picking up gold tones in that pale skin of hers, as well. It glimmered as it clung to each and every curve, the neckline a deep V that accentuated her lush body.

"It is a bit much," she said, breezing past him and moving to where her makeup bag was. She produced a tube of red lipstick, and applied it to her mouth, making her look even more of a siren than she had a moment before.

He brought her up against his side, and guided her toward the door, her figure fitting more perfectly against his than he ever could've imagined.

"When we come home," he murmured, as they got into the elevator, "I greatly look forward to stripping this dress off you."

"What exactly are we doing?" she asked.

"What do you mean? Right now, we are going to a gala."

"I mean… What are we doing? In private. Behind closed doors. Where we have no reason to be putting on a show. What are we doing? Because it was one thing when we had an arrangement, for the benefit of our son or daughter. It was one thing when we were putting on a show for the media. But this idea that we will spend our nights together… As if it's just an assumed thing… I don't understand the purpose of that."

He said nothing as they walked through the lobby of the spectacular apartment building he called his own. They were ushered into a limousine, and he took his seat right beside her, pressing his hand over the top of her small, soft one.

"I don't understand why we wouldn't burn out any chemistry that exists between us. People are so prudish about sex and attraction, but it's something that's never made much sense to me."

"I don't suppose it would. You used it as a commodity when you were young, but I did not. For me, it is about connection in some way, at the very least. It is inescapable as far as I'm concerned. I do not know of another way to see it. And I don't wish to put us in the position where things would become acrimonious between us should you decide… Should you decide that you feel an attraction for another woman. And what will happen when we decide to separate? What then? As I see it, it can only go two ways. We must decide that it is temporary, and that we are business partners. Or we must decide it's forever."

Forever.

He had never thought of anything in those terms before. Mostly because he didn't think very many steps ahead. He saw his goal, and he achieved it. And then he went on to the next. He enjoyed the excesses that he had at his disposal at any given time, with great relish. And he did nothing to concern himself with heavy things, things that pertained to the future. And she was asking him to choose. Nothing or forever.

He was a man who had no issue being decisive. And yet, he found this was one question he could not answer with an instantaneous snap of his finger.

Just another way in which this little queen confounded him.

The car rolled up to the front of the beautiful, historic hotel that the gala was being held in. The white marble shone pale in the moonlight, a beacon of all that he had ever aspired to as a boy.

And beside him there was Astrid.

A woman of pale marble, who wasn't cold to the touch, but warm and so very alive. So very enticing.

"We will speak more after the gala."

"We will speak," she said insistently. "I won't have you drowning out my common sense with your temptation."

Temptation. He would happily show her some temptation, and give her a very solid display on why they did not need to make such a definitive bargain between them.

He took hold of her hand, and pulled her forward, wrapping his arms around her and bringing her up onto his lap, so that she could feel the hardness and intensity that only she seemed to be able to create in him. And he kissed her. Not a slow tasting, but a fierce claiming. A promise. Of everything he was going to use to convince her that this heat between them needed to be thoroughly explored, and there would be no rationalizing that away on her part.

After all, she was the one who had ignited this need inside him. All of this was her fault. And her daring to try and put up a barrier between them now was something he could not let stand.

He cupped her face, taking the kiss deep, sliding his tongue against hers until he drew a fractured moan from her body. And then he pulled away.

"Yes," he said. "We will resume this discussion after the gala."

He opened the door to the limo, brushing past the driver, who was attempting to hold the door for them, and instead, held it open for Astrid before taking her arm and closing it behind them.

"You shouldn't try to do the poor man's job for him," Astrid said, clearly attempting to sound as healthy as possible and to seem unaffected by the kiss they had shared.

"You are my wife," he said. "I will be the one to hold the door for you. No other man need serve you."

"Very possessive for a man who isn't sure what he wants."

They said nothing more, because then they reached the top of the steps, and were ushered inside, where they were announced grandly, and in a fashion that Mauro would have taken a great kind of satisfaction in under any other circumstances.

He was here. Standing at the top, all these people he had looked up to all of his life, people who had kept him shut out of society, gazing up at him, as if he were the most important and powerful man in the room. Unlikely though he was, even without the inclusion of his new, royal bride.

But she brought that blue-blooded element he could not manufacture on his own.

She was carrying his child, a child who was the future ruler of a nation.

Nothing could elevate him more.

And yet, that wasn't the primary focus of his thoughts.

Mostly, he was thinking about her. Mostly, he was remembering the way her skin had felt beneath his hands.

The way she had sighed and moaned when he had kissed her. A pang of resentment hit him in the chest. That she should have such power over him. Over this moment.

He tightened his hold on her, her ultimatum ringing in his head.

They made their way down the stairs, into the center of the tangled knot of crows masquerading as aristocracy. Black dresses on the reed-thin bodies of the women, black tuxes and ties on the men.

Except for Astrid. Who was like liquid gold, shimmering before them all.

A prize. That was what he had fashioned her into. And yet, no matter how much he repeated that to himself as they circulated the room, as they made readings to those around them, Astrid with her royal ease, and him entirely absent of such a thing, all he could think was that he had revealed himself in many ways by his choices tonight.

Revealed the fact that he was not of the aristocracy, no matter that he shared half of his blood with it.

Because no one else would have dressed their wife as such an obvious prize, only to flaunt her importance.

And yet, she was beautiful. And she deserved to look as she did. As the most expensive, glorious woman in the room, and why should he have dressed her as anything else? Subtlety, he decided, might be best left to those born with money. He was not going to concern himself with it.

That was when he saw *him*.

Impossible to miss him. Broad shouldered, and taller than most of the men in the room, except for Mauro himself.

Age had not stooped the man's shoulders, and Mauro supposed that if he weren't quite so enraged at the mere existence of him, he might appreciate what that said about his genetics.

Instead, he only felt his stomach turned sour with the injustice of it all. Because his mother was dead and gone, and this man was able to stand tall, proud, well dressed and with his wife, as if he had not caused immeasurable pain over the course of years.

As if nothing troubled his conscience at all.

His eyes caught Mauro's and held them, and he whispered something to the woman at his side, who nodded in dutiful obedience, and separated from her husband, moving off to a cluster of women standing next to a tray of champagne.

Mauro gritted his teeth. "Well, it has been some time."

"Has it? I wasn't sure if we had ever met," his father returned.

"We did. I was a child. You had me thrown straight back to the slum I came out of."

"Oh, was that you? It's difficult for me to keep my slum bastards straight."

"And yet, you seem to know me well enough now."

"You've done well for yourself," he said, casting an eye over Astrid.

Mauro bitterly regretted involving her in this, the moment the old man's eyes began to roam over her luxurious curves.

Astrid, on the other hand, didn't seem regretful in the least. Astrid faced his father head-on.

"I'm Queen Astrid von Bjornland," she said, her tone frosty, her shoulders straight. Her hold on him tight. "I do not believe we've met."

"Dominic Farenzi, Duke of San Isabella."

"I see. And you are connected to my husband through accident of birth?"

She sounded perfectly civil, but he could sense she was feeling anything but.

"Yes. I had the impression you were connected to my bastard son much the same way."

Her lips curved upward. "Oh, no. I chose him. I chose him quite deliberately to be the father of my child. My heir. Because he is perfect, and everything I could possibly want, from a genetic standpoint and otherwise."

"I didn't realize the standards of perfection were lowered so."

"If this is the way that you expected you might leverage me and my status for your own personal benefit when you sought to announce your connection to my husband, you have badly miscalculated."

"You assumed it was about you? How very fascinating."

"I am queen of an entire nation. I assume many things are about me, and I've yet to be proven wrong."

"Is this what you have become?" his father asked. "Because at least when you were a boy you spoke for yourself. Now, you have this woman speaking for you." He shook his head. "But then, I am not surprised. It is the only thing that gave you any relevance in the eyes of the

media, and truly in the eyes of the world. One sin ped-
dler is essentially the same as any other. You are not only
uninteresting on your own, but unoriginal."

Mauro chuckled, and before he could grab hold of his
composure, reached out and grabbed hold of his father's
throat. "I see. I'm very sorry that I failed to produce a
surprise for you." He chuckled. "But you should understand this. If you assume that you understand me, you
will be bitterly disappointed. And if you think you can
stand here and speak to my wife, speak about my wife,
and face no repercussion, then you truly know nothing
about me at all. I have done a great many things in my
life that were rooted in calculation and self-service. But
Astrid is mine. Mine. And unlike you, I keep what is
mine. My child. My woman. You will not speak to her.
You will not speak about her. You will not sell any more
of your torrid stories to the press about my mother. If
you do anything to cause Astrid harm, I will end you.
Financially. Physically if I must. You could only lord
things over me when I was a little boy who had need.
You could only cow me, control me as long as you had
more power than I did. The tide has shifted, Father. And
now that I've made my position clear, all that's left to do
is for you to decide whether or not you want to push me.
I would suggest that you don't."

He released his hold on the old man, rage coursing
through his body. And he felt Astrid's calming touch on
his shoulder. He looked at her, the red, foggy haze of his
vision beginning to clear, and he saw that her expression
was filled with concern. "Mauro..."

"You reveal yourself," his father said. "That you would
stoop to physical threats. You might be able to put on a

suit, earn money, spend money, but you will always be what you were born. The son of a whore."

"Push me any harder and I may be the son of a dead man."

"Oh, I have no doubt. I have no interest in pushing you. I'm just making it clear, whatever narrative you think is happening, it is blood that wins. Time and time again."

"You're right about that," Mauro said. "It is blood that wins out in the end. And when mine triumphs, you had best hope it's not due to the fact that I spilled any of yours." He looked over at Astrid, who had gone pale. "Come, *cara*. I think that our time at this event has lapsed."

He had no more time for this. Had no more desire to engage in such a farce. He was going to end the evening now, and he was going to end it exactly the way he had intended on ending it before this miserable farce had began. She would see who he was.

He pulled her through the crowd, not caring that they had drawn curious stares. That they were now being subjected to scrutiny by all around them. He didn't care. He was not a good man. He was not a civilized man. He was not one of them. If it had not been apparent before, then it was apparent now.

He was Mauro Bianchi, and he was from the slums. If blood won out, then he was quite all right letting it show freely.

He signaled his driver using his phone, and by the time they reached the front of the hotel, the limo was there waiting for them. He ushered her inside, and she said nothing. That was unusual, as Astrid typically had a comment, or a snarky aside. Right now she seemed to have nothing.

Perhaps he truly had made her realize who he was. Made her realize what he was.

Now, perhaps she would find it undeniable. "I've made my decision," he said, once the limo began to move away from the hotel. "You're mine. There will be no discussion about any alternatives."

CHAPTER ELEVEN

ASTRID WAS STILL shell-shocked by the time they tumbled out of the limo and into the lobby of the apartment building that housed Mauro's penthouse. The way that his father had treated him, the way that he had treated his father…

She didn't know why she had expected anything else, actually. Mauro had all the trappings of a civilized man, but she had always known that underneath that exterior beat the heart of a barbarian.

She had not been disappointed in tonight's showing. Not on that score.

And then the way that he had… Declared his possession of her when they had gotten back into the car. But then, he hadn't spoken again. And he had not touched her.

She fidgeted, feeling restless as they stood in the lobby for a moment. Mauro seemed to take stock of his surroundings, looking for paparazzi, she wondered, and then he dragged her to the lift, the doors opening wide, as he moved them both inside. And that was when she discovered what he truly meant by being his.

He pushed her against the wall, the metal biting into her shoulder blades as he did. Then he gripped her chin between his thumb and forefinger and held her steady.

His eyes blazing down into hers. He was like a wild animal. A feral beast that she could neither soothe nor tame. One that looked completely and utterly bent on having her at his mercy.

She resisted. Everything in her resisted, because hadn't she been resisting such a thing for her entire life?

Until him. He was the beginning of that. The awakening of that desire. Feel a man's strength. To allow it to carry her own, if only for a little while. And now, even more, the temptation to allow it to overwhelm her utterly and completely.

It was intoxicating. To think that perhaps she truly could be his. She had belonged to causes. To an entire country worth of people. She belonged to Bjornland, she belonged to her duty. But to find another person who could carry all of that was a distantly hazy fantasy that she hadn't even been aware she'd ever possessed. She wanted it.

But she wasn't sure she was brave enough.

But she could see in him the anger, force, the will to bend her. To create the space that would require that submission. A space that would hold her. A space that would sustain her.

So when he kissed her mouth, she kissed him back, with all the ferocity penned up inside of her. There was no small amount of it. It was real and raw and wild. Something she had imagined might be beyond her.

But she didn't feel like another entity, not like another creature, no. Instead, she felt like she might be the truest, rawest form of Astrid. With no parents watching her every move, no press. No brother. No assistant. No council of angry men opposing her very existence.

As if she lived in a world created just for her, just for Mauro.

Not in the way she had felt when she had been pretending to be someone else, no. She felt like her. Like she was truly at home in her skin for the first time. Like she had become real, and now nothing on earth would ever be able to make her unreal. The elevator stopped, and the doors slid open, revealing his sleek and lovely penthouse, as light and view conscious as his office, with windows that she had been assured were made with one-way glass.

Affording him the view that he wanted, giving him the privacy he needed. As if reading her mind, he led her over to the window, and positioned her in front of him.

"Look at all that," he said. "All those glittering lights below. I can buy every single place and person those lights represent. Everyone. Here I am on top. And I have you."

She shivered, and he moved her hair to the side, exposing the nape of her neck. Leaning forward and pressing a firm kiss to her skin. "Yes. I have you. I want you to take that dress off."

Heat crept into her face. "Here? In front of the windows?"

"I already told you… No one can see," he said, his hand traveling down the line of her spine, stroking gently. He grasped the zipper tab that rested low on her back. "I want to see."

He drew it down slowly, the fabric parting, going loose and dropping from her shoulders, down to her hips, before it slid the rest of the way down to the floor.

The underwear she had on was whisper thin, barely there, and exposed the entirety of her backside for his enjoyment. Something he made no secret of as he reached out and grabbed her, squeezed her, growling in his appreciation.

"You're very beautiful," he said. "A beautiful trophy. All for me."

His words, rough and angry, should have upset her. Should have made her feel small and used. Instead, they sent a thrill through her body.

She was a great many things, but she had never been someone's trophy. She supposed it should make her unhappy.

But she was a woman with a great deal of power.

And within the broad scope of that power, knowing that she could call bodyguards in here at any moment and have Mauro dispatched handily. That she had an entire military at her command... That she had faced down leaders, heads of state and a great many men who had not wanted her in the position she held.

Yes, given all that, she could think of very little that made her feel threatened. It allowed her to sink into this. Allowed her to embrace it.

To give herself a moment where she was nothing more than an object for his enjoyment. A gift for him.

"I like this," he said softly, stroking her in the center of her back again. "My city laid out before me. My woman, laid out before me."

He advanced on her, pushing her closer to the glass, until her hip bones connected with the cool, smooth surface, her stomach, her breasts. Her thighs. Her palms were rested flat against it, and she looked out, having the strangest sensation that she was flying.

"You even carry my baby inside you," he said, his voice getting impossibly rough now. "You are mine.

Mine. In every beautiful, twisted-up way you possibly could be." He kissed her neck, her shoulder, gripping her hip, then the other as he continued to kiss her, tracing a line down to the waistband of her panties. He hooked his fingers in the waistband, tugging them down, before rising back to his feet and unhooking her bra, leaving her now completely naked, pressed against the glass. "The world is at your feet, my Queen," he whispered. "And I want you at mine."

He whirled her around so that she was facing him, the glass cold on her back. There was something about it that felt dangerous. This razor-thin pane between herself and the air outside. Between falling endlessly and safety. She began to work his clothes next. Wordlessly. In absolute obedience to his command. She undid his tie. Pushed his jacket from his shoulders and let it fall to the floor. She undid his shirt, her knees bending slightly with each button she pushed through the hole.

And then she did end up on her knees before him.

Ready to give him what she had last night. And more. Everything he wanted. All of her. She undid his belt, his pants slowly, taking his length in her hand and testing him, curling her fingers around all that heavy weight. He wrapped his own hand around himself, and pressed against her lips. She complied, opening to him. Taking him inside.

He bucked his hips forward slightly, gently, and she relaxed, allowing him to set the pace. Trusting him. Giving herself over to him.

He was big and strong, and he could hurt her if he chose to. But she didn't put up any defenses. She didn't do anything to protect herself.

She had seen what he was earlier, and still, she knelt

before him, offering him her throat, though she had seen him grab a man by his earlier.

His movements became less measured, more intense, and she let her head fall back against the glass as he found his pleasure, accepted his release as a strange, warm sense of satisfaction rolled through her.

She had been of service to him.

The idea made her giggle. And she didn't giggle. Particularly not after things like that.

She was buzzing, fuzzy. She looked at his body and saw that for now he was satisfied, but she found herself being pulled to her feet, lifted up into his arms. He clamped one arm around her waist, and urged her legs up around his hips, as he walked her back toward the bedroom. It wasn't any less private than the other room, large windows dominating the walls in there, as well. But there was the bed. Large and spare, with a low black headboard and a stark black bedspread.

"You will look beautiful against my sheets," he said, his voice low and harsh. "I wish to look at you." She moved over to the edge of the bed, uncertain as to how to proceed. "On your knees, facing the headboard."

She hurried to obey, getting into the center of the mattress and arching her back slightly, allowing him the full view of her body. He reached forward, pressing his fingers between her legs and teasing her where she knew she was slick with need for him.

"Turn around," he ordered.

She obeyed, still on all fours, but facing him now. She could see that he was hard again, ready for her already.

"Lie down on your back," he said. "And part your thighs for me."

Again, she did as he bid, lying back against the velvet bed cover and opening herself to him. Keeping nothing back.

She was trembling, her entire body shaking with the force of the strangeness of all of this. Of what it meant to give this kind of control.

"There," he said. "I like that. Just as I suspected. This was meant to be. You were meant to be mine."

"I am yours," she said. It felt like the right thing to say. And judging by the glint in his eye, it had been.

"You know," he said. "I told myself after that first time I met my father that I would never, ever allow myself to want without having. Ever again." He reached out, pressing his hand against her stomach, smoothing it gently over the slightly rounded bump there. "And so, I will spend my life having you, then. Because the alternative is to want endlessly, and I refuse it. I will not."

"Let me satisfy you," she said.

He growled, joining her on the bed, positioning himself between her legs and sliding inside her easily.

She gasped, arching upward, joining him in an intense, shaky rhythm that she thought might just break her apart. Might destroy them both. But she couldn't see another alternative. She needed him. Needed this.

She wrapped her legs around him and let him give all his weight to her.

And that was when she realized. The way that it worked. The push and the pull. The way he held her, kept her safe, and the way that she became the resting place for him.

Domination. Submission. Give. Take.

"Mine," he growled, as he stiffened above her, his body pulsing inside her. "Mine."

That last, possessive declaration drove her over the

edge, her release going off like a shower of sparks inside her.

And when it was through, she was shaking. Spent.

Weaker.

Stronger.

When it was through, she was his.

There would be no force on earth that could ever undo it.

"I hope you don't mind," Astrid said the next morning, sitting in the center of his bed with the regal bearing of an empress. The blankets were bunched up around her, her breasts exposed, her red hair tumbled down over her shoulders. She was clutching a coffee mug and managed to make it all look effortless and elegant.

She was such a compelling acquisition.

There was nothing, and no one, that had ever been part of his life who was quite so lovely or rare.

"You hope I don't mind what?" He was standing across the room from her, still completely naked, and he took satisfaction from the clear fact that she was enjoying the sight of him.

"I had a doctor's appointment settled in Bjornland. And, as we are here, I figured it would be easier to just have the doctor bring her equipment to us."

"Did you?"

"I didn't know when you would be through with your business here. I could have flown back, but Dr. Yang is going to meet us here instead. She's the best obstetrician in Europe, and we were going to have to fly her to be on loan anyway. Instead, she'll be bringing her equipment to us."

"My penthouse is going to be transformed into a clinic?"

"Yes," she said. "There is nothing untoward about it. People give birth at home. I might as well have my examinations done in a similarly comfortable environment. And, we won't have to contend with paparazzi."

"When do you expect her arrival? As I'm not the one meant to be in the hospital gown, perhaps I should get dressed." He bent down and retrieved his pair of dark slacks from the floor, where they had left them last night.

"Yes, perhaps you might want to do that."

"Though, we may have some time…"

It was only an hour later when the doctor showed up, and thankfully, Mauro had been able to put his legendary focus to the task and leave Astrid doubly satisfied by the time the doctor arrived. She had a warm bedside manner, and an efficiency to her movements that would have come across as brusque with most people, but with Dr. Yang it came across as a kindness. As if the time of the patient was being considered and respected.

He could see why Astrid had gone to the trouble of bringing her all this way.

"How have you been feeling?" the doctor asked.

"Well," Astrid said. "Surprisingly well. Only a bit of fatigue, and occasional nausea in the mornings, but nothing extreme."

If Astrid had been feeling nauseous this morning, she had hidden it well, and said nothing. The same with her fatigue. She was such a strong, self-contained woman, and he suddenly found himself overcome by the desire to bear some of that burden. To make it so she did not hide such things from him.

It was an ache that hit him square in the chest. A walnut-sized pain that rested there like a knot.

He didn't like it. Not one bit.

"Date of your last period?" the doctor asked.

Astrid rattled off the date effortlessly.

"Date of last intercourse?"

Astrid's face turned dark red. "That would be today's date."

The doctor didn't react to this, but Astrid was the color of a royal tomato, and Mauro took some amusement in that. It was a sweet thing, the way something like that could make her blush. It spoke of her inexperience, and of the fact that what was between them was somewhat singular.

Maybe even a bit miraculous.

That word, *miraculous*, was reinforced when the doctor had Astrid lie back on the bed and expose her stomach, squeezing some warmed gel onto it, where it was slightly distended. Then she placed the wand onto her skin and moved around, watery noise filling the room. The watery sound turned into a wish and whisper, steady and fast.

"And that's the heartbeat," she said. "Very strong. Sounds good." She moved the wand around. "It is a little bit early, but since you are sixteen weeks, we might be able to see the baby's gender. If you're interested."

"I am," Astrid said, her expression taking on a dreamy quality.

"I don't mind either way," he said. "As long as the child is healthy. It doesn't matter to me what gender." Dr. Yang and Astrid exchanged a glance, but he could not decode what it meant.

"Let me see," she said.

Suddenly, everything came into focus. The baby's head. An arm. A foot, which kicked as the doctor brought the wand down around the baby's body.

"It doesn't wish to be disturbed," Mauro said, that pit in his chest expanding, growing. As if a tree was growing from that walnut now. Becoming something large and hard and completely unmanageable.

"The baby doesn't mind," Dr. Yang said. "It's good that the baby is responsive. That's what we like to see."

He didn't know if he wanted to see it at all. It was suddenly so very real. This human inside Astrid. A child.

His child.

"We are in luck," she said. "There we go. We have a perfect view. You're having a son."

The mix of emotion on Astrid's face was strange. "I'm glad in some ways," she said. "His road will be easier. It's easier to be king."

"I would have liked to rub their faces in the fact that I was having a girl though."

She laughed. "That's a terrible reason to wish for one or the other."

He could understand what she was saying, and even the significance in her world. Producing a male heir was traditionally a valued thing. And Astrid herself was a defiance of that. But he couldn't think of that. Not now. All he could think of was that he was having a son.

A son.

A little boy, like the one his own father had taunted and sent away. A boy who would possibly look like him. Possibly look like his old man.

Redemption.

In a thousand strange and wonderful ways, this was

redemption. He craved it. And with that craving came something deep and unpleasant. Something he told himself he would not feel. Not again. This deep unending need for something he couldn't even define. This child made him hurt. And the woman in front of him, with her eyes shining so bright, she made him ache.

He felt as if his whole life had been turned inside out.

And he had been driven, driven to claim her, driven to claim the baby. He had been motivated by something he couldn't even put words to, but here in this small space, with that little life flickering on the screen in front of him, with that deep truth attached to him.

A boy.

A son.

That drive met with something different. Something dangerous. Something that had the power to wound and destroy. Something that he had told himself he wanted no part of for all that time.

It made no sense. He had her. Right here. He had the baby right here. So why did it hurt like this? Why? He could not fathom it.

"Congratulations," Dr. Yang said. She put her hand on Mauro's shoulder, and somehow in her expression he saw a wealth of things. Perhaps even sympathy, and he couldn't understand why she would feel sorry for him. Except that perhaps his own confusion was visible on his face. He despised that too. He was not a man given to confusion. He was not a man given to indecisiveness. Astrid had done something to him. She had... Damaged him in some way. And he hated it. He hated it.

"All right. I'll give you a moment with each other, and

to get dressed, and then I will have everything cleared from here, and leave you alone. The child is healthy. Congratulations."

And with that, she left them. Astrid sat up, wiping the jelly from her stomach with a warm cloth that had been placed by the bedside. "I expected that we would get to find out it was a boy. Not so soon. I'm glad… I'm glad we were together when we found out."

"You are happy?" he asked. The idea of her being unhappy with his son upset him even more than the idea of his own conflicted feelings.

"Yes," she said. "Really, his life will be easier. Easier because he's a boy. Easier because he won't have opposition to him. And I suppose what I hoped for was a chance to test out just how much we could modernize the country. But I cannot stand in his way for his gender any more than my father should have doubted me for mine. He will be a good king. We'll raise him to be."

They would raise him. Yes. They would. Of course they would. He gritted his teeth, squaring his jaw. "Yes."

"Are you all right?"

"I'm fine."

"I'm glad we're doing this together," she said. "I think I really wouldn't have wanted to do it alone."

"You won't be alone," he said, trying to harden his heart against the words.

"I guess not. Technically. I would've had nannies, and whatever else. But I am glad. I'm glad to have you. I'm glad our child will have you. Because a nanny is no substitute for a father. And what I did I did without thinking about the people involved. Not just you. But our child. It wasn't only you I would have deprived. And I'm glad things are like this. I'm glad that we'll be… I'm glad we'll be a family."

That word made him feel like he'd been cracked open. And after she spoke them, Mauro couldn't think of a single thing to say.

CHAPTER TWELVE

Mauro had gone off to work quickly after the doctor visit, and Astrid knew that something wasn't quite right, but she also could not for the life of her figure out what to do about it.

Perhaps, Mauro had legitimately needed to go into the office. That was entirely possible. Or perhaps he was running from something, which she also suspected might be true, but didn't have a clue as to what she was supposed to do if that was the case.

The idea of him running was a strange one, but in many ways she understood. She had never been more terrified in her entire life than she was when she had seen that baby. So real and vivid on the ultrasound screen. A boy. Their son. There was something undeniable about that. Something real and heavy. And if he needed a moment alone after, she would have certainly understood.

Of course, he would likely rather die than admit that.

Which is why, she suspected, he had simply excused himself.

Because the man was too alpha to function, and God forbid he have a feeling in her presence.

That very thought made a smile that curved her lips upward. She supposed the same could be said about her.

But he made her want to be not quite so soft. Not quite so stubborn and closed off.

She wondered if he needed something from her now, and simply didn't have the ability to express it.

Then she wondered why on earth she was thinking about him when she had just gotten such momentous news about her life, her future. She was having a boy. That should consume her thoughts. Utterly and totally. And yet, she found that she was consumed with him.

She was lately. Quite a bit.

She had… Feelings for him.

If she was honest with herself she had for an impossible amount of time.

She had felt a strange sort of connection with him just looking at his pictures, and while she had initially told herself it was a response to his genetics, and then had told herself it was chemistry, now she wondered if it was something more. Something that made no sense at all.

And if it hadn't been since looking at the photos, it was definitely since the first time they had made love.

The way that he touched her. The way that he made her feel… It was all a strange kind of magic. He made her feel happy to be a woman, made her glory in the way that she had been made. Made her feel as if she understood and embraced her femininity for the first time, really and truly. When Mauro finally did arrive home, he was distant. He shut himself in his home office for a time, coming out only to ask if she was hungry for dinner.

When she said that she was, he set about cooking in the small, high-gloss kitchen. She watched his movements, sure and confident as he set about preparing their food.

"I didn't know you cooked," she said.

"I'm quite accomplished at it," he said. "I can make a fairly gourmet meal out of deeply underwhelming ingredients. A skill I picked up as a boy. Of course, now I prefer to make truly wonderful food out of excellent ingredients. It's always nice when you have the option."

"Well," she said. "Yes."

"I hope you like filet mignon."

"I think I can make do," she said, smiling. "I don't know how to cook. I've never had to do it. Everyone always does it for me. And I've never seen the point in picking up a skill when it can just as easily be done."

"Sometimes it's simply good to have the skill for the sake of it," he pointed out.

"I suppose. But there's always been… An idea around me that I could concern myself with more important things. And anything that's trivial… Well, anything that's a triviality I can leave to other people."

"I can see how feeding yourself might be considered trivial," he said drily.

"Well, you don't have to be ridiculous about it."

"I'm not being ridiculous. I'm being practical."

"What are you making? In all your practicality?"

"Filet mignon with a red wine reduction. And mixed steamed vegetables. Truly. Nothing overly elaborate."

"It all seems elaborate to me," she said.

She sat back and watched him work, not at all goaded into getting up and helping simply because he had taunted her about not knowing how to cook. She enjoyed watching him work. Anyway, she was a bit fatigued. Not terribly, but just a bit more than she was used to. But this time away with him had been… Well, it had been nice. Like a snippet of another life. A life she could have had if she had been just a regular woman. One who had met a man and fallen in love by chance.

In love? Was that what this was?

Her mind went blank for a moment, nothing there except for that one word, heavy, terrifying, looming above her.

Love.

Did she *love* him?

Her first instinct was to push it down. To hide. To never, ever admit to herself that she felt these things, let alone admit it to him.

But she saw clearly, suddenly, the fabric of her life. Her parents. Her mother's ferocity, and her unfailing need for Astrid to succeed, and her father's cool indifference.

And both of those things had a wall. A firm wall between her and Astrid. She was ideological for her mother. A point of contention for her father. And they had loved her. They had.

She supposed.

But the layers that kept them back from her... Pride. All of it was protective. And it had taught her to do the same. It was what she'd always done, and so much of it was because of her position, easy to sink into naturally. But so much of it had been to protect herself. From scrutiny, from criticism. From disappointing her mother, from failing in the eyes of her father, when he so clearly imagined that she would.

It all became so clear right then.

That no wall had ever healed. That no wall had ever truly protected. She had been concerned, from the beginning, that Mauro was the barbarian at the gate. But she had not imagined how apt that description was. Not really. And something had to change. Something inside her. It had begun, all those months ago, with that trip to the club.

Continued as they had grown intimate, as they had given and taken from each other, as she had found power in her surrender.

And perhaps now this was the next stage of that lesson. Strength in vulnerability.

In becoming the one thing she had always feared she might be.

Weak. Vulnerable. Open.

But perhaps it was the only way. Perhaps, it was the only path to what was real.

Something she had not considered, not truly, as she had started out this journey, was the fact that it was about more than simply gaining independence from a council. It was about more than living in defiance of her father's last-ditch effort to control her. It was about becoming more of a person than a figurehead. It was about defying some of what her mother had instilled in her, as well. The need to be perfect. The need to be a symbol.

She didn't want to be a symbol to her son. She wanted to be his mother. She didn't want to live her life as someone worthy of being carved onto a coin. She wanted to live her life. To do the best she could. To be the best she could, but to be her. To be Astrid von Bjornland, as she was. As she was meant to be.

Not in a constant state of trying to prove herself, not in an eternal struggle to appear worthy. No. She wanted to be herself.

She was flawed. She was strong. She was weak. She was angry. She was in love. She was filled with hope for the future, and terror about it, as well.

She was everything, not simply one thing.

And it would start here. It had to start here.

"Mauro," she said slowly. "I love you."

He barely paused in his movements. "That's only because I'm cooking steak for you."

She shook her head. "No. I am in love with you. I have been. For quite some time. And today… The ultrasound, the baby… All of it crystallized something for me. I cannot be the mother that I want to be, the ruler I want to be, the woman I want to be. If I'm going to be the best mother, the best ruler, the best wife, then I have to… I have to be different. I have to break the cycle."

"What cycle?"

"This cycle where I care only for my own feelings. Honestly, that I gave even a moment's thought to wishing he was a girl, to further my own cause, this cause that I've been fighting all of my life. It shows me that my parents impacted me in ways I wish they hadn't. I know my mother did. She meant well. She believed in me. But I was a battleground. I don't want to do that to our child. I don't want to live that way with you. I don't want to live the way my parents did. I want something more. I'm willing to give whatever I need to, to make that happen. I love you, and I think that… We can be happy. I think we can be wonderful, not just an arrangement. I think we could be everything."

He turned away from her, and went back to cooking, saying nothing. Doing nothing.

"The food is finished," he said, putting the steak on a plate and dishing vegetables beside it. "Let's eat."

There with him in the dining room in stunned silence, trying to focus, while emotions were spinning through her like cracks of light. Finally, she stood.

"I'm afraid," she said. "I have been. That my father

was secretly right. I wasn't strong. That's why I never doubted myself. I couldn't afford to. Why I went forward with my crazy plan to trick you into getting me pregnant. Because I had gotten myself to a place where I was so convinced that anything that I might want was a betrayal of what I needed to be. Well, I'm not doing it. Not anymore. I'm afraid. I'm afraid I won't do a good job. But I'm doing it anyway. I'm afraid I won't be a good mother. I'm afraid you will leave me. But I… I want it enough for me. For us."

He said nothing, only assessed her with cool, dark eyes. She moved down the table to where he sat. And, heart hammering in her chest, desperation pouring into her like a fountain, she dropped to her knees in front of him. "I'm your servant," she said. "Let me give you what you need."

CHAPTER THIRTEEN

MAURO COULDN'T BREATHE. He couldn't think. He had spent the entire day away at the office for a reason.

Because everything with Astrid, with the baby, had simply been too much for him to take on board. It had been too much for him to handle. And now this. Now she was throwing herself at his feet, confessing love, prostrate before him. And worst of all, worse than watching her kneel before him, was the fact that it intensified the growing ache inside.

He couldn't even blame the child, which ultimately he had rationalized as being a natural response. Very few men faced impending fatherhood without some sort of panic. But that wasn't it.

It was her. She did this to him.

And then, she began to strip off the dress she was wearing, began to reveal her body, and he could not turn away.

"Whatever you need from me… Let me give it. Let *me* be everything you need."

It was so perilously close to what he had wished he could get from her earlier today. That he could see that vulnerability, that he could understand what scared her, what drove her, what made her. And now, it was as if she was showing him, but not only that, was asking him to do the same.

He wanted her to stop. Wanted to tell her enough was enough.

Yet he found it impossible to turn away, especially as she revealed those pale, perfect breasts for inspection, especially when all of her soft, silky beauty was laid out before him. She took everything off except for her shoes, just as she had done that first night they were together.

She stretched out on her back, on the floor in front of him, her arms lifted over her head, her wrists crossed, her knees locked criminally together, as if it might spare some of her modesty. And he no longer hungered for the food on his plate. No. All the hunger he possessed was for her. Utterly. His desire like a living thing roaring through his body, right now.

No.

Part of him wanted to run away from, from that feeling she created inside, but that same part of himself would not allow it. Would not allow for him to admit she did strange and dark, magical things that no one else had ever done.

She terrified him. Him. A man who had sold his body to survive, who had spent nights sleeping on the street, wondering if the wrong kind of people would find him, and if he would wake up at all.

He feared nothing. And yet this one, fragile queen seemed to have the power to tear him apart from the inside out.

This woman who seemed to be able to give and take in equal measure. Who seemed to be able to take charge and then give her power over at will.

He didn't understand.

He did not understand how she had spoken to him as she had, so raw and real and broken. So revealing. As if she were bulletproof. When he could see full well she was not. All that tender skin so very capable of being destroyed.

And yet… Yet. He dropped to his knees, forced her thighs apart, exposed all of that luscious body of hers.

He should turn away. Should not take her in his current state of mind. It took all of his strength to even admit that. That she'd pushed him to this place.

And he had none left to resist.

He touched her breasts, her stomach, that tender place between her legs. Let himself drink in every inch of her beauty.

He held himself back, keeping a distance between them as he undid the closure on his slacks.

He gripped himself, stroking his hardened length twice while looking down at her.

Then he reached down, gripping her thigh and draping her leg up over his shoulder, repeating the motion with the other.

Then he rocked forward, one arm like a bar over her thighs as he gripped himself with his free hand and slid himself over the slick entrance of her body, before pressing his arousal against her opening.

She gasped, letting her head fall back, and he lost himself. Poured every emotion, every pain, every deep sharp jagged thing that was making him feel, into her. He wrapped them up, let it cut them both, and he let them both get lost in the animal need that was driving him forward, making him into a thing he didn't recognize.

A thing he feared was closer to real than anything he'd allowed himself to feel for decades.

And when he came, it was on a ferocious roar, with a bastard's body pulsing around his.

And he thought that maybe, just maybe, that had fixed things. That it had drowned everything else out. But then, she lifted her hand and touched his face.

"I love you."

And he could not endure it.

Astrid could tell the moment that she had lost him. The moment when she had pushed too far.

But what could they do? What could she do? She loved him. They were married. She was having his baby. They were bonded, whether he wanted that to be true or not. And she could see something more than a lack of love in his eyes. That wasn't what she saw there at all. It was anguish. It was fear. It was abject terror. And desire. A deep, unending desire.

To take what she had offered, she was certain of it. And yet, something was holding him back. She couldn't figure out what it was, couldn't quite say where the fear was coming from, only that it was there.

"Don't do this," she said softly.

"Don't," he said. "Don't act like you can read my mind because you shared my bed. Any number of women have done this with me."

She stayed right where she was on the floor. "Any number of women have submitted themselves to you completely?"

"It is only sex," he said.

"Is it? Because it seems to be something that terrifies you. I love you," she said it again.

"That isn't what I want," he said.

"I don't care what you want."

"No. You never have, have you? You find it so easy to make proclamations, to say that you're going to change because you now realize the error of your selfish, entitled ways, but you don't actually intend to do it, do you? Because the moment that it becomes inconvenient for you, you begin to tell other people they are wrong."

"That isn't what I've done," she said, pushing back, indignation and anger filling her. "I love you, Mauro, and if that offends you so very much you might want to ask yourself why."

"That is not what I signed on for when I signed on for this marriage."

"Yes. You only signed on for forever and said that I was yours. Why would I think a little thing like love would be a simple thing for you to accept?"

"You say that you want nothing, but in the end, you will," he said. "Nothing that I do will be enough for you, now that you've entered love into the equation."

"That sounds like baggage that we haven't discussed," she said flatly. "Because I never asked for a damn thing."

"This is not the way that I operate. It is not what I do."

"No," she said. "I know. You've done anything and everything to build yourself this tower. This place where you can look down on the world. And you seem to be fine as long as we can play games, and you can look down on me when I'm naked, and I give you everything that you desire. But now that I'm telling you there's more, now that I'm telling you I want more, you find that to be a problem?"

"You're asking for the impossible. You're asking for

something I can't give," he said, his voice hard. "I don't love."

"You're not going to love our child?"

"Dammit. I already do," he said, his voice hoarse. "But I…"

"But you can't love too many people, is that it? You can't open your heart any farther? Because you might be hurt?"

"You don't understand. I had to make myself hard. I had to build myself a tower, because no one would take care of me. My mother loved me, and she did the best she could, but when she was whoring herself out, she didn't exactly enact a screening process to make sure that none of the men she brought into her home tried something with her son. And no, none of them ever succeeded, but it wasn't for lack of trying. Yes, I had to become hard. So you cannot ask for me to open up my heart on command. I'm not even certain it's possible. More than that, I'm not certain I want to. I want to have this arrangement."

"More fortification. That's what you want. You marry me, you get that."

"That is not why I married you."

"You married me for our child," she said. "And certainly not anything to do with the fact that you keep hoping if you put enough Band-Aids on this wound you'll be all right."

"I am an infamous playboy," he said, his tone hard. "I am legendary for my ability to sleep with women and move on. What makes you think you're any different?"

"I know I'm different," she said. "I am a queen, and not just that, but I am *your* queen. You are the only man that I have ever knelt before, and the only man that I ever will kneel before. But until you can set down your own pride, and you can make yourself honest, afraid, vulnerable, we can't ever be. You're right about that."

"Are you issuing ultimatums?"

"Yes. As I said before, we had to either be forever or not at all. But to me, now forever is about love. Because I lived in a family where pride and stubbornness won. I lived in a home where there wasn't…love. Not really. I won't treat our child to the same. I will not. I won't treat you to the same. I deserved more. I deserve more, and I didn't get it. Because those around me were content to let it be. While I am not. Not anymore."

"And what will you do if I say no?"

"I will get on my private jet and I will fly back to Bjornland. You may come and see me again when the baby is born. But you and I are not a couple."

"I will not allow you to keep the marriage. I will not allow you to keep your front for the benefit of the world."

"I don't care. Or have you not been listening? I don't care anymore. It isn't about image. None of this is about image. I want you. I love you. I don't care how it looks. I don't give a damn if you were a prostitute. I don't care who your mother was. I don't care who your father is. I care about us. I care about our baby. I care about what we could be. And how much happiness we could have. How much more we could have."

She touched his face. "You were fearless once. You climbed up to your father's house and faced him when you were a boy, not having any idea what you might get in return. I'm standing here guaranteeing that you will have me. All you have to do is say yes."

"No," he said. "The divorce papers will be in the mail."

"Mauro…"

Astrid had to make good on her promise. And in her

last act of paying heed to appearances, she squared her shoulders, and held her head high. She collected her clothing, and dressed in front of him, hiding nothing. Then she walked out of his apartment, out of his life.

And only when she was in her plane, up in the air and alone, did she let herself weep.

But she knew she had made the right choice. Because she was the queen of so many. The hope of a nation.

But to Mauro, she had been a woman. To Mauro, she had been Astrid.

And Astrid wanted his *love*.

She would settle for nothing less.

Mauro was a study in misery, and he stubbornly refused to believe that he had any recourse in the matter. Astrid was being unreasonable. He called his lawyer in the middle of the night, in a fit of rage, and had divorce papers drafted.

And then had spent the next three days doing nothing with them. Nothing at all. The view from his office window was tainted, and he hated it all now because of her. Because of what she'd said. That he was using it to look down and hold himself above.

"Mr. Bianchi…"

He turned around to see Carlo rushing nervously into the room, with Gunnar von Bjornland striding in front of him.

"What are you doing here?" he asked his soon-to-be former brother-in-law.

"I should think that was quite obvious. Oh, but then I forget you don't know that I have a gun hidden in my jacket."

"Are you threatening me?"

"Yes. I knew that you would hurt my sister."

"To the contrary, your sister walked away from me."

"Astrid is a sensible woman. If she walked away from you, she had a reason."

"Yes, your sister is just so damn sensible. So sensible that she sneaked away from her minders, went to one of my clubs and tricked me into getting her pregnant. Then married me. Then left me when I refused to produce the correct words of love on command. Truly, it is a miracle that I was able to walk away from such a creature."

"I will concede that her tricking you into getting her pregnant is a problem. The rest… Why don't you love her? Everyone should."

The words hit him square in the chest, because actually he could only agree with them. Everyone should love her. She was strong, and her belief in him was the strange, unfailing thing. The way that she bonded herself to him, even as he told her about his past, the way that she stood resolute, as he showed her the slums that he'd been born in.

Truly, there seemed to be nothing he could do to lower himself in Astrid's esteem. After a lifetime of finding he could not raise himself in the esteem of others no matter what he did, it was a strange and refreshing thing.

"Is it that simple to undo a lifetime of not loving?" he asked.

"I don't know," Gunnar said. "I personally have yet to overcome much of my life. And I suppose it could be argued that no matter the situation with our parents, that we have had it easier. Astrid certainly had a different situation than I did. An heir and spare cannot, and will not have the same experience. But our parents were hard on her. And if they loved, they did not show it in easy, warm ways. If Astrid loves you, then it is truly an act of bravery. Not just because there has been nothing in our lives to suggest that love is something to aspire to, but because in Astrid's world nothing has been more important than maintaining that facade that she spent her entire life cultivating. That sense of total invulnerability. That sense of perfection. And then she married you. And we all saw those headlines about you. She went with you to Italy, she made a show of being yours no matter what, and I'm not sure that you can possibly understand what that means."

"Because I'm nothing but the son of a whore."

"Because you weren't raised to care quite so much. Your entire world never stopped and turned on your reputation. But for Astrid it did. You don't know what she has given up for you. How could you understand? And yet, she gave you the gift of her love and you threw it back in her face. If you divorce her and humiliate her on top of it…"

"Is that why you're really here? To prevent embarrassment?"

Gunner shrugged a shoulder. "My function in the royal family has never been to prevent embarrassment. Whatever Astrid is, I'm her opposite. My father always felt that I should be the one ruling the country, but I can tell you with great certainty that is not true. She is strong. Not only the strongest woman I know, but the strongest person I have ever had the privilege to be acquainted with. My sister is phenomenal, and you would be privileged to have her. Not because she is blue-blooded. Not because she is a royal, and you're not. But because she has come through our lives with the ability to love, which is more than I can say for myself. The strength in her… If you truly understood it, you would be humbled. But I am not certain that you can. Not unless you find a way to do the same thing she has done."

"I'm tired of receiving lectures from poor little rich kids who imagine that their emotional struggles somehow equal the emotional and physical struggles that I endured. Unless you know what it is to sell your body for a place to stay, I'm not entirely sure we can sit here and compare war wounds."

"Perhaps not," he said. "But then..." He shrugged. "So what?"

"I'm sorry?"

"So what? Your life was hard. Maybe it was harder than mine. Perhaps harder than Astrid's. Perhaps it is a struggle now, for you to figure out how to accept love. But so what? That part of your life is over now. You have money, you could buy whatever it is you need to make your life whatever it is you want, but the one thing you cannot pay to make better, or make go away, is the situation with my sister. That requires feelings. And it requires work. And in the end, life doesn't care how hard you worked for it. But it might mean more to you. If you figure out the way through. But you won't be given instant happiness simply because it would've been harder for you to sort yourself out than it might be for me."

Gunnar straightened the cuffs on his shirtsleeves, then treated Mauro to the iciest look he'd ever received. "Remember what I said. Do not embarrass my sister. Don't give me a reason to come for you."

And then, as he appeared, Gunnar walked out of his office. Carlo looked around the corner, his expression one of comical concern.

"Leave," Mauro said.

And Carlo vanished instantly.

Mauro was hardly going to listen to the ranting of a rich prince who wouldn't know struggle if it transformed into a snake and bit him in the face. But one thing kept replaying over and over in his head.

So what?

So everything.

Everything.

Because his life had been about struggle. Had been about wanting. And Astrid created more of that feeling inside him than anything else ever had. That ache. That sense of being unsatisfied. Unfulfilled. Of needing more than he would ever be able to have. A desperate hunger that could not be satisfied by food, by money. On that score he was right, as well. Because he knew that this was something that money could not solve. Knew that it was something he would not be able to fix. And that left him feeling...

Helpless. Utterly and completely helpless.

He hated that. There was no depth he would not sink to, he had proved that. He was willing to prostitute himself. He was willing to claw his way up to the top if need be. But there was no clawing here. There were no building towers. There was only...

There was only lowering himself.

As Astrid had said. Making himself into some debased creature all for her, and he didn't have any concept of how he might do that. Of what could possibly entice him to behave in such a way.

To leave all he'd created, to lower all his shields.

To make himself less.

Love.

The need for it, the drive for it... It was the thing that

was pushing him forward now. It was the thing that was making him miserable, the thing in his chest that made him want. And he did not understand how he was supposed to do it.

How he was supposed to…

It wasn't fair. She made him ache. She made him feel things, want things, need things that he had sworn he never would again.

Is she the one making you feel this? Or is it you?

And that was when the whole room seemed to turn.

And he wondered.

Perhaps it was Astrid who made him want. Perhaps it was Astrid who existed to fulfill the want that already existed inside him, and having her there, so close, and not allowing himself to have it all.

Maybe, she was not the problem. Maybe she was the answer to a hole that had already existed. To a need that had been present.

If only he was willing to cross the divide.

If only he was willing to admit that for all his power. For all that he had…

He could not fix it on his own.

He needed her.

He needed her. And he would do whatever he needed to get her back.

"Carlo," he said, his assistant appearing as if by magic. "Ready my plane. We're going back to Bjornland."

"As you wish."

CHAPTER FOURTEEN

ASTRID WAS NOT looking forward to this year's Christmas celebration at all.

It was a massive party, and in her mind, it was a total farce. There was nothing to celebrate. Yes, the impending birth of her son was joyous, but *she* was broken and alone, and it would take some time before she felt anything beyond that.

Still, all had been planned and arranged, and she was expected to participate whether she wanted to or not.

Things at the palace had changed.

In spite of the fact that Mauro was not in residence, her situation with the council was resolved.

While they would still exist, as long as the men wished to hold the office, she would disband it formally once they all retired, or passed on to the next life. And for now they existed as figureheads, symbols, more than anything else.

Which, in her mind, was much better than her existing as such.

The room was full of revelers, crystals dripping from each and every surface of the glorious ballroom.

The Christmas tree loomed large in the corner, a glowing beacon. At least it usually was. Right now the great golden glow mocked her. A symbol of joy and hope when she could feel none of it at all right now.

All of the decorations were ornate, in a way that she didn't truly enjoy, though she'd had her bedroom redone.

The thought made her smile, if somewhat sadly. Because it was something Mauro had said she should do, and even though he had hurt her, she knew that he was right.

And every night she wished that he were there with her.

Even though she shouldn't. Even though she shouldn't wish to see him again. Not ever.

Love, it turned out, did not fade simply because someone wronged you. Love, it turned out, was a terrible inconvenience.

The ball gown she was wearing was a gossamer, floaty confection that hung loosely over her curves, which was a necessity given that they were expanding with each passing day. That was another thing that made her miss him.

He was missing all of the changes, and it made her indescribably sad that this was the case. Guests were being brought forward to where she sat, being presented to her one by one. And there were any number of ushers dressed in navy blue suits, with gold epaulets on their shoulders, traditional dress for noblemen imbuing land.

Astrid was quite bored with it, and trying her best to appear engaged. It wasn't any of her guests' fault that she was brokenhearted, after all.

Out of the corner of her eye, she saw another of the greeters moving toward her, his head bent low. His hands behind his back. He did not have a guest on his arm. She looked at him, and her heart hit the front of her chest.

"What are you…"

"My Queen," he said, bending to one knee in front of her.

Mauro. He was here. And he was dressed as… One of the ushers.

"I had to sneak into your party," he said, his voice low, "especially as my name is mud here at the palace."

"Yes," she said, feeling dizzy. "It is."

"I had to come and find you," he said. "And I took inspiration for how from you. But I have something that I think belongs to you."

He reached out from behind his back, and produced her shoe. That crystalline beauty that she had worn and left behind the night she had seduced him at the club. "I believe this is yours."

"Yes," she said, her throat dry. "It is."

"You would permit me to see, if it fits?"

A bubble of laughter rose up in her throat. "If you must."

"I must," he said gravely. "Because the woman whose foot fits this shoe has something of mine. My heart. But more than that, my everything. I thought… Astrid, I thought that you made me hurt. That you made me incomplete, but that is not true. Instead, you revealed to me the empty space in my soul, and you are the only thing that can fill it. I blamed you, but you are not the problem. You are the solution. And so… Let me see. Do me the honor of showing me if you are in fact the woman who fits the shoe. Who fits that hole inside me."

She slipped her foot out of the shoe she was wearing and held it out to him, not caring that they were drawing stares, that everyone in the room had realized just who he was.

She could see that Gunnar and Latika were barely restraining themselves, allowing her to handle the moment, out of respect for her strength, she knew. But she also knew it was testing them.

She extended her foot to him, and he slipped it on.

A perfect fit.

"My Queen," he said. "I am kneeling before you. I am not in my tower. I am at your feet. And I must humbly confess to you that I love you. But I am a broken man who is nothing more than where I came from. But I love you. I love you, and I will spend all of my days trying to prove to you that I am worthy of that love. For I am nothing without you. I am nothing without this life. And it would not matter if you were a queen, or if we lived back in those slums I worked so hard to escape. Love was the thing that was always missing. And love is the only thing I cannot buy."

"Then it's perfect," she said, sliding out of her throne and dropping to her knees with him. "Because love is the one thing that I cannot legislate. Is the one thing that I cannot bend to my will. I cannot manipulate it, I cannot find an old law that would enable me to capture it and hold it in my hands. Love is all that I need. You are all that I need."

"I love you," he said.

"I love you too."

"You have to stay at this party?"

"It's my party. It's my birthday."

"Happy birthday."

"Thank you," she said, feeling light-headed and surreal, dizzy.

"We have this? Will we have each other forever?" she asked, whispering softly.

"Yes, my Queen. We will have each other, and happily. Ever after."

EPILOGUE

WHEN THE BRAND-NEW Prince of Bjornland came into the world some months later, the media instantly hailed him as perfection. A specimen of humanity that possessed his mother's regal bearing and his father's determination, but no one was half so infatuated with him as his father. And his mother.

"He is perfect," Mauro said decisively, laying him down in the crib that first night, pressing a kiss to his soft, downy head.

"He is," Astrid agreed. "Perfection. As is our life."

"I had thought that happiness was in the top of a high-rise building. Where I had finally overcome. Where I would finally prove to my father that I had value. I climbed up that hill and begged for him to love me, and received nothing in return. Though, I realize now that I did. I realize now that I learned something I needed right now. Our son will never have to earn my love. And there is nothing he could do to lose it. What our parents did to us… It was never us. It was them. And as for me… Happiness was never alone at the top of a high-rise. It is here. With you. With him. Forever."

For the first time in his entire life, Mauro did not feel like a boy from the slums.

Astrid made him a king. Not because of her title, but because she had given him her heart.

And he had given her his.

And that was truly the most powerful thing on earth.

* * * * *

A NIGHT OF ROYAL CONSEQUENCES

SUSAN STEPHENS

For my most excellent editor, Megan, who is a joy to work with.

CHAPTER ONE

As FUNERALS WENT, this was as grand as it got. As tradition demanded Luca, who was now the ruling Prince, arrived last, to take his place of honour in the packed cathedral. He was seated in front of the altar beneath a cupola with images painted by Michelangelo. Towering bronze doors to one side were so stunningly crafted they were known as the 'gateway to paradise'. Tense with grief, Luca was aware of nothing but concern that he'd pulled out all the stops for a man to whom he owed everything. Flags were flown at half-mast across the principality of Fabrizio. Loyal subjects lined the streets. Flowers had been imported from France. The musicians were from Rome. A procession of priceless horse-drawn carriages drew dignitaries from across the world to the cathedral. Luca's black stallion, Force, drew his father's flag-draped coffin on a gun carriage with the Prince's empty boots reversed in the stirrups. It was a poignant sight, but the proud horse held his head high, as if he knew his precious cargo was a great man on his final journey.

As the new ruler of the small, but fabulously wealthy principality of Fabrizio, Luca, the man the scandal sheets still liked to call 'the boy from the gutters of Rome', was shown the greatest respect. He'd moved a long way from those gutters. Innate business acumen had made him a billionaire, while the man he was burying today had made him a prince. This magnificent setting was a long way from the graffiti-daubed alleyways of Luca's childhood where the stench of rotting rubbish would easily eclipse the perfume of flowers and incense surrounding him today. The peeling plaster and flyposting of those narrow alleyways replaced by exquisite gothic architecture, the finest sculpture, and stained glass. In his wildest dreams, he had never imagined becoming a prince. As a boy, it had been enough to have scraps he stole from bins to fill his belly and rags to cover his back.

He inclined his head graciously as yet another European princess in need of a husband acknowledged him with an enticing smile. Fortunately, he'd retained the street smarts that warned him of advantage-takers. He wouldn't be chaining himself down to a simpering aristo any time soon. Though he could do nothing about the testosterone running through his veins, Luca conceded wryly. Even freshly shaved and wearing dress uniform, he looked like a swarthy brawler from the docks. His appearance had been one thing his adoptive father, the late Prince, had been unable to refine.

Well over six feet tall and deeply tanned, with a honed, warrior's frame, Luca couldn't be sure of his parentage. His mother had been a Roman working girl. His father, he guessed, was the man who used to pester her for money. The late Prince was the only parent he remembered clearly. He owed the Prince his education. He owed him everything.

They'd met in the unlikely setting of the Coliseum, where the Prince had been on an official visit, and Luca had been stealing from the bins. He had not expected to come to the notice of such a grand man, but the Prince had been shrewd and had missed nothing. The next day he had sent an *aide de camp* with an offer for Luca to try living at the palace with the Prince's son, Max. They would be company for each other, the Prince had insisted, and Luca would be free to go if he didn't like his life there.

Young and street smart, Luca had had the sense to be wary, but he'd been hungry, and filling his belly had been worth taking a chance. That chance had led to this, which was why honouring the Prince was so important to him. He held his adoptive father in the highest esteem, for teaching him everything about building a life, rather than falling victim to it. But the Prince had left one final warning on his deathbed. 'Max is weak. You will follow me onto the throne as my heir. You must marry and preserve my legacy to the country I believe we both love.'

Clasping his father's frail hand in his, Luca had given his word. If he could have willed his strength into a man he loved unreservedly, he would have done that too. He would have done anything to save the life of the man who'd saved him.

As if reading Luca's thoughts, his adoptive brother Maximus glared at him now from across the aisle. There was no love lost between the two men. Their father had failed to form any sort of relationship with Max, and Luca had failed too. Max preferred womanising and gambling to statecraft. He'd never shown any interest in family at all. He favoured the hangers-on who flocked around him, lavishing praise on Max in hope of his favour. Luca had soon learned that, while the Prince was his greatest supporter, Max would always be his greatest enemy.

Picking up the order of service to distract himself from Max's baleful glare, Luca scanned his father's long list of accomplishments and titles with great sadness. There would never be such a man again, a thought that made him doubly determined to fulfil his pledge to the letter. 'You are a born leader,' his father had told him, 'and so I name you my heir.' No wonder Max hated him.

Luca hadn't looked for the honour of being heir to the throne of Fabrizio. He didn't need the money. He could run the country out of pocket change. Success had come when he'd nagged his father to let him bring Fabrizio up to date, and had insisted on studying tech at university. He'd gone on to become one of the most successful men in the industry. His global holdings were so vast his company almost ran itself. This was just as well as he had to turn his thoughts to ruling a country, and to filling the empty space beside him.

'If you fail to do this within two years,' his father had said on his deathbed, 'our constitution states that the throne will pass by default to your brother.' They both knew what that meant. Max would ruin Fabrizio. 'This is your destiny, Luca,' his father had added. 'You cannot refuse the request of a dying man.'

Luca had no intention of doing so, but the thought of marrying a simpering princess held no appeal. The royal marriage mart, as he thought of it, didn't come close to his love of being with his people. He would leave here and travel to his lemon groves in southern Italy, where he worked alongside the other holiday workers. There was no better way for him to learn what concerns they had, and to do something to help. The thought of being shackled to a fragile china doll appalled him. He wanted a real woman with grit and fire inside her belly.

'There are good women out there, Luca,' his father, the Prince, had insisted. 'It's up to you to find one. Pick someone strong. Search for the unusual. Step off the well-trodden path.'

At the time Luca had thought this wouldn't be easy. Looking around today, he thought it impossible.

As funerals went, this one was small, but respectable. Callie had made sure of it. It was small in as much as the only people to mourn her father's passing, other than herself, were their next-door neighbours, the rumbustious Browns. It was a respectable and quiet affair, because Callie had always felt she should counterbalance her father's crude and reckless life. There couldn't be two of them wondering where their next meal was coming from. If it hadn't been for her friends, the Browns, laughing with her at whatever life threw up, and reminding her to have fun while she could without offending other people, as her father so often had, she'd have been tearing her hair out by now.

The Brown tribe was on its best behaviour today—if she didn't count their five dogs piling out of their camper van to career around the country cemetery barking wildly, but they'd given Callie a glimpse of what a happy family life could be, and, in her heart of hearts, love and a happy family was what she aspired to.

'Goodbye, Dad,' she whispered, regretting everything they'd never been to each other as she tossed a handful of moist, cool soil on top of the coffin.

'Don't worry, love,' Ma said, putting her capable arm around Callie's shoulders. 'The worst part is over. Your life is about to begin. It's a book of blank pages. You can write anything on it. Close your eyes and think where you'd like to be. That's what always makes me happy. Isn't it, our Rosie?'

Rosie Brown, Callie's best friend and the Browns' oldest child, came to link arms with Callie on her other side. 'That's right, Ma. The world's your oyster, Callie. You can do anything you want. And sometimes,' Rosie added, 'you have to listen to the advice of people you trust, and let them help you.'

'Anywhere ten pounds will take me?' Callie suggested, finding a grin.

Rosie sighed. 'Anywhere has to be better than staying round the docks—sorry, Ma, I know you love it here, but you know what I'm getting at. Callie needs a change.'

By the time they'd all crammed into the van, Callie was feeling better. Being with the Browns was like taking a big dose of optimism, and, after the lifetime of verbal and physical abuse she'd endured keeping house for her father, she was ready for it. She was free. For the first time in her life she was free. There was only one question now: how was she going to use that freedom?

'Don't even think about work,' Ma Brown advised as she swivelled around in the front seat to speak to Callie. 'Our Rosie can take over your shift at the pub for now.'

'Willingly,' Rosie agreed, giving Callie's arm a squeeze. 'What you need is a holiday.'

'It would have to be a working holiday,' Callie said thoughtfully. 'I don't have enough money to go away.' Her father had left nothing. The house they'd lived in was rented. He'd been both a violent drunk and a gambler. Callie's job as a cleaner at the pub just about paid enough to put food on the table, and then only if she didn't leave the money lying around for him to spend at the bookies.

'Think about what *you'd* like to do,' Ma Brown insisted. 'It's your turn now, our Callie.'

She liked studying. She wanted to better herself. She aspired to do more than clean up the pub. Her dream was to work in the open, with fresh air to breathe, and the sun on her face.

'You never know,' Ma added, shuffling around in her seat again. 'When we clear out the house tomorrow your father might have left a wad of winnings in his clothes by mistake.'

Callie smiled wryly. She knew they'd be lucky to find a few coppers. Her father never had any money. They wouldn't have survived at all without the Browns' bounty. Pa Brown had an allotment where he grew most of their vegetables himself, and he always gave some to Callie.

'Don't forget you can stay with us as long as you need to, until you get yourself sorted out,' Ma Brown called out from the passenger seat.

'Thank you, Ma.' Leaning forward, Callie gave Ma's cheek a fond kiss. 'I don't know what I'd do without you.'

'You'd do more than all right,' Ma Brown insisted firmly. 'You've always been capable, and now you're free to fly as high as your mother always intended. She used to dream about her baby and what that baby would do. It's a tragic shame that she didn't live to see you grow up.'

She'd soon find out what she could and couldn't do, Callie thought as the Browns and their dogs piled out of the steamed-up van. She couldn't stick around for long. She'd be a burden to the Browns. They had enough to do keeping their own heads above water. Once her father's debts were paid, she'd go exploring. Maybe Blackpool. The air was bracing there. Blackpool was a traditional northern English seaside town with bags of personality, and plenty of boarding houses looking for cleaning staff. She'd research jobs there the first spare minute she got.

It would have been a grim task sorting through her father's things the next morning, if it hadn't been for the cheerful Browns. Ma checked every room, while Callie and Rosie sorted everything into piles for the charity shops, things that could possibly be sold, and those that were definitely going to the dump. The sale pile was disappointingly small. 'I never realised how much rubbish we had before,' Callie admitted.

'Mean old bugger,' Ma Brown commented. 'He probably took it with him,' she added with a sniff.

'I doubt there was anything to find in the first place,' Callie placated. She knew her father's ways only too well when it came to money.

'Nothing left after he'd been gambling and boozing, I expect,' Ma Brown agreed, disapprovingly pursing her lips.

'Well, that's where you're both wrong,' Rosie exclaimed with triumph as she flourished a five-pound note. 'Look what I've found!'

'Well, our Callie!' Ma Brown began to laugh as Rosie handed it over to her friend. 'Riches indeed. What are you going to do with it?'

'Nothing sensible, I hope,' Rosie insisted as Callie stared at the grubby banknote in amazement. 'It's not even enough to buy a drink, let alone a decent meal.'

She would rather have her father back either way, Callie thought, which was strange after all the years of trying to win his love, and coming to accept that there was no love in him. 'I'll put it in the charity tin at the corner shop,' she mused out loud.

'You'll do no such thing,' Ma Brown insisted. 'I'm taking charge of this,' she said as she snatched the banknote out of Callie's hand.

'Think of it as an early Christmas present from your father,' Rosie soothed when she saw Callie's distress. 'Ma will do something sensible with it.'

'It would be the first gift he'd ever given her,' Ma Brown grumbled. 'And as for doing something sensible with it?' She winked. 'I've got other ideas.'

'Sounds good to me,' Callie said with a weak smile, hoping the subject would go away now.

Knowing her friend was upset beneath her humour, Rosie quickly changed the subject and it wasn't spoken of again. The next Callie heard of their surprise find was at supper with the Browns. When the girls had finished clearing up, Ma Brown folded her arms and beamed, a sure sign of an announcement.

'Now then, our Callie, before you say anything, we know you don't gamble and we know *why* you don't gamble, but just this once you're going to take something from me, and say thank you and nothing else.'

Callie tensed when she saw the five-pound scratch card Ma Brown was holding out.

'You'll need something to scratch the card,' Pa observed matter-of-factly as he dug in his pocket for some loose change.

'Close your eyes and imagine where all that money's going to take you,' Rosie urged, glancing at the other Browns to will them to persuade Callie that this could be a good thing if she got lucky.

'All *what* money?' Callie had to smile when the Browns fell silent. Silence was such a rare occurrence in this household, she couldn't let them down.

'It's time for a change of luck,' Rosie pressed. 'What have you got to lose?'

The Browns had been nothing but kind. The money she'd get from the scratch card would likely take her as far as the hearth to toss it in the fire when it proved a dud. 'Close my eyes and imagine myself somewhere I've always dreamed of...'

'Open your eyes and scratch the bloody card,' Ma Brown insisted.

As everyone burst out laughing Callie sat down at the table and started scratching the surface of the card.

'Well?' Ma Brown prompted. 'Don't tease us. Tell us what you've got.'

'Five. Thousand. Pounds.'

No one said a word. Seconds ticked by. 'What did you say?' Rosie prompted.

'I've won five thousand pounds.'

The Browns exploded with excitement, and the next few hours were spent in a fury of mad ideas. Opening a pie and peas shop next to the pub, a sandwich bar to serve the local business park. 'I want to give my money to you,' Callie insisted.

'Not a chance.' Ma Brown crossed her capable arms across her capacious chest, and that was the end of it.

Callie made up her mind to put some of it aside for them, anyway.

'You could buy all the rescue dogs in the world,' one young Brown called Tom said optimistically.

'Or a second-hand car,' another boy exclaimed.

'Why don't you spend it all on clothes?' one of the girls proposed. 'You'll never get another chance to fill your wardrobe.'

What wardrobe? Callie thought. Her worldly possessions were contained in a zip-up bag, but she smiled and went along with this idea and they all had some fun with it for a while.

'It isn't a fortune and our Callie should do something that makes her happy,' Pa Brown said. 'It should be something she's always dreamed of, that she will remember for ever. She's had little enough fun in her life up to now, and this is her chance.'

The room went quiet. No one had heard Pa Brown give such a long speech before. Ma Brown always spoke for him, if the dogs and his brood weren't drowning him out.

'Well, our Callie,' Ma Brown prompted. 'Have you got any thoughts on the subject?'

'Yes, I do,' Callie said, surprising herself as she thought of it.

'Not Blackpool,' Rosie said, rolling her eyes. 'We can go there any weekend we like.'

'Well?' the Browns chorused, craning forward.

Reaching for the television guide, Callie opened it out flat on the table. There was a double-page spread, a travel feature, showing vibrant green lemon groves hung heavily with yellow fruit. A young family of husband, wife and two children capered across the grass, staring out towards unimaginable adventures. The headline read: *Visit Italy.*

'Why not?' Callie said as all the Browns fell silent. 'I can dream, can't I?'

'You can more than dream now,' Ma Brown pointed out with her usual common sense.

But by this time, Callie was already putting her dream on the back burner in favour of a far more realistic plan. Perhaps a weekend in a small coastal resort nearby. She could look for a job while she was there.

'Think big. Think Italy,' Rosie insisted.

'That would be a proper memory, all right,' Pa Brown agreed.

Callie stared out of the window at a grey, dismal scene. Like the rented house where she'd grown up, the Browns' opened out onto the street, but the people passing by outside had their shoulders hunched against the cold. The photo in the magazine promised something very different. Rather than traffic fumes and bed socks, there'd be sunshine and fruit trees. She glanced at the page again. It was like a window opening onto another world. The colours were extraordinary. The people in the shot might be models, but they surely couldn't fake that happiness, or the sense of freedom on their faces.

'Italy,' Ma Brown commented, her lips pressing down as she thought about it. 'You'll need some new clothes for that. Don't look so worried, our Callie. You won't need to spend much. You can do very well on the high street.'

Rosie clearly had other ideas and frowned at her mother. 'This is Callie's chance to have something special,' she whispered.

'And she should,' Pa Brown agreed, picking up on this. 'Goodness knows, she's gone without long enough.'

'A mix, then,' Ma Brown conceded. 'High Street with designer flourishes.' And with that healing remark the family was content.

'Amalfi,' Callie breathed as copying the idea in the magazine took shape in her mind. The thought of a short trip to Italy made her head reel with excitement. A change of scene was what she needed before she started the next phase of her life, and the win had made it possible.

'All that wonderful sunshine and delicious food, not

to mention the music,' Rosie commented with her hand on her heart as she thought about it.

All that romance and the Italian men, Callie's inner devil whispered seductively. She blanked out the voice. She had always been cautious when it came to romance. She'd had too many duties at home to be frivolous, and too many opportunities to witness first-hand how violent men could be.

'Come on, our Callie. Where's your sense of adventure?' Ma Brown demanded as all the Browns murmured encouragement.

She was free to do as she liked, so why not don a glamorous dress and designer heels for once? A few days of being not Callie was more than tempting, it was a possibility now. Just this once, the good girl could unleash her fun side—if she could still find it.

CHAPTER TWO

HE NOTICED THE woman sitting at the bar right away. Even from behind she was attractive. It was something in the way she held herself, and her relaxed manner with his friend, Marco, the barman. He'd just ended a call with Max, and was in the worst of moods. Max had lost no time in Luca's absence causing unrest in Fabrizio. Max had been a thorn in his side since they were boys. Thanks to his mischief, Luca should not be visiting his beautiful lemon groves on the Amalfi coast, but should return immediately to Fabrizio, but this was an annual pilgrimage to a place he loved amidst people he cared for, and nothing, not even Max, could distract him from that. Though on this occasion, he could only spare a couple of nights here.

The woman was a distraction. She was watching everyone come in through the mirrors behind the bar. Was she waiting for a lover? He felt a stab of jealousy and wondered why he cared when she could just as easily be waiting for a family member, or for a friend.

He'd dropped by the hotel to invite Marco to the annual celebrations at the start of the lemon-picking season. He and Marco had grown up together, as Marco's father had worked for the late Prince. Standing at the end of the bar where he could talk discreetly to Marco when he was free, he saw the woman clearly for the first time. She was confident and perky, and obviously enjoying the chance to trial the Italian language. Laughter lit her face when she got something wrong and Marco corrected her.

Feeling mildly irritated by their obvious rapport, he returned to working her out. Her profile was exquisite, though she seemed unaware of this, just as she seemed unaware of the appeal of her slight, though voluptuous body. She was understated, unlike his usual, sophisticated type. He couldn't help but be intrigued. Dressed impeccably, though plainly for this setting in one of the coast's most famous hotels, as if she was playing a role, she was almost too perfect. Her red hair was lush and shiny, cut short for practicality, rather than fashion, he guessed. Her eyes were green and up-tilted, giving her a faintly exotic look. A light tan and freckles suggested she'd been here no more than a week and lived somewhere cooler.

This was a lot of thought to expend on a woman who seemed unaware of his interest. Or was she? His groin tightened when she turned to stare at him boldly and was in no hurry to look away.

Interesting.

'Good evening.' After politely acknowledging the woman, he gave Marco a look that left his friend in no doubt that Luca wished to remain incognito.

Sensing mischief afoot, Marco grinned. They exchanged the usual complicated handshake, while the woman looked on with interest. She was even more beautiful than he'd first thought. Her scent was intoxicating. Wildflowers. How appropriate, he thought as Marco left them to go and serve another customer. 'Can I buy you a drink?'

She levelled a stare on his face. 'Do I know you?'

The bluntness of her question took him by surprise, as did her forthright tone. Out of the corner of his eye, he saw Marco lift a brow. His friend would call security if Luca gave the word, and the woman would be politely moved on. An almost imperceptible shake of Luca's head knocked that idea out of court.

'My name is Luca,' he told her as he extended his hand in greeting.

She ignored his hand. Intelligent eyes, framed by long black eyelashes, viewed him with suspicion.

'I don't believe we've met,' he pressed, waiting for her to volunteer her name. 'I don't bite,' he added when she continued to withhold her hand.

'But you're very persistent,' she said, making it clear there would be no physical contact between them.

Persistent? Outwardly, he remained deadpan. Inwardly, he cracked up. Women referred to his charm and thought him attentive. Clearly, this woman had other ideas. 'What would you like to drink?'

'Fizzy water, please,' she replied.

Turning to Marco, he murmured, *'Aqua frizzante per la signorina, e lo stesso per me, per favore.'*

'Sì, signor,' Marco replied, serving up two sparkling waters.

Her gaze remained steady on his as she took her first sip. There wasn't a hint of simpering or recognition in her eyes, just that desirable mouth smiling faintly. Even now she'd had time to think about it, he was a man in a bar and that was it. She had no idea who he was, and would trust him as far as a glass of water was concerned, but no further. If she was unaware that his face had been plastered all over the news lately, since he'd ascended the throne of Fabrizio, something big must have happened in her life.

So, beautiful mystery woman, he mused as she returned his interest coolly, who are you, and what are you doing in Amalfi?

Straightening the short silk skirt on her designer dress, Callie wished she had worn the Capri pants Rosie had insisted were essential to Callie's Italian adventure instead. So chic, Rosie had said as Callie had turned full circle, wishing she could get away with a new pair of jeans and a top. The Capris were still in the wardrobe upstairs in the hotel, as she'd been unsure which shoes to wear with them.

At least Capris would have been decent. The dress was anything but. Far too short, it was enticing. She could only imagine what this incredible-looking man had thought when he'd first seen her perched at the bar. How could she convey the fact that she wasn't here for *that* type of business, and that this was, in fact, a holiday? The thought of an Italian adventure had excited her, but she hadn't envisaged such a dynamite opening scene. She fell well short compared to the other, more sophisticated women in the bar. There was barely enough fabric in her skirt to cover her fundamentals. She couldn't move for fear of it riding up, and with her naked thigh so close to the man's denim-clad muscles, that was a pressing concern.

'You didn't tell me your name.'

She turned to look at him as the dark velvet voice, with its seductive hint of an Italian accent, rolled over her. Strange how sound could send shivers spinning up and down her spine. Her chin felt as if it had half a universe to travel, as she moved from scrutinising his muscular thighs, to staring into a pair of mesmerising black eyes. Mesmerising and amused, she noticed now. He hadn't missed her fascination with the area below his belt. Her cheeks burned as she volunteered with a direct stare into his eyes, 'My name is Callista.'

His lips pressed down in the most attractive way, drawing her attention to the fact that his mouth was almost as expressive and beautiful as his eyes. 'Greek for most beautiful,' he remarked. 'That explains everything.'

'Really?' She did her best to simper and then hardened her tone. 'I've heard of people being born with silver spoons in their mouths, but yours must have been coated in sugar.'

He laughed, and then affected a wounded expression. 'I'm crushed,' he exclaimed, holding both hands to his powerful chest.

'No, you're not,' she insisted good-humouredly, starting to like him more now he'd proved to have a sense of humour. 'You're the most together person I've ever met.'

He smiled. 'So what is Callista the huntress doing on her own in a hotel bar?'

'Not what you think,' she flashed back.

'What I think?' he queried.

'What are you doing on your own in the bar?' she countered.

He laughed again, a blinding flash of strong white teeth against his impressive tan. 'I'm here to see the barman. What's your excuse?'

'A holiday.' She levelled a stare on his face. 'What do you do for a living?'

The bluntness of her question seemed to take him by surprise, but he soon recovered. 'This and that.'

'This and that, what?' she pressed.

'I guess you could call me a representative.'

'What do you sell?'

'I promote a country's interests, its culture, industry and people.'

'Ah, so you're in the tourism business,' she exclaimed. 'That's nice.' And when he nodded, she asked, 'Which country do you represent?'

'Are you staying here long?' he asked, changing the subject.

The fact he'd ignored her question didn't escape her notice and she gave him a suspicious look. Then, obviously deciding it couldn't do any harm to tell him a little more, she added, 'Not long enough.'

She was enjoying the man's company and decided to prolong the exchange. He excited her. It was no use pretending when every nerve ending she possessed was responding with enthusiasm to the wicked expression in his laughing black eyes. She'd never flirted before, and was surprised to find she rather liked it. This man could turn her insides warm and needy with a look.

'Have you been dancing yet?' he enquired, shooting her an interested look.

'Is that an invitation?'

'Do you want it to be?'

'No, sadly.' She gave him a crooked smile. 'These shoes are killing me.' Twirling a foot, she stared ruefully at the delicate designer shoes with their stratospheric spiky heels. *Could anyone walk in them?*

'You could always slip them off and dance,' he suggested.

As he spoke a band struck up for the evening's entertainment somewhere outside on the terrace. Imagine dancing beneath a canopy of stars, she thought. How romantic. She glanced at her companion, and immediately wished she hadn't. He really did have the wickedest black eyes, which, for some reason, made her think of slowly stripping off her clothes while he watched. She shivered inwardly at the thought. What she should be doing was making it clear that she didn't pick up men in bars. She should collect up her things, get down from the stool and walk away. It was that easy.

Sex with him would be fun. And seriously good.

What was wrong with her? This wasn't the type of simmering heat she'd read about in novels and magazines, but hot, feral lust, that promised very adult pleasures indeed.

'You are extremely entertaining, *signorina*.'

'Really?' Goodness, she hadn't meant to be. He certainly was. Sensuality emanated from him. If she embarked on her Italian adventure with Luca, it could only lead to one place. *Fantastic!* Callie's inner harlot rejoiced, so now the thought of lying close to him, skin to skin, with those strong, lean hands controlling her pleasure—

'Signorina?'

'Yes?' She blinked and refocused on his eyes…his disturbingly experienced eyes. However attractive and compelling she found him, she had to be careful not to take these newfound flirting skills too far. *So the adventure of a lifetime is over before it begins?* The adventure of a lifetime was great in theory, but in practice it threatened all sorts of unknown *pleasures*—dangers, Callie corrected her inner demon firmly. She had more sense than to let things go too far. Concentrating fiercely on her glass of water, she tried not to notice Luca's brutal masculinity as it warred with her inner prude. She gave up in the end. He'd won this point. He was far better at flirting than she was.

What else was he good at?

Stop that now! Didn't she have enough to contend with—a crotch-skimming skirt, and heels custom-made to prevent a stylish exit—without going head to head with a sex god in jeans?

'Another *aqua frizzante, signorina*?'

How did Luca make that simple question sound so risqué? 'Yes, please.'

Oh, so her sensible self was on holiday too?

She wanted to know more about him. What was wrong with that? Chances like this didn't come around every day. *So shoot me if I'm easy.* She wasn't ready to leave yet. And, anyway, why should she be the one to go?

Marco quickly refilled her glass and Luca handed it to her. She sucked in a sharp breath as their fingers touched. He was like an incendiary device to her senses. Using the mirror behind the bar, she surveyed the other men in the room to see if any compared. No, was the simple answer. They were all without exception safe-looking guys, dressed neatly in business suits. There was no one else slouched on one hip, wearing extremely well-packed jeans and a crisp white shirt open a few buttons at the neck to reveal a shading of dark hair. She jumped guiltily when she realised that Luca was staring back at her through the mirror.

'Taking everything in?' he suggested with that same wicked look.

He couldn't be interested in her. It didn't make any sense with so many attractive women in the bar. Had he heard she'd won some money? He might be a particularly good-looking con man on the make, though he didn't seem in need of cash and Marco the barman seemed to know him. Having survived her father, she had no intention of falling for a good-looking man simply because he was charming.

Falling for him?

'You're frowning, *signorina*,' Luca murmured in a way that made all the tiny hairs on the back of her neck stand to attention. 'I hope I'm not the cause of your concern?'

'Not at all,' she said briskly as his direct stare sped straight to her core where it caused havoc all over again. On any level Luca was concerning. Lacking airs and graces, with his rugged good looks he could easily be a roustabout from the docks. Equally he could be a practised seducer. And now was not the time for her body to shout hallelujah! Instead, she should be thanking him for the drink and walking away. 'Would you like a nut?' she asked instead. Luca grinned and raised a brow in a way that thrilled her. 'Before I eat them all,' she added in a tone that told him not to tease as she pushed the bowl towards him.

'It would be easier and far tastier to come out to supper with me,' he said, angling his chin to stare her in the eyes.

Not a chance. That would be courting danger.

'Supper?' Luca pressed. 'Or more nuts?'

She glanced with embarrassment at the almost empty dish—and gasped with shock when Luca took hold of her hand. She had never felt such a shock at a physical connection with another human being. The disappointment when she realised he'd only taken hold of her hand to steady it as he poured the last few nuts from the dish onto her palm was humiliating.

'Enjoy your supper, *signorina*,' he said, straightening up.

'You're going?'

'Will you miss me?'

'Only if I run out of nuts.'

He huffed a laugh that made her heart race like crazy. 'You could come with me.'

She could singe her wings and crash back down to earth too. 'No, thank you.' She smiled, a little wistfully, maybe, but she knew she was doing the right thing. Luca was like a magnet drawing her into danger with those dark laughing eyes. She was enjoying this newfound flirting skill far too much. 'Don't let me keep you from your supper.'

'I choose to be here.'

The way he spoke made breath hitch in her throat. The way he looked at her made everything inside her go crazy. It was everything about him, the Italian accent, his deep, husky voice, and his ridiculous good looks, and perhaps most of all the mesmerising stillness of his magnificent body. She was hypnotised—and determinedly shook herself round.

'Signorina?'

He was waiting for her decision.

'Enjoy your supper.' She wanted to go with him. She wanted to be a bad girl for once in her life. Bad girls had more fun. But then she would have to live with regret. How could she not? She would regret sleeping with him and not knowing him better. She would regret not sleeping with him, and never having the chance again.

'Enjoy your nuts—'

She couldn't believe it when he walked away. Oh, well, that was that, then. Everything went flat when he walked

out of the door, and he didn't look back. He hadn't suggested they meet again, and he hadn't asked for her number. She'd probably done herself a favour, Callie reassured
herself. He'd expect too much, more than she was prepared to give, anyway.

Saying goodnight to Marco, she got down from the
barstool. She felt impatient with herself as she walked
away. She couldn't miss a man she didn't know. She'd
feel better once she was back in her room. She might
have dressed up tonight, as per Rosie and Ma Brown's
instructions, but she was still Callie from the docks inside. But not for long, Callie decided when she reached
her room. She couldn't hang around the hotel aimlessly;
she had to *do* something—get out, see more of the real
Italy. This trip was supposed to be an adventure. She
wasn't tied to the past, or frightened of the future. Roll
on tomorrow, she thought as she climbed into bed, and
whatever it might hold.

As soon as he got back to the *palazzo* he called Marco.
'Who is that woman?'

'Signorina Callista Smith? Staying at the hotel on her
own, if that's what you're asking, my friend.'

'Am I so obvious?'

Marco barked a laugh down the phone. 'Yes.'

'Do you know anything else about her?'

'Only that she comes from the north of England and
that her father died recently, so this is a rebooting exercise for Callie. That's how she described it while we were
chatting. And that's all I know about her.'

'Okay. It explains a lot, though I'd guessed some of it.'

'And?' Marco prompted.

'And it's none of your business,' Luca told his old

friend. 'See you on the estate for the celebrations to-morrow night?'

'The start of the lemon-picking season,' Marco confirmed. 'I wouldn't miss it for the world, but can you spare the time? I thought Max was kicking off in Fabrizio.'

'I have controls in place to keep Max on a leash.'

'Financial controls?' Marco guessed.

'Correct,' Luca said calmly. Max's allowance was generous under their father's rule, and was even more so now that Luca had the means to increase it. Max had never liked to work and with no other source of income he looked to Luca to support him.

'And before you ask,' Marco added, 'Signorina Smith is booked into the hotel for another few days.'

'You've been checking up on her?'

Marco laughed. 'You sound suspicious. Do you care?'

He was surprised to discover that he did. 'Back off, Marco.'

'That sounds like a warning.'

'And maybe I've discovered a conscience,' Luca suggested. 'She's innocent and she's alone, and you are neither of those things.'

'You feel responsible for her already?' Marco commented knowingly. 'This sounds serious.'

'I'm a caring citizen,' Luca remarked dryly.

'I'll do as you say,' Marco offered with his customary good humour. 'And I'll watch with interest to see how long your concern for Signorina Smith's innocence lasts.'

He told Marco what he could do with his interest in Callista Smith in no uncertain terms, reminded him about the celebrations, and then cut the line.

What was he doing? He was a driven man with a country to care for, and a practically out-of-control brother to deal with. And he had to find a bride to provide an heir and continue the dynasty. He shouldn't be wasting time on contemplating an affair—wouldn't be, if he hadn't found Signorina Smith so appealing. He had to remind himself that she was an ingénue with her life ahead of her, and, yes, everything to learn. If they never saw each other again it would be better for both of them. She should learn about sex and the harsh realities of life from a man who could make time for her.

Just don't let me run into that man, Luca reflected dryly as he sank into the custom-moulded seat of his favoured bright red sports car. He'd have to kill him. *No!* He had no time to waste on romancing a woman who might have intrigued him tonight, but who would surely bore him by tomorrow when she proved to be as shallow as the rest.

Gunning the engine, he drove into town with his head full of Callista Smith. He planned to eat at his favourite restaurant. She should have been with him. Top international chefs worked at the *palazzo*, but Signorina Smith had put him in the mood for more robust fare. Tomorrow he would work alongside his seasonal staff in the lemon groves. In lieu of more challenging distractions, for which he had to thank Signorina Smith for providing some very entertaining images to keep him awake tonight, he'd fuel up on good food instead.

'Hey, Luca... Alone tonight?' The restaurant owner, who'd known Luca since he was a suspicious child tagging along behind his newly adoptive father, rushed out of the kitchen to give him a warm hug.

'Unfortunately yes. But don't worry. I can eat enough for two.'

'You always had a huge appetite,' the elderly owner approved.

True, Luca mused dryly as he ran his experienced eye over the women seated at the tables. They all stared at him with invitation in their eyes, but not one of them had the power to hold his interest. Not like Callista Smith.

She was surely the most ungrateful person in the world, Callie concluded as she woke to yet another day of sublime Italian sunshine. And frowned. She was staying in the most beautiful place imaginable in the most fabulous hotel, and yet still she felt as if something was missing. But how could that be, when she was nestled up in crisp white sheets, scented with lavender and sunshine, wearing the ice-blue, pure cotton nightdress trimmed with snowy white lace that Ma Brown had said Callie must have for her trip of a lifetime.

If money can't make me happy, what can I do next?

Well, she'd spent most of the money on staying at this hotel, so she wouldn't have to worry about her win on the scratch card and what it felt like to have some extra cash at her disposal for too much longer, Callie concluded with her usual optimism. Leaping out of bed, she threw the windows open and the view snatched the breath from her lungs. Steep white cliffs dropped down to pewter beaches where the shoreline was fringed by the brightest blue water she'd ever seen. Closing her eyes, she inhaled deeply. Flowers and freshly baked bread, overlaid by the faint tang of ozone, prompted her to take a second breath, just so she could appreciate the first.

What was so terrible about this?

She was lonely, Callie concluded. She missed the Browns. She missed her colleagues at work. Maybe it hadn't been much fun at home with her father being drunk most of the time, but the Browns more than made up for it, and even caring for her father had taken on a regular and predictable pattern. She still felt sad when she thought about him and his wasted life. He could have made so much more of himself with his natural charm and undeniable good looks, but instead had chosen to gamble and drink his life away, putting his trust in unreliable friends, rather than in his daughter Callie, or the Browns.

It was no use dwelling on it. She was determined to make a go of the rest of her life, which meant that decisions had to be made. She wasn't going to sit around in the hotel doing nothing for the rest of her stay. Nor was she going to monopolise Marco and risk bumping into the man with the devastating smile again. Luca was out of her league, the stuff of fairy tales. She had wracked her brains to try to find a film star or a celebrity who could eclipse him and had come up short. There was no one. It wasn't just that Luca was better looking, or had presence to spare, but the fact that he was so down to earth and made her laugh. And thrill. She liked him so much it frightened her, because that wasn't normal, surely? You couldn't just meet a man in a bar and never stop thinking about him…imagining his arms around her, his lips pressed to hers…body pressed to hers… That was ridiculous! She was being ridiculous, Callie concluded, pulling away from the window to retreat into the airy room. She could fantasise about Luca all she liked—well, had done for most of the night, but she had enough sense to stay well away.

'Room service…'

She turned and hurried across the room to answer the door. 'Sorry I took so long. I slept in today.'

'I can come back,' the young maid offered.

'No. Please,' Callie exclaimed. 'Your English is very good. Can I ask you something before you go?'

'Of course. My name is Maria,' the young woman supplied in answer to Callie's enquiring look. 'If I can help you, I will.'

Maria wasn't much older than Callie. Her long dark hair was neatly drawn back, but her black eyes were mischievous, and she had the warmth of Italy about her that Callie was fast becoming used to. 'If you wanted to work outside in the sunshine, Maria—we don't get very much where I come from,' Callie explained ruefully. 'Where would you look for a job?'

'Oh, that's easy.' Maria's face brightened. 'This is the start of the lemon-picking season when the demand for casual labour is at its highest. There's a big estate belonging to the Prince just outside town. They're always looking for temporary staff at this time of year.'

'The Prince's estate?' Callie exclaimed. 'That sounds grand.'

'It's very friendly,' Maria assured her. 'It must be for the same people to come back year after year.'

'Do you think I could get a job there?'

'Why not?' Maria frowned. 'But why would you want to work as a picker?'

Callie could see that it must seem odd for her to be staying at a five-star hotel, yet jumping at the chance to work in the fields. 'I need a change,' she admitted, 'and I'd love to work in the open air.'

'I can understand that,' Maria agreed. 'I'd go today if I were you, so you don't miss the party.'

'The party?' Callie queried.

'There's always a party at the beginning of the season,'

Maria explained, 'as well as at the end. Apart from exporting lemons around the world, they make the famous liquor Limoncello on the Prince's estate, and his parties are always the best.'

'Is the Prince very old?'

Maria snorted a laugh. 'Old? He's the hottest man around.'

Two of the best-looking men in one town seemed impossible, but as she wasn't likely to bump into the Prince, and was determined to avoid Luca, her heart could slow down and take a rest. 'I can't thank you enough for this information,' she told Maria.

'If there's anything else you need, anything at all, Signorina—'

'Call me Callie. You never know when we'll meet again,' Callie added, thrilled at the prospect of having a real goal to aim for.

'In the lemon groves, maybe,' Maria suggested.

'In the lemon groves,' Callie agreed, feeling excited already at the thought of working in lemon groves that she'd only seen in a photograph before.

She was excited and couldn't wait to embark on her new plan, Callie mused as she took her shower. She wouldn't be Callie from the docks for much longer, she'd be Callie from the lemon groves, and that had a much better ring to it.

This was his favourite place in the world, Luca concluded as he swung a stack of crates onto the back of a truck. Hard, physical labour beneath a blazing sun, surrounded by people he loved, who couldn't have cared less if he were a prince or a pauper. Max had been dealt with for now, and was cooling off after his drunken rampage in the local jail, Luca's royal council had informed him. He should take this last chance to celebrate at the party tonight, his most trusted aide Michel had insisted. 'I'll come back right away, if you need me,' he'd told Michel. Luca had never resented the shackles of royal duty. He felt humbled by them, and honoured that the late Prince had trusted him with the responsibility of caring for a country and its people. The only downside was picking a princess to sit at his side, when so far none of the candidates had appealed to him.

To lie at his side, to lie beneath him, to give him children.

He ground his jaw and thought about Callista. She could lie at his side and lie beneath him, though he doubted she'd remain calm or accepting for long. If he were any judge, she'd want to ride him as vigorously as he thought about riding her, with pleasurable thoroughness and for the longest possible time. Callista had more spirit in her little finger than all the available princesses put together possessed in their limp and unappealing bodies. But the fact remained: he had to choose a wife soon. His father's elderly retainer, Michel, had point-blank refused to retire until Luca took a wife. 'I promised your father I'd watch over you,' Michel had said. 'What this country needs is a young family to inject life and vitality into Fabrizio, to lead the country forward into the future.'

He'd sort it, Luca concluded. He always did. The buzz of interest surrounding him at his father's funeral suggested suitable breeding stock wouldn't be too hard to find. A very agreeable image of Callista chose that moment to flash into his mind. Callista naked. Giving as good as she got, verbally, as well as in every other way. She might be young and inexperienced, but her down-to-earth manner promised the type of robust pleasure that an insipid princess would be incapable of providing.

And how does this advance my hunt for a wife?

Loading the last crate of lemons, he groaned as he remembered Michel's words: 'Yours will be a bountiful reign with a harvest of children as abundant as the lemons on your estate,' Michel had assured him. Right now it was Luca's face that looked as if he'd sucked a lemon when he contemplated the current selection of brides.

Work over, he tucked his hands into the back pockets of his jeans and eased his shoulders, grimacing as he thought about the stack of neglected folders on his desk. Leafing through them had confirmed his worst fears. All the princesses were excellent contenders for the role of his wife, but not one of them excited him.

What would Callista be doing now? *She'd better not be sitting at that bar.* He'd drag her out, and—

Really? He grinned, imagining her reaction to that. There was nothing insipid about Callista. She wouldn't fall into line, or be content to bask mindlessly in luxury while working dutifully on creating an heir and a spare. Even Michel would find Callista difficult to lure into the royal fold.

Grazie a Dio! The last thing he needed was a headstrong woman fighting him every step of the way!

But a bolt of pure lust crashed through him as he imagined her in his arms. Finding a suitable princess could wait a few days.

Callie stared up in wonder at the royal gates marking the boundary of the Prince's estate. They were everything she'd expected and more. They were regal and imposing with gilt-tipped spears crowning their impressive height, while lions, teeth bared, grinned down at her. 'Hello,' she murmured, giving them a wink. The lions scowled back.

'Very welcoming,' she managed on a dry throat. Should she be using another entrance? Was there a back entrance? Well, it was too late now. She was here. And then she spotted a notice. It was only about twelve feet high. 'Numbskull,' she muttered. Turning in the direction indicated by the bright red arrow, she walked over to a disappointingly modern control box attached to the far side of the gate. Pressing the button, she jumped with surprise when a metallic voice barked, *'Sollevare la testa, si prega.'*

'I'm sorry, but I don't speak Italian very well...'

'Look up, please,' the same metallic voice instructed.

She stared at the sky.

'At the camera.'

Okay, numbskull squared, that small round lens just in front of me is a camera!

The metallic voice hadn't shown any emotion, but Callie could imagine the person behind it rolling their eyes. Finally, she did as instructed.

'The photograph is for security reasons,' the metallic voice grated out. 'If you don't wish to enter the estate, please step back now.'

'No—I do. I mean, yes. I'm here to apply for a job. I'm sorry if I should have used another entrance...' Her mouth slammed shut as the massive gates swung open.

'Report to the foreman in the first barn you come to.'

'Yes, *signor*...um...*signora*?' The sex of The Voice would remain a mystery for ever, Callie thought as she stepped into a very different world.

This was a world of control and order, Callie concluded, as well as extreme magnificence on every level.

Awestruck, she stared down the length of an incredible avenue composed of a carpet of glistening, white marble beads. At the end of this lay a pink stone edifice, bleached almost white by the midday sun. Both elegant and enormous, the *palazzo* boasted turrets and towers that could have come straight from a book of fairy tales. Cinderella's castle, she mused wryly. The driveway leading up to the palace was broad and long, with stately cypress trees lining the route like sentries. Butterflies darted amongst the colourful flowerbeds lining her way, and birds trilled a welcome as she walked along, but there was no sign of the barn The Voice had referred to.

'*Hey! Per di qua!* This way!'

She turned at the sound of friendly voices to see more pickers following her into the palace grounds. They'd halted at what she could now see was the shrubbery-concealed entrance to a pathway.

Callie scolded herself as she hurried to join them. There was another sign, and it was a huge one, but she'd missed it completely, being too busy ogling her surroundings. The sign read, '*Benvenuto ai nostro personale stagionale!*' Even she knew what that meant. 'Welcome to our temporary staff!'

It was certainly a warmer greeting than the stained sheet of lined paper pinned up on the noticeboard outside the pub, which warned staff to use the back door not the front, on pain of immediate dismissal.

The pickers had waited for her and were all in high spirits. She blended right in with denim shorts and a loose cotton top, teamed with a pair of market-find trainers. She was ready and excited for whatever lay ahead. This was an adventure. This was what she'd been waiting for. This was something to tell the Browns.

It was good news to hear she could start right away and be paid in cash if she wanted. That suited Callie. She planned to check out of the posh hotel and move to a small bed and breakfast in town to extend her stay. She'd already called to confirm the B & B had rooms. She wanted to get to know the real Italy, and, with her father's example behind her, she knew better than to fritter her money away. She'd tasted the high life, and was glad to have done so, but had come away feeling slightly let down. This was so much better, she concluded as she trooped out of the barn with the other pickers. There were no airs and graces here, and, more significantly, no need to wear those excruciatingly painful high-heeled shoes.

The Prince's estate was like a small town. She hadn't guessed how big it was from the road. There were dozens of gangs of pickers working throughout the spectacular lemon groves. This was heaven, Callie thought as she straightened up and paused for breath. Yes, the work was hard, but the sun was warm, the scent of lemons was intoxicating. She had thick gloves to protect her hands and a tool to pick the lemons that were out of reach. The camaraderie was incredible. Everyone wanted to help the newcomers. The party Maria had told her about at the hotel was definitely on tonight, and all the pickers were invited. What could possibly be better than this?

She soon returned to the rhythm of picking. With a lightweight bucket tied around her waist, dropping fruit into it as she went, she loaded the lemon gold into crates that were taken away on gleaming tractors. By the time the blazing sun had mellowed into the amber glow of early evening, she felt as if she'd been working there all her life.

She'd even made a new friend called Anita, a big, bonnie woman, as Ma Brown would have called her, with a ready smile as big as Texas. Anita came from the north of England each year to pick lemons, to feel the sun on her face, to prepare her for the long, cold winter, Anita said. 'I'm on my own,' she'd explained to Callie, 'but when I come here, I have a ready-made family.'

That was when Callie told Anita about the Browns. 'It's people that make things special, isn't it?' she'd asked.

This wasn't just a great way to extend her stay in Italy, Callie concluded as Anita offered to show her the way to the cookhouse, this was an entirely new slant on life, if she had the courage to seize it.

Seize it she would, Callie determined. Her limbs might be aching from all the unaccustomed exercise, but she felt exhilarated for the first time in years. This, *this* was freedom.

CHAPTER THREE

HER ADVENTURE HAD only just begun, Callie realised as excitement for the upcoming party built inside her. Anita had shown her to one of the many well-groomed courtyards surrounding the palace where the celebration was to be held. She couldn't help glancing through the brilliantly lit windows of the palace, to see if she could spot the Prince. Of course, there was no one who looked remotely like a prince, and there was no special buzz in the crowd, so he probably wasn't here. Anita and she accepted a small glass of iced Limoncello from a passing waiter and started to chat. They hadn't been talking long before Callie felt compelled to turn around. She gasped. 'Luca?'

'Someone you know?' Anita asked with surprise.

'Sort of,' Callie admitted. She'd just caught a glimpse of him, but now there was a crowd clustering round, so she could only see the top of his head. She wasn't surprised by all the interest. It was his magnetism that had first gripped her. 'He didn't tell me he worked here,' she told Anita.

'He's a regular—are you all right?' Anita had been about to say something else about Luca, but was responding to the look on Callie's face.

'I'm absolutely fine,' Callie insisted on a dry mouth. Which was an absolute lie. She had to put her glass down and cross her arms over her chest to hide her arousal as Luca looked at her. And he didn't just glance her way. Their stares locked and held.

'Uh-oh. He's coming over,' Anita warned. 'I predict things are about to change for you,' Anita commented sagely. She had to nudge Callie, who was as good as in a trance. 'Better make myself scarce…'

'No, Anita! Stay—' Too late. Anita had already disappeared into the crowd.

Luca saluted Callie with a bottle of beer, and his slanting smile of recognition was infectious and made her smile too. Her heart raced out of control. It was so exciting to see him again. *Too exciting.* She should follow Anita. What was she thinking of, standing here, waiting for a man who looked as if he ate brass tacks for breakfast with a virgin on the side?

Quite simple, Callie concluded, lifting her chin. She didn't run away from anything, and she wasn't about to start now.

And he was quite a magnet. Luca looked better than ever in his banged-up work clothes. Swarthy-faced, with an unruly mop of thick black hair and an indecent amount of sharp black stubble, he was everything better avoided for those in search of a quiet life. *But I'm here in search of adventure,* Callie reminded herself with a secret inner grin. Tousled and rugged, with scratches on his powerful forearms and hard-muscled calves, he even looked sexy when he wiped smudges of dirt from his face with the back of his arm. The bonfire behind him was throwing off flames that provided the perfect showcase for a man who looked like a dark angel from hell come to wreak havoc on novice flirters.

'Luca,' she said pleasantly as he came over, acting as if her senses weren't reeling.

'Signorina Callista Smith,' he countered with a slanting grin. 'What a pleasant surprise.'

'You know my name?' He must have been talking to Marco the barman, Callie realised. She wasn't sure how she felt about being discussed by the two men.

'You can't expect to be ignored, signorina.'

As Luca made a mock bow, she tried not to notice they'd become the centre of attention. She didn't flatter herself that he'd picked her out for any particular reason. If he was a regular as Anita had suggested, she was fresh meat.

His top was tight and skimmed the waistband of his low-slung shorts. It was impossible not to notice the arrow of dark hair that swooped beneath his zipper, or indeed the quite preposterous bulge that lay beneath. To say he looked amazing was an understatement. Even when she tried to focus on something harmless, like his tanned feet in simple thonged sandals, she realised they were sexy too. Her interest travelled up his legs to powerful calves, and on again to where she definitely shouldn't be looking. She had to stop this right now, and *concentrate*!

No! Not there!

She was about to meet a very challenging man for the second time, and she'd better be ready for it, Callie warned herself firmly. Fixing her gaze on Luca's darkly amused face, she determined not to let her gaze wander, but then thought, why not stare? Luca had never been shy about staring at her, and interest wasn't a one-way street. His bronzed and muscular torso, barely covered by the ripped and faded top, invited attention. He was an outstanding specimen. A statue should be raised in the town square for everyone to admire.

'Nice to see you at the party,' he said, smiling in that faint way he had that made her body burn. 'I hope they're serving nuts tonight.'

She gave him a look, half smile, half scolding. He'd stopped within touching distance. His heat enveloped her. And that voice. Dark chocolate tones strummed her senses until they were clamouring for the sort of pleasure she guessed Luca knew only too much about. He towered over her in a way that blocked out the light, which was enough to warn her to be careful. She didn't stand in anyone's shadow. 'Are you here on your own?' she asked, diplomatically stepping away.

'I am,' he confirmed.

His voice curled around her, making her skin tingle. 'No one waiting for you back home?' she enquired casually.

'My dogs, my cats and the horses,' he said.

'I think you know what I mean,' she insisted.

'Do I?' Luca stared at her in a way that made heat curl low in her belly. 'Do you always put people you've only just met through the third degree?'

When they look like you, and have who knows what secrets, yes, I do, she thought. 'That depends who I'm talking to,' she said.

'So why do I get the third degree?'

'Do we have enough time?' she demanded, and when he laughed, she said honestly, 'I just didn't expect to see you here, so it's a bit of a surprise.'

'A surprise I hope you're getting used to?'

His black eyes were dancing with laughter, so, responding in kind, she shook her head and heaved a theatrical sigh. 'I'm trying to be tactful, and I realise now that blunt is much easier for me.'

'I'm with you there,' he said. 'So be blunt.'

'Are you married?' she asked flat out. 'Or do you have a partner, a special friend?'

Luca grinned. 'You weren't joking about blunt.'

'Correct,' Callie confirmed. 'Before I say another word, I need to know where I stand.'

'Do I look married?'

'That's not an answer to my question,' she complained. 'In fact, I'd call it an evasion.'

'I'm not married,' Luca confirmed as she turned to go. She stilled when he caught hold of her arm. His touch was like an incendiary device to her senses. 'I'm unattached, other than being briefly joined to you,' he said as he lifted his hand away. She felt the loss of it immediately. 'Does that satisfy your moral code?'

'My moral compass is pointing in a more hopeful direction,' she agreed.

'You're an intriguing woman, Callista Smith.'

'Callie.' She enjoyed the verbal sparring with him. 'And you must have led a sheltered life.'

He laughed out loud at that suggestion, making her wish they could carry on provoking each other for the rest of the night. Electricity sparked between them. He made her feel good. Primal attraction, she thought. Sex, she warned herself flatly. Who couldn't think about sex with Luca?

He looked like a natural-born hunter who thought he'd found his prey. While under her blunt manner, Callie was sugar and spice and all things nice, and determined to remain that way. Her body could argue all it liked that sugar and spice could still enjoy verbal sparring, but she had no intention of taking things any further. Luca might be everything she'd fantasised about while she was on her knees scrubbing floors in the pub, but this was reality, not a dream world, and the safest thing she could do now was leave. 'I was about to go home,' she explained, glancing away down the drive.

'Aren't you enjoying yourself?'

Too much. 'I am.' She couldn't lie. She'd enjoyed everything about today, and now the food smelled amazing, the band was playing, and it was a beautifully warm evening beneath a canopy of stars. And then there was Luca. 'But I've got work tomorrow.'

'So do I,' he said smoothly.

'You're making this difficult for me.' And hard to breathe, she silently added.

'Why deny yourself the reward for a hard day's work?'

That depended on the reward. Good grief, he was beautiful! His stillness reminded her of a big, soft-pawed predator preparing to pounce. She didn't need a wake-up call, Callie concluded. She needed a bucket of ice-cold water tossing over her head.

'Hey, Luca!'

They both swung around to see Marco coming over. It broke the tension for a while as Luca greeted Marco, but once the two men were done with complicated handshakes and Marco moved on, the two of them were alone again. 'I thought you'd have gone in search of nuts by now,' Luca remarked dryly.

'I was waiting to say goodbye to you.'

'Ah.'

Was he convinced, Callie wondered, or had he guessed that she was trapped like a rabbit in headlights by his brazen masculinity?

'So why are you here, mystery woman? You're staying at a five-star hotel, but work in the fields picking lemons?'

'What's wrong with that?' she challenged.

'Nothing.'

'Well, now we've got that sorted out, I'll say goodnight.' To give him his due, there was no more questions. Luca shrugged and stood aside to let her go, but as she passed he reached out to smooth a lock of hair from her face. His touch thrilled her. Her skin tingled, and her nipples tightened, while tiny pulses of sensation beat low down in her belly.

'Stay,' he insisted. 'You'll have more fun.'

That was what she was afraid of. 'Should I be flattered by your suggestion?' she asked coolly, searching his eyes.

'No,' he said bluntly. 'You should be on your guard.'

She made a point of glancing around. 'Are there many predatory men at this party?'

'None that stand a chance of getting close to you.'

'Will you keep them away? I would have thought you had better things to do.'

'And I thought you were leaving,' he countered.

'I am.'

He could hardly believe it when she walked away. This wasn't a woman he could tease into his bed, but a woman to be reckoned with. Good. He needed a challenge. There was only one woman who could hold his interest tonight. He could hardly believe the transformation from butterfly at the bar, to working girl in the lemon groves. It was a good mix. That stubborn chin clinched it for him. He was done with insipid. She had a great walk too. He feasted his eyes as she walked away from him with her head held high and her shapely butt swaying provocatively beneath the simple clothes. She hadn't a clue who he was. He doubted it would have made any difference. Status meant nothing to Callie, as proved by her easy transition from luxury living in the five-star hotel, to some of the hardest physical work in the area.

The sun had been kind to her today. Flushed from physical activity, she looked good enough to eat, something he'd put on hold until later in the evening, he reflected dryly. He watched as she met up with her friends. She was more relaxed than she'd been at the hotel. Laughing easily, she mimed words when the different languages spoken became a problem. Nothing seemed to faze her. Apart from him.

She was comfortable around everyone, as he was, and far more beautiful than he remembered. Young and natural—even the smear of dirt on her neck only made him think about licking it off. It was time he stopped thinking about Callie naked in his arms, or he'd be walking around the party uncomfortably aroused.

And, before he committed himself to taking her to bed, there were questions to be answered. Why was she picking fruit for a few euros a day when she was staying at a five-star hotel? Was it just for the experience? Who was funding her? Why was she in Italy? Was this a holiday or an escape? If she was escaping, from what? He had no intention of allowing Max to lure him into a honey trap that could discredit Luca, and expose the principality of Fabrizio to corruption beneath his half-brother's rule. It was time to find out more.

As he approached Callie her friends melted away. 'Where are they going?' she asked with surprise.

They were diplomatically giving him space. Callie

couldn't help but be oblivious to the dynamics that existed between a prince and his people. However much he would have liked it to be different, obstacles between him and Utopia were not in his gift to remove.

'Anyone would think you'd got the plague,' she said, bringing a comic slant to bear on the situation.

'Let's hope it's not that serious,' he said, loving the way she could pop the pomposity bubble before it even had chance to form. She had raw, physical appeal, he mused as she stared up at him. It was all too easy to imagine her limbs wrapped around him as she sobbed with pleasure in his arms. 'Dance?' he suggested, curbing baser needs.

'Not if I can help it,' she exclaimed.

The response was pure Callie. 'Why not?' he demanded, play-acting wounded.

'Because I have two left feet and the sense of rhythm of a hamster on a wheel.'

He shrugged. 'Should be interesting. I'm a fast mover myself.'

She raised a disapproving brow, but her eyes betrayed her interest.

'Perhaps I can slow you down?' he suggested. 'Show you an alternative to racing to the finish?'

Her cheeks flushed red. She'd got the sexual message in his words loud and clear, but she hit him with a blunt response. 'You must be wearing steel-capped boots to feel so confident. And I'm going to sit this one out.'

He was nowhere near finished and caught hold of her arm. Momentum thrust her against him. She felt sensational, strong, lithe, and yet softly plump in all the right places. She was so tiny compared to him, but they fitted together perfectly.

'You're taking a lot for granted.' She frowned, but made no attempt to move away.

'I don't see you rushing off,' he countered softly.

'Caveman.'

'Nut freak.'

'Nut freak?' She stared into his eyes. Her lips were just a tempting distance away.

'You're quaint,' he said, meeting her jade-green eyes head-on.

'Quaint?' she queried.

'Old-fashioned.'

She appeared to consider this, and then said, 'There's nothing wrong with tradition. Someone has to take responsibility for keeping standards high.'

Yes. That was him. He stared at a mouth he could have feasted on until she fell asleep with exhaustion. 'Talk to me,' he murmured.

'About what?' she asked, her brow crinkling in enquiry.

He didn't care. He just loved to watch her lips move as she goaded him. The thought of teasing those lips apart with his tongue to claim all the dark recesses of her mouth, along with everything else, fired him up until the hunger to take her was all-consuming. 'That dance we talked about?'

'You talked about.' But she didn't resist when he steered her towards a space that miraculously, as far as Callie was concerned, had opened for them on the packed dance floor.

When Luca pressed her close she gasped at the intensity of feeling. She was conscious that people were staring at them and whispering, which she guessed was only to be expected when she was dancing with the hottest man at the party. Why he'd chosen her to dance with, she had no idea. She hadn't exactly made it easy for him. When he nuzzled her hair aside and kissed her neck, she didn't care what his reasons were. She didn't care about anything. The world and everyone in it simply dropped away.

CHAPTER FOUR

RISK VERSUS PLEASURE, Callie thought as she flicked a
glance into Luca's eyes. Even the briefest look sent heat
surging through her. She could trust herself for one dance,
she decided, which might have had something to do with
the fact that when Luca took hold of her hand a thrill raced
through her. When his other hand slipped into the hollow
in the small of her back, she could think of nothing but
closer contact. Fighting the urge, she kept a sensible distance between them. Other couples had made space for
them, so there was no need to cling to him like a limpet.

Luca was really popular, she realised as they started
to move to the music. They were attracting lots of interested glances and smiles. In fact, she would call it more
of a buzz, so maybe the Prince was close by. She glanced
around and realised that she wouldn't know the Prince
if she tripped over him. Everyone was probably wondering how she got so lucky, but she couldn't shake the
feeling that she was missing something. There was no
chance to dwell on it. It was far more important to keep
her wits about her. Dancing with Luca was a high-risk
sport, she concluded as the sinuous melody bound them
closer together. There was only thing more intimate they
could do and be this close, and that was to make love—

She could put that out of her head right now! She was going to have one dance, and then she was going home. To pull away from Luca before the music ended would be rude. To fall into the trap of relaxing in his arms was stupid. Control would be her watchword. *At least for now.* Another, far more reckless side of Callie wanted to know why she couldn't see this adventure out. She wasn't Callie who scrubbed floors for a living now, but Callie from the lemon groves, who had a whole world of adventure tucked up inside her.

She made herself relax. Luca was right about dancing with him being easy. For some reason her feet seemed to know what to do. Her body moved instinctively with his. They could have been alone on the dance floor. She looked up to see him smiling a lazy, confident smile. He was good. He was very good. Luca might look rugged and tough, but when it came to seduction, he was smooth. So long as she was aware of it, she'd be okay, Callie reassured herself as they danced on.

But he must feel her trembling with arousal. Her body was on fire for him. Her heart was banging in her chest. She'd never played such dangerous games before. Luca was so brazenly virile she couldn't think straight. She wanted to lace her fingers through his hair, and explore his body. She wanted to feel his sharp black stubble rasp her skin, and his firm, curving mouth tease hers into submission. *While his big strong hands position me for pleasure...*

No! She had to leave now.

But she didn't.

And then an annoying drone buzzed overhead. 'It's only just checking who's around,' Luca reassured her when she looked up.

'Like we're so important,' she said dryly. 'I guess the Prince must be around.'

'It's a natural precaution when there's a crowd,' Luca explained.

Hmm. She loved to watch his mouth tilt at the corners when he smiled. 'You've worked here before, so you're used to it,' she pointed out, 'but this is all new to me.' *And how!* And how fabulous, Callie thought as the music started up again, and one dance segued smoothly into two.

'Tell me about home for you,' Luca prompted.

'I'm from a small town in the north of England.'

'What's it like?'

His hands were looped lightly around her waist as he pulled his head back to stare at her. A sensible question was welcome. A return to reality was exactly what she needed when their bodies were an electric hair's breadth apart. But how to explain to a man who lived in one of the most beautiful countries in the world that her life back home was not like this? She settled for the truth. 'I'm very lucky. I have the best of neighbours, a good job, and wonderful friends.'

'So you live alone?' he pressed as they danced on.

It was hard to concentrate on anything while she was this close to Luca, but she shook her mind back to the facts. 'I lived with my father until recently. He died a short time before I came to Italy.'

'I'm very sorry.'

'He was killed in a drunken brawl,' she explained. Luca had sounded genuinely concerned, and she didn't want to mislead him, but her eyes brimmed as she said this. It had been such a tragic waste of life. 'The world keeps turning,' she said, to deflect Luca's interest from the confusion on her face. Guilt had always played such a large part in her thinking where her father was concerned. She had never had any influence over him, but had always wished she could have changed things for the better for him.

'And now you're spreading your wings,' Luca guessed, bringing her back on track.

'I'm trying different things,' she confirmed, brightening as she thought about the short time she'd been in Italy. 'I love it here. I love the warmth of the people, and the sunshine, the glamour of a party beneath the stars— who wouldn't love being here on the Prince's estate? I feel free for the first time in a long time,' she admitted carelessly. 'Sorry. My mouth runs away with me sometimes.'

'No. Go on,' Luca encouraged. 'I'm interested. I want to hear more.'

She was careful not to add the word adventure to her gush of information. He would definitely get the wrong idea. She told him a little more, and then his arms closed around her. His embrace was worryingly addictive and people were packed around them on the dance floor, making dancing close inevitable. Luca was easy to talk to and soon she was telling him things that perhaps she shouldn't, like the camaraderie down the pub where she worked that could so easily erupt into violence when people had had too much to drink.

'*Dio*, Callie, how could your father let you work there?'

She frowned. 'No one gave me permission, and it was a well-paid job. Good, honest work,' she emphasised, and then she laughed. 'They had to pay their staff well, in order to keep them in such a rough area.'

'It sounds horrendous,' Luca remarked, not seeing anything amusing in what she'd said.

'We needed the money,' she said honestly, 'and there aren't too many options where I come from.'

Luca was a passionate Italian male, Callie reminded herself, and they could be very protective. He might look hard as rock, but he was no brute. And she was no saint, Callie thought as his hard thigh eased between hers. She tried using force of will to pretend nothing was happening, but that was the biggest fail yet. He was so big and she was so small that relaxing against him soon became snuggling into him, which felt ridiculously good, almost as if it was supposed to be. Music quickly restored her moral compass when the beat speeded up. She thought he'd let her go, lead her off the dance floor, but instead he caught her closer still.

'You're a good dancer.'

'Only because you lift me off my feet.' She laughed, then reviewed what was happening to her body while they were brushing, rubbing, nudging. It was both sensational and addictive. She wanted more. She wanted to toss her moral compass away.

As if sensing the way her thoughts were turning, Luca whispered in her ear, 'I'm sure you've had enough dancing for now.'

She pulled back her head to stare into his eyes, which was dangerous, because now she discovered she was addicted to danger too. The camera drone chose that moment to intrude. 'If the person behind those controls wants to take a better look at us, why don't they just come down here and say so?'

'I doubt we're the sole object of the controller's attention.'

'You could have fooled me.' She glared at the drone.

'Do you think it's so interested because the Prince is here?'

'Possibly,' Luca agreed.

'I haven't seen him yet. Have you? I mean, you've worked on the estate before, so you must know him.'

'I'm offended,' Luca said, half grinning, which suggested he wasn't offended at all. 'All you want to talk about is the Prince.'

'It's something to tell them about back home.'

'What about me?' he growled.

'Don't look for compliments. You won't get them from me.'

He laughed and swept her off her feet.

'Put me down this instant,' she exclaimed.

'Not a chance,' he said. Amusement coloured his voice. 'Don't you want to know where your adventures could take you?'

'I've got a pretty good idea, which is why I hope your tongue is firmly planted in your cheek. Just for the record, I'll be sleeping on my own tonight,' she added as Luca strode on across the courtyard with her safely locked in his arms.

'Brava,' he said, showing no sign of slowing down.

The crowd parted like the Red Sea, she noticed. She should put up some sort of token struggle, but it was a magical night, a magical moment, and not too many of them came along.

Her senses rioted when Luca dipped his head to brush a kiss against her neck. She would see this adventure through, so long as it only took her from one side of the courtyard to the other. 'I have to go,' she insisted, when he lowered her to her feet to acknowledge some boisterous partygoers.

'No. You have to stay,' he argued when he was done, and so close to her ear that it tingled.

'Are you determined to lead me astray?'

'Would I?' Sweeping her up before she had chance to protest, he strode on towards the palace gardens.

She was dangerously aroused, but for one night, she was going to be Callie from the lemon groves, without fear or guilt, or any of the dutiful thoughts that had curbed her in the past.

'Where are you taking me?' she asked as Luca opened a gate leading to lemon groves.

'Wait and see.'

He didn't stop until they reached the riverbank where he set her down. She had free will. She could do what she liked. She didn't have to do anything she didn't want to. Conscious he was watching her, she smiled, but Luca wasn't fooled. 'What's worrying you?' he said.

'I'm not worried.' Apart from the longing to have more nights like this, which she knew in her heart of hearts would not be possible. Moonlight lit the scene. Sparkling water rushed by. The bed of grass beneath her feet was soft and deep, and the midnight-blue sky overhead was littered with stars. It was the perfect setting on the perfect night, and Luca was the perfect man. Reaching out, she linked their hands.

Luca soothed and seduced her with kisses, with touches, and with the expression in his eyes. She believed they were connecting on a deeper level. He made her want to know more about him, and for this to be the start of something, rather than the grand finale. His hands worked magic on her body. His strength seduced her, his scent seduced her... everything about Luca seduced her. He was a man of the earth, a man of the people, who worked with his body, his mind, and good humour, as well as unstinting loyalty towards his Prince, which he'd proved when he had refused to point him out to her.

This adventure might have its ups and downs, but Luca had featured large in every part of it. He made her spirit soar, and her body cry out for his touch.

They couldn't keep their hands off each other. There was no chance she was going anywhere any time soon. She was a woman with needs and desires, who saw no reason for self-denial. She hadn't prepared for this, but had taken the usual precautions, more in hope than expectation of a love life some time in the far distant future. She hadn't planned anything, because placing trust in a man was a huge deal for Callie, but Luca was different. He made her feel safe. He made her believe she could trust him.

His mouth was warm and as persuasive as sin, and, though she was tentative at first, she soon matched his fire. He was more controlled. She was not. She was new to this, and had had no idea how the fire could take hold and consume her. Luca kept his touch tantalisingly light, far too light for her frustrated body. The urge to know every part of him intimately was clawing at her senses. 'I want you,' she said as she stared up into his eyes.

He knew she was suffering. Of *course* he knew. He was responsible for it. She was hardly playing hard to get, and Luca was available for pleasure. Tracing his magnificent torso over his insubstantial top tipped the balance from caution to action. 'Take it off,' she instructed, 'and then the rest of your clothes.'

His eyes fired with interest and amusement. 'You first,' he countered. 'Or at least, match me.'

And so the game began. It was a game with only one

conclusion. Once started, it couldn't be stopped. Without breaking eye contact, she began unbuttoning her blouse. She did so slowly, and felt heat rise between them. It was her turn to make *him* wait. Pushing the soft fabric from her shoulders, she let it drop.

He frowned. 'You're wearing a bra.'

'I'd say you're overdressed too,' she murmured.

He smiled.

'You should have drawn up your rules before this started,' she teased, 'because now you have to take off your flip-flops too.'

Maintaining eye contact as he kicked them off, she whispered, 'And now your shorts.'

'Are you sure about that?'

'Absolutely sure.' She would keep her eyeline level with his.

'Take off your trainers,' he suggested.

'If that's a ruse to give me chance to have second thoughts, save it. I won't change my mind.'

'I'll take my chances.' Luca's stare was long and steady. 'By the time I've finished, you won't have a stitch of clothing on,' he promised.

She shrugged, pretending indifference, but her heart was banging in her chest. 'If you'd rather not?'

'Oh, I'd rather,' he said with a look that made her body flame with lust.

She toed off her trainers, wishing she'd dressed for the Arctic and had more clothes to remove. Luca was in serious danger of winning this game. How would such an experienced man judge her when he saw her naked? But it was exciting and fun, and every bit the adventure she'd dreamed about…the adventure she wouldn't be telling the Browns about.

She should have known he'd go commando. He'd lowered his zipper and allowed his shorts to slide down his lean frame. Currently, they were hanging on his thighs. Reaching down, he pushed them the rest of the way and, stepping out of them, he stood in front of her, unconcerned. 'You still have some way to go,' he commented.

She would not look down. 'My rules state—' She gasped as Luca yanked her close.

'Your rules count for nothing,' he assured her in a seductive growl as he nuzzled his stubble-roughened face against her neck.

'*Oh*—' Breath shot from her lungs. She couldn't help but rub her body against his in the hunt for more contact between them, but Luca held her firmly away.

'Not so fast,' he said, all control, while she was a gasping mass of arousal. 'I can see I have some training to do.'

'Please,' she said, making his eyes flare with amusement.

'Nice bra,' he commented as he deftly removed it.

Now that was definitely going to give him the wrong idea. She'd chosen something frivolous for Italy. It had seemed such fun at the time. And safe. When she had been shopping in a brightly lit department store with not a single good-looking man around, the flimsy bra and thong had seemed harmless. The brand was quite exclusive, meant for show rather than practicality. Designer lingerie in bright pink silk chiffon bordered with palest aquamarine lace was hardly Callie's usual choice. She was more of a sensible white cotton type. She could only imagine what Luca was thinking.

'You're beautiful,' he murmured, reassuring and disarming her all in one breath.

'No, I'm not.'

'I guess there's only one way to convince you,' he said, laughing softly.

He drew her closer, inch by inch, and then he kissed her. And this was not a teasing brush of his lips, but something more that drew emotion out of her, until she was happy and sad, excited and confused, all at once. She was happy to be here with him, and sad because she knew it couldn't last. He excited her. Her body was going crazy for more—which he knew. And she was apprehensive too, in case she got this terribly wrong. There were *so* many ways she could get this wrong.

'Stop,' Luca murmured against her mouth. 'Stop thinking and just allow yourself to feel for once. Go with your instincts, Callie.'

Her instincts were telling her to rub herself shamelessly against him, to part her legs and find relief as quickly as she could for the throbbing ache of frustration that he'd put there. And she had mightily encouraged, Callie conceded. She wanted this badly. Even more than that, she wanted the connection between them to last, but she had to face facts: Luca was an itinerant worker, as was she, and so they'd both move on.

He kissed away her doubts as he lowered her slowly to the ground. Stretching out his length against hers on the cool swathe of grass, he made sure that the world faded away, leaving just the two of them to kiss and explore each other. It was as if time stood still. Water still bubbled nearby, and a light breeze still ruffled the leaves overhead, but they were in another world where her senses were totally absorbed in Luca's warm, clean man scent, and the feel of his powerful body against hers. His chest was shaded with just the right amount of dark hair that rasped against her nipples as he moved. She was filled with desire for him, and only felt a moment of apprehension when he reached into the pocket of his discarded shorts and she heard a foil rip. She was glad he had the good sense to protect them both, because she had no intention of pulling back. She had no regrets. None.

When he dipped his head to suckle her mind exploded with sensation. Moving her head on the cushioned earth, she bucked her hips repeatedly, involuntarily, responding to the hungry demands of her body. In the grip of sexual hunger, she reached for his shoulders and held on tightly, as if she were drowning and Luca was her rock. She had stifle a gasp of excitement when he moved over her. The weight of him against her thighs was new to her, and a little frightening. She had to tell herself that this was what she wanted, and that nothing was going to stop her now, nothing.

'I'm right here,' he soothed as if he could sense her apprehension.

'Don't I know it?' she joked half-heartedly.

'Seriously. Stop worrying. I would never hurt you.'

She stared into his eyes and saw the truth behind his statement. It was as if that had opened the floodgates to hunger, to curiosity, which left her fierce with passion, as well as uncertain as to what Luca was used to. Goodness knew, her experience was limited, to say the least. She was on a journey of discovery, Callie consoled herself, and this was an adventure that would carve a memory so deep she would never forget this moment, or this man.

Luca whispered against her mouth, 'Trust me, Callie,' and then his hands worked their magic and she was lost.

'*Oh*…that's…'

'Good?' he suggested in a low, amused murmur.

Her answer was a series of soft, rhythmical sighs. 'Better than good,' she managed to gasp.

'More?' he suggested.

The hands cupping her buttocks were so much bigger than hers, and his skilful fingers could work all sorts of wickedness.

'Would you like me to touch you here?'

His tone was low and compelling. 'So much,' she admitted, sucking in a shaking breath.

One of Luca's slightly roughened finger pads was all it took to send her mindless with excitement. He knew exactly what to do. He started stroking steadily, rhythmically, applying the right amount of pressure at just the right speed.

'Good?'

Was she supposed to answer? She daren't speak. She was frightened of losing control.

'Would you like me to tip you over the edge?'

'I'm not sure.'

'Yes, you are.'

Staring into Luca's laughing eyes, she knew he was right.

He kissed her as he explored her, a shallow invasion at first with a single finger, and then deeper, with one, two, and finally three fingers. 'You're so ready,' he commented with approval.

She rocked her body in time to the steady thrust of Luca's hand. It wasn't as good, or as immediate as when he attended to her achingly sensitive little nub. It was a different feeling, and one just as compelling in its way. It made her want him to lodge deep inside her. The urge to be one with him was overwhelming.

Nudging her thighs apart with his, he continued to

touch her in the way that took her mind off everything else. The delicious sensation of having him enclose her buttocks in his big, warm hands while he touched her lightly at the apex of her thighs was startlingly good. He found new ways to tease her, moving his body up and down until she was so aroused he could slide in easily, but then he pulled out again, provoking her more than ever. 'Don't stop!' she exclaimed with frustration.

He ignored this plea and continued to tease her. Wild for him, she begged for more in words she'd never used before.

'Like this?' Luca suggested in a low growl.

She gasped with shock when he sank deep. For a moment she didn't know if she liked it or not. He was very slow and very careful, but that only gave her chance to realise how much he stretched her. Every nerve ending she possessed leapt instantly to attention. The sensation was sudden and complete. She couldn't think, she could only feel. *'Yes,'* she sighed, moving with him.

Luca maintained a dependable rhythm, taking her to the edge and over, and he still moved intuitively, steadily, to make sure that her ride of pleasure continued for the longest possible time. She might have screamed. She might have called his name. She only knew that by the time she quietened her throat was sore, and with a gasp she collapsed back against the grass.

'And we're only just getting started,' Luca promised with amusement.

Still lodged deep, he began to move again, persuasively and gently to take account of her slowly recovering body. He kept up this sensitive buffeting until the fire gripped her again and she wound her legs tightly around his waist as he thrust deep. She didn't wait to be tipped over the edge this time, but worked her hips with his, falling fast and hard, while Luca held her firmly in place so she received the full benefit of each deep, firm stroke.

'Greedy,' he approved as she gasped for breath.

'You make me greedy.' Luca was still hard. She was still hungry. She reached for him and he took her again.

Callie was unique in his experience. It was as if they'd been lovers for years, but could enjoy the first, furious appetite that came with discovery of someone special. Not only could she match him, she fired him like no other. He was driven by the primitive urge to imprint himself on her body, her mind, and her memory. Pinning her down beneath him with her arms above her head, he thrust firmly to the hilt. She growled, and bucked towards him, as hungry as she had ever been. She was wild and abandoned, as he'd imagined Callie would be once he discovered what lay beneath her carefully cultivated shell. When they were still again, she turned towards him, as slowly as if her bones had turned to lead. Smiling, she managed groggily, 'You're amazing.'

'And so are you,' he replied softly.

CHAPTER FIVE

THEY BATHED IN the stream, seemingly unaware of the chill of the water, and dried off on the bank next to each other, kissing and staring into each other's eyes. Luca seemed surprised when she insisted she would go home on one of the staff buses, but she wasn't ready to spend the night with him. She needed to clear her head and come to terms with the fact that this might have been a life-changing experience, but it had no future.

Let this be, she thought as Luca smiled against her mouth before kissing her. Let it remain shiny and special. Allow nothing to taint it. She had those same thoughts when she boarded the bus, but by the time she walked into the hotel lobby her mood had changed, mainly because the concierge was waiting for her, and he looked worried to death.

'Thank goodness, Signorina Smith. This came for you.'

She looked at the envelope he was holding out. It was obviously urgent. She ripped it open and started reading. There was some confusion about her room at the bed and breakfast. She had intended to move hotels tomorrow, but now it seemed her room at the B & B was no longer available. Crumpling the note in her hand, she frowned as she wondered what to do next. She couldn't afford to stay on here.

'Signorina Smith?'

The concierge was hovering anxiously. 'Yes?'

'Forgive my intrusion, but I can see how concerned you are. Please don't be worried. The manager at the establishment you had hoped to move to left that note for you. He has informed us of a problem, and so it is arranged that you continue to stay here.'

Callie's cheeks flushed with embarrassment. 'I'm afraid I can't afford to stay here,' she admitted frankly. The concierge looked as embarrassed as she felt and this wasn't his fault. 'I'd love to stay on,' she added warmly. 'Everyone's been so kind to me, but I need to find somewhere cheaper. Maybe you can help?'

'Please, *signorina*,' the concierge implored, shifting uncomfortably from polished shoe to polished shoe. 'There will be no charge. You have been let down. This is a matter of local pride. The management of this hotel and the staff who care for you will be insulted if you offer payment.'

'And I'll be insulted if I don't,' Callie said bluntly. 'I really can't stay on if I don't pay my way.'

'The cost of your room has been covered.'

She swung around in surprise. 'Luca! Are you following me?'

'Yes,' he admitted.

'What do you know about this?' she demanded. Luca, tousled and magnificent, couldn't have looked more incongruous in the sleek, polished surroundings of the five-star hotel. She had to curb a smile as she glanced down at her clothes, and then at his. They both looked exactly what they were, labourers from the fields, which was another reason for decamping to another, much plainer establishment. Not that her body could have cared less what Luca was wearing. As far as her body was concerned, Luca looked better naked, anyway.

A million and one feelings flooded through her as they stared at each other. 'Are you responsible for this?' she asked, holding out the letter. Out of the corner of her eye, she could see the concierge, who'd returned to his booth, looking more anxious than ever. Something was definitely going on. Luca knew Marco. Had they pulled strings between them so that she would have to stay with Luca? She refused to be manipulated, especially by Luca.

'I couldn't help overhearing that you were having difficulties,' he began.

She bit her tongue and decided to wait to see what he said next. When he shrugged and smiled, threatening to weaken her resolve, she said, 'I don't suppose you know anything about my mysterious benefactor, or the fact that the hotel is refusing to charge me?'

He raised a brow. 'Don't you like it here?'

'That's not the point,' she insisted. It hadn't escaped her notice that Luca was speaking as calmly as if he were a tour operator dealing with a quibbling client, rather than a controlling alpha male who seemed to think that everything and everyone should run to his prescription. He might have quite literally swept her off her feet at the party, but post-party common sense had had time to set in.

'My only concern is that you have somewhere comfortable to stay,' he insisted.

She bristled. 'Well, thank you, but I'm quite capable of making my own arrangements.'

'They had a burst pipe at the small establishment

where you booked a room,' Luca explained while the concierge nodded vehemently. 'Marco alerted me to this, and the concierge was only trying to help.'

'How did Marco know I was planning to move to the B & B?' she asked suspiciously.

'I'm sorry, Callie, but you can't live in a small town like this and not know what's going on.'

'So Marco told you?' How could she have been so dim?

'Stay on at the hotel,' Luca offered, as if he were the owner of the sumptuous building. 'You'll be closer to the lemon groves here.' He shot her a questioning look. 'That's if you intend to continue working on the Prince's estate.'

'Of course I do,' Callie confirmed. She loved it on the Prince's estate, and was nowhere near ready to leave yet.

'So, come back with me.'

Luca was waiting at the lobby door, as if it were all a done deal. Did he mean go back to the party with him? Or did Luca have something different in mind? She had paid for the hotel until tomorrow, and packing could wait until the morning. Meanwhile...*adventure beckoned*!

More adventure? Why not? Luca was everything virile and masculine, drawing her deeper into the adventure she'd always dreamed about. 'Thank you for your concern,' she said, knowing she needed time to think more than ever now. 'And, thank you,' she added to the concierge as she walked away.

Callie avoided him the next day. His pride was piqued. However, everyone broke for lunch in the afternoon and congregated at the cookhouse. She was there, and they nodded to each other as they stood in line.

'Luca.'

Her greeting was cool. She hadn't appreciated his interference at the hotel, he gathered. He was hot from the fields, and hot for Callie, who had spent the morning in an air-conditioned facility the size of an aircraft hangar. Small, neat and clean, she slammed into his senses in her prim little buttoned-up blouse. Her denim shorts were short and they displayed her legs to perfection, as well as a suggestion of the curve of the bottom he'd caressed last night. That was all he needed before an afternoon's work.

'Excuse me, please,' she said politely, waiting with her loaded tray to move past him.

The urge to ruffle those smooth feathers and make her wild with passion again was more than a passing thought. Weighing up the bandana he wore tied around his head to keep his crazy hair under control, she moved on to scrutinise the ancient top skimming his waist, though was careful not to look any lower. He took charge of her tray. Her gaze settled on his hands, and then his wrists, which were banded with leather studded with semi-precious stones, collected for him by the children of Fabrizio so he wouldn't forget them while he was away. 'I can manage, thank you,' she said, trying to take the tray off him.

'I'm sure you can,' he agreed, 'but sometimes it's good to let people help you.'

Her brow pleated in thought as if she'd heard this somewhere before.

'Are you staying on at the hotel, or have you found somewhere else to stay?' he enquired lightly as he carried her tray to the table where Anita was waiting for Callie to join her.

'Is that why you're here? To question me?' Callie probed with a penetrating look.

For a moment he couldn't decide whether to shrug off her question or throw her over his shoulder like the caveman she thought him. He did know one thing. The tension between them couldn't be sustained.

'See you later,' he said, turning to go.

'Not if I see you first,' she called teasingly after him.

A little frustration would do them both good, he decided. Ignoring the buzz of interest that accompanied him to the door, he saluted the chefs and left the cookhouse.

Infuriating man! How was it possible to feel so aroused, and yet control the impulse to jump on Luca and ravish him in front of everyone? Which was probably exactly how he expected her to feel. The tension in the cookhouse had been high, and made worse because people were obviously trying hard not to stare at them. She had tried to start a conversation with Anita, but couldn't concentrate and kept losing her train of thought.

'If you take my advice, you'll get it over with,' Anita advised, glancing at Callie with concern.

'Get what over with?' Callie demanded, frowning.

'Sex. You need to sate yourself.'

'I beg your pardon?'

'Oh, come off it, Callie. You'll be no good to anyone, least of all yourself, until you do.'

'Anita, I'm shocked!'

'No, you're not, you're frustrated,' Anita argued. 'No one would think any the worse of you if you glut yourself on that one.' She glanced in the direction Luca had gone.

'This isn't an adult playground. It's a place of work.'

'Listen to yourself,' Anita protested with a forkful of crisp, golden fries poised in front of her mouth. 'Take precautions and don't involve your heart. You're here for adventure, aren't you?'

It might be too late to do as Anita said, Callie reflected as she left the cookhouse ahead of her friend. Her heart was already involved. She couldn't last a minute without wondering if she'd see Luca again soon.

Turning onto the dusty track leading through the lemon groves, she headed for the storage facility where she'd been working that morning, only to see Luca coming towards her.

'Shall I show you a short cut?' he offered.

A short cut to what? she wondered as he grinned and took hold of her hand.

It was no good. He couldn't get through the afternoon without it, without her, without Callie, without being up against a tree kissing her as if they were the last couple on earth and time was running out fast.

'Luca—we can't—'

'Yes, we can,' he insisted. Pressing his body weight against her, he slowly moved his body against hers until she was sucking in great gulping sobs of frustration.

'I need you,' she gasped out.

'I know,' he whispered.

He found her with his hand over the rough, thick denim shorts and stroked firmly. He could feel her heat and his imagination supplied the rest. He couldn't wait. Neither could she. They tore at her shorts together. Removing them quickly, he tossed them away. There was no time for kissing, or touching, or preparing, there was only this. He freed himself. She scrambled up him. He dipped at the knees and took her deep. She came violently after a few firm thrusts. Tearing at him with hands turned to claws, she threw back her head and howled out her plea-sure as each powerful spasm gripped her. When he felt her muscles relax, and her hands lost their grip, he gave it to her again, fast and hard.

'Yes!' she cried out as he claimed her again. 'More,' she begged, blasting a fiercely demanding stare into his eyes.

'You can have all you want,' he promised as he worked her steadily towards the next release. 'But not right now,' he murmured, still thrusting, 'because we have to go back to work.'

'You're joking.' Her eyes widened. 'How can I go back to work after this?'

'That discipline we talked about?'

'*You* talked about.'

He ended the argument with a few fast thrusts, and she screamed out her pleasure as they both claimed their most powerful release yet.

'You're right,' she accepted groggily a long while after she'd quietened. 'They'll be short a team member if I don't go back, and I can't let everyone down.'

He could have sorted this out for her with a few words in the appropriate ear, but that would be taking advantage of his position, and so he huffed an accepting laugh and lowered her down to the ground. They were both bound by duty. Groping for his phone, he clicked it on to see the time. What he saw was a line of missed calls. Spring-ing up, he dislodged her. 'Sorry, I have to take this,' he explained as he walked away. Sorting himself out as the call connected, he tucked the phone between ear and his shoulder and asked a few pertinent questions. Having cut the line, he beckoned to Callie. 'Sorry, but there's some-where I have to be.'

'Your afternoon shift?' she queried, frowning.

'Something like that, but I'll have to leave the estate.'

'Is there anything I can do to help?' she asked, feeling his tension.

'Nothing.' He sounded abrupt, but there was no time for explanations.

Callie was hurt. She refused to meet his eyes. His sharp response had shocked her. And no wonder, when one minute they were totally absorbed in each other, even if that was up against a tree, and the next he couldn't wait to leave. It couldn't be helped. He'd see her again, if and when he came back.

She didn't have much experience of love affairs, but she knew enough to know Luca's behaviour wasn't acceptable. His intended departure was brutal and sudden, and only went to prove she didn't know the man she was with. She didn't know him at all. Shame and humiliation swept over her in hot, ugly waves as he paced impatiently while she struggled to put on her shorts as fast as she could. For Luca it was just sex, necessary like eating and breathing, and now it was done, he couldn't wait to leave.

What a mug I am, Callie thought as she pulled up her zipper. Even her well-used body mocked her as she dressed. It was so tender and still so responsive, while her mind continued to whirl in agitated spirals as she flashed glances at a man who seemed to have forgotten she existed. She'd been swept up in a fantasy, but as far as Luca was concerned they were two healthy adults who'd wanted sex. Now that was done there was nothing left. She couldn't even be angry with him. She'd been a more than willing partner. She was just puzzled as to how they could seem so close, and now this.

She glanced at him. He glanced back, but only to check on her progress. There'd be no more conversation or confiding, no more intimate jokes. Smoothing her hair as best she could, she looked at the time on her phone and grimaced. She was already late for the afternoon shift and would have to take a shower before returning to work. It must have been her heavy sigh that prompted Luca to say, 'There are facilities next to the building where you're working. You'll find everything there—towels, shampoo—'

Did he do this on a regular basis? Callie wondered. 'Thanks.' Why wouldn't he? Luca came here every year. She couldn't be the first woman to fall for his blistering charm. Her face flamed red as she pictured him with someone else. She'd thought they were special, which only went to prove how little she knew about men. She could understand he was in a hurry, but couldn't there be just the slightest pleasantry between them, to allow for an exit with dignity?

'So that's it?' she said as she checked her top was properly tucked in.

'Should there be more?' he demanded.

His response was the slap in the face she badly needed. Something had to bring her to her senses. Reality had landed. Hooray. He was right. What more should there be?

Callie was angry, but they were hardly at the stage where he could confide state secrets. She controlled herself well, but the tension in her jaw and the spark in her eyes told their own story. It couldn't be helped. News of Max's attempted coup was for his ears only. He strode on ahead as soon as Callie was ready. His mind was already elsewhere. Stabbing numbers into his cell, he told his staff to prepare the helicopter. He had to get to Fabrizio fast. He would just have time to shower and change before it arrived to pick him up. Max and his cronies had been causing trouble again, and, though they had been swiftly suppressed, the people of Fabrizio needed the reassurance of seeing their Prince.

'So, you're not even going to wait for me?' Callie called after him.

He turned around, shrugged impatiently then kept on walking. She was no longer his priority. However much he might want her to be, he couldn't put his own selfish pleasures first.

'What's got under your skin?' Anita asked when the two women bumped into each other outside the shower block. 'A man? One man in particular?'

Anita sounded so hopeful that Callie couldn't bear to disillusion her. 'Tell you later,' she promised as she hurried off for her afternoon shift.

'Wave goodbye to the Prince before you go,' Anita called after her.

Callie stopped and turned around. 'Where is he?'

Shielding her eyes, Anita stared up at a large blue helicopter with a royal crest of Fabrizio on the side.

'Apparently he's been called back to Fabrizio to deal with an emergency,' Anita explained as both women protected their eyes against the aircraft's downdraft, which had raised dust clouds all around them. 'Don't worry. It won't be an emergency when Luca gets there.'

'Sorry?' Callie froze.

'Prince Luca's will is stronger than any army his brother Max could raise, *and* his people adore him,' Anita explained. 'The people don't trust Max as far as they could throw him. I read in the press today that Prince Luca intends to buy Max off. Max will do anything for money,' Anita explained, 'and that includes relinquishing his claim to the throne. Max needs Luca's money to pay his gambling debts. He'd bleed the country dry, if he became ruler. The late Prince, their father, knew this. That's why he made Prince Luca his heir—Callie? Are you all right?'

'Why didn't you tell me that Luca was the Prince?' Callie stared at her friend in total disbelief, but how could she be angry with Anita when Callie was guilty of ignoring what had been, quite literally, under her nose?

'I'm sorry,' Anita said as she enveloped Callie in a big hug. 'I thought you knew. I thought, like the rest of us, you were being discreet by not naming him, or talking about him. We all know that's what Prince Luca prefers. If I'd guessed for a moment—'

'It's not your fault,' Callie insisted. 'I'm to blame. I only saw what I wanted to see.' She stared up at the helicopter as it disappeared behind some cloud. Luca hadn't told her anything, let alone that he was the Prince. What a fool she was. How could she have missed all the clues? They were as obvious to her now as the bright red arrow she hadn't noticed when she'd first arrived at the Prince's estate. Only worse, much worse, Callie concluded. She didn't blame Luca. Was he supposed to act like Prince Charming in a fairy tale? He was a man, with all the cravings, faults and appetite that went along with that, and she hadn't exactly fought him off.

'Why are you laughing?' Anita asked.

Callie was thinking that Luca didn't have to excuse his actions. He simply called for his helicopter and flew off. But into a difficult situation, she reminded herself.

Even if Luca and his brother had never been close, no one needed to remind Callie how much a barb from within the family could hurt.

'I thought he was one of us,' she admitted to Anita.

'He is one of us,' Anita confirmed hotly.

Callie smiled, knowing there was no point in arguing with Anita, one of Luca's staunchest supporters, but she still couldn't get her head around her own clumsy mistake. It was so much easier to think of Luca as a worker, rather than a prince, but how she could have been so wrapped up in her Italian adventure that she hadn't guessed the truth before now defeated her.

'Max's uprising was over before it began,' Anita explained as she linked arms with Callie. 'You can't fault Prince Luca for keeping his word to his father, the late Prince. Luca's been coming here for years to work alongside the pickers, but nothing's more important to him than the pledge he made to keep his country safe, and we all understand why he had to go back to Fabrizio.'

All except Callie, who was still floundering about in the dark wondering why Luca hadn't told her his true identity. Perhaps there were too many people who only wanted to be close to him for the benefits they could gain, apparently like his brother, Max. She could forgive him if that were the case. Well, sort of. Luca expected her to trust him, but he clearly didn't trust her.

And was she always truthful?

The only time she'd reached out since arriving in Italy was to text Rosie to reassure the Browns that everything was going well. She'd explained that she was going to extend her stay, but had kept her answers to Rosie's excited questions bland in the extreme. She was staying on because she wanted to learn more about Italy, Callie had said, which explained why she had taken a part-time job. She just hadn't expected to get her heart broken into pieces and trampled on in the process. 'I'll be leaving soon,' she mused out loud.

'Must you? Oh, no. Please don't. Was it something I said? I didn't mean to probe,' Anita assured Callie with concern, 'and I'll understand completely if you don't want to tell me why you're leaving.'

Callie responded with a warm hug for her new friend. 'You've done nothing wrong,' she assured Anita. 'If anyone's at fault, it's me. I could have asked Luca more questions, but chose not to. I didn't want reality to intrude, I suppose. It's better if I go home and get real. It's too easy to believe the dream here.'

How true was that? She couldn't believe she'd made such a fool of herself with Luca.

'Can't you stay a little longer?' Anita begged. 'We're only just getting to know each other, and I'll miss you.'

Tears sprang to Callie's eyes at this confession, and the two women exchanged a quick, fierce hug. 'I hope you'll come and visit me?' Callie insisted. 'I don't want to lose touch, either.'

'No chance,' Anita promised stoutly as they stood side by side on the dusty path that ran through the groves. 'When I go home, it's to a damp northern mill town not too far from your docks, so there's no reason why we can't meet up.'

'Come for Christmas,' Callie exclaimed impetuously. 'Please. I'll ask Ma Brown. The more, the merrier, she always says. Promise you will.'

'Are you serious?' Anita looked concerned, and then her face lit up when she realised that Callie meant every word. 'I usually spend Christmas alone.'

'Not this year,' Callie vowed passionately with another warm hug. 'I'll speak to Ma and Pa Brown as soon as I get back, and I'll send you the details.'

'You're a true friend, Callie,' Anita said softly.

'I won't forget you,' Callie promised.

Casting one last wistful look around the sun-drenched lemon groves, Callie firmed her jaw. She might be Callie from the docks when she returned home, but she would always be Callie from the lemon groves in her heart.

CHAPTER SIX

'WHERE THE HELL is she? Someone must know.'

The staff stared at him blankly. He was back in the warehouse where the lemons were stored. As soon as he'd sorted the problems in Fabrizio, he'd returned to his estate expecting to find Callie still working there. He hadn't realised how much he'd miss her until she wasn't around. 'Callie Smith?' he exclaimed, exasperated by the continued silence. 'Anyone?'

Apologetic shrugs greeted his questions. No one knew where she was. Or they weren't telling, he amended, glancing at Anita, who was staring fixedly six inches above his head. He'd made it back just before the end of the season when the casual workers left. Most of the pickers had already gone home, but some had stayed on to make sure everything was stored properly and they were set fair for next year. *Why would Callie stay when I've been so brusque?*

Wheeling around, he strode to the exit. Fresh from re-solving a potential uprising in Fabrizio, he could surely solve the mystery of one missing woman. Max had accepted a pay-off equivalent to the GDP of a small country, and Luca had paid this gladly with the proviso that Max stayed out of Luca's life and never returned to Fabrizio.

He had the funds to buy anything he wanted, even freedom from Max, but could he buy Callie? In the short time he'd known her, he'd learned that, not only was Callie irreplaceable, she was unpredictable too. Her newfound freedom after years of duty to her father had lifted her, and in the space of a couple of days Luca had succeeded in knocking her down. Throwing money at a problem like Max worked. Callie was just as likely to throw it back.

He entered the office on the estate and everyone stood to attention. In a dark, tailored suit, Luca was dressed both as a prince and a billionaire, and not one member of staff had missed that change. 'Relax, please. I'm here to ask for your help.'

As always, his people couldn't have been more accommodating. They gave him Callie's home address from her file. Now there was just Callie to deal with, he reflected as he left the building. He doubted she'd be quite so helpful, and his smile faded. He'd never been unsure of an outcome before, but he couldn't be sure of Callie.

He took the helicopter for the short flight to the airport, where his flight plan to the north of England was already filed. He'd fly the jet himself. The thought of being a passenger appalled him. He needed something to do. Callie occupied every corner of his mind. The unfinished business between them banged at his brain. There was no time to lose. He didn't leave loose ends, never had.

Could it really be more than two months since she'd first met Luca? It was certainly time to take stock of her life. That didn't take very long. She was living in one freezing, cold room over a dress shop where she worked six days a week to fund her studies at night school. She was determined to get ahead by building on the Italian language she'd already picked up on her trip to Italy. Her love affair with the country was in no way over, and it had turned out that she had a flair for languages. She had moved to another town, because she didn't have a home to go back to as such. Her old home next door to the Browns had new tenants, and though the Browns had begged her to stay on with them, Callie had insisted that they'd done enough for her, and that it was time for her to go it alone. 'I wish I could have brought you more exciting news from my adventures,' she'd told them.

'Exciting enough,' Rosie had exclaimed, her eyes fever bright when Callie talked about the Prince.

Callie hadn't told anyone about the time she'd spent locked in the Prince's arms, and had deflected Rosie's questions by telling her that staying in a five-star hotel had kept her away from the real Italy. 'The posh hotel was lovely,' she'd explained, 'but it was bland.'

'Unlike the Italian men?' Rosie guessed, still digging for information.

'And so I looked for a job amongst the people,' Callie had driven on in an attempt to avoid Rosie's question. She had never lied to her friend, and she never would.

'You're too hard on yourself, love,' Pa Brown had insisted when Callie explained that without the young maid's suggestion she would still have been sitting in the hotel, rather than experiencing the lemon groves she had grown to love. 'You wanted to get out and do an honest day's work. You asked for help to find some. There's nothing wrong with that. We all need help sometimes.'

Pa Brown's words resonated with Callie more than ever now. He was right. In her current situation, she would have to ask for help at some point.

Yes. From Callie Smith, Callie concluded. Like millions of women who'd found themselves in this situation, she'd get through, and get through well. Though there were times when she wished she'd agreed to see Luca when he first flew to England to set things straight between them.

'Why won't you see him?' Rosie had asked with incredulity on the first occasion. 'He's an incredible man and he cares about you. He must do, to leave everything to fly here to find you. And he's a prince, Cal,' Rosie had added in an awestruck gasp, 'as well as one of the richest men in the world.'

Callie remembered firming her lips and refusing to add to this in any way. She had simply given her head a firm shake. The money meant nothing to her and neither did Luca's title. She couldn't risk her heart being broken again, and the feelings she had for Luca were so strong they frightened her. But Rosie knew her too well. Realising Callie wouldn't change her mind, Rosie had put an arm around Callie's shoulders and hugged her tight. 'I know you love him,' Rosie insisted. 'And one day you'll know that too. Just don't find out when it's too late.'

It hadn't ended there, of course. Luca wasn't the type to meekly turn around and go home. He didn't know how to take no for an answer. He'd called several times, sent flowers, gifts, notes, hampers of dainty cakes and delicacies from a famous London store. He'd even despatched an elderly statesman called Michel to plead his case. Callie had felt particularly bad about the old man, but Ma Brown had made up for her refusal, treating Michel to a real northern afternoon tea before politely telling him that his Prince had no chance of changing Callie's mind at the moment. 'You shouldn't even have given him that much hope,' Callie had insisted. 'I don't want to be any man's mistress and Luca's a prince. He's hardly going to take things in the direction I...'

As her voice had tailed away, Pa Brown had piped up, 'The direction you want is love, Callie. Love and respect is the direction you're entitled to want, when you give your heart to someone special.'

As Ma Brown had sighed with her romantic heart all aflutter, Callie had known it was time to move on. Her relationship with Luca, such as it had been, had started to affect the Browns, so she'd told them what she planned to do, and had packed her bags. And here she was three months later in Blackpool, the jewel of the Fylde coast. It was blustery and cold this close to Christmas, but there was an honest resilience about the place that suited Callie's mood. And there were the illuminations, she mused with a rueful grin as she glanced out of her top-floor window at the light-bedecked seafront. Known as the greatest free light show on earth, one million bulbs and six miles of lights brought tourists flocking, which meant there were plenty of part-time jobs.

The irony since she'd been here was that Luca was never out of the press. She couldn't believe she'd spent so much time in blissful ignorance as to his identity when his face stared out of every magazine and newspaper. Even when she went to the hairdresser's, she couldn't escape him. She had read every column inch written about him, and knew now that Luca had won his position in Fabrizio thanks to his sheer grit and determination. That, and the love of an adoptive father who had always believed his 'boy from the gutters of Rome', as Luca was referred to in the red-tops, was an exceptional man in the making.

Callie had become an expert in press releases and

could quote some of them by heart. Luca, who was already a titan in business, was now equally respected in diplomatic circles. A tireless supporter of good causes, he had just completed a world tour of the orphanages he sponsored.

The photos of him were riveting. Luca relaxing, looking hot as hell in snug-fitting jeans, or Luca riding a fierce black stallion, looking like the king of the world. He could be cool and strong on state occasions, when he was easily the most virile and commanding of all the men present. In a nutshell, the new ruler of Fabrizio currently dominated world news, which made him seem further away to Callie, and more unreachable than ever. Much was made in the press of his lonely bachelor status, but Luca clearly had no intention of changing that any time soon. Flowers arrived regularly at the Browns', a clear indication that he hadn't given up his search for a mistress yet.

The flowers were still arriving, Rosie had informed Callie only last night, together with the handwritten letters bearing the royal seal, which Rosie had insisted on squirrelling away for Callie. 'You'll look at them one day,' she'd said, not realising that Callie steamed them open and had read every one.

She'd never fit into Luca's glitzy life, Callie concluded, however much affection and humour he put into his letters. But there were deeper reasons. Her mother had died believing her father's lies, and Callie had listened to them for most of her life. 'Tomorrow will be better,' Callie's father would promise each day. But it was never better. He always gambled away the money, or drank it, and so Callie would do another shift at the pub. Did she want another man who lied to her, even if not telling her that he was a prince was a lie of omission by Luca to test how genuine she was? She would be the one lying if she couldn't admit to herself that each time she saw a photograph of Luca, she longed for him with all her heart.

'The trick is knowing when to say thank you, and get on with things,' Pa Brown had told her in their last telephone conversation, when Callie had asked what she should do about the flowers. 'You can send us your thank-you notes, and we'll pass them on. Don't you worry, our Callie, Ma Brown's loving it. She's like Lady Bountiful, spreading those flowers around the neighbourhood so they do some good. You can thank that Prince Luca properly when you see him in person. I certainly will.'

We won't be seeing him, Callie had wanted to say, but she didn't have the heart.

'Stop beating yourself up, girl,' Pa Brown had added before they ended their most recent call. 'You went to work in the lemon groves, which was what you'd dreamed about. You turned that dream into reality, which is more than most of us do.'

She should have kept a grip on reality when it came to Luca, Callie thought with a sigh. But she hadn't. She had allowed herself to be swept up in the fantasy of a holiday romance. And now there was something else she had to do, something far more important than fretting. Reaching into her tote, she pulled out the paper chemist's bag. She couldn't put the test off any longer. While her periods had always been irregular this was a big gap, even for her. Now, she had to know. It was a strange thing, becoming pregnant, Ma Brown had told Callie before the last baby Brown was born. There could be barely any signs for a doctor to detect, but a mother knew. For a couple of weeks now Callie had tried to believe that this was an old wives' tale, but she couldn't kid herself any longer. She might not be a mother, or have personal experience of becoming pregnant, but she did know when she wasn't alone in her body and there was a new, fragile life to protect. She had considered that this feeling might possibly be nothing more than the product of an overactive imagination. There was only one way to find out.

She stared at the blue line unblinking. Not because if she stared long enough it might disappear, but because she was filled with the sort of euphoria that only came very rarely in life. It was a moment to savour before reality kicked in, and she was going to close her eyes and enjoy every moment of it. When she opened them again, her biggest fear was that the kit was faulty. Surely, there had to be a percentage that were?

Leaning forward, she turned on another bar of the ancient electric fire and pulled the cheap throw that usually covered the holes in the sofa around her shoulders as she tried to stop shivering. Part of that was excitement, she supposed, though her hands were frozen. She couldn't believe it was December next week. Where had the time gone? It only seemed five minutes since she had been basking in sunshine in Italy. That was almost three months ago. Three months of life-shattering consequence, Callie reflected as she stared, and stared again at the blue line on her pregnancy test. One thing was certain. She'd have to see Luca now.

He knew Callie was pregnant since he'd tracked her down to England. He'd been tied up with his enthronement once the dispute with Max was settled. That stiff and formal ceremony was over now, with the celebratory garden party for thousands of citizens of Fabrizio still to come.

He loved being amongst his people and looked forward to it, but it was time to concentrate on Callie. They were similar in so many ways, which warned him to tread carefully, or Callie would only back off more determinedly than ever. And hormones would be racing, so the mother of his child, the one woman he could never forget, would have more fire in her than a volcano. Once more into the breach, he thought as the royal jet, piloted by His Serene Highness, Luca Fabrizio, the most frustrated and most determined man on earth, soared high into the air.

Blackpool Illuminations Requires Tour Guides. Callie studied the headline. She was going to need more money soon. Her bank account was bouncing along the bottom, and when the baby arrived… Touching her stomach, she was filled with wonder at the thought; when the baby arrived there would be all sorts of expenses. A wave of regret swept over her, at the knowledge Luca should be part of this. The sooner she told him, the better, but he must understand she didn't want anything from him.

But the baby might need things.

Might need the father she'd never really had, Callie mused, frowning. But what would that mean? Would Luca be a good father? Instinct said yes, but would he and his royal council control their every move? What about the lack of freedom that being royal would mean for a child? She wrapped her arms protectively around her stomach as, hot on the heels of excited disbelief and the marvel of a new life, came a very real fear of the unknown. What if she was a hopeless mother?

She couldn't afford to be frightened of anything, Callie concluded with a child on the way. Grabbing her coat and scarf, she quickly put them on. Leaving the bedsit, she locked the door behind her. The baby came before everything. She had to make some money, even save a little, so she could move to somewhere bigger, hopefully somewhere with a garden. Long before that, she had to buy clothes and equipment for the baby.

Remembering not to rattle down the stairs at a rate of knots as she usually did, she walked sensibly, thinking about the baby. She was already feeling protective. She was confident of one thing. She would not be separated from her child. Luca would have to know they were expecting a baby but, Prince or not, billionaire or not, she would not allow him, or his council, to take over. She would raise her child to have values and warmth, and teach it to be kind. The Browns would help. Maybe she'd have to move back to the docks, but not yet. Burying her face in her scarf to protect it from the bitter wind, she prepared to brave the weather to find a job.

And Luca?

He was an Italian male. Of course he'd want to be part of this. But he would also want to found a dynasty, and for that he needed a princess, not Callie from the docks.

She exchanged a cheery hello with the kindly shop owner who had rented Callie the flat and paused to help with a string of tinsel. 'Thank you, darling,' the elderly shop owner exclaimed, giving Callie a warm hug. 'I can't believe how you're glowing. You look wonderful. Don't you get cold outside, now.'

'I won't,' Callie called back over her shoulder as she stepped out into the street.

He saw the car coming from the end of the street. Driven at speed, it was being chased by a police vehicle, sirens blaring.

No!

He wasn't sure if he shouted, or thought the warning, but he did know he moved. Sprinting like a cheetah, he hurtled down the road. Shoving pedestrians from the path of the car, his sightline fixed on his goal. Time remained frozen, or so it seemed to him, with countless variables of horror possible.

Most people hadn't even realised there was a problem. Callie was one of them. She was still walking across the street, oblivious to the danger hurtling towards her. Launching himself at her, he slammed her to the ground. There was a thump, a screech of brakes, and for a moment the world went black, then the woman in his arms, the woman he had cushioned from the edge of the pavement with his body, battled to break free.

'Are you okay?' she exclaimed with fierce concern, lifting herself up to stare at him.

Winded, he was only capable of a grunt. She stared at him in disbelief. 'Luca?'

He gulped in a lungful of fumes and dust, mixed with Callie's warm fragrance, then, as his brain clicked back into gear, he had only one concern, and that was Callie. 'Are you hurt?'

'No.' She hesitated. 'At least, I don't think so.'

Colour drained from her face. He could imagine the thoughts bombarding her brain. She was pregnant. Was the baby okay? Could she reel back the clock and walk across the road a few seconds later or sooner? Did she have any pain? She squeezed her eyes tightly shut, making him think she was examining her body, searching for signs of trauma, particularly in her womb. She slowly relaxed, which he took to be a good sign. And then she remembered him. He saw the recognition and surprise in her eyes turn to suspicion and anger, and then back again, when she remembered where they were and how they had got there.

'You saved me,' she breathed.

'Grazie Dio!' he murmured.

Her gaze hardened again. *He* was back. The man she had thought she knew had turned out to be someone else entirely. She'd flirted with him, and had had sex with a man she had believed to be an itinerant field worker, who had turned out to be a billionaire prince, and an important figure on the world stage. He could imagine her affront when she'd found out. It wouldn't have taken her long. Settling back into her normal life, she could hardly avoid seeing his face in the press after his enthronement. In shock, she would be trying to process every piece of information, amongst which had to be what the hell was he doing here?

He followed her gaze as she glanced around to see if anyone else was hurt. He saw the tyre marks on the pavement left by the car as it had mounted the kerb, and realised how kind fate had been. Pockets of survivors were checking each other out. Numbers were being exchanged and arms thrown around complete strangers. This was human nature at its best. From what he could see, everyone was shaken up, but thankfully unharmed. Quite a crowd had gathered. People were calling on their phones. The emergency services would arrive soon. The police were already on the scene. The youth behind the wheel of the speeding car had been captured. Patrol cars had his vehicle boxed in.

'Luca,' Callie gritted out, managing to fill that single

word with all the bitterness and uncertainty prompted by his supposed deception. When she was calm, she might realise they'd both been escaping their normal lives during their time in the lemon groves. Both had seized the chance to escape and explore a different, looser version of themselves. But none of that mattered now. All that mattered was that Callie was safe. However, she, understandably, took a rather different view. 'I can't believe this,' she said, staring at him. 'What are you doing here?'

Ignoring her understandable surprise, he concentrated on essentials. 'Take it easy. Slowly,' he advised as she struggled to sit up. 'You might feel dizzy for a while. You've had a shock.'

'To put it mildly,' she agreed. 'Are you all right?' she asked tensely.

'Don't worry about me.'

'You came down with quite a bang.'

He wasn't interested in discussing anything but Callie, and was only relieved that he'd reached her in time.

'Sorry.' She started to giggle. Hysteria, he guessed. 'But we must stop meeting like this.'

He couldn't agree more. They were lying in the road on a bed of grime and oil patches. Hoping that laughter signified her body's resilience to the blow it had just received, he huffed wryly, and for a moment they weren't at loggerheads, but just two people caught up in an unexpected incident on a cold and wintry street.

'Oh, no!' Callie was staring at the stolen vehicle, which was planted in what appeared to be a dress shop window. 'My landlady,' she exclaimed, starting to get up.

'Let me help you.'

She pushed him away in panic. 'I have to make sure she's all right.'

'You have to get checked out first,' he argued.

'What *are* you doing here?' she demanded as he shrugged off his jacket and draped it around her shoulders.

'You're in shock, Callie. You need to go to hospital for a check-up now.'

'I'm fine,' she insisted, starting to pull his jacket off.

He closed it around her. 'You're shivering. You're in shock,' he repeated, 'and until the paramedics get here and check you out, I'm not taking any chances.'

'So you freeze to death instead?'

'I don't think it will come to that,' he soothed, 'do you? I'm just glad I got here when I did. I couldn't get here any sooner.'

'I heard you'd been busy,' she admitted.

A paramedic interrupted them. 'You all right, love?' he asked, proffering a foil blanket. 'Let the gentleman have his jacket back, or he'll catch his death of cold.'

'I've been trying to give it back to him,' Callie explained, 'but he won't take it.'

'Well, if he's happy for you to keep it.' The paramedic shrugged as he arranged the foil blanket over the jacket for extra warmth. 'Not too many gallant gentlemen left, love,' he commented. 'Better hang onto this one.'

Callie hummed and smiled, though Luca wondered if her smile was for the paramedic's benefit. 'Was anyone else hurt?' she asked. 'The lady in the dress shop?'

'Had just gone to make herself a cup of tea,' the paramedic reassured her. 'She was working in the shop window, she told me, only minutes before the car struck.'

'What a relief,' Callie gasped. 'I was with her. I live over the shop,' she explained.

'It's thanks to the quick thinking of your knight in shining armour that a young mother and her baby were also shoved to safety and saved from injury. He's a real hero. Aren't you, sir?'

'I wouldn't say that.' Luca had acted on instinct. There had been no planning involved. There'd been no time to think. He'd done what was necessary to avert disaster, in his view, and that was all.

'Accept praise when it's due, sir. You're a genuine hero, sir,' the paramedic assured him. 'Now, excuse me, miss, but we'd better get you to hospital for a check-up. If the gentleman wants to come too—'

'He doesn't want to come,' Callie said with a glance his way. 'You obviously know where I live,' she added, narrowing her eyes, 'so we'll speak later.'

Shepherding her to one of the two waiting ambulances, the paramedic steadied her as she climbed inside. 'What are you doing?' Callie demanded when he swung in behind her.

'Collecting my jacket?' Luca suggested dryly.

The paramedic gave him a broad wink, but had the good sense to appear busy with paperwork when the doors closed and the ambulance set off. Callie disapproved of him accompanying her to the hospital. Too bad. As she had been a member of his staff, he had a duty of care towards her, and with a baby on the horizon that duty had doubled.

'You saved her, mate,' the paramedic put in as he settled down.

This wasn't how he'd pictured his reunion with Callie. He just wanted her to be safe.

'Have you been spying on me?' Callie asked, careful not to let their companion hear her conversation.

He shrugged. He wasn't going to lie. It was a fine line between his security team's protection service and over-stepping the mark. 'Your welfare and that of our child is my only concern.'

She blenched. He didn't think he'd ever seen anyone so pale. 'Are you all right? Pain? You're not—'

'No. At least, I don't think so.' Her eyes were wide with fear as she stared at him. She reached for his hand. For the first time, she looked vulnerable. This was a very different woman from the Callie he'd met in Italy. This was a woman afraid for her unborn child, and discover-ing she cared for that child far more than she cared for herself. 'Don't,' she said. 'Don't look at me like that.'

'Like what?'

'As if I'm special and you're glad you're here.'

'You are special. You're about to become a mother, the mother of my child. And if I am looking at you, it's only because you're covered in grit and filth and need a good wash.'

'Charming, mate,' the paramedic piped up, proving that he wasn't lost in his work after all. 'Which charm school did you attend?'

'I didn't go to school until I was ten,' Luca admitted wryly. 'And then it was the school of hard knocks.'

'Hey, wait a minute,' the paramedic exclaimed, turn-ing to stare at Luca intently. 'Aren't you that billionaire bloke who started life in the gutters of Rome and became a prince?' And when Luca didn't reply, he added, 'What are you doing in Blackpool?'

He winked at Callie. 'I've been checking out a new set of gutters, mate.'

'Don't you worry,' the paramedic told Callie. 'I won't tell a soul. And you're going to be okay, love, we'll make sure of that.'

The atmosphere lightened a little, and Callie didn't resist when Luca put his arm around her and drew her close.

CHAPTER SEVEN

LUCA WAS BACK. Callie's mind was in turmoil, and as for her heart... What a time for him to choose to come back! The best time, she conceded gratefully as the ambulance raced towards the hospital. She knew shock was playing a part in her mixed-up feelings, but on top of the accident and Luca returning to find her, and above all the fear that her recent fall had harmed the baby, her thoughts were spinning around and around.

'Okay?'

Had she really believed that putting distance between them would lessen her feelings for him? This wasn't the Amalfi coast where she could make the excuse of her senses being heightened by sunlight and laughter, but a grey northern coastal town in winter, and yet Luca was as compelling as ever.

'Hey,' he whispered. 'You're safe now.'

His arms seemed designed to protect. They had certainly protected Callie when she'd needed him. And now Luca's embrace was sending a very different kind of shiver spinning down her spine.

'Look at me,' he whispered. 'I said, you're safe.'

Even with his hair tousled and grazes down one side of his face, Luca looked what he was: a hero, her hero.

When they'd first met it had been lust at first sight for Callie, but now it was something much more.

'Callie?'

Instinctively nursing her still-flat stomach, as if to protect the child inside, she stared into Luca's eyes.

'We're here,' he explained gently. 'We've arrived at the hospital.'

'Oh…'

The paramedic stood aside as Luca helped her down from the ambulance. She clutched the foil blanket tighter as the wind whipped around her shoulders. The only part of her that felt warm was her hand in Luca's. His grip was warm and strong, and it was with reluctance that she broke free from him in the screened-off cubicle when a doctor came to check her over.

'I want an exhaustive examination. Whatever it costs,' Luca emphasised.

'She'll have the best of care,' the doctor assured him. 'We'll be careful that nothing escapes our notice.'

'She's pregnant.'

Luca knew everything. He probably had a drone positioned over the house. But when he thanked the doctor and turned around, she could only feel warm and thankful that he was back.

He was unharmed and impatient to leave, but first he had to make absolutely sure that Callie was okay. He'd wait as long as it took. Mud spattered his clothes. His jeans were ripped. Every bit of exposed skin had taken a battering. The nurses wanted to treat his wounds, but all he cared about was Callie. He sat outside the exam room while she was put through various tests. They were both ecstatic at the outcome. Babies in the womb were surprisingly well protected against trauma, the doctor told them both, and Callie had got off lightly with a sprained ankle and a colourful selection of scrapes and bruises. Apart from the shock, she was fine and could go home. The medical staff had been superb at every stage. He showed his gratitude with a generous donation, which was very well received.

'And now for your bath,' he told Callie as he escorted her off the hospital premises.

'My bath?' she queried, looking at him in bemusement.

'Yes.' They'd cleaned up her minor injuries in the emergency room, but like him she was still covered in dirt from the road, and he had plans. A short drive to the airport would be followed by a flight to his superyacht where Callie could enjoy a rest at sea. Heading south to the sun would be the perfect remedy, allowing her to chill out in privacy while they discussed the future.

'I can have a bath at home,' she said. 'Leave me here. I'll take a cab. Thanks for all you've done—'

'You will not take a cab,' he assured her. 'You can play tough all you like, Callie Smith, but the rules changed when you got pregnant.'

'It took two for me to get pregnant,' she reminded him.

'Which is why I'm prescribing rest for you.'

She gave him a look and then pulled out her phone.

'What are you doing?'

'Calling my landlady to check she's okay, and calling a cab. And guess what,' she added after a few moments of conversation with someone on the other end of the line. 'Turns out an unknown fairy godmother has waved a magic wand, so builders and window fitters are already on site at my landlady's shop, securing the building. I don't suppose you'd know anything about that?'

'Fairy godfather, please.'

She hummed and gave him a look.

'About that cab,' he said.

'Please respect my independence, Luca.'

'I do,' he assured her.

'Anywhere *I* want to go could easily turn into wherever you plan for me to go, and I need to get used to you being back first.'

He had no answer for that. She was right.

'Are you going to log my every move?' she asked with a welcome return of her customary good humour.

'Only some of them,' he said straight-faced.

'My lift is on its way,' she said. 'Give me a chance to think things through. It's all been such a shock. And I don't just mean the accident. Finding out your true identity, and then the months we've spent apart. The gifts you sent. The notes you wrote.'

'Would it have been easier if I hadn't contacted you?'

A brief flash of pain in her eyes said it would have been hell. The same went for him.

'I knew we had to talk when I discovered I was having your baby. I would never leave you in the dark. I just need time to process everything that's happened today. Just the fact that your security team has been watching me is unnerving. I realise you're a prince and I'm having your child, but that doesn't give you the right to put me under surveillance.'

'Your safety will always be my concern.'

'Just don't let it become your obsession.'

'My security team check out anyone I'm seen with.

They report to me, and I can hardly avoid reading what they put in their reports.'

'I accept that,' she said, 'and I thank you for being so honest with me. And most especially for saving my life,' she added in a softer tone.

'I don't want your thanks. I want your time.' He was impatient for a very good reason. The royal council was pressing him to find a bride. The country was waiting. He needed an heir, and Callie's pregnancy had set a clock ticking. He needed things settled between them before the ticking stopped.

'You left me without an explanation, Luca, and now you're back I'm supposed to snap to attention?'

'I never misled you.'

'You never told me you were a prince, either,' Callie pointed out. 'You allowed me to believe that you and I were on the same level.'

'As we are,' he insisted.

She laughed and shook her head. 'That's a fantasy. You're a prince and a billionaire, and who am I?'

'The most determined woman I've ever met.'

'Flattery doesn't wash with me, Luca. We had sex, the deepest intimacy of all, and then you simply turned your back and walked away. That means one thing to me. You're incapable of feeling.'

'You disappeared and pitched up here. Is that so different?'

'I was never going to stay in Italy for ever. It was a once-in-a-lifetime opportunity for me. I always knew I'd come home at some point. And now I intend to study and go on to make a purposeful life. You might be used to women throwing themselves at you, but—'

'Not in the way that just happened,' he said dryly.

She couldn't bear this. She couldn't bear the mash-up of feelings inside her. Her body was bruised. Her thoughts were in turmoil. She was in love with Luca. Their short, passionate time in Italy had left an indelible brand on her heart, but he was a man she could never have. He knew that as well as she did, surely?

'There's fault on both sides,' Luca insisted. 'You didn't reply to my letters. You refused to see me. You rejected my gifts. And, yes, I can see it must have seemed to you that I'd callously walked away, but I hope you can see now that there was a very good reason for my absence. Spend some time in Fabrizio. See the type of life our child will have.'

Fear speared through her at his words. *Hormones.* She knew she was overreacting, but he would sweep her away if she let him. He would expect the royal child to live with him. Yes, she should get to know his world. Luca was no ordinary man. She could never compete with his wealth, or royal status, but she believed just as strongly in her own values, and in her ability to bring up their child. They had to talk, but not right now. 'My cab's here—' She looked at his hand on her arm.

'What are you proposing, Callie?'

Luca's tone had changed, hardened. Their baby wouldn't benefit from parents at war. 'Truce,' she said. 'I'm proposing a truce. You're a hero. You saved me. You saved our child's life. I can never thank you enough for that. If nothing else, I'm sure we can be friends.'

'Friends?' Luca frowned.

'Please? For the sake of our child.'

Her cab rolled up at the kerb. Talking was done. He ground his jaw. Why wouldn't she take the lift he'd offered? He could call up a diplomatic limousine in minutes. Was this how it was going to be? He couldn't allow Callie a free hand. The heir to Fabrizio was too precious for that.

'I can't believe my new phone is still in one piece,' she said, glancing at it before putting it away.

'Give me your number.' He pulled out his phone.

'Give me *your* number,' she countered, 'and I'll call you when I'm ready.'

'Can I at least know where you're going,?'

'I'll call you,' she said as she climbed into the cab.

Seething inside, he gave her his number. After the accident and the shock of seeing him, he had to cut her some slack, but seeing Callie again was non-negotiable. He had every intention of keeping track of his unborn child. Grinding his jaw as the cab drove away, he had to remind himself this wasn't the end of anything, but just the start of their return match.

If her feelings had been mixed up before, they were ready to explode by the time she walked down the steps of the civic building to find Luca waiting outside. Lounging back against a sleek black car, he was staring at her with the lazy confidence that suggested he knew exactly what had happened at her job interview. *Of course he knew.*

Firming her jaw, she quickened her step towards him. The sooner they got this over with, the better. She'd had her suspicions at the start of her interview. It hadn't taken her long to realise she was never going to get the job, and the director of tourism was just curious to meet her. Even he'd admitted she was everything they were looking for; gregarious and well informed, she had read up on the history of the famous illuminations from the nineteenth century to the present day.

'And I know every nook and cranny of the town,' she'd assured him, explaining she'd visited Blackpool on numerous occasions.

'In short, you're perfect for the job,' he agreed, just before he shuffled awkwardly in his seat and explained that the vacancy was no longer available.

So why see her at all? Callie had wondered, until the director of tourism had added, 'Don't look so disappointed. I'm told you have a glittering future ahead of you.'

'What did it cost you?' she challenged Luca tensely. She'd come to a halt in front of him, and was determined to get the truth out of him, whatever it took.

'Cost me?' He frowned.

'How much did it cost you to spoil my chances for that job?' she demanded tight-lipped.

'Nothing,' he admitted.

'You're lying,' she said quietly.

'I think you should calm down,' Luca remarked as he opened the passenger door of his car. 'Climb in.'

'Not a chance.'

'Please.'

She started to walk past him, but he caught hold of her arm. 'Where do you think you're going?' he asked. 'You can't go back to the shop. It's all boarded up.' His voice was still low and even, but it had taken on an edge. 'Your landlady is spending the night in a very comfortable local hotel while my builders complete their repairs.'

'*Your* builders,' she snapped. 'That says it all. *Your* hand in my failure at interview just now. And you say you're not controlling? What else do you have in store for me, Luca?'

Releasing her arm, he stood back. 'I provided a faster

solution for your landlady than her insurance company could hope to offer, and that is all. As for your job interview, how are you going to work as a tour guide when you're heavily pregnant? I can't risk the mother of my child being exposed to people who might exploit her to get at me. Your situation has changed, Callie, whether you like it or not.'

'It certainly has,' she agreed. 'I was free and now I'm not.' She was furious. 'How did you get an appointment to meet with the Director of Tourism so fast?'

'His secretary recognised me.'

'Of course she did. Since your enthronement you're all over the news. "The world's most eligible bachelor",' she quoted tensely, 'who just happens to have a pregnant and discarded mistress on the side.'

'Very dramatic,' he said.

'Dramatic? Since you came into my life, everything's been dramatic—' She bit off her angry words, remembering that without Luca she'd probably be dead and so would their unborn child. Hormones again, she realised. Definitely hormones. The next thing she knew there were tears in her eyes. She drove them back. 'You said it cost you nothing to stand in the way of me getting that job. What *did* you do, Luca? You must have said something?'

'I did,' he confirmed, shielding her as the wind blasted them. 'I offered reciprocal marketing of our two very different holiday destinations.'

'There must be more.'

'There was,' he confirmed evenly. 'I told him I wanted you to work for me.'

'What?'

'Get in the car.'

She was shivering violently. It was freezing cold. They

stared at each other, unblinking. They both knew there could be no walking away this time. Callie had very little money left, and nowhere to stay tonight. Even a simple boarding house at this time of year, when the illuminations were drawing crowds to the resort, cost far more than she could afford to spend.

'Where will you take me?' she asked.

'I thought you had a sense of adventure.'

'I don't like surprises.' But her options were zero. They had to speak at some point. Why not now? Surely two intelligent human beings could come to an amicable agreement?

Seriously?

Yes, because this wasn't about either of them, but about their child, and with their histories Callie was prepared to bet that both of them would put that child first.

The passenger door closed with a soft clunk, enclosing Callie in a very different world. This was a world that only the super-rich could afford. It wasn't the spicy warmth of the lemon groves, or the anodyne interior of a five-star hotel, but was so comfortable that it could easily muddle her mind. It was far too tempting to relax and not think of anything but getting to her destination, wherever that might be, safely and warmly. Soft classical music played in the background, while the scent of soft leather assailed her senses. In spite of all the warnings to self, she relaxed and drank it in.

This was the scent of money, she thought as Luca swung into the driver's seat. He only added to her pleasure with his natural warmth, and the scent of warm clean man, laced with the light, exotic fragrance he always wore. He pressed a button and the engine purred. The sexy black car pulled effortlessly out into the flow-ing traffic. There were no brash noises, no sharp edges, nothing to alarm. The vehicle was precision engineering at its finest, rather like the workings of Luca's mind.

He drove as smoothly and as skilfully as he did everything else. They were heading out of town, she noticed, towards the airport. She had some decisions to make, and had better make them fast. She had agreed to get in the car, but had she agreed to travel out of the country? The thought of seeing Luca on his home turf was an exciting prospect, but she was wary of being seduced into giving up her freedom. Even now she knew his true identity, he was still the most brutally handsome and desirable man. Her body ached and longed for him. Her mind told her they needed to talk. Her soul said they were meant to be together. On a far baser level, pregnancy had made her mad for sex, and there was only one answer to that.

CHAPTER EIGHT

THE ROYAL JET was waiting. On this occasion he would not be the pilot. He escorted Callie on board as if she were already his Princess. He understood her need for freedom. Theirs would be a marriage for practical reasons, tying neither of them down. Its sole purpose would be to provide Fabrizio with the longed-for heir. Would she agree to that proposal? Better this woman he cared for than some unknown princess from Michel's list, and it would fulfil Callie's wish for independence.

Callie would certainly agree to sex. Pheromones were threatening to drown him. Electricity wasn't just snapping, it was threatening to bring down the national grid. Taking her by the wrist, he led her straight to the rear of the plane where his private quarters were located. He had given instructions that they were not to be disturbed under any circumstances, short of an aviation meltdown. They didn't speak. They didn't need to. Callie's needs were flashing like neon signs. They'd talk later. Opening the door to his lavish suite, he ushered her inside.

'Luca—'

'Too much talking.' She was still wearing high heels and her prim interview suit. 'Keep the shoes on.'

'What?'

'You heard me. Take everything else off.' She had the best legs on earth, elongated by the high-heeled shoes, and a figure to die for. The height of the heels thrust her hips forward in a way he found irresistible. Caging her with his arms either side of her face, and his fists planted against the door, he brushed his lips against hers for the sheer pleasure of hearing her moan.

'All my clothes?' she asked, snatching a breath.

'Yes.'

Erotic heat clouded her eyes. 'You haven't told me where you're taking me.'

'You're going to love the surprise.'

'Let me decide,' she insisted. 'Tell me, then I'll take my clothes off.'

She was teasing *him*?

'You don't play fair,' she gasped as he pressed his body against hers.

'Have you only just noticed?'

Rolling his hips, he rubbed his body against her while she groaned. When he pulled back she moved frantically towards him in an attempt to repeat the contact. The jet engines whined into life right on cue. The aircraft was ready for take-off. Any time soon there would be the most enormous thrust and they'd take to the sky. 'You're overdressed,' he commented.

'Why couldn't we talk in Blackpool?' she asked, playing for time, he guessed.

'In a hotel, somewhere anonymous and clinical? Wouldn't you rather be here?'

She gasped as he found her. 'I can't.'

'I think you'll find you can.' He dropped a kiss on her shoulder.

'Who lives like this?' she said, staring past him at

the designer-led living quarters on board his state-of-the-art jet.

'Stop trying to distract yourself and enjoy.'

'No. I can't. *I can't...*'

'You must. I insist.' Using his tongue to tease his way into her mouth, he deepened the kiss and pressed her back against the door. Every inch of her felt amazing. Had he really thought he knew how much he'd missed her, missed this? He didn't have a clue. Using his thigh to edge her legs apart, he finished what he'd started. She went quite still and then cried out repeatedly. It was some time before she quietened.

Her eyes remained closed, Her breathing remained hectic. He caressed her breasts while she recovered, teasing nipples that had tightened into prominent buds very lightly with his thumbnail. Gasping out his name, she rested her head against his chest as he stroked and teased her.

'I think we should take this to bed,' he said at last.

She gave him a teasing look.'Shouldn't we be strapped in?'

'If that's what you'd like?' he offered.

'You're bad,' she said as he took her to see the specially designed bed belt. 'For the billionaire who has everything, I presume?'

'For the turbulence,' he confirmed.

'Do you expect much turbulence?'

'I expect a great deal of turbulence.'

'You're worse than I thought,' she said, laughing and relaxed now.

'Worse than you know.' Bringing her into his arms, he kissed her. When he let her go she searched his eyes in a way that touched him somewhere deep. Callie didn't see herself as he saw her. She was a refreshing change. Most women of his acquaintance were overly self-aware, while Callie was oblivious to how attractive she was.

'Why are you looking at me like that?' she asked him softly.

'I'm anticipating having sex with you.'

'That's convenient.'

'Is it?'

'Yes.' She bit back a smile. 'Because I'm doing the same.'

He moved over her. She writhed beneath him. She opened herself to him, inviting him to explore. 'Now,' she said with a kitten smile that made him hungrier than ever. She quivered with arousal beneath his hands as he teased her lips apart with his tongue. As he deepened the kiss she melted against him. He pressed her into the bed to rediscover the contours of her body. She was driving him crazy with lust. He was driving them both crazy, with delay. Lifting her on top of him, he caressed her buttocks, stroking them as she sighed and groaned, until finally he clasped them to position her. Reversing positions, he brought her under him.

'What about your clothes?' she asked.

He started to undress, but Callie was ahead of him. Ripping off his clothes, she wasn't satisfied until they were both completely naked. Taking hold of her shoulders, he held her away from him so he could give her a long, hard look. 'I've missed you,' he ground out.

'I've missed you too.' She was trembling with excitement and anticipation, asking him with her body to be held, to be kissed, and to be pleasured until she was exhausted. He had no intention of falling short in any way. Throwing her onto her back, he hooked her legs over his shoulders. He took a long, appreciative look, and then dipped his head and feasted while Callie groaned and bucked.

'The bed straps,' she gasped out.

'Are you asking to be restrained?'

'Sounds as if we're about to take off,' she warned, turning her head on the pillows to listen.

He shrugged as the whine of the engines turned into an imperative roar. 'I think you could be right,' he agreed dryly. 'I definitely think you should be held firmly and safely in place.' Securing her in a few deft moves, he returned to finish what he'd started.

She didn't last long. *'Aaaah...'* The cry of pleasure seemed torn from her soul. It escalated into a series of rhythmical, primal sounds deep in her throat. They tormented him. She tormented him. His was a seriously painful state.

'Ah...ah...' she gasped out repeatedly, bucking so furiously that even the straps and his hands had a battle to contain her. Once she was capable of speech, she instructed, 'I need you inside me now,' with her customary bluntness.

This coincided with the pilot applying full thrust. Pinning Callie's hands above her head on the bank of soft cushions, he did the same. The sensation as the aircraft soared and they did too, was mind-numbing. Whatever he'd imagined about sex with Callie again was nothing compared to this. She was perfection. Her inner muscles gripped him with a vigour he could never have anticipated, and from there it was a wild, furious ride to satisfaction. By the time the jet had levelled out, Callie had enjoyed at least three noisy climaxes, and was ready for more. When she was done, he turned her on her side. 'Curl up and let me touch you. I want to watch.'

They were both blunt in bed when it came to what they liked. Callie didn't just agree to his proposition, she used colourful language to outline exactly what was expected of him. She lifted her thigh to tempt him even more, and angled her hips so he could see everything. He sank deep with a groan of contentment. 'More,' she insisted. 'More.'

He felt as if his climax started at his toes and then flooded his entire body. They were engaged in a very primitive act. He was claiming his mate. She was claiming hers. Where this could lead he had no idea, and he wasn't in any condition to reason things through sensibly. 'I only have one complaint,' he said, bringing her on top of him when they were quiet again.

'A complaint?' she queried.

'You should always wear more clothes so there are more to take off.'

She relaxed and smiled, and, sighing with contentment, she added, 'Well, that's your Christmas present sorted out.'

Then she fell silent. He realised it was only a matter of days before Christmas. There had been so much going on he hadn't even realised. 'Hey,' he whispered, seeing Callie frown. 'We're definitely going to be together at Christmas.'

'Are we?' Her voice was matter of fact. Her stare was deep and long.

'Yes,' he confirmed, stroking her back to soothe her. 'You're not going to be spending Christmas in one room over a shop. I want you to see where I live.'

'I know where you live.'

'I mean Fabrizio.'

'It's still a palace.' She sighed as if picturing a world filled with art treasures, flunkeys and hushed decorum, when the truth was a modern palace that was more of a workplace. He had homes across the world where he enjoyed complete privacy, but since his enthronement the palace had become his main residence. He had an apartment there. The palace in Fabrizio was the engine of the dynasty, but his wing was elegant and private. The boy from the gutters had come a long way. 'Where I live overlooks a lake and gardens, and has every comfort a child could need,' he reassured Callie.

Better than one room over a shop, he could see her thinking. 'I'm sure it's lovely,' she agreed, tense now. Turning her back on him, she pulled up the covers and pretended to sleep. She did drift off eventually, while he lay at her side with his arms folded behind his head, checking his plan to make sure there'd be no hitches.

When she woke, she sat up and spotted the selection of outfits on a rail immediately. 'Where did they come from?'

'The cabin attendant wheeled them in.'

'While I was asleep? In your arms?'

'You were well covered up. I asked my private secretary to make sure there were some dresses and accessories on board for you, for when you disembark.'

'I've got my suit.'

He glanced at the creased skirt and jacket, still lying on the floor where she'd dropped them. 'Well, I have to say, this is another first.'

'What is?'

'A woman refusing to look at a rail of clothes.'

'Chauvinist.' Grabbing a sheet around her, she swung

off the bed. 'I didn't say I wouldn't look at them, but I must insist on paying for whatever I choose.'

'I would expect nothing less of you,' he assured her, straight-faced.

'Are you mocking me?' she demanded.

'Maybe a little,' he admitted wryly.

For a few seconds as they stared at each other, he was stunned by how Callie made him feel. He had always guarded his emotions, but with Callie that wasn't possible. Even with the Prince, his late father, it had been very much a man-to-man relationship. He'd never had any softening influences in his life. Women had always been accessories in the past, a deal that worked well both ways, but Callie was different, special. Tousle-haired and flushed from sleep, she was drowsy-eyed with contentment, but still ready to take him on if she felt it necessary. His groin tightened at the thought. Unfortunately there wasn't time. They'd be landing soon. 'I'm looking forward to seeing which outfit you choose.'

She hummed and shot him a warning look.

That was all it took. He'd been inactive long enough. Crossing the cabin, he yanked her close to plant a hard, hot kiss on her tempting mouth. 'Surprise me,' he whispered.

'Don't I always?'

He kissed her again.

'What was that for?' she demanded.

'A down-payment on later.'

'I won't be bribed,' she warned.

He laughed as he left the cabin. They'd slept together, made love together, and been happy together. Now they had a deal to make that both they and Fabrizio could live with. He was sure of Callie in so many ways. She was full of light and love and passion, and was honest and direct to a fault. That didn't mean he could predict how she would react to the idea of raising their child in Fabrizio, but for him that outcome was non-negotiable.

She chose a simple outfit of jeans, crisp white shirt and a smart navy-blue blazer, teamed with a pair of mid-heeled boots. She felt comfortable, confident, and happy—until she saw the royal chauffeur, standing by the side of the big royal limousine. The imposing black vehicle flying the crimson and gold flag of Fabrizio on its bonnet, above a shield that displayed Luca's royal house in images of a lion, a rearing black stallion and a mandolin, was a real punch between the eyes, reminding her that Luca was a royal prince with all the money, power, and influence he could ever wish for, while she couldn't even get a job.

The chauffeur stood proudly to attention as Luca appeared at the door of the aircraft. He ushered her ahead of him. She felt exposed. The blazer and jeans didn't seem enough somehow now that Luca had changed into a smart, dark linen suit with a pale blue open-necked shirt. If he'd looked stunning before, he looked like a prince now. Then, she thought, *Stand tall, you've got as much right as anyone else to fall down the steps of an aircraft.*

'Take my arm,' Luca directed, making sure she didn't have another accident.

'Are you sure?' she asked, thinking he would not want to be seen with her in a way that could compromise him.

'Of course, so long as you give it back,' he said.

Lifting a brow as he stared at her, Luca made her laugh.

Turned out, it wasn't so hard, this royal business. Luca's humour helped. She smiled. The chauffeur smiled back. He saluted as he opened the door of the fabulous royal limousine, and she thanked him when he saw her safely inside.

'That wasn't so bad, was it?' Luca demanded as the chauffeur closed the door, enclosing them in the heavy silence Callie was fast becoming used to in these luxury vehicles.

'Not bad at all,' she admitted. 'Why are you doing that?' she asked when he lowered the privacy screen.

'Because I want you.'

Luca was as blunt as she was. Reaching across the wide expanse of soft cream kidskin, he dragged her onto his lap. 'You should have chosen a dress.'

'Luc—' She was about to protest, but he cut her off with a blistering kiss, and at the same time his hand found her. 'Oh, no,' she groaned, yielding to the inevitable as she opened her legs a little more. 'Oh, no?' he queried. 'Does that mean you want me to stop?'

'Don't you dare,' she whispered, rubbing her still-tender lips against his sharp black stubble. 'I wish I'd chosen a dress too.'

'I'm sure we can manage,' Luca said as his fingers worked deftly on the fastening at her waist. 'It's not as if we're stuck for space.'

'But do we have time?' she asked as he pulled off her jeans and she pulled off her jacket, this time remembering to fold it neatly.

'Enough time,' Luca ground out. 'Now your thong?' he suggested, settling back to watch.

'What about your clothes?'

'What about my clothes?' Lowering his zipper, he freed himself, proving he was more than adequately prepared. Reaching out, he brought her onto his lap. 'Straddle me,' he insisted, 'and make it slow.'

She felt deliciously exposed with her legs widely spread, and deliciously excited when Luca's hand found her. He was right about taking it slowly. She would never grow used to the size of him.

He felt so good. Linking her hands around his neck, she allowed him to guide her carefully down. He decided the pace, while she concentrated on sensation. She cried out with disappointment when his grip tightened on her buttocks, and he lifted her almost off him. Her cries of complaint brought a smile to his face, and he slowly lowered her again. Pressing down on her buttocks made sure that the contact between them was complete. And then he began to move. His hips thrust, sending him deep inside her, and he upped the tempo with each stroke until she could only bury her face in his jacket and wait for release. When it came it was incredible, and he knew just how to prolong it.

'Better now?' he asked quietly as she subsided into a series of soft, rhythmical sighs.

Callie lifted her head. 'Is there time for more?'

With a soft laugh against her mouth, Luca obliged.

CHAPTER NINE

FABRIZIO WAS BEAUTIFUL and quaint, with winding cobbled streets, and tree-filled parks at every turn. People waved and cheered when they saw the royal car, and Luca lowered the window when Callie was dressed again, so he could wave back. His timing, as always, was impeccable. She had caught her first sight of his fabulous palace when they were a few miles away. Surrounded by ancient city walls, the royal palace of Fabrizio sat atop a hill from where the defenders of old could see their enemies coming for miles around. It was the most beautiful building she had ever seen with a grandeur that even his *palazzo* in Amalfi couldn't match. Where that had been wedding-cake pretty, this was royal splendour cast in stone, wrought iron and stained glass. When the royal limousine drew up in front of a wide sweep of stone steps, Luca helped her out of the car and then left her in the care of his housekeeper and a maid, while he hurried off into the building.

Having crossed an exquisite hall, full of shields and swords and ancient portraits, Callie was taken up a sweeping staircase to the first level where she was shown into the most beautiful light and airy apartment. Knowing it would be hers for the duration of her stay was just incredible. The delicately decorated French furniture, the Aubusson rugs yielding softly underfoot, the twinkling glass and antique ornaments, the gilded mirrors—*what was she doing here?*

She thanked the stiffly formal housekeeper and the maid tasked with looking after her. Waiting until the door closed behind them, she headed for the unbelievably beautiful bathroom to take a shower in an enclosure big enough to house an entire rugby team. There was every conceivable type of potion, cream and bath foam, not in their original containers, but in the most exquisite cut glass jars and jugs. Lifting the fragile lid on one of these, she inhaled deeply. And sneezed. She was a little bit allergic to scent. But not to Luca's scent, Callie reflected wryly as she turned full circle to admire the pink-veined marble walls. What was he doing now? she wondered as she glanced at the internal telephone. She didn't want him to think her desperate. Let him call her, she decided. *Please.*

There was no such thing as the hot water running out at the palace. She basked in the luxury of heat and fragrant scent until she felt thoroughly clean, cosy, and fresh again. Then she donned a fluffy robe and wondered what to do about clothes. Pushing her feet into slippers she found ready in the bathroom, that matched the robe, she returned to the bedroom with its panelling and paintings, and floating silk voile, drifting romantically in front of the open window. She suddenly felt incredibly homesick and reached for her phone. What she needed was someone down to earth to confide in, someone she could trust to act as an honest sounding board. Ma Brown answered on the first ring.

'Ma...'

'Yes, dear?'

Ma Brown's concerned tone both bolstered Callie and provided a much-needed wake-up call. She had never been a moaner, and she wasn't about to start now that she was about to become a mother. 'I don't want you worrying about me,' she stressed, 'so I'm giving you an update.'

'Ooh, lovely,' Ma Brown enthused.

Callie could just picture her dear friend, pausing mid baking, or ironing, or dusting, or stirring a pot of something delicious on the stove, to hear what Callie knew she had to make into a Christmas fairy tale so that Ma Brown would smile and share it with the family, rather than fret about Callie over Christmas. 'I'm in Fabrizio,' she began.

'I knew it!' Ma Brown exclaimed. 'You're with the Prince.'

'Yes. But there's something else—'

'You're pregnant!' Ma Brown shrieked before Callie had chance to say a word.

'I had intended to break it to you gently—'

Ma Brown wasn't listening. 'Has he proposed yet?'

'No,' Callie admitted.

'Why ever not?' Ma Brown demanded good-humouredly. 'Do you need me to come out there and prompt him? I will, if you like. I can easily catch a flight.'

'No,' Callie said again, this time laughing. Ma Brown's voice had soared at least an octave. She probably didn't need a phone to be heard in Fabrizio. 'I promise I can deal with it.'

'Tell me about his country, then,' Ma Brown compromised, snatching a noisy breath as she attempted to calm down.

To a casual listener, their conversation might have

seemed a little blasé under the circumstances, but Ma Brown could always imply more by her tone than she said in words. The simple phrase, tell me about Fabrizio, for instance, promised that the subject of Callie's pregnancy had not been forgotten, but merely put on the back burner for now. One thing was certain. Ma Brown would always be on Callie's side. Missing out the fact that she should have been planning her future, rather than scrambling over Luca, having sex in his jet and then in his car, Callie cut straight to the particulars. 'Everything in Fabrizio looks as if it has been polished to a flawless sheen. Think Monte Carlo with a touch of Dubai—'

'Oo-er,' Ma Brown exclaimed, breathless with excitement. 'Go on,' she prompted.

'Luca's palace looks like something out of a fairy tale. It's like Cinderella's castle with turrets and crenellations. There's even a drawbridge over the moat.'

'Imagine the staff needed to look after that,' Ma Brown breathed in awe.

'And everyone wears uniform,' Callie confirmed to add to the picture. 'Sentries stand guard wearing black velvet tunics braided with gold—'

'Goodness,' Ma Brown cut in. 'Isn't that all a bit intimidating?'

You have no idea, Callie thought, but what she actually said was, 'Poof! Not for you and me, Ma.'

'That's the spirit,' Ma Brown exulted. 'I've read about the palace and how fabulous it is. The countryside around it is supposed to be equally beautiful. Tell me about that now.'

Hmm. Difficult topic, Callie thought as the silence extended. 'I was so excited on the drive from the airport to the palace I didn't take much notice,' she admitted truthfully. 'I'll make sure to check it out next time and let you know.'

Ma Brown hummed thoughtfully. 'I've taken quite an interest in your Prince since he rode to your rescue.'

'He's not *my* Prince, Ma.'

Ignoring this, Ma Brown continued, 'The late Prince has ancestry stretching back to the mists of time.'

Unlike Luca's, which stretched back to the gutters of Rome. Or her own, Callie reflected, which extended to a row of small, back-to-back houses in the same neighbourly terrace as the Browns, which she wouldn't exchange for the world. She couldn't imagine how she'd have got on when she was younger without the wonderful support of the family next door.

'When are you coming home, our Callie?'

'I'm not sure,' Callie admitted.

'If I were you, I'd stay there as long as you can,' Ma Brown cheerfully recommended. 'There's a grand ball soon in Fabrizio to celebrate Prince Luca's enthronement. You can't miss that. I want to hear all about it.'

'I doubt I'll be invited,' Callie confessed. Luca hadn't mentioned a ball. She couldn't imagine he'd want her there. Thank goodness. Her stomach flipped at the thought of attending such a grand occasion, and then flipped at the thought of Luca attending the ball with an eager princess on his arm. He was better off with someone like that, she told herself, someone who was used to public occasions. Callie would probably say the wrong thing, or trip over her own feet.

'Don't let me down,' Ma Brown warned. 'When you said you were going on an adventure, a ball at the Prince's palace was exactly the sort of thing I had in mind.'

'I'm not Cinderella,' Callie reminded her good friend ruefully, 'and I don't have a fairy godmother.'

'I wouldn't be too sure about that,' Ma Brown insisted. '*And* I want an invitation to the wedding.'

Before Callie had chance to respond, Ma Brown had bustled off the line, no doubt to attend to more motherly duties.

A diet of romance, Ma Brown's favourite reading matter, had obviously distanced her from reality, Callie concluded, but she was both thrilled and relieved at the way her good friend had taken the news of the pregnancy. Ma Brown was right. Pregnancy was normal. Attending a royal ball was not. But she'd have a go, if she were invited. She owed it to Ma Brown to attend the ball if she got the chance.

Ten minutes later she changed her mind again. *I don't belong here.* Burying her head in her arms, Callie took a deep, steadying breath, and then lifted her chin to stare at herself in the ornately gilded dressing-table mirror. Her reflection appeared in what was surely a priceless antique like everything else in her elegant suite of rooms. How on earth had she ended up here?

'I'll tell you how,' Callie's snarky inner critic butted in. 'From good girl to a hussy in no time flat, that's you, Callie Smith!'

Fair play, Callie agreed. The fairy tale wasn't quite as she'd described it to Ma Brown. She never knew where she stood with Luca, and the worst of it was, a few months ago, she'd known exactly where she was heading. Her short adventure in Italy would be a harmless interlude to look back on with pleasure. She'd go home after a couple of weeks, pick up her studies, go to college, and get a better job. Pregnancy had changed all that. Her priorities had completely switched around. The baby came first. It always would. Every decision Callie made from now on would be in the best interests of her child.

Luca's child also.

Closing her eyes, she reviewed what she'd seen of Luca's life to date. From the vast, echoing hallway, with it frescoes on the lofty ceiling, to the foot of a wide sweep of crimson-carpeted stairs, her head hadn't stop whirring as she gazed around. Did she need more proof that she didn't belong here? It hardly seemed possible that just a few hours ago she had been planning to make do and mend to raise a child she already loved. In the palace she was surrounded by so much...*everything.* The five-star hotel she'd thought so lavish was a mere potting shed compared to this. She had to stop short of pinching herself to make sure it wasn't all a dream. When a knock came at the door and it opened without Callie saying a word, she sprang up guiltily.

'Oh, sorry, madam, I—'

'No—please, come in. And please call me Callie...'

Callie paled as the maid stood back against the wall to allow a team of footmen to wheel several gown rails into the room. These were laden with a sparkling array of full-length ball gowns. Cinderella had nothing on this, Callie concluded, frowning. 'There must be some mistake,' she said.

'No mistake, madam,' the maid assured her. 'As it's rather short notice, His Serene Highness apologises for not sending you an invitation to the ball, but he wants you to know that you are free to choose any of these dresses to wear.'

'His Serene Highness expects me to attend the ball?'

'He does, madam.'

Then, His Serene High and Mightiness could have the courtesy to come and tell her that himself, Callie thought, but she thanked the maid, who was the innocent messenger. 'I hope this hasn't put you to too much trouble?'

'None at all, madam. As soon as you've made your choice, if you ring this bell…' the maid indicated a silken tassel hanging on the wall '… I'll return immediately to help you dress.'

'The ball's tonight?' Callie exclaimed in panic.

'Oh, no, madam. This is just to give you chance to choose your gown and try it on. The Prince has instructed me to tell you that he will be with you by seven o'clock this evening to discuss your choice of gown.'

Hmm, Callie thought. And take it off, if she knew Luca. She couldn't imagine he cared less what she wore. He was far more interested in removing her clothes.

As soon as the maid had gone, she walked over to the rail to check out the selection of dresses. She'd never seen so many fabulous outfits before. There were gowns in every colour in the rainbow. Some were beaded, some had frills, and some had gauzy ribbon. Nearly all of them had low necks, and/or big slits up the side and plunging backs. She guessed she was ungrateful for thinking all of them a bit over the top. She was frightened to touch them in case she soiled them, but she had to choose one. Picking out an aquamarine gown, her favourite colour, she held it up against her, but it was so heavily beaded it weighed a ton. She had to admit that the scent of fine silk, and the sight of such expert tailoring, did take her breath. There was boning inside the bodice, so no need to wear a bra, and the skirt was such a slender column, she'd have to hop, Callie reflected wryly as she returned it to the rail.

One after the other she discarded the dresses. She couldn't see herself wearing any of them. They were far too fancy, and didn't look at all comfortable to wear. Crossing the room, she rang the bell.

'Yes, madam?' the maid enquired politely.

'We're around the same size. Could you lend me a pair of jeans and a top so I can go shopping?' There must be a high street in Fabrizio, she reasoned.

'Go *shopping*, madam?' the maid repeated as if Callie had suggested dancing naked in the street. 'I'll have a selection of outfits delivered to you within the hour.'

'Really?'

'Of course.'

'Okay, but be sure to give me the—' Before she had chance to say, 'receipt, so I can pay the bill,' the maid had left the room and closed the door.

Callie heaved a sigh. What was she supposed to do now? She tried to ring Luca, but that was like trying to get hold of the Queen of England. She went through half a dozen people and none of them would put her through to him. It was already nine o'clock in the evening. He'd left her alone to stew. Talking of which, she was hungry. Picking up the internal phone, she rang the kitchen to order a tray of sandwiches and a pot of tea. Hmm. So much for the high life! And so much for the discussions they were supposed to be having. Could matters of State be so much more important than their child?

She drank the tea, ate the sandwiches, then walked around the apartment until she knew every inch of it by heart. It was a gilded cage for the Prince's pet bird, Callie concluded. It was impersonal. The drawers were empty. There wasn't even a book to be found. There certainly wasn't anything as crass as a TV. Opening the glass doors onto her private veranda, she sat down at the wrought-iron table. Listening to the night sounds soothed her. It was a beautiful evening, but where was Luca? She should have known by now that sex meant nothing to him, and he could just walk away, forget it, forget her.

She went back into the room when it began to get chilly. She'd forgotten that the maid had promised to have more clothes delivered, and the room was full of them. She couldn't deny that rooting through the boxes and carrier bags was fun. Choosing a pair of jeans and a loose sports top, she exchanged her fluffy robe for a casual look that would take her through to bedtime.

More tea?

More tea.

She was just concluding, with a return of good humour, that wading through such a vast selection of clothes was exhausting, when the door opened and Luca walked in.

'Tea, madam?'

She almost jumped out of her skin. Even with a tray of tea in his hands, he was everything she could desire in a man. Dark, tall, and powerfully built. She would never get used to the breath-stealing sight of him. He'd changed into jeans and a crisp white shirt with the sleeves rolled up. *Those arms!* His jeans were cinched with a heavy-duty belt that drew attention to his washboard waist. His shoulders were epic and his powerful forearms were tanned and shaded with just the right amount of dark hair.

Those arms belonged around her, she concluded, forgetting her good intentions as he strode across the room. She was supposed to be having a serious discussion with him, not falling victim to his dazzling charm. *Be objective*, she told herself firmly.

'Ah, the dresses have arrived,' he commented as his stare swept over the gown rail. 'Now for the fashion show.' Throwing himself down on a finely upholstered chaise longue, he made a gesture she could only presume was supposed to goad her into action.

'Are you going to model them for me, then?' she asked. 'You mentioned a fashion show?' she prompted when Luca raised a brow.

For a moment he looked bemused and then he laughed. 'You never change, do you?'

'I hope not. Hooking up in a car does not a future make, Prince Luca. You and I have some serious talking to do.'

'Soon,' he promised. 'But first a toast,' he insisted, standing up.

'In tea?' she queried.

'I can send for champagne—'

'I can't—'

'Of course you can't.' With a grimace, he reached for her, and, jerking her close, he linked their fingers in a way she found very hard to resist. 'Forgive me,' he whispered, slanting a grin. 'I had forgotten why we're here for the moment.'

'Don't,' she warned with a straight look into his eyes.

'I was about to propose a toast to the heir to the principality of Fabrizio,' he explained.

She hummed. 'In that case, I'll forgive you.'

When Luca smiled his wicked smile, if it hadn't been for the sexual tension between them they were close enough in that moment to be just two friends enjoying a moment of trust between themselves.

'Have you chosen your ball gown yet?' he asked, turning to glance at the packed gown rail.

'I want you to feel comfortable. I know you'll look beautiful. It's going to be a special night for both of us, because this is my chance to introduce you to my guests.'

'As what?' she asked.

Luca appeared to ponder this. 'My personal assistant? No.' His lips pressed down as he shook his head. 'What about Keeper of the Crown Jewels? More accurate?'

'This is serious,' Callie warned. 'Please stop teasing me. If I'm going to attend my first ball with you, I need to know where I stand. That's the only way I'm going to feel comfortable.'

'Comfortable was the wrong word. I can see that now,' Luca admitted. 'I want you to feel sensational. As the ball is tomorrow evening you'd better choose one of these gowns to make sure you do.'

But that wasn't what she was here for. She had come to Fabrizio to talk about their baby.

What about the promise she'd made to Ma Brown to send a full report on the ball? Callie glanced at the glamorous gowns twinkling on the rail. She wouldn't be able to get into any of them in a few months' time, not that she'd have any use for a ball gown when she went home. 'I'll look ridiculous,' she fretted as she rifled through the rail.

'You'll look beautiful,' Luca argued, making himself comfortable. 'Let's make a start.'

'I'll change in the dressing room,' she said, picking out the aquamarine gown that had first caught her eye. 'And I'm not coming out if I look a freak.'

Safe behind the door to her dressing room, Callie stared at herself in the mirror and grimaced. The gown that had looked so pretty on the rail did fit well, but, apart from being so heavy, it was too tight. It pushed her breasts up and her confidence down. But that wasn't what really worried her. When she emerged from the dressing room, Luca agreed. 'You look like a mermaid,' he said as she wiggled her way across the room.

'Thank goodness that's a no.'

'Unless you plan to hop into position at my side?' he suggested.

'I could drift towards you in this,' she suggested when she had changed into the next dress, a coral number with long chiffon floats flying from each shoulder.

'Nah. You'll only get caught in the door.'

'You know me too well.'

'I'm getting there,' Luca admitted dryly as Callie chose another dress.

'This one?' she asked uncertainly, blowing fronds of fern-like decoration away from her face.

'You look like a market garden,' Luca dismissed as she performed a twirl.

True enough, the big floral pattern wasn't her best look.

'What about this one?' he suggested, selecting a plain, intricately beaded flesh-coloured gown.

'Yes. That's nice,' she agreed. 'I'll try it on.'

With the dressing-room door closed between them again, Callie stared at her reflection in amazement. She actually looked quite good. Smoothing the delicate fabric over her frame, she had to admit that the gown Luca had chosen was both elegant and sexy. She might have known he'd have exquisite taste. The shade of the fabric matched her skin tone so exactly it was almost possible to imagine she was naked. Naked and shimmering with a slit up the side of the dress that almost reached her waist. Taking a deep breath, she opened the door.

Luca said nothing at all. His face was completely expressionless. This was Luca at his most dangerous, she thought. 'No,' she warned when he stood up and prowled towards her.

'Why not?' he husked. 'It's not as if I can make you pregnant.'

'Luca!'

He swallowed her protests in a kiss, and it wasn't just a kiss but a whole-body experience that made her hunger for him eclipse everything. His hands were warm on her body. He knew every slope and curve. The gown was so sheer, so delicate, that his touch transmitted effortlessly through it as if they were both naked. Memories bombarded her, memories of pleasure, memories of trust.

'I want you,' he growled. 'Right here. Right now. I can't wait.'

'Neither can I,' she assured him fiercely.

Luca had already found the slit at the side of the dress. She only had to move slightly for his fingers to brush dangerously close to where she needed him. Her breath caught as he handled her with the skill that promised so much more. She was wearing nothing beneath the gown but a flimsy thong. Held together with not much more than a hope and a prayer, the thong stood no chance against Luca's assault. Ripping it off, he cast it aside and rammed her up against the wall. Breath shot out of her as his hand found her. With teasing strokes, he tested her readiness. That didn't take long. Freeing himself, he nudged his thigh between her legs and, dipping at the knees, he took her in one long, firm thrust. From there it was a wild, noisy ride to their goal, but even when she shrieked as she lost control he kept on plunging until her throat was hoarse, and her body was alight with pleasure.

'I can't feel you,' she complained when she was able to talk again.

'What?' Luca demanded, frowning into her eyes.

'Not that—' She groaned with pleasure as he flexed inside her. 'I mean your naked body,' she explained. Tugging at his shirt, she made her meaning clear. 'I want to feel all of you hot and hard against me.' They ripped his clothes off between them and tossed them aside. 'Better!' she approved as his heat rasped against her body.

'Still not enough for you,' he guessed. Taking hold of her hands, he pinned them above her head, and with his other hand locked around the front of her dress, he ripped it from her body.

The beautiful gown was shredded, ruined. Disaster. But she didn't care. All that mattered was this. Rubbing her breasts against him tormented her nipples until they were taut little buds, composed entirely of sensation. They had a direct link to her core, and her hips worked involuntarily in her desperation for more contact. She couldn't remain still. She couldn't remain quiet. She was noisy and demanding. Scrambling up him, she locked her legs around his waist.

'More?' he suggested in the deep, gravelly voice with its flavour of Italy that could always make her tingle.

'Are you purposely withholding pleasure from me?' she demanded.

Luca laughed softly. 'As if I'd dare.'

'Don't make me wait,' she warned.

His answer was to nuzzle her neck with his sharp black stubble until she was a seething mass of lust. 'I just asked, did you want more?' he reminded her.

He surely didn't expect an answer to that question.

CHAPTER TEN

THE BALL GOWN was ruined. No point worrying about that now. She'd skip the ball. That was the last thought in Callie's head as Luca made rational thought impossible. He was making love to her. This wasn't just sex. They were natural together. This was so good, so right. This was fierce. When the moment came, she was wild with fear of the precipice she was facing, but Luca husked soothing words of reassurance and encouragement in his own language as he kissed her over the edge.

'Greedy,' he whispered when she quietened.

'You make me greedy,' she complained, smiling with contentment as she crashed against his chest.

Finding the nook just below his shoulder blade, she snuggled close as he carried her to the bed. A deep sense of this being right filled her completely. They belonged together. He laid her down gently on the bed and came to lie with her. When he brought her into his arms, her breathing slowed and her limbs grew weightless. Problems nagged at the back of her mind, but they could wait until tomorrow. Right now she could do nothing more than close her eyes and drift away.

He held Callie in his arms all night, watching her sleep. As he did so, he went over what lay ahead of her.

It wouldn't be an easy transition for her from the freedom of a normal life to all the restrictions of royalty, but if anyone could cope, she could. And he'd be with her every step of the way. He was confident that Callie would adapt to royal life as quickly as he had. He'd rebelled at first, but then he'd been very young. Callie was clever and kind, and her sense of humour would ease her through the sticky patches. Her common sense would get her through the rest. Not only would he have the longed-for heir, but a new, fresh style of Princess who would care for the land he had come to love as deeply as he did.

Careful not to wake her, he left Callie at dawn. Breakfast meetings were the norm for him. With her hair tousled, and her face still flushed with sleep, she had never looked more desirable, but he was a slave to duty. Both his royal council and his business concerns called him this morning. And then there was the ball tonight. He grimaced as he glanced at the gown he'd ruined. But there were plenty more on the rail. Callie would have to forget about being understated for one night, and just choose one of them.

Callie woke slowly, cautiously. At first she didn't know where she was. Her head was ploughed into a stack of pillows scented with lavender and sunshine. The bed was firmer than she was used to, the duvet softer...and her body felt very well used. With a groan of contentment, she turned her face, relishing the touch of the smooth white cotton, and inhaled deeply. Slowly, it all came back to her. Reaching out a hand, she searched for Luca, and stilled when she discovered the bed at her side was empty. Sitting up, she could see the indentation of his head on the pillow, so she hadn't imagined last night. She really was at the palace. *The palace!* In the most sumptuous suite of rooms imaginable. *Incredible.* But it was very quiet. She stilled and knew at once she was alone.

Hearing a knock on the door, she hastily pulled up the sheet to cover her naked body. 'Yes?' It had to be the maid. Spotting what remained of the glamorous gown still strewn on the floor, she called out, 'Just a minute,' and leapt out of bed. Gossip would spread like wildfire in the palace. Why fan the flames? Gathering up the dress, she brought it back to the bed, and stuffed it out of sight beneath the bedding. 'Come in,' she called out brightly.

The maid entered carrying a breakfast tray. There was a single red rose in a silver vase on the tray. 'From His Serene Highness,' the maid explained as she set down the tray. 'He has suggested that you rest this morning in preparation for the ball.'

Recover, he meant, Callie thought dryly, showing nothing of her thoughts on the passionate night before on her face. 'Thank you for bringing my breakfast,' she said warmly, 'but I will be getting up.'

'Oh, and this arrived by courier,' the maid said as she handed Callie a package she had lodged under her arm.

'For me?' Callie exclaimed with surprise.

She bolted breakfast as the maid opened the curtains and threw the windows wide. She couldn't wait to open the unexpected parcel, but wanted to do so when she was alone.

'Anything else I can get for you?' the maid asked politely before she left.

'Nothing. Thank you.'

Turning over the large padded envelope, Callie smiled broadly. The bold handwriting gave the game away, as did the UK stamp. 'Ma Brown,' she breathed. 'What have you done now?'

What Ma had done was to go shopping at a popular high street store, where she'd found the perfect dress for Callie to wear at the ball. Callie gasped with pleasure as she held it up and saw her reflection. The dress was simple and elegant. At last, a dress she could feel comfortable in. She'd take a shower and then she'd try it on.

The fine flesh-coloured fabric slithered over Callie's naked body like a second skin. It couldn't have fitted her better. The design was uncannily similar to the gown that lay ruined on the bed. The popular brand was a known fast follower that could have catwalk looks available for sale within hours. She would go to the ball, Callie concluded with amusement as she slipped on a pair of high-heeled shoes, and in a dress worth infinitely more to her than all those expensive gowns on the rail put together. Picking up her phone to thank her best of friends, she smiled with pleasure. 'Oh, Ma Brown, you've really come up trumps this time,' she murmured as she waited for the call to connect.

It was the evening of the grand ball and all his guests had arrived, but where was Callie? He wasn't accustomed to waiting. Tonight of all nights, a late arrival was unacceptable. Her maid had been given strict instructions regarding timing. Royals were expected to be punctual. Everything ran to clockwork precision. There was no leeway for a few minutes either way. With impatience, he turned his attention from the entrance where Callie was due to appear, to the guests who were waiting to meet him.

Laughter and excitement filled the room. There was a huge sense of expectation. No one had refused his invitation to the ball. There were rumours of an announcement tonight and interest was running high. He felt a great sense of love and gratitude for the restoration his father, the late Prince, had carried out so efficiently on the glorious old building, and this did soothe him to some small degree. The ballroom was a glittering spectacle with huge chandeliers glittering like diamond globes beneath a domed sky of priceless frescoes. An orchestra of the most talented Viennese musicians set the mood. Waiters in black dress trousers and short white jackets, braided with the royal colours, carried solid gold trays bearing a selection of canapés prepared by the world's top chefs. There were two champagne fountains, as well as tall crystal flutes of vintage champagne being offered to guests at priceless French ormolu tables that lined the room. Nearly every country was represented. Splendidly dressed royals dripping in family jewels mingled with diplomats and top-ranking soldiers. No one was too proud to sup at his table. Guessing that tonight would be talked about for years had winkled out even the most standoffish royal. Everyone was keen to see how the boy from the gutters had transformed into a prince.

So where was she?

There was no excuse for this. He had instructed his private secretary to commission the finest hairdressers and beauticians to assist Callie with her preparations for tonight. He couldn't believe her personal maid had failed to get her out on time. Did Callie hope to slip in unnoticed? Was she coming at all?

He gave a grim shrug. Callie Smith was the one woman he could never predict. Summoning a footman, he sent a message to Signorina Smith's maid to ask how much longer she would be. The man hurried off, leaving Luca to seethe in silence.

* * *

Well, this was it, Callie concluded as two liveried foot-men swung the gilded double doors wide. She had po-litely asked the hairdressers and make-up artists to leave, preferring to get ready by herself, and now there was just this small hurdle of a ballroom packed with the great and good to overcome. She inhaled sharply at the scene of dazzling glamour, and was almost blinded by the flash of diamonds and the light flaring from countless chan-deliers. *Trust me to forget my tiara tonight*, she mused wryly. Lifting her chin, she walked forward.

'Signorina Callista Smith.'

Callie glanced around as the disembodied voice of a famous television personality announced her arrival at the ball.

'That's you, miss,' one of the friendly footmen who'd opened the door for her prompted in an exaggerated stage whisper.

'Thank you,' she whispered back.

In the time it had taken Callie to say this, every head had turned her way. Even the orchestra paused, leaving her at the top of a dizzying flight of marble steps. The solid mass of people below her looked impenetrable, and not exactly welcoming. Her throat dried. She clenched her hands into fists at her side. She could only pray the stiletto heels fairy was on her side tonight.

'Wait…'

Every head swivelled to stare at Luca. His familiar voice stripped the tension from her shoulders. Her gaze fixed on him as the crowd parted to let him through. Whatever remained of her breath flew from her lungs as he strode forward. In full dress uniform, with his sash of office drawing attention to his powerful chest, this was the man she remembered, the man her body rejoiced in, the man she laughed with, slept with, and enjoyed challenging, as Luca relished tormenting her, and right now he looked good enough to eat.

'May I?' he asked, offering his arm as he prepared to lead her down the stairs.

'Thank you.' She smiled—graciously, she hoped.

If a pin *had* dropped, it would most certainly have deafened her. It appeared that no one breathed, let alone spoke, as Luca steered her safely down the steps.

'You look beautiful,' he whispered.

'I'm sorry I took so long,' she whispered back. 'The hairdresser made me look like a freak, so I had to redo everything. And don't even ask about the make-up.'

'But you aren't wearing any.'

'Exactly,' she murmured. 'If you'd seen me with false eyelashes and red-apple cheeks you'd have run a mile.'

'Would I?' he murmured, sounding unconvinced.

They'd reached the dance floor by this time. Everyone was staring, but just being with Luca reassured her, and she didn't hesitate when he asked her to dance.

Callie came into his arms like a rather lovely boat floating effortlessly into its mooring. The intimacy between them must have been obvious to everyone, and the shocked silence that had first greeted her changed at once to a buzz of interest.

'I can just imagine what they're saying,' she breathed.

'Do you care?' he replied.

'No,' she assured him. 'I just wish I was barefoot. You're in serious danger of being stabbed.'

'Not a chance,' he whispered.

He laughed. She relaxed, and the glamorous ball continued.

'Where did you get the beautiful dress?' he asked. 'You look stunning. It's so elegant. I didn't see it on the rail. It's so delightfully simple, compared to other women's more elaborate gowns.'

'That's the secret of its allure,' she assured him with a cheeky smile. 'Ma Brown,' she whispered discreetly.

'Well, wherever it came from, you couldn't look lovelier.'

'Well, thank you, kind sir…you don't look too bad yourself.'

She was in his arms, and, as far as he was concerned, that was all that mattered. 'Do you find it warm?' he asked.

'Is this another of your euphemisms, which could be interpreted as let's find a tree?'

'Callie Smith,' he scolded softly with his mouth very close to her ear.

'You left me alone, abandoned me, and now you can't get enough of me?'

'Correct.'

'Don't you have any scruples?'

'Hardly any,' he confessed. 'I'm planning to take you to see a magical gazebo.'

'Filled with your etchings?' she guessed.

He laughed, and was further amused by the fact that people dancing close to them were hanging on their every word. Leading Callie off the dance floor, he led her through towering glass doors onto a veranda stretching the entire length of the palace. Even this late in the year, plants illuminated by blazing torches still flowered profusely, and their fragrance filled the air. He wouldn't usually notice such things, but being with Callie always heightened his senses. A pathway led through the formal lawn gardens, and where they ended there was a lake with an island at its heart. Lights glinted on the island, and a rowing boat was moored alongside the small wooden pier that stretched out into the lake.

'Really?' Callie queried with a pointed glance at her dress and shoes.

'Where's your sense of adventure?' he demanded.

Slipping off her shoes, she accepted his steadying hand as she gingerly boarded the boat. 'I used to escape the palace by rowing out to the island,' he explained when he joined her. He'd left his uniform jacket and white bow tie on the shore with his highly polished shoes. Freeing a few buttons at the neck of his shirt, he sat across from her and reached for the oars.

'I can understand why you might want to be alone here,' Callie agreed as she trailed her fingertips in the water. 'It's so beautiful and peaceful on the lake.'

'I didn't notice that when I was a youth,' he admitted, plunging the oars into the mirror-smooth water. 'It took time for me to trust the Prince, my father, and sometimes I was just angry for no reason and just wanted to get away. Now I think I was afraid of disappointing him. I'd only known rare acts of kindness on the streets, and the fact that he never gave up on me seemed to be just one more reason for me to put him to the test.'

'That's only natural.'

'I was lucky.' He put his back into the stroke and as he saw Callie's appreciative gaze focus on his bunching muscles his impatience to reach the opposite shore grew.

'How did you live,' she asked, 'back before the Prince found you?'

He shrugged and dipped the oars again. 'I cleaned around the market stalls in return for spoiled fruit, stale bread, and mouldy cheese. I had some good feeds,' he remembered, 'but the stallholders had many calls on their time, and I was proud even then. I might have been filthy and wearing rags but I vowed that I would never sink any lower and would always strive to rise. My bathroom was the Tiber, and my bedroom better than most people could boast.'

'What do you mean by that?' she asked.

'I slept at the Coliseum,' he explained. 'I came to know a member of the security staff, and he turned a blind eye when I curled up in the shadows of that great arena.'

'You make it sound romantic,' Callie said with a frown, 'but you must have been freezing in winter.'

'It was certainly a challenge,' he recalled, 'but atmospheric too. I used to sleep in Caesar's box, rather than in the dungeons where the poor victims used to languish as they awaited their terrible fate. I had nothing in the material sense,' he added as their small craft sliced through the water, 'except when it came to determination. I had plenty of that, as well as the freedom to change my condition, which I did.'

'What age were you when this was happening?'

'I was grubbing around the streets from the age of four. That was when my mother died,' he explained. 'The whorehouse where she worked kicked me out. In fairness, no one could spare the time to take care of me. I think now that I was better off by myself. The clientele at the brothel weren't too choosy who they abused, if you take my meaning.'

'I do. But how did you manage on your own on the streets at the age of four?'

'There were other, older children on the streets. They showed me how to stay alive.'

'How did you end up at the Coliseum?'

'A lot of homeless children slept there. I saw the tourist posters advertising this colossal building, and I wanted to see it for myself. Getting inside was easy. I just joined the queue of tourists and walked straight in. I soon learned that if I pretended to be a lost child, concerned attendants would feed me. It worked for quite a while until they began to recognise me, but by then they had developed a soft spot for the boy from the gutters and so they turned a blind eye. The people who worked at the Coliseum didn't have much money, either, and so they saved food from the trash for me to root through. There were plenty of half-eaten burgers and hot dogs for supper. I don't remember being hungry. The Coliseum was like a hotel for me, growing up, so don't feel sorry for me. I did fine. The Coliseum was both my home and my school. I saw everything you can imagine during my time there. I learned about sex, violence, thieving, unkindness, and great acts of kindness too.'

'Can you remember your parents?' she asked as he took a deep pull on the oars.

'Nothing I care to bring to mind,' he admitted dryly. 'My mother was always harassed and often sick. I think now that she was what we would call depressed. No surprise there, but a child can't understand why a person behaves the way they do. A child only knows that it's hungry, or frightened, and I knew I had to fend for myself long before she died.'

'And your father? Did you ever meet him?'

'He turned up one night,' Luca recollected. He huffed a short, humourless laugh. 'My mother's colleagues pelted him with rotten fruit and worse. I remember him standing on the street, shouting up at her open window.

I remember his angry voice, and his soiled white shirt and the glint of his gold earrings.'

'He doesn't sound very nice.'

He shrugged. 'Who knows?'

'And now you're a prince with a country to rule and a palace to live in. It must all seem quite incredible, even now?'

'No. It seems right,' he said thoughtfully. 'If there was luck involved, it was that I met the Prince, the best of men, and a man who changed my life. Though even that wasn't as simple as it sounds,' he admitted. 'After everything I'd seen, I wasn't easily impressed—not even by the Prince of Fabrizio.'

'How did he persuade you to leave the streets and come to live with him?'

'He was a patient man,' Luca said, thinking back. 'From the moment he found me stealing food from the bins and the buffet table during his royal visit to the Coliseum, he was determined to save me. He told me this years later.'

'What did he do about your stealing?' Callie asked as he shipped the oars.

'He asked his attendant to find me a shopping bag, so I didn't have to hide my hoard down my shirt.'

'Cool,' she said, smiling.

'Oh, he was that,' he agreed as he sprang onto the shore to moor up.

She placed her hands in his as he helped her onto the dock. He wanted to take her right there. Throw her down on the cool wood and make love to her until she didn't have the strength to stand, but delay was its own reward.

It was just a small island. She could probably walk around it in ten minutes, Callie thought. The grass was cool and green, and felt lush and thick beneath her naked feet. Picking up the hem of her dress, she stared around. The clustering trees were lit with thousands of tiny lights in celebration of the ball. And then she saw the gazebo he'd talked about ahead of them. 'Is this where you used to come and sulk?' she asked.

'How did you guess?'

As he swung around to face her, the pulsing heat of desire surged through her. 'I've been a teenager too.'

He laughed and held out his hands. She felt so safe and warm when he took hold of her, and Luca's kisses were always a drugging seduction. They seemed even more so here on this magical island. Just occasionally, fairy tales did come true. She wanted to believe it so badly as he kissed her again. She'd spent so much of her life bottling up emotion, but Luca knew how to set it free, and as his kisses grew more heated she knew she would take any and every chance to hold onto happiness.

He swung her off her feet and strode quickly to the entrance to the gazebo. Lowering her down, he steadied her and then pressed her back against the wooden structure. Caging her with his arms either side of her face, he brushed his lips against her mouth and smiled. It was the most romantic moment, but if she'd written the fairy tale herself she could never have predicted what he'd say next. 'Marry me, Callie. Marry me and become my Princess.'

At first she thought she was imagining it, and it was all a dream, until Luca repeated softly, 'Marry me, Callie.'

She stared into his eyes, struggling to compute what he'd said. Embarrassed, uncertain, she resorted to teasing him. 'Shouldn't you be down on your knees? Or, one of them, at least?'

'I need an answer,' Luca said, refusing to respond to

her lighter tone. 'Just a straight yes or no will do. Or are you playing for time?'

'No,' she argued. 'I'm playing for the highest of stakes of all. I'm playing for my heart, and for the future of our child.'

'Then, marriage makes perfect sense,' he insisted.

'Does it?' She frowned.

'You know it does.'

Smiling into her eyes, he kissed her again, and because she wanted him she was foolish enough to believe in the fairy tale for now.

CHAPTER ELEVEN

'TRUST ME,' LUCA said as he took her slow and deep. They had been making love on the soft cushions in the gazebo for what felt like hours. 'Trust me,' he said again as he soothed her down.

'Shouldn't you get back to the ball?' she asked. She was snuggled up tightly against Luca, whose protective arms wrapped securely around her.

'If you're ready, we'll go back,' he murmured as he planted a kiss on the top of her head.

'Bathe in the lake first?' she suggested.

They swam, then dried off together, and Callie dressed quickly, thanking her lucky stars she had short hair that didn't take long to dry in the warm night air. Slipping her simple dress on, she took hold of Luca's hand and they walked back to the boat; back to reality, she thought, but if he could carry this off—their absence would have been noted—then so could she.

'My lords, ladies and gentlemen, I have an announcement to make…'

Silence fell the instant Luca's deep and distinctive voice was heard through the hidden speakers in the ballroom. 'I realise the clock is about to strike midnight, so I won't keep you long.'

A ripple of laughter greeted this remark.

'I'm taking this opportunity to introduce you to the woman I intend to marry.'

Not the woman he loved, Callie thought, cursing herself for being such a doubter. Luca had to wait a moment until the exclamations of surprise had died down.

'Signorina Callista Smith is an exceptional woman, whom I am lucky to have found.'

As he beckoned Callie forward and she joined him in the centre of the ballroom, the surprise of the sophisticated onlookers gradually turned to muted applause. They were shocked to the heels of their highly polished footwear, she thought as Luca lifted his hands for a silence that had already fallen deep and long.

'It goes without saying,' he added, 'that all of you will receive an invitation to our wedding.' He gave a fierce, encouraging smile into Callie's eyes, before turning back to address his riveted audience. 'I invite you all to enjoy the rest of your evening, while I continue to celebrate with my beautiful fiancée.'

As if by magic the orchestra struck up a romantic Viennese waltz, which allowed Luca to prove that not only could he sweep Callie off her feet, but he could provide the prompt necessary to shake everyone out of their stupefied trance, and soon the dance floor was ablaze with colour and the flash of precious jewels.

Callie told herself that everything would work out. Yes, there would be problems, but they'd get through them. Luca was right. This was the best solution. It was only when the clock struck midnight, and he was briefly distracted by one of the many ambassadors present, that everything changed.

She'd seen pictures of Max in various magazines back home. In the flesh, he was even more striking. As tall as Luca, he looked quite different, which was only to be expected when they weren't related by blood. Where Luca's features were rugged and sexy, Max's face was thin and hard, and, quite unlike Luca, Max's manner was unpleasantly autocratic.

Dressed entirely in black, his blood-red sash of office the only bright thing about him, Max was the haughtiest man in the room by far. And he was heading her way surrounded by cronies, all of whom were viewing Callie with what she could only describe as amused contempt. There was a beautiful woman on Max's arm, who was also dressed in black, with the addition of half a hundredweight of diamonds. Her tiara alone could have settled most countries' debts, Callie guessed. Knowing she was the target of the advancing party, she stood her ground and lifted her chin, then shrank inwardly when Max stopped directly in front of her.

'Well, my dear,' he said, keeping his stare fixed on Callie as he turned to address his obviously heavily pregnant companion, 'this is the little snip my brother intends to put on our throne.'

'Surely not?' his elegantly dressed companion protested as she stared disapprovingly at Callie. 'Who is she, anyway? And *where* did she get that dress?'

Callie ground her jaw, refusing to demean herself by responding. Max's friends could laugh all they liked. They wouldn't drive her away.

'Goodness knows, my dear,' Max replied, still staring at Callie through mocking eyes. 'Perhaps she got it from the same thrift store that sold her the dye for that ridiculous hair colour.'

As everyone laughed Callie reached up instinctively to touch her hair, and regretted the lapse immediately. She hated letting them see they'd upset her. 'Well, at least I don't have a cruel tongue,' she said mildly.

'Oh, she speaks,' Max exclaimed, turning to look at his friends. 'I imagine she learned that skill in *the pub back home*.' He made each vowel sound grotesque and ugly.

As Max and his friends roared with laughter, Callie made sure to remain impassive.

'He only keeps her around because she's pregnant,' Max drawled, quirking a brow in an attempt, Callie thought, to elicit some sort of response from her. 'He's desperate for an heir, and when you're as desperate as Luca I suppose it's a case of any port in a storm. Seeing you pregnant,' he added to the woman at his side, 'must really have disturbed him. That's the only reason he's chosen this girl. He's trying to compete with me—imagine that?'

'He's quite obviously failed,' one of Max's cronies derided.

'That's all this is,' Max assured Callie, bringing his cruel face close. 'Don't think for one moment that you've bagged yourself a prince, let alone that this is a fairy tale. This is a cold-blooded transaction, my dear. Luca doesn't want you. He doesn't want anyone. The only thing Luca wants is an heir. That's the only way he can hope to keep the throne of Fabrizio. It's written into our constitution. Two years, one baby at least, or I take over.' Coming even closer, he sneered. 'You're nothing more than a convenient womb. Shall we?' he added to his gloating companions with an airy gesture. 'I've had enough of this ball. The quality of guests at the palace has really gone down. The casino beckons. A few spins of the wheel holds far more appeal than these provincials can ever hope to provide me.'

'She's gone? What do you mean, she's gone?' Luca stared down at Michel in surprise. The elderly retainer seemed more than usually confused. 'Take your time, Michel. I'm sorry. I didn't mean to shout at you.'

'I saw her talking to Max,' Michel told him in a worried tone.

'What?'

'You said you wouldn't shout,' Michel reminded him.

'You're right,' he admitted, placing a reassuring hand on the older man's shoulder. 'But who invited Max?'

'Does Max need an invitation to visit his family home?'

Luca ground his jaw. He should have known that Max would never keep to their agreement that he stay out of Fabrizio. 'So, where the hell is she?' he repeated as he raked his hair with tense fingers.

'I saw her running out of that door not ten minutes ago,' Michel informed him, staring across the ballroom towards the French doors leading onto the garden and then the lake. 'And that was straight after talking to Max.'

'Ten minutes?' Luca exclaimed, frowning. 'Did I leave her alone for that long?'

'The ambassador can be garrulous and difficult to get away from,' Michel said in an obvious attempt to placate him. 'And His Excellency was more than usually talkative tonight.'

Luca could not be placated. His one concern was Callie. He should have told her long before now what she meant to him. The convenient plan that had fallen into place when he found out she was pregnant hadn't figured in his thinking when he'd made the announcement that they would be married.

All right, so maybe it had, he conceded grimly as he made a visual search of the ballroom to make sure she'd gone. Would he stick around under similar circumstances? So, where could she be? In her room, or had she tried to return to the island? His heart banged in his chest at the thought that she might have taken the rowing boat. Navigation was easy for him in the dark. He'd been rowing on the lake for most of his life. So he knew about the clinging weeds and treacherous rocks. If Callie took the wrong route, she could be in serious trouble. He didn't wait to consider his options. Cutting through the crowd, he hurried away.

He ran to the shore. The boat was gone. There was no sign of Callie. Everyone had been shocked by his announcement of their engagement, and now Max was causing trouble again. He had a stark choice to make. Callie, or the future of Fabrizio. There was no choice. Stripping off his clothes, he dived into the lake.

Relief surged through him when he spotted her pacing the shore. 'Callie,' he exclaimed, springing out of the water. Striding up to her, he seized hold of her and demanded she look at him. 'What's wrong? What happened back there?'

'You happened,' she said.

Her voice was faint, but the fire in her eyes was brighter than ever. She was hurt, bitterly hurt. He knew all the signs. Max had always been an expert when it came to wounding with words.

'Thank you for telling me how badly you needed an heir,' she said tensely, sarcastically.

'Meaning?' he demanded.

'I'm told your constitution demands it, if you're to keep the throne.' There were tears of anger and distress in her eyes. 'I would have been quicker off the mark getting pregnant, if you'd told me.'

'Don't be ridiculous,' he flared. 'What on earth has Max said to you?'

'Only the truth, I believe.'

A muscle jerked in his jaw. He couldn't even deny it, and had to listen to his brother's poison flooding from Callie's mouth.

'Max said that making an heir is the only reason you had sex with me.'

'I didn't have sex with you,' he insisted. 'I made love to you.'

'Maybe.' She hesitated a little. 'But how do I know that's true, now I know you had a motive?'

'Why can't you believe in yourself, Callie? Why won't you believe how much I need you?'

'Because it's convenient for you to have me,' she exclaimed. 'A convenient womb, Max called me. He says your primary concern is to build a dynasty.'

'My primary concern is you,' he argued fiercely.

'It doesn't feel that way to me, Luca. You made the announcement of our engagement without asking me first, without giving me chance to consider what I'm getting into. My late father used to tell me what I could and couldn't do, and I swore that I would never fall into that trap again.'

'This isn't a trap. You're not thinking straight, Callie.'

'I'm thinking perfectly,' she fired back. 'It's just a pity I haven't been thinking perfectly from the start.'

'That's your hormones talking.'

'Don't you dare,' she warned him. 'What was your plan, Luca? We marry, I have the baby, and then your people organise a convenient divorce? You don't have much time to play with, do you? Pregnancy sets a clock ticking, and so does the constitution of Fabrizio, Max tells me. Tonight was the perfect opportunity for you to announce our engagement. I imagine you'd have had us married by the end of the month, so that everything would be finalised before my pregnancy becomes obvious.'

He couldn't argue. So much of what she said was true, but his feelings when he'd discovered Callie was pregnant had been real and strong. A baby. A child. A family. Everything he'd always dreamed of had been suddenly within his reach. For a man used to subduing or ignoring his emotions, he'd been overwhelmed, and not just because Callie would provide him with the longed-for heir. She was the perfect woman, who would become the perfect mother. She would be his perfect bride, and would transition seamlessly into a much-loved princess. 'What's so terrible about becoming my wife?'

'If you don't know,' she said, sounding sad, 'I can't tell you. I suggest you forget about me, and ask one of those princesses to be your wife. You'll hardly be short of replacements for me.'

'Aggravating woman!' he roared. 'I don't want a replacement. I want you.'

'You can't have everything you want, Luca.'

'Are you saying no?' he demanded with incredulity.

'I'm saying no,' Callie confirmed.

'But you'll be a princess.'

'Of what?' she demanded. 'All you're offering is a temporary position, an empty life in a foreign country with a man who only wants me for my child-bearing capabilities.'

'That's Max talking. Don't listen to him.'

'I don't want that for our child,' she said, ignoring him, 'and I don't want to be a princess in a loveless marriage. I can't snuggle up to a tiara at night. I'd rather be back home in one room with my baby.'

'That isn't your choice to make,' he said, adopting a very different tone.

'Are you threatening me?' she said quietly.

'I'm reminding you that you're carrying the heir to the principality of Fabrizio, and that neither you nor I can change that fact.'

'And thank God for it,' she whispered as blood drained from her face. 'But there is something I can do.'

'Which is?' he demanded suspiciously.

'Unless you intend to keep me here by force, I can return home to spend Christmas with friends I can trust. You took my trust and abused it,' she accused. 'And tonight I learned that you took my body and used that too.'

'*What? Dio!* Never!' He raked his still-damp hair with frustration. 'Don't we know each other better than this? Yes, passion drove us initially. And yes, your pregnancy was convenient. I won't deny it. But it means so much more to me now. *You* mean so much more. I'm still coming to terms with the fact that I feel—' He stopped. He couldn't even put into words how many feelings he was dealing with. For a man who'd spent most of his life avoiding emotion, he was drowning in them. 'I respect you and I always will,' he stated firmly. 'Please give some thought to what becoming my wife will mean.'

'I have,' Callie assured him quietly, 'and it's not what I want.'

'What do you want?' he demanded fiercely. He'd do anything to put this right.

'I want love and respect on both sides,' she said without hesitation. 'I want friendship that makes both of us smile, and I want trust like a rock we can both depend on. I want to honour the man who is my lover, my friend, and the father of my child, as he honours me. And I want my independence. I've fought too hard to lose that now.'

'You'll have it as my wife,' he asserted confidently.

'And as your Princess?' When he didn't answer, because he knew only too well the restrictions that royal life imposed, she continued, 'I've spent too much of my life caged, and I won't exchange one cage for another, however big an upgrade that might seem to you. And it's not what I want for our child. I want us all to be free. I know I'm a fantasist,' she added in a calmer voice, 'and I know I want too much. I should have realised that from the start.'

'Callie!'

'No. Don't try to stop me,' she called back as she ran back to the lake. 'We were never meant to be together. Max is right. I can't marry a prince—this is over,' she flared, trying to shake him off when he caught up with her.

'It doesn't need to end here,' he said firmly, holding her still.

'Yes, it does.' With a violent tug she broke free. 'Goodbye, Luca—'

'But I love you.'

She stopped on the edge of the lake. Whether she intended to swim back or row back, he had no idea. He did know she was furious. 'You love me?' she said tensely. 'Yet you didn't think to tell me this before tonight? It sounds like you're desperate to keep me here.'

'I am desperate, but not for the reasons you think. You're more to me than you could ever know, more than Max could even comprehend.'

She shook her head. 'You had to be sure of me, didn't you, Luca? That's why you made the announcement of our engagement tonight in front of so many witnesses.'

'You're not listening, Callie. I love you. And you're right. I should have told you long before now, but I didn't realise it myself. I didn't recognise the symptoms,' he admitted ruefully, raking his hair with frustration. 'I'm not exactly familiar with love in all its guises.'

'Your father didn't love you?' she challenged with an angry gesture.

'The Prince loved me, but it wasn't easy for me to trust him enough to return his love, not as soon as he wanted, anyway.'

'He must have been a patient man.'

'He was.'

'Know this, Luca. Nothing will change my mind. I don't want a work in progress, while you discover your feelings. I want the boy who made his home in the Coliseum and dreamed of what he would one day become. I want the man who made that happen. Don't you dare make your past an excuse. I haven't.'

That was true. She shamed him. 'How can I prove that I love you?'

'By letting me go,' she said with her usual frankness.

* * *

Back home at the Browns', the ache in Callie's heart at the absence of Luca was like a big, gaping wound that refused to heal. Even the Browns' famously over-the-top Christmas preparations couldn't do anything to mend it. Seeing Anita again had helped, Callie conceded as she smiled across the room at her friend from the lemon groves. Anita had become a most welcome fixture at the Browns'. On her return, Callie had persuaded Anita, who lived alone in a rented room, to take a job close by, and the Browns had offered to rent her a room. They always welcomed help with the younger children and Anita would never be alone again, Ma Brown had promised. Anita had a proper family now—if she could stand the noise and chaos. Anita could certainly do that, and had fitted right in.

'Come on, our Callie,' Ma Brown insisted as she bustled into the room they called the front parlour. 'Anita, I need you to help me in the kitchen, and, Rosie, you and Callie still have the rest of those crêpe paper streamers to hang.'

'And make,' Rosie pointed out as she glanced at the uncut reams of crinkled paper and then at Callie's preoccupied face. 'Come on, I'll help you.' Kneeling down at Callie's side, Rosie waited until her mother had left the room before putting an arm around Callie's shoulders. 'I know you haven't said anything in front of the family, but you can't keep bottling this up. And you can't keep refusing to speak to him,' Rosie added. 'If Prince Luca comes to England to see you—'

'Do you know something?' Callie asked. Her heart soared at the thought of seeing Luca again, even as her rational mind told her she could never be a princess, so it was better not to see him at all.

'Not exactly,' Rosie admitted uncomfortably. 'I'm just saying that if Luca did turn up, you should see him.'

'I don't have to see anyone,' Callie argued stubbornly, but her heart was beating so fast just at the thought of seeing Luca again that she could hardly breathe. Was he in the country, maybe somewhere close by? There was no smoke without fire, she concluded, glancing at Rosie, who refused to meet her eyes.

'We'd better get these streamers made,' Rosie said, acting as if the lack of paper decorations was the only crisis looming, 'or there'll be hell to pay.'

CHAPTER TWELVE

CALLIE FROZE. THEY had just sat down to the most mouth-watering Christmas feast when an imperative knock sounded at the door.

'I'll answer it,' Pa Brown insisted when Callie moved to get out of her chair.

'Let him go,' Ma Brown said to everyone with a calming gesture. 'Whoever's there, we can't leave a stranger on the doorstep today.'

That was no stranger, Callie thought, shivering inwardly with excitement as the distinctive sound of Luca's dark, husky voice made everyone sit up and take notice. The air changed, stilled, and was suddenly charged with electricity as, quite improbably, His Serene Highness, Prince Luca of Fabrizio, stood framed in the narrow doorway. Radiating glamour, presence, and an irrational amount of heat, Luca was a starry visitor to the homey Christmas at the Browns'. His stare locked briefly with Callie's. That short look carried more heat, more passion and determination than she could stand. It was almost a relief when he turned to greet everyone else in the room.

'This is wonderful,' Luca exclaimed, sucking in a deep, appreciative breath as Pa Brown relieved him of his rugged jacket. 'I didn't realise how hungry I was, until

I smelled this delicious food.' His gaze swept over Callie before he smiled at Ma Brown. 'Do you have room for one more?'

'Most certainly,' Ma Brown exclaimed, leaping up from the table.

In a midnight-blue fine-knit sweater that clung lovingly to his magnificent frame, and beat-up jeans moulding his muscular thighs, Luca was an improbable giant in their midst. Callie couldn't help but remember having those thighs locked around her as they made love, and her longing for Luca surged as his stare found hers and this time lingered. Her heart was gunned into action. She hadn't realised how much she'd missed him. Snow dusted his ink-black hair, making it twinkle and gleam. If she'd never met him before and didn't know his history, if someone had told her that Luca was a cage fighter she'd have believed them. He certainly wasn't her childhood idea of Prince Charming. But fairy tales were a long way behind them now. Sex radiated from him like sparks from a Catherine wheel, though his eyes were full of warmth for the Browns, and for Anita. 'Don't I know you from Italy?' he asked Anita.

'You do, Your Serene Highness,' Anita admitted, blushing.

'Call me Luca,' he said. 'You know the rules.'

As Anita and Luca laughed together, Callie thought him so infectiously warm, so vital and compelling. 'I hope I'm not intruding,' he said, noticing that the Browns were all staring at him open-mouthed.

'Not at all,' Pa Brown was quick to reassure him.

'Good,' Luca declared, 'because I'm here to claim my bride.'

The younger Browns stared at Luca, while the rest

carried on as if nothing unusual had occurred. Callie moved first. Pushing her chair back, she put down her napkin. If it hadn't been for Pa Brown's restraining hand on her shoulder, she would have left the room and taken Luca with her. What right did he have to come storming in like some medieval feudal lord, interrupting the flow of everything around the Christmas table and demanding that she be his bride. 'Steady girl,' Pa Brown murmured discreetly.

Everyone closed their mouths and pretended to concentrate on their food as Callie sat down again. All except one. 'You can have my chair, if I can have a ride in your sports car,' young Tom Brown told Luca.

'Sounds like a deal to me,' Luca agreed with a smile.

'My name's Tom,' the youngster supplied as he and Luca bumped fists.

'Come on, everyone…shuffle up,' Ma Brown instructed. 'Let's make room for the Prince.'

'Now, there's a phrase you don't hear said every day,' Pa Brown ventured, only to receive a stern look from his wife.

For a while everything was good-natured chaos as chairs were swopped around, and new cutlery was brought out of the drawer. Once crockery and glassware had been located, everything was settled for their guest.

'I envy you,' Luca told his hosts midway through the most succulent meal of turkey with all the trimmings.

'You envy us?' Pa Brown exclaimed, only to receive a second hard stare from his wife, who sensibly steered the situation.

'More gravy with that extra helping of meat, Luca?'

'Yes, please.'

With Ma Brown setting the tone, all the Browns began

to behave as if His Serene Highness were any other neighbour who'd called around to share their Christmas cheer. Now that was class, Callie thought. Stuff Max and his cronies. They couldn't hold a candle to these genuine folk. The meal could have been tense, and Christmas could have been ruined, but with Luca at his relaxed best, and Anita and the Browns just being themselves, the irreverent, good-natured banter soon resumed.

'So, what's it like being a prince?' young Tom enquired.

'Busy,' Luca told him economically.

'Don't you have to smile at people you don't like?' another boy asked.

'That's called diplomacy,' Pa Brown put in. 'Something you could all do with a lesson in.'

'No, he's right,' Luca intervened. 'That's why it's so good to be here.' He flashed a wry glance at Callie, who raised a brow.

'Didn't you have anywhere else to go at Christmas but here?' young Tom demanded.

Luca's lips quirked as he thought about this. 'I had a few places, but nowhere as special as here.'

'Pudding?' Ma Brown enquired.

'Yes, please,' Luca confirmed. 'But first…' He glanced at Callie, and then jerked his head towards the door.

'Of course,' Ma Brown agreed. 'I'll keep the pudding warm for both of you.'

Callie wasn't sure how she felt. She didn't feel any more forgiving towards Luca, but they did need to talk, and the sooner, the better.

'So now you know,' she said. Having wrapped herself up warmly in her winter coat and scarf, she was sitting in the front seat of Luca's bright red car.

'Know what?' he asked with a frown as he started the engine.

'Where I come from.'

'You're lucky. It's wonderful. That's the best Christmas I've ever been part of.'

'And it hasn't even started yet,' Callie said wryly. 'Wait until they start playing parlour games.'

'Parlour games?' Luca queried.

'What people used to do before TV.'

He shot her a sideways look. 'Sounds interesting.'

'You said you'd give me time, Luca,' she reminded him as he pulled into the light Christmas Day traffic.

'How much time do you need?'

'More,' she insisted.

'I'm afraid that's not possible. I have other places to be.'

'You said you'd let me go.'

'I didn't say I wouldn't come after you.'

Callie shook her head while her heart went crazy. 'I belong here, Luca.'

'You belonged in the lemon groves too. You belonged in the five-star hotel, whether you chose to believe it or not. The staff there love you. You belong anywhere you choose to be. You have a positive slant on life that infects the people around you. That's why they love you. That's why I love you, and want you for my wife.'

'And a royal princess, mother of your heir,' she said quietly.

'So you're going to believe Max, not me.'

'I make my own decisions. This has nothing to do with Max.'

'Who has been reminded that he'd agreed to stay away

from Fabrizio for life,' Luca explained, 'in case you were wondering.'

'Stop here.'

'What?'

'Here,' she insisted. 'There's a park. We can walk.'

Luca dipped his head to stare around. 'I had intended taking you somewhere more romantic.'

'It's all a matter of scale,' Callie insisted, 'and this is fine. This patch of green might not look much to you, but I can tell you that it's appreciated around here as much as you appreciate your royal parks.'

'I didn't play in royal parks as a boy,' Luca reminded her as he slowed the car. Parking up, he killed the engine. Getting out, he came around to open the passenger door. She accepted his help and climbed out.

The same thrill raced up her arm. Luca's quiet strength was so compelling. He broke the silence first as they went through the entrance into the small inner-city park, and her breath caught in her throat when he said, 'I refuse to believe you don't know how right this is between us.'

'But you're a prince,' she protested.

'I'm a man.' Wrapping his big hands around her lapels, he drew her close. 'And that man knows we belong together. But though I've confided in you, you've told me nothing.'

Shoulders hunched against the freezing wind, Callie lifted her head and stared into Luca's strong, rugged face. 'Why do you want to marry me, when you can have your pick of every princess in the world, and all the heiresses, if that grand ball was anything to go by?'

'I keep asking myself that same question,' Luca admitted dryly.

'This isn't funny,' she said.

'This I know,' he agreed. 'All I can come up with is that there is no reason to love. You either do or you don't.'

They had stopped in front of the bandstand where, only that morning, she'd sung carols with the Browns while the local band played their hearts out.

'I know why you don't trust easily, Callie. You had a hard life with your father. Ma Brown told me a lot of it over the phone.'

'She shouldn't have.'

'Yes, she should,' he argued. 'She cares about you, and the Browns thought I should know. When you didn't answer my letters, I got in touch with them. They told me to stay away and give you time to take everything in. Has it worked?' He gave her a fleeting smile.

'And love,' she said. 'What conclusion did you come to?'

He considered her question. 'I came to the conclusion that love isn't rational, and there are no answers. There's only this…' Dragging her close, he kissed her, gently to begin with, and then with increasing fire, until they were kissing each other as if they were the last two people on earth.

It felt as if they were finding each other all over again. 'I've missed you,' she breathed when they finally broke apart.

'You have no idea,' Luca murmured as he smoothed her hair back from her face. 'When I say that I want to know all about you, I'm not talking about the heavily edited facts you've fed me in the past, but the truth, all of it, good and bad. I want to face the trials and triumphs together, so we can share the feelings we've both steered clear of in the past. I'm still learning when it comes to emotion, but I owe it to my country to change, and I owe it to you most of all. If we don't know sadness, how can we recognise happiness, and if we don't feel regret, how can we look forward and plan for the future? Tell me everything,' he insisted. 'I'll know if you're holding back.'

She thought back, and started with her mother. 'I can't remember her…' She paused, saddened. 'My father blamed me for her loss. She died in childbirth,' Callie explained. 'And he could have been so much more,' she said as she thought about her father.

'But none of this is your fault,' Luca insisted. Taking hold of her hands, he brought them to his lips and kissed them. 'You don't need to tell me how hard you've worked. Your hands speak for you.'

Callie laughed ruefully. She didn't exactly have a princess's hands. They were red and work-worn, having never quite recovered from scrubbing floors at the pub, but they were part of her, and she would rather have her work-roughened hands than all the pale, floaty things she'd seen at the ball.

'What was life like before your father died?' Luca prompted when she fell silent.

'Life's always been great, thanks to the Browns. Well, most of it,' she conceded. 'But if I didn't have the Browns…' That didn't bear thinking about.

'Good friends are beyond price,' Luca agreed. 'But now you have to ask yourself what *you* want out of life now.'

You, she thought, but you without complications, and she knew that wasn't possible. 'I wish life were simpler,' she said. 'I wish we could go back to working in the lemon groves, when I thought we were both holiday staff.'

'We're the same people we were then.'

'But now you're a prince,' Callie argued.

'I'm a man in love with you.'

Or in love with the thought of great sex going forward with the woman carrying his child? she wondered. 'I just don't know if it could work out,' she said, speaking her doubts out loud. 'The Princess bit, I mean.' Lifting her chin, she stared directly at Luca. 'Being royal seems so confining to me.'

'Not once you learn how to pin on a tiara,' he said. 'I'm sure you'll soon get the hang of it.'

She shot him a warning look, but Luca was in no way deterred. 'I've got homes across the world where we can be alone as much as you want, and I've got a superyacht to escape to.'

'That's just the point, isn't it? This is all normal to you, but it's crazy mad to me.'

'So?' he prompted.

'So, no, thank you.'

'Think about it carefully.'

'I have,' she assured him.

'I realise it's a huge commitment to make. Most people would jump at the chance of marrying into royalty and wouldn't give a second thought to the practicalities. But that's not you, Callie. You're cranky, challenging, and real, and that's why I want you at my side.'

'Compliments?' she said dryly. It was hard to remain neutral when Luca was working his charm. She was already warming and thrilling inside, and she didn't need anyone to tell her how dangerous that was. 'Or are you saying I keep your feet on the ground?'

'That's not the reason I want you,' Luca assured her with one of his dark, gripping looks. 'And, in the interest of clarity, I should make it clear that your feet won't be on the ground for long.'

* * *

'So,' Callie murmured, shooting him a troubled look when they got back in the car. 'You love me.'

'I do.'

'And you want to marry me.'

'Correct.'

'And not just because I'm pregnant with your convenient heir?'

Pressing back in the driver's seat, Luca sighed heavily. He owed her nothing less than the truth. 'When I first found out, I'll admit that it suited my plan.'

'You needed an heir,' she supplied.

'Yes, I did. And great sex.'

'Luca—'

'Regularly.'

'You're impossible.'

'Seriously?' he asked. 'If you want to know what I want? I want a family like the Browns.'

'Fourteen children?'

'One at a time?' he queried, sliding her a look. 'That's not so bad.'

'For you, maybe,' Callie said, biting back a smile. But then she turned serious. 'Callie from the docks, the Princess of Fabrizio?'

'Callie from the lemon groves, and my beloved wife,' Luca argued as he pulled away from the kerb. 'So, what's your answer, Callie?'

'The same as it was before,' she said tensely. 'I still need time to think.'

'All you need is time to assess your character and abilities to realise that you have everything it takes and more to be my Princess. So I'll give you until we get to the Browns', and then I want your answer.'

'And if it's no?' she pressed.

'We'll deal through lawyers in the future.'

Her face paled. 'That sounds like a threat.'

'It's the only practical option I can come up with. Or you can give me your answer now, if you prefer?'

She refused to be drawn, and by the time he had stopped the car outside the Browns', he could feel Callie's tension. Helping her out of the low-slung vehicle, he kept hold of her hand as they walked to the front door. Each time they talked, he learned a little bit more about her, and what he'd learned today had confirmed his opinion that they weren't so different. They both had principles, loyalty, and trust printed through them like sticks of rock. Callie was honest to a fault, and still overcoming the scars of a difficult childhood. He'd had the most enormous stroke of luck when he'd met the Prince at the Coliseum, and Callie had experienced a small taste of luck with her surprise win on the scratch card that had allowed her to travel to the lemon groves. It was strange how fate set things in motion. Experience had taught him that sometimes it paid to go with the flow.

'Come in, come in,' Pa Brown invited as he threw the front door wide.

Luca might live in a palace with servants on every side, but he hadn't been joking when he said that he envied the Browns. This was the type of family he had imagined being part of when he was a boy on his own each night with only the ghosts from the past for company. He and Callie were welcomed back into the warm heart of the Brown family just as the Christmas gifts were being opened and happy noise was at its height. Dogs and children were racing around colliding with each other, while Anita tried in vain to keep up with the amount of wrapping paper flying through the air. Rosie was attempting, without much success, to dissuade the younger Browns from opening each of the crackers before they were pulled, to discover what gifts lay inside.

'We saved some crackers for you,' she explained to Callie and him, as Pa Brown insisted on taking Luca's jacket.

'And I've saved two big dishes of plum pudding,' Ma Brown added from the doorway.

'I'd like a few moments of Ma and Pa's time. If I may,' he said.

Silence dropped like a stone. Every head turned his way, and then the focus switched to Callie, who shrugged, giving him no clue as to what her answer would be to his proposal.

'Of course,' Pa Brown agreed, breaking the tension as he exchanged a look with his wife. 'Come into the kitchen where we can be private, Luca. Would you like Callie to join us?'

'No. It's something I want to ask both of you. It involves Callie, but she knows all about it.'

'Do I?' Callie demanded, making him wonder yet again if he had misjudged the moment.

She was unreadable, and where women of his acquaintance were concerned that was a novelty, and, for a man who had everything money could buy, novelty was the most valuable currency of all.

'You should know how I feel about you by now,' he insisted, and, grabbing her close, he kissed her, which in front of the younger Browns was tantamount to making a public announcement.

Before he had chance to leave for the kitchen, young Tom piped up, 'You'll need this...' Holding out a blue plastic ring from his cracker, Tom stared up at Luca expectantly.

'*Grazie!* Thank you, Tom. Your timing couldn't be better.' He stowed the ring away in the back pocket of his jeans, and left Callie to have his conference with the Browns. When he came back, he knelt at Callie's feet—which wasn't as easy as it sounded with all the toys scattered around. 'Will you do me the very great honour of accepting this priceless ring, which has been especially chosen for you by Signor Tom?'

'I'm overwhelmed,' Callie admitted, starting to laugh.

The situation was bizarre admittedly, and could only happen, he figured, at Christmas. 'Take it,' he muttered discreetly, 'or I won't be responsible for my actions.' As the younger Browns cheered he sprang up and put the ring on Callie's finger. There were a few tense moments when she didn't say a word, but then she laughed and threw her arms around his neck, and everyone cheered.

'A Christmas wedding, then,' Ma Brown exclaimed, clapping her hands with excitement.

'A bit late for Christmas, Ma. It will have to be New Year,' Pa Brown, who should have known he could never win, argued, frowning.

'Ah, that's where you're wrong,' Ma Brown assured him, 'because Christmas is celebrated in January in Fabrizio. Isn't that right, Luca?'

'Quite correct, Mrs Brown.'

'Still, not much time,' Ma Brown said, frowning as she thought about it. 'But enough time, if I know our Callie.'

'You do know Callie,' Luca asserted, giving Ma Brown the warmest of hugs. 'You know her better than anyone except me.'

'I'll accept that,' Ma Brown stated as Callie narrowed her eyes in mock disapproval.

'How long have you three been conniving?' Callie enquired, raising a brow as she looked at Luca and then Ma and Pa Brown in turn.

'Four,' Rosie put in. 'Don't forget me.'

'Why, you—' Callie was still laughing when Luca swept her off her feet. Swinging her around, which was quite a risky manoeuvre in a room full of Browns and Anita, he planted a breath-stealing kiss on her mouth. 'Have you kept my letters?' he asked as he set her down. 'I was just thinking that you might want to read them now.'

'Read them *now*?' Rosie exclaimed. 'The paper they're written on is almost worn through. Don't let Callie kid you, Luca. You are the love of Callie's life.'

EPILOGUE

IT WAS UNSEASONABLY cold in the north of England. Brilliant white snow was falling in soft, silent drifts, slowing the traffic and muffling the noise of hooves as Callie's horse-drawn wedding coach arrived outside the Browns'. To counterbalance the frigid temperatures, every house on the street was brilliantly lit to celebrate the holiday season, which would go on well into the New Year. In the town, stores and corner shops were still crammed with reindeer and stars, and sleighs and plump-cheeked Santa Clauses, as if no one could bear to let go of the Christmas cheer.

There would never be another wedding like this one, Callie was sure of that. She was going to marry Luca in the area where she'd grown up, surrounded by her closest friends the Browns, Callie's landlady from the shop in Blackpool, and Anita, and Maria and Marco, who had travelled from Italy. She was wearing a dress chosen by Ma Brown and approved by Rosie. In ivory lace, it fitted her like a second skin—something she wouldn't be able to indulge in for very much longer, Callie thought, smoothing her hands over her slightly rounded stomach as Rosie arranged her veil.

The ceremony would be a simple affair in the local

church, followed by a small reception at the Browns'. Callie had wanted the people closest to her to know how much they meant to her, and that even when she became a princess and lived in the palace in Fabrizio, they would still be a big part of her life. As far as the world of royalty was concerned, Callista Smith would marry Prince Luca of Fabrizio at a grand ceremony in that country's cathedral in a couple of weeks' time.

'You look beautiful,' Pa Brown said as he took charge of the young woman he thought of as a daughter. 'I'll be a proud man giving you away—though I'm only lending you out,' he added, frowning. 'I want you to keep in touch, our Callie, and never lose sight of your roots.'

'I never will,' she promised, giving Pa Brown a warm kiss on the cheek as Rosie draped a warm, faux-fur cape around Callie's shoulders. 'And you must all come and visit me regularly in Fabrizio.'

'Only if I can watch the match while I'm there,' Pa fretted with a frown.

'I'm sure it can be arranged,' Callie soothed, knowing how much the Saturday football match meant to Pa Brown.

They stepped out of the house straight into a snowdrift. Callie howled with laughter as she pulled her foot free from the glistening snow. 'Not a great start,' she admitted, 'but nothing can spoil today.'

The day was so Christmassy, with crisp snow underfoot and robins chirruping in the trees. It was so evocative of all the optimism inside her. Luca had insisted she must travel to the local church by horse and carriage and she was glad of the hot-water bottle waiting for her beneath the blankets on the leather seat. Two beautiful dapple-grey ponies with white plumes attached to their headbands were waiting patiently to draw her to the church. There were silver bells on their bridles that jingled as they trotted along. People stopped to stare, and waved frantically with friendly approval when they recognised the local girl who was soon to become a princess.

She'd never change, Callie thought. She'd always be Callie from the docks and Callie from the lemon groves too. All that mattered was love and friendship, and the man waiting for her inside the church.

Luca's face was full of pride when he turned around as the grand old organ struck up the wedding march. She had never seen anyone more handsome in her life. In a plain dark suit, without any of his orders of office, or the royal sash with its ornate jewelled insignia, Luca couldn't have looked hotter if he'd tried. What more could she want than this? Callie thought as Pa Brown transferred her hand from his to Luca's.

'You may kiss the bride.'

'I may kiss the love of my life,' Luca whispered so that only Callie could hear, 'the only Princess I'll ever need.'

'The only Princess you're ever going to get,' she teased him softly before they kissed. She stared down at the band of diamonds that Luca had whispered could never replace the blue plastic ring from the cracker, but he hope she liked it. Liked it? She loved it. And there will be another ring, he'd told her. 'When we marry in Fabrizio, you will have a ring made in Fabrizian gold.'

'The blue plastic ring was enough for me,' she had assured him. 'What I feel for you is in my heart.'

As they stepped outside the ancient church hand in hand, a crystalline scene of snow and icicles greeted them. Luca turned to Callie beneath the stone archway decorated with white winter roses and floating silk ribbons, to draw her winter bridal cape more snugly around her shoulders. 'Warm enough?' he asked.

She gave him one of her looks. 'Is that a serious question?'

Pulling her close against his muscular body, Luca gave Callie the only answer *she* would ever need, in a kiss that was more than hot enough to keep out any chill.

Michel, Luca's elderly aide, had advised on all things formal to make sure that protocol was followed for Luca and Callie's second ceremony in Fabrizio, but the magic, as always, was provided by the Browns, who had a far more relaxed take on what went into making the perfect wedding day. Callie only knew that it took one man to make her day perfect and he had just snuck into her suite at the palace, when she was fresh from the shower and naked beneath her fluffy towelling robe.

'You shouldn't be here,' she whispered, glancing over her shoulder to check that the door was securely locked.

'Why?' Luca demanded, looping his arms around her waist. 'You're not in your wedding dress, are you?'

'Exactly,' Callie exclaimed, shivering with desire as he teased the sensitive skin just below her ear with the lightest of rasps with his stubble. He looked beyond amazing, wearing nothing more than a white T-shirt and banged-up jeans. 'You parked the shave?' she reprimanded in between hectic gasps of breath.

'I know how much you like a good rasping,' he murmured, transferring his attention to her lips, which he now brushed with the lightest of kisses.

And she did like a good rasping. Far too much. 'You have to stop,' she gasped out.

'Or you won't be accountable for your actions?'

'Something like that,' she agreed on a dry throat as Luca's experienced hands traced the outline of her breasts.

'Do you know how long it is since we made love?' he demanded.

'Too long?'

'That's right,' he confirmed. 'It must be an hour since. What's this?' he asked, frowning as he extracted the fine gold chain that disappeared between her breasts.

'My something blue?'

'The plastic ring,' he exclaimed, smiling. 'I hope you won't mind if I replace it with something more substantial today?'

Callie's heart beat nineteen to the dozen. What type of rings did princesses have to wear? Her knowledge of such things was confined to magazines and newspapers, and those rings always looked so clunky and as if they would ruin all her clothes. 'So long as it's nothing too flashy.'

Luca hummed and frowned. 'I'm afraid I can't promise that.'

And Callie couldn't fail to be impressed. In fact, she was speechless when she saw the obviously priceless diamond ring that Luca had so casually pulled out from the back pocket of his jeans. The large, blue-white oval stone glittered wildly in the light as if it contained countless hopes and dreams just waiting to be set free. It was the most stunning piece of jewellery she'd ever seen, apart from the diamond ring Luca had surprised her with in the church in England. 'I don't need this,' she felt it only fair to tell him.

'But I want you to have it,' Luca insisted. 'Our children will expect you to have beautiful gifts from their father, a man who loves you more than anything else in the world.' As he spoke Luca placed his hand on her not quite so flat belly, as if he were making a pledge to both Callie and their baby to love and protect them with his life. 'You'll have to wear the engagement ring on your right hand with the eternity ring from England,' he said as he brought her fingers to his lips. 'According to tradition in Fabrizio, your wedding band goes on this left hand, because it is said to contain the vein the ancient Romans believed connected directly to your heart. We still call it the *vena amoris*, the vein of love, and for that finger you will wear something very different.'

'Fabrizian gold,' she said, remembering as their stares connected.

'As strong and as direct as you are,' Luca confirmed in a way that made her heart go crazy. Thrusting his hand for a second time into the back pocket of his jeans, he brought out the simple band. 'No frills,' he said. 'Just plain, honest perfection like you. I hope you enjoy wearing it.'

'I love it,' Callie exclaimed. 'You couldn't have chosen anything better. This is the most precious ring I'll ever wear.'

'And the plastic ring?'

'I'll never forget it, but this,' she said as Luca drew her close, 'will be the ring of my heart.'

He dipped his head to kiss her just as Ma Brown called out from the other room, 'Are you ready to get dressed, Callie? We can't keep that carriage waiting.'

'Punctuality is the politeness of kings,' Luca teased.

'And my time-keeping's dreadful,' Callie fretted.

'Lucky for you I'd wait for ever if I had to.'

Luca had turned serious in a way that made her body ache for him, but with the briefest of kisses he was gone.

* * *

The second royal winter wedding was perfection, if a little grander than the first. The streets were packed with people eager to see their new Princess, and they weren't disappointed. There were food stalls and bands, and Christmas decorations still glittered everywhere. The theme was white and silver, which made everything seem filled with light. There might not be snow in Fabrizio at Christmastime, but beneath the flawless blue the gentle sunshine warmed the throngs of wedding guests as they cheered their new Princess dressed in yards of white silk chiffon that floated behind Callie as she walked along, and yet moulded her body so beautifully. The finest lace covered her arms and shoulders, while her train was almost twenty feet long. Anything shorter than that, and there wouldn't have been enough fabric for all the young Browns to take a handful of, Ma Brown had proclaimed ominously, but all the small bridesmaids and pageboys behaved perfectly on the day. There wasn't a spill or a smudge from any of them, and under the Browns' and Anita's prudent shepherding, Callie felt as if she were floating down the aisle of the glorious cathedral in Fabrizio before she finally halted at Luca's side.

'Who giveth this woman—'

'We do,' Pa Brown piped up, to be heartily shushed by his wife.

No one in the congregation noticed anything amiss, as they were all too busy watching the way Luca gazed at his bride. There was no doubt in anyone's mind that this was a royal love match, and one that would benefit all.

'Happy Christmas,' Luca murmured, and as Callie's gaze dropped instinctively to his mouth he added in a sexy whisper, 'Remind me. How long is it since we made love?'

'Too long,' Callie whispered back, her gaze locked on Luca's. 'Must be almost three hours now.'

'We may have to miss the reception,' he said with a mock frown.

'Almost certainly,' she agreed. And then the announcement rang out that His Serene Highness, Prince Luca of Fabrizio, could now kiss his bride. 'We may have to ask the congregation to leave,' Callie said dryly when Luca kissed her and she felt his very obvious impatience for herself.

Turning Callie, so that now they faced the packed body of the church together, Luca announced in a firm, strong voice, 'My Princess.' And as everyone applauded, he added, 'The love of my life.'

'There are no affairs of state for me to deal with for the next two weeks,' Luca told Callie as their horse-drawn carriage made its stately progress along the gracious main boulevard lined with cheering crowds. 'There's just my long-running affair with my wife to concentrate on now.'

'After our wedding feast,' she reminded him as she waved happily to the crowds.

'Did I mention we'll be delaying our arrival?'

'Really?' she asked, pretending to be shocked.

'I have commanded the carriage pause at our private entrance to the palace, so we have chance to…freshen up.'

'You think of everything,' Callie remarked dryly.

'I try to,' Luca confirmed.

If the staff at the palace was surprised by the sight of their Prince and Princess racing full tilt, hand in hand, across the grand hall, the bride with her tiara askew and her lengthy train bundled up beneath her arm, they of course made no comment. Minutes later, the happy couple had slammed their bedroom door behind them. Frantic seconds later Luca had opened every button down the back of Callie's beautiful gown. She barely had chance to remove her tiara before he swept her into his arms and carried her to the bed. The room was full of flowers and the scent was divine. 'And all for you,' he said.

'They're so beautiful,' Callie gasped when Luca gave her the briefest of chances to take everything in. 'Everyone's gone to so much trouble.'

'For you,' he declared as he took her deep, groaning with pleasure as she claimed him. 'For ever,' he whispered.

'Or even longer than that,' Callie agreed.

* * * * *

THE PRINCESS PREDICAMENT

LISA CHILDS

To Tara Gavin and Melissa Jeglinski, with deep appreciation for your professional expertise and your warm friendship!

Chapter One

Six months earlier...

"I'm going to kill him! Let me in there!"

Whit Howell had been hired as the king's bodyguard to protect him from political threats and criminals—not from his own daughter. But as furious as Princess Gabriella St. Pierre was at the moment, she posed the greatest threat Whit had encountered yet during the ten weeks he'd been on the job.

"Your royal highness," he addressed her as protocol required even though they were alone in the hallway outside the door to the king's wing of the palace. "Your father has retired for the night and will not be disturbed."

"You damn well better believe he's going to be disturbed," she said, her usually soft, sweet voice rising to a nearly hysterical shout. "He'll be lucky to be alive when I'm done with him!" She rushed toward the double mahogany doors, but Whit stepped in front of them.

She slammed into him, her breasts flattening against his chest. With her stiletto heels on, her forehead came to his chin. Her hair—a thick golden brown, was falling over the tiara on her head and into her face and rubbing against his throat.

With her face flushed and caramel-brown eyes flashing with temper, she had never been more beautiful. He doubted she would graciously accept that compliment, though, so he bit his tongue to hold it back. Of course he had noticed she was attractive before but in the kind of untouchable, one-dimensional way that a model in a magazine was attractive. She hadn't seemed real then.

She certainly hadn't acted like any woman he'd ever known. Not only was she beautiful but also sweet and gracious—even to the people her father considered servants. She had seemed more fairy-tale fantasy than reality.

She was real now. And quite touchable. She put her hands on his arms and tried to shove him aside, so she could get through the doors to her father's rooms.

While she was tall, she was slender—with not enough muscle to budge him. She let out a low growl of frustration and then fisted her hands and started pounding on his chest. "Get out of my way! Get out of my way!"

Damn. If she raised her voice any louder, she was likely to disturb the king. And Whit couldn't lose this security job. Assignments like this had been hard to come by the past three years. So he stepped closer to her, using his body to gently push her back from the door. She kept swinging even as she stumbled. So he caught her around the waist and lifted her— up high to swing her over his shoulder. Then he touched a button on the two-way radio in his ear.

"Aaron?"

"Put me down!" Princess Gabriella screamed, pounding on his back now.

He crossed the wide hall, moving farther away from the tall wood doors to the king's wing. Then he touched the button again to call his partner. Former partner. They were no longer in the security business together. They had actually been hired separately to protect the king.

It was Aaron's night off, which he'd had to postpone until after the ball that had been held earlier that evening. But usually Aaron would still be on the job; the man was always on the job.

"Aaron? Timmer?"

Maybe his partner answered but Whit couldn't hear him over the princess's shouts. Her yelling had drawn some of the other palace guards to the hall outside the king's private quarters. Whit gestured at one of the men he'd personally hired, a man with whom he'd served in Afghanistan, like he had with Aaron Timmer. He could trust him to guard King St. Pierre while he deposited the princess in her private rooms.

"Stop! Put me down!" she ordered, her tone nearly as imperious as her father's.

There was none of the sweetness and graciousness Whit had seen in her the past couple of months that he'd been guarding the king. While she had always talked to him as she did to all the *help,* with him she had seemed especially shy and nervous—nothing like the woman currently pounding on his back. The sweet woman had attracted him; the angry woman exasperated and excited him.

As he carried her past the other guard, she implored the man, "Stop him!"

Like he trusted the guard, the guard trusted Whit, a lot more than Aaron trusted him now. The guard let them pass.

"You creep!" she hurled insults as she pounded harder on his back. "You son of a bitch!" She added some even more inventive insults, using words he wouldn't have thought someone as privileged as she would even know. Then she ordered him, "Get your hands off me!"

She wriggled in his grasp, her breasts pushing against his back while her hip rubbed against his shoulder. She had curves in all the right places—curves that he wanted to touch…

But he shouldn't have been able to get his hands on her in the first place. Since the day, as an infant, she had been brought home to the palace, there had been threats to her safety. People had tried to kidnap her to ransom her for money or political influence from the king. To make sure that none of those abduction attempts were successful, she had been protected her entire life but never more so than now. Usually…

"Where the hell's *your* bodyguard?" he wondered aloud. Even though he hated the woman who protected the princess, he couldn't criticize how the former U.S. Marshal did her job. She went above and beyond to keep the young heiress safe; she had even had plastic surgery so that she looked exactly like Gabriella St. Pierre.

Could it be that they had switched places… It made more sense that the woman he'd slung over his shoulder was the bodyguard than the princess…because the bodyguard rarely let the princess out of her sight. Unless she had secured her in her rooms and was now masquerading as her.

For what purpose?

To attack the king?

After the announcement her father had made at the ball that evening, the princess had more reason—a damn good reason—to want to hurt the man who had so hurt and humiliated her. Whit had done the right thing to not let her into the monarch's wing of rooms. Because if she really was the princess, he could understand why she was so pissed, and he wouldn't have blamed her had she wanted to kill her own father. But he couldn't let her— or her bodyguard—complete the task.

Which woman was she?

It mattered to him. He didn't want his pulse racing like crazy over the bodyguard. He didn't want his hands tingling with the need to touch her wriggling body. He had never been attracted to the former Marshal, and he didn't want to be.

Charlotte Green had already cost him too much. Just like every other woman he'd ever had contact with, she hadn't given a damn about him. Maybe she didn't really give a damn about the princess, either.

No guard stood sentry at the entrance to the princess's suite. He pushed open the unlocked door and strode down the hall to her private rooms and found no security there either. If the princess had been left in her wing of the palace, Charlotte Green had left her unprotected. No matter how much he despised her, he doubted she would have done that. But she wouldn't have let the royal heiress go running off on her own, either.

Sure, they were *inside* the palace. But that didn't mean they were safe, especially with guests from the ball spending the night in the palace. And even if they weren't, sometimes the greatest threats to one's life were the people closest to them. The princess had learned that tonight.

She must have also learned that yelling and struggling wasn't going to compel him to release her because she'd fallen silent and still. Her body was tense against his. And warm and soft…

And entirely distracting.

He needed to deposit her in her rooms and get the hell back to his post. Using his free hand, the one not holding tight to the back of her toned thigh, he opened the door to her sitting room. Painted a bright yellow, the room was sunny and completely different from her father's darkly paneled rooms. After going inside, he released her, and she moved, sliding down his body—every curve pressing against him. He bit back a groan as desire overwhelmed him, and he was the tense one now.

As her feet touched the floor, she stepped back, and then stumbled and fell against him. He caught her shoulders in his hands to steady her, and he realized she'd lost a shoe somewhere along the route to her room. She stood before him in only one stiletto slip-on sandal. She really was a fairy-tale princess; she was freaking Cinderella.

No, that wasn't right.

His mom had taken off early in his childhood, leaving him with a father who'd had little time to read him fairy tales. But Whit had picked up enough from movies and TV shows based on them to realize he'd gotten it wrong. If she was Cinderella, then she would be the bodyguard and not Gabriella.

"Who are you?" he asked.

Beneath the hair falling across her brow, lines of confusion furrowed. Then she blinked brown eyes wide with innocence. Real or feigned?

"You know who I am," she haughtily replied.

"No one can really know who you are," he said, "but you."

She shivered, as if his words had touched a chord deep inside her. As if he'd touched her. And he realized that he held her yet and that his fingers almost absently stroked over the silky skin of her bare shoulders. Her gown was strapless and a rich gold hue only a couple shades darker than her honey-toned skin. She was so damn beautiful.

But beauty had never affected Whit before. He wasn't like his partner—his former partner. Aaron Timmer fell quickly and easily for every pretty face. Not Whit, though. He was a professional.

So he forced himself to let go of her shoulders and step back. And that was when he heard it. Her little shuddery gasp for breath as if she'd been holding hers, too—as if she'd been waiting for him to do something. Else. Like move closer and lower his head to hers…

But besides her gasp, he heard another noise—a low thud like someone bumping into something in the dark. Despite the brightly painted walls, the sitting room was dimly lit, but small enough that Whit would have noticed someone lurking in the shadows. However, a door off the room stood ajar, darkness from her bedroom spilling out with another soft thud.

Someone was already waiting to take Princess Gabriella to bed. But she gasped again—this time with fear—and he realized she'd heard the noise, too. And she wasn't expecting anyone to be inside her bedroom.

"Stay here," he whispered and reached beneath his tuxedo jacket to pull his gun from his holster. Armed, he headed toward her bedroom.

"Be careful," she whispered back, her sweet voice trembling with concern. For him?

Her words touched something inside Whit—something that he'd closed off years ago—the part of him that had yearned to have someone—anyone—give a damn about him. Of course she didn't really care, but those words...

Distracted him enough that when he stepped inside the bedroom, the intruder got the drop on him. Before his eyes could even adjust to the darkness, something struck his head—knocking him down and knocking him out—leaving the princess at the mercy of the intruder...

BLOOD SEEPED INTO his blond hair, staining the short silky strands. Gabriella pressed her fingers to the wound, gauging the depth of it.

Would it need stitches? Had he been hit hard enough for the injury to be fatal?

She moved her fingers to his throat. He had already loosened the collar of his silk shirt and undone his bow tie, which dangled along the pleats of the shirt. So she had easy access to the warm skin of his neck. At first his pulse was faint, but then it suddenly quickened.

She glanced at his face and found his dark eyes open and staring up into hers. How could he be so blond but have such dark, fathomless eyes? The man was a paradox—a mystery that had fascinated her since the day he'd walked into the palace to guard her father.

She had been able to think of little else but him. No matter where she'd been—fashion show or gallery opening or movie premiere—her mind had been on him—which had probably made her even more distracted and nervous every time the press had interviewed her.

She had been looking forward to tonight—to seeing him in a tuxedo. To blend in, all the security team had worn black tie. But she had seen only Whit, looking like every young woman's fantasy of Prince Charming. Then her father had made his horrible pronouncement and shattered all Gabriella's illusions of a fairy-tale happily-ever-after…

"You're alive?" she asked.

While he'd opened his eyes, he had yet to move—to even draw a breath. Of course he wasn't dead, but he must have been stunned. In shock? Concussed?

Finally he nodded, then winced and repeated her ridiculous question, "You're alive?"

Her lips twitched into a smile. "I'm fine."

"The intruder didn't take you," he said, as if surprised that she wasn't gone.

"No." She shuddered at the thought of being abducted, as she had nearly been so many times before…until the former U.S. Marshal had become her bodyguard a few years ago. As well as protecting her, the ex-Marshal had taught her how to defend herself. Fortunately Gabriella hadn't been put in that position tonight. But she wished she could have defended Whit and saved him from the blow he'd taken to the head.

"Who hit me?" he asked, "Charlotte?"

She chuckled at the thought of her bodyguard knocking him out in the dark. Charlotte would not have been so cowardly, as cowardly as Gabby had been when she'd allowed her father's pronouncement at the ball to stand instead of immediately speaking up. And when she had finally gathered her courage and her anger, this man had stopped her from talking to the king. She should have been angry with him. But she only felt relief when he had finally opened his eyes. The three minutes he'd been unconscious had seemed like a lifetime to Gabby.

"Charlotte?" he repeated but his tone was different now, as if he suspected that *she* might actually be her bodyguard.

That was nearly as ridiculous as Charlotte striking him. "It all happened so fast that I have no idea who it could be. After hitting you, he ran out the door. All I saw was that he was dressed in black pants and a black sweatshirt with the hood pulled tight around his face."

"It was a man?"

She nodded. "Tall and thin with no curves. But I suppose it could have been a woman." At all those fashion shows and movie premieres, she had met many tall, thin women. "But not Charlotte."

"No," he agreed, but tentatively, as if he debated taking her word for it.

"You don't trust me?" she asked, wondering if she should be offended or amused. Certainly it wasn't good to be thought a liar but that wasn't the issue for her.

Most people didn't consider her clever enough to be able to pull off any deception.

The public believed she was an empty-headed heiress. They weren't being cruel or unfair. Because she was naturally shy and introverted, nerves got the better of her during interviews, and she usually babbled incoherently—earning the nickname of Princess Gabby.

"I'm not even sure who you are," he admitted, his dark eyes narrowing with suspicion as he studied her face.

He really believed she might be Charlotte Green. Again she was flattered instead of offended. Most people might mistake the former U.S. Marshal for her—from a distance. Along with already having the same build and coloring, Charlotte had had plastic surgery so their faces looked alike, too. Except Charlotte had a beauty and wisdom that came with being six years older and so much more worldly than Gabriella. Her bodyguard was tough and independent while Gabby was anything but that.

Charlotte would not have been passed off tonight from one fiancé to another—publicly humiliated during the ball. What was worse was that the man who had traded Gabriella to the highest bidder like a brood mare at auction was her own father.

She expelled a ragged breath of frustration. "I wish I was Charlotte," she admitted. "Then I wouldn't be engaged to marry a stranger. I wouldn't have had people trying to kidnap me since I was a baby just so they could get to my father. No one would even care who I am."

"I would care," he said, with a charm of which she had not thought him capable.

She had thought him tough and cynical and dangerous and ridiculously handsome and sexy. She'd thought entirely too much of Whitaker Howell since he had stepped inside the palace ten weeks ago. She had also talked about him, asking the men he'd served with in Afghanistan to tell her about him. And the more she'd learned, the more fascinated and attracted she had become.

Now he was lying on her bedroom floor with her straddling his hard, muscular body while she leaned over him. Her fingers were still in his hair. No longer probing the wound, she was just stroking the silky blond strands.

He must have become aware of their positions, too, because his hands clasped her waist—probably to lift her off. But before he could, she leaned closer. She had to know— and since he would probably never be this vulnerable again, she had only this chance—so she pressed her mouth to his to see how he would taste.

Like strong coffee and dark chocolate—like everything too rich and not good for her. Instead of pushing her away, his hands clutched her waist and pulled her closer. And he kissed her back.

No. He took over the kiss and devoured her—with his lips and his teeth and his tongue. He left her gasping for breath and begging for more. And instead of ignoring her, as he had earlier, he gave her more. He kissed her deeply, making love to her mouth—making her want him to make love to her body. She leaned closer, pushing her breasts against his chest.

He reached for the zipper at the back of her dress, his fingers fumbling with the tab before freezing on it. "We can't do this," he said, as if trying to convince himself. "I—I need to report the intruder—need to lock down the palace and grounds..."

She would have been offended that he thought of work instead of her...if she couldn't feel exactly how much he wanted her.

"We have guests staying overnight," she reminded him. "You can't disrupt the whole palace looking for what was probably a member of the paparazzi who passed himself off as either a guest or part of the catering staff. He was probably snooping in my rooms or waiting with a camera to get some compromising photos." And if he hadn't given himself away, he might have gotten some good shots—of her and Whit.

"I still need to report the breach of security," he insisted. "And I need to make sure you have protection. Where the hell is Charlotte?"

"I gave her the night off," she said.

"And she took it?" he asked, his brow furrowing with skepticism of her claim.

"She thought I'd be safe." Because Gabriella had sworn she wouldn't leave her rooms.

His dark eyes flashed with anger. "She thought wrong."

"I will be safe," she said softly, her voice quavering with nerves that had her body trembling, as well. "If you stay with me…" She drew in a deep breath and gathered all of her courage to add, "…all night…"

SHE AWOKE ALONE in the morning—her bed empty but for the note she found crumpled under her pillow. She had obviously slept on it.

Her fingers trembled as she unfolded the paper and silently read the ominous warning: "You will die before you will ever marry the prince…"

Whitaker Howell had not left her that note. So the intruder must have. He or she hadn't been just an opportunistic guest looking for a souvenir or a member of the paparazzi looking for a story. The intruder had broken into her rooms with the intent of leaving the threat. Or of carrying it out…with Gabriella's death.

Chapter Two

Present day...

For six months Princess Gabriella St. Pierre had been missing—vanished from a hotel suite in Paris. A hotel suite that had become a gruesome crime scene where someone had died. For six months Whit Howell had been convinced *she* had been that someone. He had believed she was dead.

Just recently he'd learned that Gabby was alive and in hiding. Her life had been threatened. And instead of coming to him for protection, she had left the country. She hadn't trusted him or anyone else. But then maybe that had been the smart thing to do. Her doppelgänger bodyguard had been kidnapped in her place and held hostage for the past six months.

If Gabriella hadn't gone into hiding...

He shuddered at the thought of what might

have happened to her. But then he shuddered at the thought of what still could have happened to her since no one had heard from her for six months.

Could someone have fulfilled the prophesy of that note? The man, who had accidentally abducted the bodyguard in Gabby's place, claimed that he hadn't written it. Given all the other crimes to which he'd confessed, it made no sense that he would deny writing a note. But if not him, then who? And had that person followed through on his threat?

Whit had to find Gabby. Now. He had to make sure she was safe. He knew where she'd gone after leaving the palace. Her destination was on the piece of paper he clutched so tightly in his hand that it had grown damp and fragile.

"Sir, are you all right?" a stewardess asked as she paused in the aisle and leaned over his seat.

He nodded, dismissing her concern.

She leaned closer and adjusted the air vent over him. "You look awfully warm, sir. We'll be landing soon, but it may take a while to get to the gate."

"I'll be fine," he assured her. Because he would be closer to Gabriella—or at least closer to where she had been last. But after the woman moved down the aisle, he reached up to brush away the sweat beading on his forehead. And he grimaced over moving his injured shoulder.

He had been shot—a through-and-through, so the bullet had damaged no arteries or muscles. But now he was beginning to worry that the wound could be getting infected. And where he was going, there was unlikely to be any medical assistance.

He didn't care about his own discomfort though. He cared only about finding Gabriella and making damn sure she was alive and safe. And if he found her, he had to be strong and healthy enough to keep her safe.

Because it was probable that whoever had threatened her was still out there. Like everyone else, her stalker had probably thought her dead these past six months. But once they learned she was alive, they would be more determined than ever to carry out their threat.

"She's alive."

Gabriella St. Pierre expelled a breath of relief at the news Lydia Green shared the moment the older woman had burst through the door. For six months Gabby had been holding her breath, waiting for a message from her bodyguard. Actually she'd been waiting for the woman to come for her.

Especially in the beginning. She hadn't realized how pampered her life had been until she'd stayed here. The floor beneath her feet was dirt, the roof over her head thatch. A bird that had made it through her screenless window fluttered in a corner of the one room that had been her home for the past six months.

Once she had stopped waiting for Charlotte to come for her, she had gotten used to the primitive conditions. She had actually been happy here and relaxed in a way that she had never been at the palace. And it wasn't just because she had been out of the public eye but because she had been out from under her father's watchful eye, as well.

And beyond his control.

She had also been something she had never been before: useful. For the past six months she had been teaching children at the orphanage/school Lydia Green had built in a third-world country so remote and poor that no other charity or government had yet acknowledged it. But she had learned far more than she'd taught. She realized now that there was much more to being charitable than writing checks.

Lydia Green had given her life and her youth to helping those less fortunate. She'd grown up as a missionary, like her parents, traveling from third-world country to third-world country. After her parents had died, she could have chosen another life. She could have married and had a family. But Lydia had put aside whatever wants and needs she might have had and focused instead on others. She had become a missionary, too, and the only family she had left was a niece.

Charlotte. The women looked eerily similar. Lydia had the same caramel-brown eyes, but her hair was white rather than brown even though she was still in her fifties.

"Charlotte called?" The first day Gabriella had arrived, somewhere between the airport and the orphanage, she had lost the untraceable cell phone her bodyguard had given her. But it probably wouldn't have come in as far into the jungle as the orphanage was.

Lydia expelled her own breath of relief over finally hearing from her niece and nodded. "The connection was very bad, so I couldn't understand much of what Charlotte was saying…"

The orphanage landline wasn't much better than the cell phone. There was rarely a dial tone—the lines either damaged by falling trees, the oppressive humidity or rebel fighting.

"Did she tell you where she's been and why she hasn't contacted us?" Not knowing had driven Gabriella nearly crazy so that she had begun to suspect the worst—that Charlotte was dead. Or almost as bad, that Charlotte had betrayed her.

Lydia closed her eyes, as if trying to remember or perhaps to forget, and her brow furrowed. "I—I think she said she'd been kidnapped…"

"Kidnapped?" Gabby gasped the word as fear clutched at her. That would explain why they hadn't heard from the former U.S. Marshal. "Where? When?"

"It happened in Paris."

Gabriella's breath caught with a gasp. "Paris?"

She was the one who was supposed to have gone to Paris; that was what anyone who'd seen them would have believed. Whoever had abducted Charlotte had really meant to kidnap Gabby. She shuddered in reaction and in remembrance of all the kidnapping attempts she had escaped during her twenty-four years of life. If not for the bodyguards her father had hired to protect her, she probably would not have survived her childhood.

"Is she all right?"

"Yes, yes," Lydia replied anxiously, "and she said that the kidnapper has been caught."

"So I can leave…" Gabby should have been

relieved; months ago she would have been ecstatic. But since then she had learned so much about herself. So much she had yet to deal with…

"She said for you to wait."

"She's coming here?" Nerves fluttered in Gabby's stomach. She was relieved Charlotte was all right, but she wasn't ready to see her.

Or anyone else…

"She's sending someone to get you," Lydia replied, with obvious disappointment that she would not see her niece.

Gabriella was to be picked up and delivered like a package—not a person. Until she'd met Lydia and the children at the orphanage, no one had ever treated Gabriella like a person. Pride stung, she shook her head and said, "That won't be necessary."

"You're going to stay?" Lydia asked hopefully.

"I would love to," she answered honestly. Here she was needed not for *what* she was but *who* she was. She loved teaching the children. "But I can't…"

She had no idea who was coming for her, but she wasn't going to wait around to find out. Given her luck, it would probably be Whit, and he was the very last person she wanted to see. Now. And maybe ever again…

Lydia nodded, but that disappointment was back on her face, tugging her lips into a slight frown. "I understand that you have a life you need to get back to…"

Her existence in St. Pierre had never been her life; it had never been *her* choice. But that was only part of the reason she didn't plan on going back.

"But I would love to have you here," Lydia said, her voice trembling slightly, "with me…"

They had only begun to get to know each other. If they had met sooner, Gabriella's life would have been so different—so much better.

Tears burning her eyes, Gabriella moved across the small room to embrace the older woman. "Thank you…"

Lydia Green was the first person in her life who had ever been completely honest with her.

"Thank you," she said, clutching Gabriella close. "You are amazing with the kids. They all love you so much." She eased back and reached between them to touch Gabby's protruding belly. "You're going to make a wonderful mother."

The baby fluttered inside Gabriella, as if in agreement or maybe argument with the older woman's words. Was she going to make a wonderful mother? She hadn't had an example of one to emulate. Her throat choked now with tears, she could barely murmur another, "Thank you…"

She didn't want to leave, but she couldn't stay. "Can I get a ride to the bus stop in town?"

She needed a Jeep to take her to a bus and the bus to take her to a plane. It wasn't a fast trip to get anywhere in this country while the person coming for her would probably be using the royal jet and private ground transportation. She needed to move quickly.

"You really should wait for whoever Charlotte is sending for you," Lydia gently insisted. "This is a dangerous country."

Sadness clutched at her and she nodded. That was why they had so many orphans living in the dorms. The compound consisted of classroom huts and living quarters. If disease hadn't taken their parents, violence had.

"I've been safe here," she reminded Lydia.

"At the school," the woman agreed, "because the people here respect and appreciate that we're helping the children. But once you leave here…"

"I'll be fine," she assured her although she wasn't entirely certain she believed that herself.

"You have a bodyguard for a reason. Because of who you are, you're always in danger." Lydia was too busy and the country too remote for her to be up on current affairs, so Charlotte must have told her all about Gabby's life.

Gabriella glanced down at her swollen belly. Her bare feet peeped out beneath it, her toes stained with dirt from the floor. "No one will recognize me."

Not if they saw her now. She bore only a faint resemblance to the pampered princess who'd walked runways and red carpets.

But she wasn't only physically different.

She didn't need anyone to protect her anymore—especially since she really couldn't trust anyone but herself. *She* had to protect her life and the life she was carrying inside her.

A WALL OF HEAT hit Whit when he stepped from the airport. Calling the cement block building with the metal roof an airport seemed a gross exaggeration, though. He stood on the dirt road outside, choking on the dust and the exhaust fumes from the passing vehicles. Cars. Jeeps. Motorbikes. A bus pulled up near the building, and people disembarked.

A pregnant woman caught his attention. She wore a floppy straw hat and big sunglasses, looking more Hollywood than third world. But her jeans were dirt-stained as was the worn blouse she wore with the buttons stretched taut over her swollen belly.

It couldn't be Gabby.

Hell, she was *pregnant;* it couldn't be Gabby...

His cell vibrated in his pocket, drawing his attention from the woman. He grabbed it up with a gruff, "Howell here."

"Are you there?" Charlotte Green asked, her voice cracking with anxiety. "Have you found her yet?"

"The plane just landed," he replied.

He had only glanced at his phone when he'd turned it back on, but he suspected all the calls he'd missed and the voice mails he had yet to retrieve had been from the princess's very worried bodyguard.

"But Whit—"

"Give me a few minutes," he told her. "You're not even sure she's still here."

Wherever the hell *here* was; from his years as a U.S. Marine, he was well traveled but Whit had never even heard of this country before. Calling it a country was like calling that primitive building an airport—a gross exaggeration.

"I finally reached my aunt Lydia this morning," Charlotte said. "She confirmed that Gabby is still at the orphanage."

He exhaled a breath of relief. She was alive. And not lost. "That's good."

Nobody had kidnapped the princess as they had her bodyguard. Gabby was right where Charlotte had sent her six months ago. Why hadn't she answered the woman's previous calls then?

"She's all right?"

"No." Static crackled in the line, distorting whatever else Charlotte might have said.

He stopped walking, so that he didn't lose the call entirely. Reception was probably best closest to the airport, so he took a few steps back into the throng of people.

"What's wrong?" Whit asked, the anxiety all his now. "Has she been hurt?"

"Yeah…"

And he realized it wasn't static in the line but Charlotte Green's voice breaking with sobs. He had never heard the tough former U.S. Marshal cry before—not even when armed gunmen had been trying to kill them all. His heart slammed into his ribs as panic rushed through him. "Oh, my God…"

It had to be bad.

Not Gabriella…

She was the sweetest, most innocent person he'd ever met. Or at least she had been…

"Charlotte!" He needed her to pull it together and tell him what the hell had happened to the princess. In a country as primitive as this, it could have been anything. Disease. A rebel forces attack. "What's wrong?"

"It's my fault," she murmured, sobs choking her voice. "It's all my fault. I should have told her. I should have prepared her…"

"What?" he fired the question at her. "What should you have told her? What should you have prepared her for?"

The phone clanged and then a male voice spoke in his ear, "Whit, are you there?"

"Aaron?" He wasn't surprised that his fellow bodyguard was with Charlotte. Since Aaron Timmer had found her after her six-month disappearance, the man had pretty much refused to leave her side. "What's going on?"

"Don't worry about that," his fellow royal bodyguard advised. "It's just personal stuff between Charlotte and Princess Gabriella."

When the princess and her bodyguard had disappeared, Whit and Aaron had launched an extensive search to find them. Aaron had reached out for leads to their whereabouts. Whit had done the same, but he'd also dug deeply into their lives and discovered all their secrets, hoping that those revelations might lead him to them. So now he knew things about Princess Gabriella that she had yet to learn herself.

Or had she finally uncovered the truth? She must have and that was why Charlotte was so upset; she was probably full of guilt and regret. He recognized those emotions because he knew them too well himself.

"Damn it!" If that was the case, Gabby had to feel so betrayed. He added a few more curses.

"Whit," Aaron interrupted his tirade. "Just find Gabriella and bring her home to St. Pierre Island. We'll meet you there. The royal jet is about to land at the palace."

"The king is still with you?" The monarch was really their responsibility, one that both men had shirked in favor of protecting the women instead. King Rafael St. Pierre hadn't seemed to mind.

"He's secure. Everything's fine here," Aaron assured Whit. "What about there?"

"I just got off the plane." The third one. It had taken three planes—with not a single one of them as luxurious as the royal jet—over the course of three days to bring him to this remote corner of the world. And it would take a bus and a Jeep to get him to the orphanage deep in the jungle where the princess had been hiding for the past six months. "I haven't had a chance to locate Gabby and assess the situation."

Shots rang out. And he dropped low to the ground while he assessed this new situation. Who the hell was firing? And at whom? Him?

Nobody knew he'd been heading here but Charlotte and Aaron. Not that long ago he would have been suspicious; he would have considered that they might have set him up for an ambush. But the three of them had been through too much together recently. And if they'd wanted him dead, they wouldn't have had to go to this much trouble to end his life. They could have just let him bleed out from the bullet wound to his shoulder.

But the shots weren't being fired at him. They weren't that close, nowhere near the dirt street where Whit stood yet. But the shots were loud because they echoed off metal. Someone was firing inside the airport. His hand shook as he lifted the cell to his ear again.

Aaron was shouting his name. "What the hell's going on? Are those shots?"

"I'm going to check it out," he said as he headed toward the building—shoving through the wave of people running from it.

"You need to get Gabriella," Aaron shouted but still Whit could barely hear him over the shrieks and screams of the fleeing people.

Whit flashed back to that woman getting off the bus and heading inside the airport. "Gabby! Is Gabby pregnant?"

"Yes—according to Charlotte's aunt."

It was hardly something the woman would have lied about. But how? But when? And whom?

"She's probably six months along," Aaron added.

Realization dawned on Whit, overwhelming him with too many emotions to sort through let alone deal with.

Oh, God...

"That's Gabby…" Inside the airport where shots were being fired.

He shoved the phone in his pocket and reached for his gun before he remembered that he didn't have one on him. He hadn't been able to get one on the first plane he'd boarded in Michigan and hadn't had time to find one here.

Would he be able to save her? Or was he already too late?

Chapter Three

As disguises went, the hat and the glasses were weak. But it had fooled Whitaker Howell. He had barely glanced at her when she'd disembarked from the crowded bus. Of course he had seemed distracted, as he'd been reaching for his phone while moving quickly through the crowd milling from and to the airport.

She'd had to fight the urge to gawk at him. He had looked so infuriatingly handsome and sexy in a black T-shirt and jeans. But the sense of betrayal and resentment and anger overwhelmed her attraction for him. She didn't want to see Whit Howell much less be attracted to him any longer.

When she'd glimpsed him through the window, she'd thought about staying put in her seat. But since he was probably the one who'd been sent to retrieve her, he would have boarded the bus for the return trip and she would have been trapped.

When Charlotte had become her bodyguard three years ago, that was one of the first self-defense lessons she had taught Gabriella. Avoid confined places with limited exits. And given her girth, the exits on the bus had definitely been limited for her since it wasn't likely she'd been able to squeeze her belly out one of those tiny windows. So she had gotten off the bus and hurried toward the airport.

That was another of Charlotte's lessons. Stay in crowded, public places. So Gabriella had breathed a sigh of relief when she'd walked into the busy airport. She needed to buy a ticket for the first leg of the long journey ahead of her. She still had most of the cash Charlotte had given her to travel. She hadn't needed it at the orphanage. Even though she was using cash, she would still have to present identification. She fumbled inside her over-stuffed carry-on bag for the fake ID that Charlotte had provided along with the cash.

She couldn't even remember the name under which she'd traveled. Brigitte? Beverly? As she searched her bag for the wallet, she stumbled and collided with a body. A beefy hand closed around her arm—probably to steady her.

"I'm sorry," she apologized. She glanced up with a smile, but when she met the gaze of the man who'd grabbed her, her smile froze.

It wasn't Whit. He had probably already boarded the bus on its return trip to the orphanage. She didn't know this man, but from the look on his deeply tanned face, he knew her—or at least he knew of her. Most people thought her life a fairy tale; she had always considered it more a cartoon—and if that were the case, this man would have dollar signs instead of pupils in his eyes.

"Excuse me," she said and tried to pull free of the man's grasp.

But he held on to her so tightly that he pinched the muscles in her arm. "You will come with me," he told her, his voice thick with a heavy accent.

She was thousands of miles from home, but it had come to her. First Whit and now this man, who sounded as though he was either from St. Pierre Island or close to it, probably from one of the neighboring islands to which her father had promised her. Well, he'd promised her to their princes, but she would belong to the island, too. Like a possession—that was how her father treated her.

And it was how this man obviously intended to treat her. She glared at him, which, since she'd taken off her sunglasses in the dimly lit building, should have been intimidating. Charlotte hadn't had to teach her that glare—the one that made a person unapproachable. Gabriella had learned that glare at an early age— from her mother, or the woman she'd always thought was her mother.

The man, however, was not intimidated, or at least not intimidated enough to release her.

So she pulled harder, fighting his grip on her arm.

"Let me go!" she demanded, the imperious tone borrowed from her father this time. No one had ever dared refuse one of *his* commands, no matter how very much she had wanted to.

The first time he'd offered her as a fiancée she'd been too young and sheltered to understand that arranged marriages were archaic and humiliating. She'd also been friends with her first fiancé—she and Prince Linus had grown up together—spending all her holidays home from boarding school with him.

But the night of the ball her father had broken that engagement and promised her to another man, a prince who'd already been engaged to one of Gabriella's cousins. So her father had actually broken two engagements that night. He hadn't cared about the people— not that he'd ever considered her a person— he'd cared only about the politics, about using

her to link St. Pierre to another, more afflu-
ent country.

The man moved, tugging Gabriella along
with him. He pulled her through people—toward one of the wide open doors that led to the
airstrip in the back and the private planes. The
planes for which a person didn't need a ticket
or even a flight manifest in this country...

And if Gabriella got on that plane, she would
probably never get off again. Or at least she
would never be free again. Panic overwhelmed
her, pressing on her lungs so that she couldn't
draw a deep breath.

Don't panic.

Charlotte was undoubtedly still thousands
of miles away, but it was her voice in Gabriella's ear, speaking with authority and confidence. And hopefully, in this case, the truth
for once.

Gabriella exhaled a shaky breath and then
dragged in a deep one, filling and expanding
her lungs with air. It was stale and heavy with
the humidity and the odor of sweaty bodies
and jet fuel and cigarette smoke. There was
no airport security to help her. She had to take
care of herself.

Assess the situation.

Despite the lies, Charlotte had helped her.
Perhaps she had even considered her lies help-

ing Gabriella, protecting her. But Charlotte had known there would be times like this when she wouldn't be there, so she had taught Gabby how to protect herself.

The man wasn't much taller than she was. But he was heavier—much heavier even with the extra pounds she was carrying in her belly. Most of his extra weight was muscle. He had no neck but had a broad back and shoulders. And at the small of his back, there was a big bulge. He had definitely come in on a private plane and from some airport with about the same level of security as this one. None.

Choose the most effective mode of protection.

Charlotte had been trained to fight and shoot and had years of experience doing both. She had taught Gabby some simple but *effective* moves. But Gabriella's experience using those methods had been in simulated fights with Charlotte, whom she hadn't wanted to hurt. Then.

A sob caught in her lungs. She didn't want to hurt her now, either. Or avoid her like she'd initially thought. She wanted to see Charlotte and talk to her, give her a chance to explain her actions and her reason for keeping so many secrets. But Gabriella couldn't do that if she didn't get the chance—if she wound up held hostage or worse.

And by effective, I mean violent...

Charlotte Green had lived a violent life, and she possessed the scars to prove it. Both physical and emotional.

Gabby only had the emotional scars until now.

She wouldn't be able to use her simulated fight moves to fend off this muscular man— probably not even if she wasn't six months pregnant. But because she was six months pregnant, she couldn't risk the baby getting hurt.

So instead she reached for the gun and pulled it from beneath the man's sweat-damp- ened shirt. The weapon was heavier than she remembered. She hadn't held one in the past six months. But before that she'd held one several times. With both hands, using one to hold and balance the gun while she focused on flicking off the safety and pulling the trig- ger with the other.

But the man held one of her hands. When he felt her grab the gun, he jerked her around and reached for the gun. So she fumbled with it quickly, sliding the safety and squeezing the trigger.

Because she hadn't wanted to hit anyone

else in the crowded airport, she'd aimed the barrel up and fired the bullet into the metal ceiling. Birds, living in the rafters, flew into a frenzy. And so did the people as the bullet ricocheted back into the cement. She breathed a sigh of relief that it struck no one. But the cement chipped, kicking up pieces of it with dust.

The man jumped, as if he'd felt the whiz of the bullet near his foot. And he lurched back. When he did, he released her arm. Now she had two hands, which she used to steady the gun and aim the barrel—this time at the man's chest.

People screamed and ran toward the exits. They thought she was dangerous. The man didn't seem to share their sentiment because he stepped forward again, advancing on her.

"I will shoot!" she warned him.

He chuckled. Then, his voice full of condescension, said, "You are a princess. What do you know of shooting guns?"

"More than enough to kill you…" Like the simulated fights, she hadn't shot a weapon with the intent of hurting anyone…except for all the targets she had killed. She was good at head shots. Even better at the heart-kill shot.

Of course those targets hadn't been moving. And the man was—advancing on her with no regard for the weapon. He was mad, too, his eyes dark with rage. If he got his hands on her again, he wasn't just going to kidnap her. He was going to hurt her. And hurting her would hurt her unborn child.

So when he lunged toward her, she fired again.

ANOTHER SHOT RANG out. But it didn't echo off metal as the earlier shot had. It was muffled— as if it had struck something. Or someone...

Gabriella...

Whit held back the shout that burned his lungs. Yelling her name might only put her in danger—if she wasn't already—or increase the danger if she was. Maybe that hadn't been Gabby he'd glimpsed getting off the bus. Maybe she was still back at the orphanage. If she'd known someone was coming for her, wouldn't she have stayed and waited?

Or maybe she hadn't wanted to be found. If the shooting involved her, she had been found, but the wrong person had done the finding. The person who'd written that threatening note?

Whit shoved through the screaming people who were nearly stampeding in their haste to escape the building. There was no sign of the pregnant woman he'd glimpsed getting off the bus. She wasn't with the others running away.

And then he saw her and realized that she was the one they were all running from—she was the one with the gun. She gripped it in both hands.

As Whit neared her, he noticed the blood spattered on her face, and his heart slammed into his ribs with fear for her safety.

"Gabby," he spoke softly, so as to not startle her, but she still jumped and swung toward him with her body and with the barrel of her gun.

He barely glanced at it, focusing instead on her face—on her incredibly beautiful face but for those droplets of blood.

Anxiously he asked, "Are you hurt?"

A groan—low and pain-filled—cut through the clamor of running people. Gabriella's lips had parted, but she was not the one who uttered the sound. Whit lowered his gaze to the man who had dropped to his knees in front of Gabby. The burly man clutched his shoulder and blood oozed between his fingers.

Whit flinched, his own shoulder wound stinging in reaction. "What the hell's going on?"

Gabby took one hand from the gun to tug

down the brim of her hat—as if her weak disguise could fool him twice.

The man took advantage of her distraction and looser grip and reached for the gun. But he could only grab at it with one hand, as his other arm hung limply from his bleeding shoulder. He had the element of surprise though and snapped it free of her grasp.

She lunged back for it, her swollen belly on the same level as the barrel of the gun. But Whit moved faster than she did and stepped between them. Before the man could move his finger to the trigger of the gun, Whit slammed his fist into the wounded man's jaw. The guy's eyes rolled back into his head as his consciousness fled, and he fell back onto the cement floor of the airport, blood pooling beneath his gunshot wound.

Whit's shoulder ached from delivering the knock-out punch, and he growled a curse. But his pain was nothing in comparison to the fear overwhelming him. He'd only just learned where Gabby was and he'd nearly lost her again.

Maybe forever this time—if the man had managed to pull the trigger before Whit had knocked him out.

"What the hell were you thinking?" he shouted the question at Princess Gabriella.

His fear wasn't for himself but for her, and he hadn't felt an emotion that intense since the night before she disappeared. The night she'd begged him to stay with her. At first he'd thought she'd only wanted protection but then he'd realized that she'd wanted more.

She'd wanted him. But then the next morning she'd left him without a backward glance. So he'd probably just been her way of rebelling against her father's attempts to control her life. That was what that night had been about, but what about today?

"I—I was defending myself," she stammered in a strangely hoarse tone, as if she'd lost her voice or was trying to disguise it. She ducked down and reached for the gun that had dropped to the floor with the man.

But Whit beat her to the weapon, clutching it tightly in his fist. "No more shooting for you, Princess."

"I'm not a princess—"

"Save it," he said. "I damn well know who you are." He had no idea why she was denying her identity to him, though. But that wasn't his most pressing concern at the moment.

He leaned over to check the man for a pulse. He was alive, just unconscious. And that might not last long. "Who is this? And why did you shoot him?"

"He tried to kidnap me," she said, apparently willing to admit that much even though she wouldn't admit to who she was. "So I grabbed his gun."

Whit uttered a low whistle of appreciation. Even without a weapon, the guy would have been intimidating, yet she'd managed to disarm him, too. Maybe she wasn't Princess Gabriella. "How do you know he was going to kidnap you?"

"He tried to drag me out there," she gestured toward the big open doors in one of the metal walls, "to a plane."

As Whit glanced up to follow the direction she pointed, he noticed men—about four of them—rushing in from the airfield. They must have heard the shots, too. And they were armed.

"We have to get the hell out of here," he said.

Or the man's friends were liable to finish what he'd started—abducting Gabriella. And Whit with his shoulder wound and his borrowed gun were hardly going to be enough protection to save her.

She must have seen the men, too, because she was already turning and moving toward the street. Whit kept between her and the men.

But they saw the guy on the ground, and they saw the gun in Whit's hand.

And they began to fire.

"WHAT'S WRONG?" Charlotte asked anxiously. "What did Whit say?"

It wasn't so much what he'd said as what Aaron had overheard when he'd been on the phone with his friend. But Charlotte was already worried about Princess Gabriella; he didn't want to upset her any more.

She settled onto the airplane seat across from him. After her trip to the restroom, her eyes were dry and clear. She'd composed herself. But how much would it take for her to break again?

She'd already been through so much—kidnapped and held hostage for six months. And she was pregnant, too, with his baby.

Aaron's heart filled with pride and love. But fear still gripped him. He wasn't like Whit; he couldn't hide his emotions. Whit usually hid them so well that Aaron had often doubted the man was even capable of feeling. But he'd heard it in his voice—his fear for Princess Gabriella's safety—once he'd realized she was also where the shooting was.

"I know something's wrong," Charlotte persisted, but she pitched her voice low and glanced toward the back of the jet where the king had retired to his private room. "Tell me."

Aaron uttered a ragged sigh of resignation and admitted, "I heard shots…"

Charlotte's eyes widened. "Someone was shooting at Whit? He wouldn't have had time to get a gun yet. He won't be able to defend himself."

On more than one occasion, Aaron had seen Whit defend himself without a gun. But he hadn't been injured then. "Whit wasn't the one getting shot at."

She gasped. "Gabby? Was it Gabby?"

"I don't know," he said. But from the way Whit had reacted to the news that the princess was pregnant, too, he was pretty sure that it was her. "It's a dangerous country. It could have been rebel gunfire. It could have been anything…"

"Call him back!" She reached across the space between them and grabbed for the cell phone he'd shoved in his shirt pocket.

But Aaron caught her hand in his and entwined their fingers. "He won't answer," he told her. "He needs to focus on what's happening. And there's nothing we can do from here anyway."

That was why he hadn't wanted to tell her. She would want to help, and that wasn't possible from so many miles away. That feeling of helplessness overwhelmed Aaron, reminding him of the way he'd felt when Charlotte had been missing. He'd been convinced that she was out there, somewhere, but he hadn't been able to find her.

Now Whit needed help—Whit, who'd so often stepped in to save him—and Aaron was too far away to come to his aid.

Panic had tears welling in her eyes. "We can have the pilot change course—"

"We're almost to St. Pierre," Aaron pointed out. "We'll be landing soon."

Panic raised her voice a couple of octaves. "Once we drop off the king, we can leave again—"

"No," he said. "There's a doctor meeting us at the palace. You need to be checked out." Even after he'd rescued her from where she'd been held hostage, she'd been through a lot.

She shook her head, tumbling those long tresses of golden brown hair around her shoulders. "I need to protect Gabby."

He knew it wasn't just because she was the princess's bodyguard. But he had to remind her, "You need to take care of our baby first."

"We shouldn't have let Whit go alone," she said. "He's hurt too badly to protect her."

"We hadn't thought she would need protecting," Aaron reminded his fiancée.

"We did," Charlotte insisted, squeezing his fingers in her distress. "Six months ago someone left her that note threatening her life. That's why I sent her into hiding." And set herself up as a decoy for the princess. Her plan had worked. Too well.

"But nobody knows where she is." Or the paparazzi would have found her, no matter where she'd been. And there would have been photographs of Princess Gabriella on every magazine and news show, as there had always been.

"If those shots were being fired at her," Charlotte said, her beautiful face tense with fear, "then someone must have figured it out."

"How?" he asked. "Nobody but you and I and Whit know where she is."

She glanced to the back of the plane. "After I talked to my aunt and confirmed that Gabby was actually still with her at the orphanage, I told the king. I thought he had a right to know."

"Was he furious?" Aaron asked. Charlotte had done much more than just violating protocol as a royal bodyguard.

"He called St. Pierre and sent out another plane with a security team as Whit's backup."

She drew in a deep breath, as if trying to soothe herself. "They should be there within a few hours."

Aaron had heard the shots. He wasn't re-assured. In fact he was disheartened. He had wasted so many years being mad at Whit for something that hadn't been the man's fault. Had he repaired his friendship only to lose his friend?

If Princess Gabriella had been involved in the shooting, then Whit would have stepped in and done whatever was necessary to try to save her life—including giving up his own.

By the time the security team made it to where Whit and Gabriella were, they would probably be too late to help. With Whit injured and unarmed, it was probably already too late.

Chapter Four

Gabby pressed her palms and splayed her fingers across her belly, as if her hands alone could protect her baby from the bullets that began to fly around the airport—ricocheting off the metal roof and cement floor. She wanted to help Whit, but she had no weapon—nothing to save him. So she ran.

He returned fire as he hurried with her to the entrance. Keeping his body between her and the men, he used himself as a human shield. She would have been moved—if she hadn't known that it was bodyguard protocol to put themselves between their subject and any potential threat.

These men weren't potentially a threat; they were definitely a threat. To Whit more than to her. They probably wouldn't want to risk fatally injuring her—if they intended to kidnap her. It was hard to collect a ransom on a dead hostage. But if they'd been hired by whoever had left her that letter, then she was in as much danger as Whit was.

Maybe more.

She ran out of the building, but the street was as deserted now as the airport was. All the people had scattered and left. It was no safer out here than it had been in the deserted metal building.

But she had Whit. He'd stayed with her, his hand on her arm—urging her forward—away from the danger. But the danger followed them. Shots continued to ring out. Whit's gun clicked with the telltale sound of an empty magazine. He cursed.

Panic slammed through Gabby. The men chasing them were not about to run out of bullets—not with all the guns they had. Should she and Whit stop and lift their arms in surrender and hope they were not killed? Before she could ask Whit, he made the decision for them.

He lifted her off the ground and ran toward the street. Gabby didn't wriggle and try to fight free as she had six months ago. Instead of pounding on him, she clutched at him, so that he wouldn't drop her. He leaned and ducked down, as if dodging bullets.

Gabriella felt the air stir as the shots whizzed past. But with the way he was holding her—she wouldn't feel the bullets. They would have to pass through Whit's body before hitting hers. Again, it was bodyguard protocol, but she couldn't help being impressed, touched and horrified that he might get killed protecting her.

He ran into the street, narrowly avoiding a collision with a Jeep. The vehicle screeched to a halt, and Whit jerked open the passenger door and jumped inside. He deposited her in the passenger seat and forced his way into the driver's seat, pushing the driver out of the door.

The man scrambled to his feet and cursed at him. Then he ducked low and ran when the gunmen rushed up behind him, firing wildly at the vehicle. Whit slammed his foot on the gas, accelerating with such force that Gabriella's back pressed into the seat. She grabbed for the seat belt, but there wasn't one.

"Hang on tight," Whit advised.

She stretched out her arms and braced her hands on the dash, so that she wouldn't slam into it and hurt the baby. "Please, hurry," she pleaded. "Hurry—before they catch up to us."

"Where the hell am I going?" he asked. "Which way to the orphanage?"

Panic shot through her, shortening her breath as she thought of the danger. "No. No. We can't—we can't risk leading these men back to the orphanage." Those children had already lost so much to violence; she wouldn't let them get caught in the cross fire and lose their lives, too.

"I'll make sure we're not followed," Whit assured her. "But we have to hurry."

She hesitated. She'd been uncertain that she could trust anyone again, let alone him. But this wasn't her heart she was risking. It was so much more important than that. Whit was good at his job. Charlotte wouldn't have had the king hire him if he and Aaron hadn't been good bodyguards. So she gave him directions, leading him deeper and deeper into the jungle.

The Jeep bounced along the rutted trails, barely passing between the trees and the other foliage that threatened the paths. Gabby left one hand on the dash and reached for the roll bars over her head with the other, holding tight, so that she didn't risk an injury to her unborn child. She also kept turning around to check the back window and make certain that they had not been followed.

"No one's behind us," Whit assured her with a glance at the rearview mirror. "I've been watching."

She uttered a breath of relief that they wouldn't be leading danger back to the orphanage. At the speed that Whit was driving, they arrived in record time at the complex of huts and larger wood-and-thatch buildings that comprised the orphanage.

"This is it," she said with a surge of pride and happiness, which was the polar opposite from the way she'd felt when she'd first seen the complex six months ago. When she'd accepted that it was really where Charlotte had sent her, her heart had been heavy with dread and her pulse quick with panic. "We're here."

Whit stepped on the brake but didn't put the transmission into Park. Instead he peered through the dust-smeared windshield at the collection of crude outbuildings that made up the orphanage complex.

"This is it?" he echoed her words but his deep voice was full of skepticism.

"This is it," she confirmed. Now that she knew how hard it was to build in the jungle, she was even more impressed with what Lydia had achieved—and with what Gabriella had helped her manage during her stay. "Pull around the back of that hut. That's mine."

He followed her direction, parking the Jeep where she pointed. But before she could open her door, he reached across her. His hand splayed over her belly. He leaned close, so close that she felt his breath warm her face when he asked, "Is this mine?"

She shivered at his closeness and the intensity in his dark eyes. But she couldn't meet his gaze and lie to him. So she glanced down and noticed the blood that trickled down his arm. And she gasped in shock and horror. "You were shot!"

Perhaps it had only been his duty as a royal bodyguard, perhaps it had been his concern for the child he suspected might be his—but he'd taken a bullet that had been meant for her. And after being hit, he'd driven the Jeep over tough terrain to get them to safety.

"We need to get you inside," she said, fighting back her panic and concern. During her time at the orphanage, she'd learned to not let the children see her anxiety when they were hurt because it only upset and hurt them more. "And I'll have Lydia call for the doctor."

She opened the door and slipped out from under his hand. Then she hurried around to the driver's side and opened his door.

In addition to the blood trailing down his arm and turning the shoulder of his shirt an even darker black with wetness, he had sweat beading on his brow and upper lip. It was hot and humid in the jungle. But she'd heard the other guards talking about Whit's deployments to the Middle East—usually because she had asked them to tell her about the blond bodyguard—and they had always said how he had never perspired—not in the heat—not under pressure.

Was he hurt that bad?

She lifted his arm and slid beneath it, in order to help him from the driver's seat. But he didn't lean on her. With a short grunt of pain, he unfolded himself from beneath the wheel and stepped out of the Jeep to stand beside her. Close beside her, his tense body nearly touching hers. He leaned down, so that their gazes met and locked.

"I don't need a doctor," he said, dismissing her concern. "I need the truth."

She had given up denying her identity to him. She'd only been able to fool him once, but he obviously had no doubt about who she was now. So what did he mean? "The truth about what?"

His throat moved, rippling, as if he swallowed hard. And after clearing his throat, he asked, "Is that baby you're carrying mine?"

The baby shifted inside her, kicking at her belly, as if he, too, wanted to know the answer. She placed her palms over her stomach again, protectively. And because she felt so protective, she wasn't willing to share her baby with anyone.

Not even the baby's father.

Whit moved to lift his arms—probably to grab her and maybe shake the truth out of her—but the movement had his handsome face contorting with a grimace of pain. And a groan slipped from between his gritted teeth.

"Doctor first," she insisted. "Then we'll talk..."

Maybe by the time she had Lydia summon the doctor from the clinic in the more populated town close by, she would have figured out if she was going to tell Whit the truth.

WHIT GLANCED DOWN at the dirt floor beneath his feet and peered up at the thatched roof. The hut was primitive and small. There was only enough space for the double bed that stood in the middle of the room, enshrouded in a canopy of mosquito netting. He sat on the edge of that bed, so he had a clear view out the window and the doorway. To make sure no one had followed them from the airport.

There was no screen or glass in the window; it was just a hole to the jungle. There was no door either—just the threshold through which Gabby passed as she returned from wherever she'd gone to summon a doctor.

Her bodyguard had sent her here to keep her safe? Anger at Charlotte Green coursed through him. Any animal—two-legged or four-legged—from the jungle could have come inside and dragged her off never to be seen again. After he had learned all the secrets about Gabriella St. Pierre, he'd begun to question Charlotte's motives. Now he questioned them again.

"This is where you've been staying?" he asked, still shocked that the princess of St. Pierre would have spent one night in such primitive conditions let alone six months.

Gabby glanced around the tiny hut, and her lips curved into a wistful smile. "Yes..."

Not only had she stayed here but she seemed to have actually enjoyed it.

"I'm sorry I was gone so long," she said, "but Lydia was with a class. My class, actually." Her smile widened. "And the children were so thrilled that I came back..."

"You've been teaching here?"

"Yes, it's a school as well as an orphanage." She peered through that hole in the wall as if checking the jungle for threats. "Are you certain that no one followed us?"

"They would have been here already," he pointed out. Because they would have had to follow them directly from the airport in order to find this place. But he looked out the window, too. "You're safe."

"It's not me I'm worried about..." Her palms

slid over her belly, as if protecting or comforting the child within. "Those kids have already been through so much…"

When he had first met Princess St. Pierre, he had been impressed that someone as privileged and probably pampered as she must have been seemed to actually care about people. She had showed genuine interest in the lives of the palace staff. But here she had taken that interest to a whole other level, sacrificing her own comfort to care for others. She wasn't just a princess; she was a saint.

He had nothing to offer a princess; he had even less to offer a saint. All he could give Princess Gabriella St. Pierre was his protection. He stared at her belly. Unless he'd already given her something else…

He opened his mouth to ask again the question that had been burning in his mind since the minute he had realized the pregnant woman from the bus was Princess Gabriella. Was that baby his?

But before he could ask, she hurriedly said, "The doctor should be here soon. The clinic is just a mile away."

"I don't need a doctor."

"You've been shot," she said, moving her hands from her belly to his arm.

Blood still trickled slowly from the old

wound in his shoulder, over his biceps, down his forearm, over his wrist to drip off his fingertips onto the dirt floor.

"Yes, I was shot," he admitted with a wince of pain as he remembered the burn of the bullet ripping through his flesh. "But not today."

Her brow furrowed in confusion. "But you're bleeding…"

He shrugged and then winced again as pain radiated throughout his shoulder and his fingers tingled in reaction. "The wound must have reopened."

"When you carried me…"

Despite the men chasing them, firing shots at them, he had enjoyed carrying her. He had savored her slight weight in his arms, the heat of her body pressed against his, her hands clutching at him—holding him close. It had reminded him of that night—that night he had taken on the responsibility of guarding her.

But he hadn't really protected her…not if that child was his. He groaned.

"You are hurting," she said and commanded him, "Take off your shirt." But she didn't wait for him to obey her royal order. She lifted his T-shirt, her fingers grazing his abdomen and then his chest as she pulled the damp fabric over his head. Expelled in a gasp, her breath whispered across his skin.

Despite the oppressive heat, he nearly shivered in reaction to her touch. For six interminable, miserable months he'd thought she was dead. He had thought he would never see her again. That he would never touch her...

Was she real? She was so beautiful that he doubted it, as he had the first time he'd met her. She couldn't be real. Maybe he had been shot again, and this time he'd died and found an angel. He snorted in derision of his ridiculous thought. As if he would ever make it to heaven...

"This wound isn't very old," she observed, her teeth nibbling at her bottom lip with concern. "When were you shot?"

"Five or six days ago..." He couldn't remember exactly; everything had happened so quickly and then it had taken him so many days and flights to reach her. Maybe he should have waited for one of the royal jets to be available. But the king had needed to return to St. Pierre so he had taken his, and Whit hadn't wanted to wait for one to come in from St. Pierre. He hadn't wanted to wait another minute to see Gabriella and make sure she was safe. He had never imagined he'd find the Princess of St. Pierre like this...

Literally barefoot and pregnant.

"You should be in the hospital," she admonished him, as she rose up on tiptoe and inspected his wound.

"I saw a doctor already," he assured her. "I'm all stitched up. I'm fine." So they could talk. And maybe he would have insisted on it already if he wasn't worried about what she would tell him. Several years ago he had sworn he would never become a father. Or a husband. He'd had no intention of ever attempting a long-term relationship.

"You were shot!" she snapped at him, temper flashing in her eyes. "How did that happen?"

He shrugged and then cursed as the movement jostled his wounded shoulder, sending pain radiating down his arm until his fingers tingled.

Damn it...

He shouldn't be the one to tell her any of this. He was only supposed to retrieve her from her hiding spot and bring her back to the opulent palace on St. Pierre Island. Then her father and her bodyguard could explain everything...

The king and the others had probably landed on St. Pierre by now, so they could send the royal jet here. And Whit could bring her home where she belonged—with her family and her fiancé. He grabbed his cell phone from the front pocket of his jeans, but the screen was illuminated with a disheartening message. No service.

"That's not going to work," she informed him. "You're not stalling…"

"Stalling?" he scoffed. "I'm trying to call the palace."

Her breath caught, and her eyes widened with panic.

And he realized something. "You weren't in that airport to take a flight home."

"Home?" she repeated.

"The country of which you're the princess," he reminded her. "Where you grew up, where you live…"

"I grew up in a boarding school," she said. "And I've been living here."

At another boarding school/orphanage. Was that how she'd felt growing up? Like an orphan? Or was that feeling new because of what she might have learned about herself and all those secrets he'd uncovered?

"You know what I mean," he said. "You weren't heading back to St. Pierre." She'd been running again. And that was probably why she had worn the disguise and tried to deny her identity to him. She hadn't wanted him to bring her back to St. Pierre.

Instead of denying his claim, she changed

the subject. "Tell me why you were shot," she urged him. "I know Charlotte was kidnapped. The telephone connection was bad but Lydia understood that much."

And knowing that, she hadn't intended to go back to St. Pierre? Charlotte's concern that Gabby was upset with her might have been warranted.

"I know Charlotte's safe now," Gabriella said, as if she'd read his mind.

Or his expression, which would have been odd given that everyone—even those to whom he'd been closest—always claimed that he had a poker face, that they could never tell what he was thinking or feeling. Or if he even felt anything.

"The kidnapper was caught," she continued. "Did you get shot rescuing Charlotte from him?"

"Aaron rescued her," he said. Because his fellow royal bodyguard was madly in love with Charlotte. "I got shot when we went back to where she'd been held captive and tried to discover who was behind the kidnapping."

She drew in a quick, sharp breath. "But he was caught, right?"

He nodded, wishing again that he'd been part of the takedown. But he'd been knocked out cold from the painkillers the doctor who'd stitched up his gunshot wound had given him.

"Who was it?" she asked, her eyes wide with fear. She must have figured out that she—not Charlotte—had been the kidnapper's intended hostage.

He drew in a deep breath, hoping to distract her. He was only responsible for her safety, not a debriefing. "We need to get back to St. Pierre, and the others can explain everything."

Anger flashed in her eyes again, and she narrowed them. "If you're not going to tell me what I want to know, why should I tell you?"

Debriefing wasn't part of his job, but he hadn't made any promises to lie to her. Only to keep her safe. "The kidnapper was Prince Linus Demetrios."

She gasped at the name of her ex-fiancé. "No. Linus wouldn't have shot you. He would never hurt anyone. He's not capable…"

As sheltered as her life had been, she had no idea of what desperate men were capable. He hoped she never found out.

"He actually wasn't responsible for my gunshot wound," Whit admitted. "But he was responsible for Charlotte's kidnapping."

"He thought she was me?" she asked, her voice cracking with emotion and those dark eyes filling with guilt.

He didn't want to tell her, didn't want to make her feel worse. But he wouldn't lie to her, as everyone else had. So he just nodded.

"But why would Linus want to kidnap me?"

"He didn't want to lose you," Whit said. While he didn't appreciate the man's methods, he understood his reasoning.

"How was kidnapping me going to keep me?" she asked. "Did he intend to never let me go? To hold me captive forever?"

Whit sighed and figured he might as well explain the man's twisted plan as best he understood it. "He intended to get you pregnant, so he would have a claim to St. Pierre through an heir."

Hurt flashed across her face. "Of course he didn't really want me. He wanted my country." Her eyes widened with shock. "Did he…hurt Charlotte?"

"No. He was going to go about it artificially, but she was already pregnant—"

"Charlotte's pregnant, too?"

"Yes," he said. "With Aaron's baby."

Her pain and indignation forgotten, she smiled. "That's wonderful. And the baby is all right despite her being abducted?"

"Fine," he assured her. "She's fine. You can see for yourself soon enough."

She shook her head. "No…"

Was she refusing to return or was she denying something else entirely? "What do you mean?"

"That plan couldn't have been Linus's alone. He wasn't that clever or that conniving," she said. "But his father…"

"His father?" At the ball, he'd been warned to be especially vigilant of King Demetrios after Gabby's father made his announcement changing her engagement. The man had been enraged, but he hadn't spoken a word, just left in a blind fury.

"King Demetrios was determined to join his country to St. Pierre," she explained. "He could have masterminded the whole plot."

And if that plot had been thwarted, would he have stepped in again with the help of the man who tried grabbing Gabby in the airport? Maybe his son's arrest hadn't stopped his machinations.

"Is everything all right?" a woman's voice— as soft and sweet as Gabby's—asked.

Whit turned toward the doorway, toward the woman who, except for having white hair instead of golden brown, looked exactly like Gabby. He glanced from her to the princess and back—just in confirmation of what he already knew.

And seeing the look of understanding and

betrayal on Gabriella's face, she realized that he'd known. And anger chased away her guilt.

THE SENSE OF betrayal overwhelmed Gabriella. She'd told herself that Whit wouldn't have known—that he might not have been keeping secrets like everyone else in her life had. But when he'd looked from her to Lydia and back, he hadn't been surprised by their uncanny resemblance.

He'd known that they were related. He'd known that Charlotte Green was more than Gabby's bodyguard; she was her sister, too—an illegitimate princess.

But then so was Gabby. Just like the baby she carried was an illegitimate royal. She pressed her palms over her belly as the baby shifted inside her, kicking so hard that Gabby's stomach moved. Her sister was also pregnant, her baby probably conceived the same night that Gabby's had been.

Gabriella was happy for her, but she didn't want to be with her. Not yet. Six months hadn't been long enough for her to come to terms with how she had been betrayed—by her father. By her sister…

She hadn't thought of Charlotte as just her bodyguard; she'd considered her a friend. She'd been such a fool…

Whit had gone with Lydia back to her office, so that he could use the landline phone—so that he could call for the royal jet to take her back to St. Pierre. He'd saved her from a kidnapper only to kidnap her himself—to take her somewhere she didn't want to be.

She glanced out through that open window to where he'd parked the Jeep. The keys dangled from the ignition. During the past six months, she'd learned to drive a manual transmission.

She grabbed up her backpack from the bed and headed out to the Jeep. It would take a while for Whit to get his call through, and even longer for him and whoever he called to understand what each other was saying. By the time he finished with his call, she would be almost back to the airport.

Authorities must have been called. Someone would have reported the shooting and Whit stealing the Jeep. With the local police swarming the airport, nobody would try to kidnap her again. She would probably be safer there than here with Whit.

But her hand trembled with nerves as she lifted the handle and pulled open the door. She stepped up into the Jeep and slid beneath the wheel. But before she could swing the door shut behind herself, a strong hand jerked it from her grasp.

She didn't look to confirm her fear of being abducted. But that hand couldn't belong to Whit. He couldn't have returned to the hut yet.

Had the men actually followed them but stayed out of sight until they'd found her—alone and vulnerable?

Chapter Five

Whit had left her alone and vulnerable. Some damn bodyguard he was.

And when he had stepped inside her hut and found it empty, he'd felt every bit as sick as he had when he'd seen that trashed hotel suite in Paris. The walls had been riddled with bullets, the rug and hardwood floor saturated with blood. He'd thought her dead then.

He didn't think her dead now. He thought her pissed off. So he wasn't surprised to find her trying to take off in the Jeep.

But she was surprised to see him. Her lips parted in a gasp when he stopped the door from closing. Then he reached for her.

She slapped at his hand and then turned, kicking out with her leg. Her foot connected squarely with his kneecap, which caused his knee to buckle and nearly give beneath his weight.

"Damn it!" he cursed her. And Charlotte.

Her bodyguard had taught her some self-defense moves—in addition to teaching her how to shoot.

If the guy in the airport hadn't been trying to abduct her, Whit might have felt sorry for him taking the bullet in his shoulder. He knew too well how that felt. His throbbed with pain, but he ignored the discomfort as he tugged her from the vehicle. "Where the hell do you think you're going?"

"Whit?" She finally focused on him, her eyes widening with surprise. She stopped fighting and allowed him to guide her back inside the hut. "I thought you were calling St. Pierre."

St. Pierre. Not home.

Whit could relate. He'd never really had any place he had called home. After his mom had left, he and his dad had moved around a lot—his dad following the seasonal work of construction. Then Whit had joined the marines, going from base to base, deployment to deployment. And becoming a bodyguard had brought Whit into other people's homes without ever giving him a chance to make one of his own.

"Your aunt is making the call for me," he said. He had asked her to the moment he'd realized he shouldn't have left Gabby alone—because of her safety both physically and emotionally.

"You know who she is." Her usually sweet soft voice was sharp with resentment, and her eyes darkened with anger. "You were just like everyone else keeping secrets from me and using me."

Not only was she angry, she was in pain, too. He reached for her, trying to close his arms around her to offer comfort and assurance. "I didn't—"

But she jerked away from him, as if unable to bear his touch. But then she touched him, pressing her palms against his chest to push him back.

"How could you…" her voice cracked with emotion "…how could you be with me that night and not tell me what you knew?"

If anyone had used anyone that night, she had used him—probably to get back at her father for humiliating her at the ball. She must have figured having his daughter sleep with the hired help would shame the king.

"I didn't know, that night, that you and Charlotte were related," he said. But he should have noticed the resemblance sooner since he'd known the U.S. Marshal before her plastic surgery; the surgeon hadn't had to change much to make her Gabby's virtual twin.

She stared at him, her eyes still narrowed with skepticism. She probably thought he should have known, too.

He continued, "I didn't find out until after you'd disappeared." And remembering his anguish over that, his temperature rose and his blood pumped faster and harder in his veins. She'd let him and her father and her fiancé believe she was dead. She was hardly the saint he'd painted her to be. "How could you?"

"How could I what?" she asked, her brow furrowing with confusion.

Images of that hotel suite flashed through his mind again, bringing back all those feelings of fear and loss and...

"How could you just take off?" he asked. And leave everyone behind worried sick about her.

"I had a threat," she replied. "That person who hit you over the head that night left something under my pillow."

"A letter threatening your life," Whit said. If she hadn't distracted him from doing his job that evening, he would have been the one to find the note. Or if he'd followed his instincts and locked down the palace, he might have found the person who'd left the threat. "I know."

"Then you must know why I disappeared," she said, as if he were an idiot unable to grasp a simple concept. "I was in danger."

"Still are." His gut tightened with dread at the thought of that man pointing the gun at her and her unborn baby.

She shook her head. "The kidnapper was caught."

"Then who were those men at the airport?" he asked. "They sure as hell looked dangerous to me. Then again I didn't get a good look at them—I was too busy dodging the bullets they were firing at us."

"They probably thought we'd killed their friend," she said, making excuses for the men. "I shot him, and you knocked him out."

Whit nodded. "Yes, because he was threatening your life—just like the person who'd left the note. So you are definitely still in danger."

She shrugged, apparently unconcerned. "The man who grabbed me was an opportunist. He recognized me, saw that I was unprotected and tried to take advantage of the situation."

"Why was he here?" Why? Had he followed Whit right to her? And if he'd followed him from the place Charlotte Green had been held captive in Michigan, then he could have followed him to the orphanage.

"This country is a war zone full of rebels and mercenaries," Gabriella said.

"Then why the hell would your bodyguard send you here?" Maybe his doubts about Charlotte's motives had been right. Maybe she hadn't been trying to protect Princess Gabriella when she'd had plastic surgery to look just like her; maybe she had been trying to take her place as the legitimate heir to the country of St. Pierre and the fortune of the king.

But Charlotte had seemed to genuinely care about her assignment. About her *sister*. Then he realized the answer to his own question. "She couldn't tell you. The king had sworn her to secrecy with the threat of firing her if she told you the truth."

Gabriella gasped and then blinked furiously as tears pooled in her eyes. "My father wouldn't allow her to tell me?"

He had begun to appreciate Charlotte Green when she'd saved his life four or five days ago. But he really appreciated her now, for finding a way around the king's royal decree. "So she showed you. She had to know that once you met her aunt you would figure it out."

Charlotte had found a way around the king, but with the way she'd handled the situation,

Gabriella had been alone when she'd learned the truth. Even though Lydia was related to her, she was a stranger. There had been no one there for Gabby who could have held her, who could have comforted her.

His arms ached, not from the gunshot wound, but with the need to hold her, to have been the one who comforted her when her world had turned on its axis. And when everything that she had believed to be true had become a lie.

She expelled a shaky breath. "I figured out that my father, that *my family*," her voice cracked as emotion overwhelmed her, "has made a fool of me my entire life."

He reached for her again, and this time she didn't fight him off. Instead she wrapped her arms around his shoulders and clung to him. And his arms, which had ached to hold her, embraced her.

He ignored the twinge of pain in his shoulder. He ignored everything but how warm and soft she was and how perfect she felt.

Then, even as close as they were, there was a movement between them. The baby shifted in her stomach, kicking him as he or she kicked Gabby. While it was only a gentle movement, Whit felt the kick more violently than he had the princess's when she'd tried to fight him off at the Jeep.

This baby inside her could possibly be his. He could be a father?

GABBY FELT HIM tense, so she pulled back—embarrassed that she had clung to him. More embarrassed that she'd wanted to keep clinging to him. She had missed him, missed his touch—his strength. That night he'd guarded her he had made her feel safer than she'd ever felt. He'd made her feel *more* than she had ever felt.

Even now, her tumultuous emotions were all mixed up about him. She had to remind herself that, like that night, he was just doing his job. She meant nothing more to him than a paycheck from her father. She'd realized that when she'd woken alone the next morning and even more so when she'd left for Paris and he hadn't tried to stop her.

She'd felt like such a fool for throwing herself at a man who really hadn't wanted her. And then she had come here…and discovered exactly how big a fool she'd been.

"I could never figure out why my mother—the queen—hated me so much," she admitted.

The woman had never shown Gabby an ounce of affection or approval. On her deathbed, she had even refused to see Gabriella—not wanting hers to be the last face she ever saw. She had never been able to tolerate even looking at Gabby. That was why she'd sent her off to boarding schools when she'd been scarcely more than a toddler.

"But she wasn't really my mother," Gabriella said. She had actually been relieved to learn that; it had explained so much. It wasn't just that she was so unlovable her own mother hadn't been able to love her. The queen hadn't been her mother. But then her biological mother hadn't loved her either since she'd so easily given up her baby.

"The queen couldn't have any children," she continued. He undoubtedly already knew this, but she needed to say it aloud—needed to bring the secrets to light since she had been left in the dark too long. "So the king had his mistress give him another baby—one he intended to claim and make the queen pretend was hers. Unlike Charlotte, whom he never claimed."

"He has now," Whit said, as if it mattered.

The king had denied the paternity of his eldest for thirty years. And for twenty-four years he'd denied Gabby a relationship with her sister and her aunt. Gabriella would never be able to forgive him that—let alone hav-

ing traded her from one fiancé to another like
livestock. But, as things had turned out, he
had been right to break her engagement to
Prince Linus. Despite her friendship with him,
he hadn't been the man she'd thought he was.

Even if he hadn't masterminded the kidnapping plot, he had gone along with it. He'd put
Charlotte's life and the life of Gabby's future
niece or nephew at risk. But he hadn't done it
out of love. He'd done it so he could make a
claim on her country.

Nobody in her life had actually been the
person she'd thought he or she was.

As if on cue, Lydia Green stepped through
the doorway and entered the hut. Her gaze
went immediately to Gabby, as if surprised
to find her still there and emotionally intact.

Gabby was surprised, too. But then if Whit
hadn't caught her, she might have been half-
way to the airport by now.

"Did the call go through?" Whit asked.

Gabby held her breath, hoping that it hadn't.
She didn't want the royal jet being sent for
her—because she knew there was only one
place that jet would bring her. Back to St.
Pierre.

But Lydia nodded. Her gaze still on Gabby,
her eyes filled with regret. She knew this

wasn't what Gabriella wanted. She was the first one who actually cared what Gabby wanted.

"When are they going to send the royal jet?" Whit asked.

Her aunt still wouldn't look at him, continuing to stare at Gabby—much as she had the first time Gabriella had shown up at the orphanage. When her sister had signed off her parental rights to her youngest child, Lydia had thought she would never see the baby again. She had been elated when she'd realized who Gabriella really was.

Gabby had been devastated. Her biological mother had basically sold her. Unlike Lydia who'd followed her parents into missionary work, Bonita Green had resented never having material possessions. She'd spent her life conning people out of theirs until one of those marks had cut her life short.

Gabby would never have the chance to meet the woman—not that she ever would have wanted to. The queen and a former con artist were her only maternal examples. Gabby rubbed her belly, silently apologizing to her baby. It wasn't really a question of if she would screw up; it was more a question of how badly.

"Are they going to send it?" Whit anxiously prodded Lydia for a reply.

Her aunt continued to focus on Gabby.

"They already sent it—several hours ago actually. It should be here soon."

She obviously wondered if Gabby still wanted to go. Gabby had actually never intended to go back there. But she wasn't going to put Lydia in the awkward position that Charlotte had when she'd sent Gabby here. So she nodded her acceptance and forced a smile.

Her aunt released a soft sigh, but Gabby couldn't tell if it was of relief or disappointment.

"Before you leave for the airport, come say goodbye," Lydia said, "again."

"We will," Whit answered for them both.

Once her aunt had gone, Gabby admonished him, "You shouldn't have spoken for me."

His jaw tensed; perhaps he clenched his teeth in response to her imperious tone. But he didn't apologize or argue. He only headed for the doorway, as if she were going to blindly follow him.

"I'm not leaving," she explained. She had no intention of going where she couldn't trust anyone.

THE WOMAN INFURIATED him. From the moment he'd met her, he hadn't been able to figure her out. She was unlike anyone else he'd ever known. "If you're not leaving, why the hell did I just stop you from taking off in the Jeep?"

"I was trying to get away from you," she said dispassionately, as if her words weren't like a knife plunged in his back.

"Why?"

"Because I can't trust you," she said—again so matter-of-factly that it was obvious she had never considered trusting him at all.

But before he could defend himself, she continued, "I can't trust anyone on St. Pierre. That's why I'm not going back."

He understood her reasons. But he had a job to do—protect her. And after the close call at the airport, he wasn't convinced he could do that alone. Especially not here. He had a gun but no bullets, a shoulder throbbing with pain and a possible infection. "You can't stay here."

She let out a wistful sigh. "I know."

She'd been leaving earlier, and in a disguise, because everyone knew where she was now. He couldn't blame her for wanting to stay hidden.

"Where were you going?" he asked again.

She chuckled but without humor. "You really are just like everyone else," she mused. "You think I'm an idiot. But you shouldn't believe my image. It's a lie just like the rest of my life has been."

He'd already learned that for himself.

She lifted her chin with stubbornness and pride. "I'm not telling you where I'm going."

"Fine," he said. "I'll tell *you*. You're going with me." Back to St. Pierre? Could he bring her back there? To the family who'd lied to her? To the stranger she didn't want to marry?

His stomach churned with revulsion over the thought of her marrying anyone, of her lying in anyone else's bed, in anyone else's arms...

He forced away the repugnance and the twinges of jealousy. He had no right to either. Unless...

"We are leaving," he continued. "As soon as you tell me who the father of your baby is."

She flinched, as if he'd slapped her. Or insulted her. Because she'd often been photographed with movie stars and athletes, the media had painted her as a promiscuous princess. But he had intimately learned exactly how wrong they had been about her—as wrong as when they'd claimed she was ditzy.

She was neither.

"You've been working for my father too long," she said. From the disdain in her voice, the comment was obviously more complaint than compliment. "You're beginning to act just like him."

He winced now, definitely offended. Fortunately he had only been hired to protect the man, not to like him. King St. Pierre was tough to like. He was a difficult man. Period.

"Since I do work for your father, I need to carry out his orders," Whit replied, choosing to ignore the insult and focus on what was more important. "He wants you safely back in St. Pierre."

She snorted—a sound he would have thought her entirely too ladylike to make. Wouldn't some princess etiquette class in one of those fancy boarding schools she'd attended have polished the ability to snort right out of her?

She lifted her chin again, looking every bit the royal ruler despite her dirty jeans and blouse. "You're crazy to think I will be safe in St. Pierre."

He might have agreed with her if he hadn't just re-established his friendship with Aaron. He trusted that man with his life and hers. "You'll be safer there than you are here where you were just nearly abducted and shot at…"

She might have been right about it being a crime of opportunity. Maybe it was just a dangerous country with dangerous men. Maybe he hadn't been followed straight to her…

"That can happen in St. Pierre, too," she pointed out.

"I will make sure it doesn't happen," he said. "I will protect you." And with Aaron and Charlotte helping, he had a good possibility of actually keeping her safe.

"You will protect me from kidnappers and killers," she agreed—again with that damn calmness that infuriated him. "But will you protect me from my father?"

He couldn't say that her father wouldn't hurt her—because he already had. With his lies. With his manipulations...

Maybe she had learned some of her father's moves because she had veered the conversation away from what he wanted to know. She'd stalled him long enough. Maybe it was her form of payback for having had to wait twenty-four years before she'd learned the truth.

"Gabby," he began, about to urge her to stop the cycle of secrets now.

But the roar of a Jeep engine drew his attention to the doorway. If he'd missed a tail from the airport, he had lost his ability to do his job properly—then he couldn't protect the princess.

But there was only one man in the Jeep. Both the man and the vehicle must have been familiar to the kids because they came out of nowhere to greet him, dancing around his feet like puppies as he hopped out of the vehicle.

The kids hadn't greeted him and Gabby like that. Maybe they'd been in class. Or maybe they had been taught to never approach a strange vehicle or a strange man. This man wasn't unfamiliar to them.

Despite the black medical bag clutched in his hand, he looked too young to be a doctor.

Whit should have cancelled the house call Lydia had arranged; he didn't need a doctor. He needed the truth from the princess; he needed to know the paternity of her baby.

"Gabriella," the man said. With the familiarity of a frequent visitor, he stepped through the hut doorway without knocking and waiting for her permission to enter. "I am sorry I took so long getting away from the clinic."

She offered this man the smile she used to give Whit when they'd first met. It was a smile full of warmth and welcome and beauty. Whit wondered if she would ever smile that way at him again.

"Dominic, it's fine," she assured the doctor, her concern for Whit's injury obviously long forgotten. "I know how busy you are."

The guy answered her smile with a wide grin. Not only was he young but good-looking, too, since women seemed to like that whole tall and dark thing. Or at least that was what he'd witnessed with the women who'd gone for Aaron Timmer over the years. As easily as his partner had fallen for women, they had responded to him, too.

This guy also had charm. His grin widened as he took Gabby's hand in his with a familiarity and possessiveness that had Whit gritting his teeth. "If you had been the patient, I would have dropped everything…"

For her. Not for Whit. The doctor had clearly fallen for the princess.

Maybe Whit had been wrong to assume the child she carried was his. Maybe her baby belonged to this man.

Whit should have been relieved that he might not be the father. But his heart dropped with regret. And then possessiveness gripped him.

He did not want Princess Gabriella or the baby she carried belonging to any man but him.

Chapter Six

"The doctor gave me a clean bill of health."

Aaron Timmer grinned at the news. He was apparently as relieved as she was that their baby was all right. But Charlotte wasn't worried only about the baby she carried. She was worried about the baby sister she'd failed to protect as she'd sworn she would.

"I'm clear to travel," she said. "Clear to do my job."

Aaron shook his head. "You don't have a job anymore," he reminded her. "The king doesn't want you working for him."

King St. Pierre claimed that he wanted Charlotte as a daughter now, not as an employee. But she worried that he'd dismissed her because he no longer trusted her to safeguard the princess—not after she had already failed. Charlotte had spent six months in captivity and during that time all kinds of unimaginable horrors could have happened to Gabriella—since she'd been left completely unprotected.

"She's pregnant, too," Charlotte said, as with awe, she remembered her aunt's words the first time they had talked. The phone connection hadn't been good, but she'd not misinterpreted that.

Aaron sighed. "Did you tell your father that news?"

Charlotte tensed—not used to thinking of the king as her father even though she'd known for a few years now. Gabby had just discovered her real parentage. So she was dealing with all those conflicting emotions while she was going to become a mother herself.

"I haven't told him yet," Charlotte admitted. "I'm concerned…"

"About how he will react?"

The king had never treated Gabby with the respect she deserved. He'd never treated her like what she was—an independent, modern woman. "He already arranged for her to marry another man."

"You don't think the baby she's carrying is Prince Tonio Malamatos's?" Aaron asked, referring to Gabby's fiancé.

The prince had been waiting at the palace when they arrived. As soon as the king had notified him that the princess had been found, he had come from his country with an entourage that included his ex-fiancée. When Charlotte had stepped off the plane, he'd mistaken her for Gabby and tried to embrace her. She shuddered as she remembered the man's clammy hands touching her arms, of his pasty cheek trying to press against hers.

Gabby never would have let that man touch her. Charlotte shook her head. "And neither do you. You know who the father is."

He expelled a ragged sigh. "Whit. If they'd been involved before she disappeared, it would explain why he was acting so strangely when you and Gabby went missing." Aaron had admitted that he'd been suspicious his old partner had been involved in their disappearances. "And why he was so anxious to bring her back once you told him where she was."

"I knew she had a crush on him," Charlotte admitted. "But I hadn't thought Whit would ever act on her vulnerability to him."

"Neither did I," Aaron admitted. "He's always been the professional, unemotional one."

Charlotte smiled as she thought of her sister. "Gabby has a way of getting to a person, of stealing her way into your heart."

But that hadn't worked with their real mother or with the queen. The person actually had to have a heart for Gabby to work her way inside. From everything Charlotte had heard about him, Whitaker Howell didn't have a heart either. But he had acted very worried about Gabriella and her safety.

Charlotte was also anxious about her sister. "I hope she's had access to medical care. And that she's not in need of it now."

"She's fine," Aaron said, referring back to Charlotte's most recent conversation with her aunt, who had called the palace at Whit's request. "Whit rescued her at the airport."

Charlotte breathed a soft sigh of relief. Whit had saved her. Just because he'd been doing his job? Or because he cared about Gabby?

In order to board the royal jet and return to St. Pierre, they would have to go back to the airport. And what if the gunmen were waiting there to try to grab Princess Gabriella again?

"We still should be there, too," Charlotte insisted. While the doctor had cleared her for flight and work, he'd cautioned her to take it easy. She'd been restrained to a bed for the past six months, so she'd lost some of her strength and stamina.

"The other jet has already taken off," Aaron said. "They're hours ahead of us and may have already landed."

"But they're not you and me," she pointed out. "And I'm not sure if Whit should trust anyone but you and me." Not with his life and certainly not with Gabby's.

Aaron snorted. "That shouldn't be a problem since Whit rarely trusts anyone."

"That's what's kept him alive for the past thirty years," Charlotte pointed out. But the problem was that he was traveling with a woman who trusted everyone, who always saw the good in people no matter what they'd done. Gabby would forgive Charlotte—eventually. But she wouldn't be able to do that unless Whit could keep her alive.

Six months ago Whit had been willing to let her marry another man, but today he had barely let the doctor speak to her before he'd ushered Dominic Delgado back to his Jeep. Dominic was an irrepressible flirt. Was Whit jealous?

Hope fluttered in her heart—and in her belly as the baby kicked with excitement. Could Whit care enough to feel jealousy?

He strode back through the doorway. "We have to leave now. The royal jet may have already landed."

So he hadn't been jealous at all. Just impatient to carry out his orders to bring her back to St. Pierre and her father. Disappointment quelled her flash of hope. But then she didn't want him to be jealous of her. Because if Prince Linus had been acting of his own accord and not his father's, then it must have been his jealousy that had cost Charlotte six months of her life.

She doubted he'd acted alone, though, because she doubted he'd cared enough to be jealous of her.

"You really want to bring me back to St. Pierre?" she asked. And her disappointment grew.

She had been right to leave him six months ago. Despite that night they'd shared, he hadn't cared anything for her—not enough to stop her from leaving. Not enough to stop her from marrying another man.

"You need to go back to St. Pierre," he stubbornly insisted. A muscle in his lean cheek, beneath the couple of days' worth of stubble and above his tightly clenched jaw, twitched.

"Why?" she asked. Nobody on St. Pierre genuinely cared for her—at least not enough to have ever been honest with her. "So my father can force me to marry Prince Tonio Malamatos?"

"That is not the reason why the king wants you home," Whit said.

She wasn't foolish enough to entertain any flutters of hope this time. Her question was more rhetorical than curious; despite the secrets he'd kept, she still knew her father well. Too well. "So he's broken that engagement for me, too?"

Good thing her question had been rhetorical because he didn't answer it. That muscle just twitched in his cheek again.

"Maybe Prince Tonio took my disappearance as a rejection and resumed his engagement to my cousin?" Actually Honora Del Cachon wasn't her cousin since Gabby wasn't really the queen's daughter. Like the queen, Honora had never liked Gabby, either. The night of the ball—when she'd been publicly humiliated—instead of blaming the king, Honora had glared at Gabby with such hatred that she shuddered even now, remembering it. "They could actually be married by now." And she fervently hoped that they were.

Whit shook his head. "Prince Malamatos refused to break your engagement until he had proof that you were dead."

"He waited for me?" she asked. Unlike Prince Linus, he didn't even know her. They had only met a few times over her lifetime, and had rarely spoken more than a couple of words to each other. So his loyalty wasn't personal.

Was her country that important to him?

Whit jerked his chin up and down in a rough nod. And for a second she wondered if he'd read her mind. But he probably only meant that the prince had waited for her.

"So he still intends to marry me when I return?" Panic rushed up on her now, so that she struggled to draw a deep breath. "And my father will expect me to obey his royal command and marry the prince."

"You can talk to him this time," Whit said, "instead of running away."

His words stung her pride. "You think I ran away six months ago?"

He gave a sharp nod. "I know that's what you did."

"I was threatened," she reminded him. Physically and emotionally. "And Charlotte thought I would be safer here." From both threats.

"Charlotte thought wrong."

"I was safe for six months," she said. And happy, despite feeling like a fool for giving her love to a man without a heart and for believing her family's lies. "I was safe until you came here."

He flinched but didn't deny that he might be responsible for the danger she'd stumbled into at the airport. "You're not safe anymore," he said. "We need to leave."

Distress attacked her again, making her

heart race and her stomach flip. "You don't care about me." She'd realized that long ago but it still hurt to know she'd given him so much and he'd given her so little.

She touched her belly. Actually he'd given her much more than he'd realized.

"Gabby," he said, his breath expelling in a ragged sigh of exasperation. Then he lifted his arms and reached for her, as if he intended to offer her comfort or reassurance.

But she held up a hand between them, holding him off. "And that's fine. I don't care that you don't care what'll happen to me on St. Pierre. But what about your baby? Don't you worry what will happen to him?"

There. She'd done it—she'd told him the truth. He was about to be a father.

But why would he care since he obviously didn't spare a thought for the baby's mother? She would try not to take it personally; perhaps Whit Howell cared about nothing and no one.

ALL THE BLOOD rushed from Whit's head, leaving him dizzy while heat rushed to his face. Sweat beaded on his brow. He brushed it away with a shaky hand. Maybe he should have let the doctor examine him, so he could have known for sure that he wasn't on the verge of having a stroke.

His heart raced, pounding fast and hard. And his lungs were too constricted for him to draw a deep breath. He had been in some of the most dangerous places and situations in the world, but he'd never felt such panic and fear before.

"Are you all right?" Gabby asked. Moments ago she'd pushed him away, but now she reached for him, her small hands grasping his forearms.

He nodded. But it was a lie. He wasn't all right. He was about to become a father—one of several things he'd sworn he would never be: a father, a husband, a besotted lover...

By leaving them, his mother had destroyed his father, sinking him deeper into the bottle, so that he hadn't been able to hold a job. Three years ago, when Whit had lost a job and struggled to get another, he'd felt like he was becoming his old man. And he had become more determined than ever to not even risk it. That was why he'd put up with the king and his asinine royal commands—because he hadn't wanted to lose another job. But now he risked losing so much more than just a job.

"Are you sure?" he asked.

She jerked her hands off his arms as if his

skin had burned her. Maybe it had. He felt like his face was on fire. And he still couldn't draw a deep breath.

But then she lifted her face toward his, and her big brown eyes were bright with indignation. "You know there was only you…"

His muscles tensed like they had that night when he'd realized she was a virgin, that despite all the media reports to the contrary, she had never been promiscuous. She had never been with another man before. Whit had tried to pull back, had tried to stop, but they'd both been too overcome with passion. And she'd urged him to take her—to take her innocence.

He'd done it because he'd wanted her so much and because he had really believed she'd wanted him. But the next morning when he'd returned to his room to change his clothes so that no one would realize that he'd spent the night with her, she had packed up and booked her flight to Paris. And he'd realized that he'd probably just been an act of rebellion for her, that she'd used him as revenge against her father.

"I know that I was the only one before you disappeared." He heard the Jeep's engine droning in the distance. "But you've been here six months…" Close to a man who had obviously fallen for her.

She lifted her hand, as if she intended to slap him, but then she drew in a breath and her control. And instead of touching him, she pressed her palm to her belly. "I am six months along. I was already pregnant when I came here."

He waited for more, waited for her to assure him that she'd slept with no other man but him. She offered no such assurances about her love life.

She only assured him, "This baby is yours."

But only the baby. She was not his. And she would never be.

If he brought her back to St. Pierre, her father might very well do as she feared; he might force her into marrying a strange prince. It was King St. Pierre's country, his rules. And he sure as hell wasn't going to let his princess become involved with a bodyguard.

"Where were you going?" he asked.

She blinked and then narrowed her eyes in confusion. "Six months ago?"

"No. Today," he clarified. "At the airport. If you had time to buy a ticket, where were you going to go?"

"The United States."

She'd be safer there than St. Pierre.

"Any state in particular?" he wondered.

She pressed her lips together, as if refusing

to answer him. Obviously she still intended to give him the slip, and she didn't want to make it easy for him to find her again.

"I'm not letting you out of my sight," he said. Especially not after what had happened at the airport. She could have been kidnapped or killed. And if he took his eyes off her for a moment, she would try to lose him again—leaving herself and their baby vulnerable.

Their baby?

He waited for the panic to surge back, but he could still breathe. His heart was beating—strong and steady—instead of the frantic pace it had when he'd first realized her baby was really his.

"Then why does it matter where I was going?" she asked with a slight shrug.

He fought an internal battle between following the rules and following his gut, between betraying friends and betraying her. His shoulder throbbed, as if his struggle had been physical as well as emotional. Or maybe it was infected. He really should have let Dr. Dominic examine it. But he ignored the pain and mimicked her shrug. "Because I want to know where we're going when we get to the airport."

She gasped in surprise over his admission. "You're not taking me to St. Pierre?"

He couldn't. Even before she'd told him

the baby was his, he doubted he could have brought her back to the people who'd betrayed her—who'd manipulated and lied to her for her entire life. She deserved better than that.

She also deserved better than him.

Maybe he should leave her here with the doctor and Lydia—people who were able to love and already loved her. That would be the right thing to do, but Whit rarely did what was right. Because even if it was right, it wasn't safe to leave her in a country where a man had already tried to abduct her and had nearly shot at her.

"No," he replied. "But we can't stay here, either."

"Because everyone knows where we are," she said, as if she'd read his mind again. But she continued to stare up at him, as if debating whether or not to trust him.

After discovering how many people had lied to her and for how long, she shouldn't trust anyone. Ever. Again.

He could figure out another place for them to go. During his years in the service, he had traveled so much that he had discovered some places where a man could hide. But a pregnant princess?

"I was going to Michigan," she said.

"Michigan? How did you know that's where

Charlotte was held for six months?" Had she already forgiven her sister and wanted to check on her?

Her brow furrowed with confusion. "I didn't. Where in Michigan was she held?"

"At a private psychiatric hospital called Serenity House." He nearly shuddered as he remembered the place that had been Charlotte's prison for six months and had nearly been where Whit had breathed his last.

She flinched with obvious regret and embarrassment. "I told Linus about Serenity House."

"How did you know about it?" he asked. She was inquisitive by nature; his men had told him that she'd often asked them about him. But he hadn't realized how knowledgeable she was.

"Someone told me about it," she replied, evasively avoiding his gaze.

Nothing had been less serene than a pregnant woman being held captive there for six months, restrained to a bed. It was also where Whit had been shot and would have been killed had it not been for Charlotte. He owed her his life. Could he keep her sister from her?

"Who did you talk to?" he asked, more worried than curious.

She shrugged. "Just somebody who lives near there."

"Did you meet her through Charlotte?"

She nodded. "Charlotte met her while she was still a U.S. Marshal. I think it was on her last assignment that they met."

And Whit's last assignment as Aaron's partner before they dissolved their business and their friendship. "Josie Jessup?"

Gabby shook her head. "That's not her name."

"It probably isn't now," he said. "But I bet it sure as hell was. I know who she is. And I've always known where she was in northern Michigan—not that damn far from Serenity House."

He had betrayed Aaron to make sure that Josie stayed safe, when he'd helped Charlotte fake his and Aaron's former client's death to put her in witness relocation. So to make sure she was safe, he'd found out where the U.S. Marshal had hidden her.

Gabby nipped at her bottom lip and then nodded. "Charlotte called her JJ."

"Charlotte shouldn't have told you anything about her." A man had been killed trying to find out where the woman, heiress to a media mogul's empire, was hiding. Whit had been forced to kill the man in order to save

Aaron's life and Josie's. His shoulder throbbed just thinking about the danger her knowledge put Gabriella in.

"Why the hell would Charlotte tell you where she is?" he asked. "Nobody should know." Maybe that was why the man at the airport had tried to grab Gabby—not because of who she was but of what she might know. It was information that someone had already killed for—information over which Whit had nearly died. Before he'd killed the man, the man had had gunmen try to kill him and Aaron. That was when Whit had taken the hit to the shoulder.

"She trusts her," Gabby explained. "And if anything happened to Charlotte, she trusted JJ and me to help each other."

While he'd been protecting her over three years ago, Whit had figured out that Josie Jessup was a smart, resourceful woman. What he hadn't realized was how smart and resourceful Gabriella St. Pierre was.

"We can't go there," he said.

"Of course not now," she agreed. "Charlotte would look for me there. That would have been a stupid place to hide." She shook her head, apparently disgusted with herself for considering it.

Gabby had yet to realize how intelligent and

capable she was. She must have read and believed too much of what was printed about her. Whit knew, intimately, how wrong the media had always been about her.

"If Charlotte was still missing, you would have been smart to go to Josie," he admitted.

With the former U.S. Marshal's help, Josie had learned how to disappear. And maybe that was what Gabby needed to do—not just for six months but for the rest of her life. It might be the only way she would escape her father's archaic insistence on ruling her life like he ruled his country—as a sole dictatorship.

"Why didn't you go to Josie earlier?" he asked, wondering why she hadn't the minute she'd discovered Charlotte had been keeping secrets from her.

Gabby glanced around that primitive hut. "I didn't want to leave here."

It obviously wasn't the conditions that had made her want to stay. So it was either the orphans, her aunt or Dr. Dominic. He hoped like hell it wasn't the doctor.

WHAT DID HE think about becoming a father?

Gabriella kept studying Whit's handsome face, but he revealed nothing of his feelings—after the initial shock. Maybe he was still in shock. But that could have been from the gunshot wound more than over what she'd told him.

"You really should have had Dominic examine you," she admonished him.

Whit shook his head. "I don't need a doctor. I need to get you out of here. Did you have all your stuff packed up?"

She nodded. Everything she needed was in her big backpack-style bag. She could no longer wear anything she'd brought with her six months ago. The clothes either didn't fit or hadn't stood up to the elements or how hard she had worked.

"Then we need to go," he said, heading toward the doorway.

But Gabriella stayed where she was, standing next to the bed, fingering the edge of the mosquito netting. "Can I really trust that you're not going to bring me back to St. Pierre?"

She had debated with herself before telling him about Michigan. While Charlotte hadn't trusted her with the secret that affected her own life, she had told her all about Josie Jessup and how Whit helping her relocate the woman had ruined his friendship with Aaron. So she knew he was very familiar with Josie's situation. Gabriella had no intention of putting JJ in danger. She'd only wanted to put herself and her unborn baby somewhere safe.

But apparently Michigan wasn't safe, either. But at least in Michigan, no one would make her marry someone she didn't know, let alone love.

He uttered a ragged sigh. "I'd like to think that you're wrong about your father—that he won't force you to marry Prince Malamatos…"

"You don't know my father like I do," she said.

After what she'd learned about her biological mother, she had to accept that she didn't know her father very well, either. Not that she didn't believe he would have cheated on the queen but she didn't believe he would have fallen for a con artist. Then again he hadn't fallen for the woman or he wouldn't have stayed with the queen. Or would he—just for the sake of propriety? Hell, the only thing she knew for certain was that nothing mattered to him as much as his country—certainly not either of his daughters.

Whit nodded his head in agreement. "That's why I can't risk it."

"Why do you care if I'm forced to marry the prince?" she asked.

He clenched his jaw again, so tightly that he had that muscle twitching in his cheek.

"Don't worry," she said. "I know you haven't suddenly developed feelings for me."

When he had so obviously not given a damn about her before now. "I know it must be because of the baby."

"I don't want another man claiming *my* child," Whit said, his voice gruff.

"So *you're* claiming your child?" she asked.

His chest lifted, pushing against his black T-shirt, as he drew in a deep breath. Then he nodded. "I believe you—that the baby's mine."

"But that doesn't mean you have to claim him," she pointed out, especially since he'd reacted to the news as if she'd shot him.

His already dark eyes darkened more with anger and pride. "You think I could walk away and pretend I don't have a child growing inside you?"

"So if I wasn't carrying your baby, you could walk away?" She needed to know that— needed to face the fact that it didn't matter that they were having a child together. They had no future together.

"I didn't say that."

"You didn't have to," she said. She grabbed up her bag from the bed and headed toward the doorway.

But he caught her arm, turning her back toward him.

"What?" she asked. "I thought you were in

such a hurry to leave that you couldn't even take a minute for the doctor to examine you."

"Forget the damn doctor!" he snapped.

"I think you mean that." Literally. That he wanted her to forget about Dominic. Did he think she'd been involved with the flirt?

"I spent six months thinking about you," he said, almost reluctantly as if the admission had been tortured from him, "thinking that you were dead and blaming myself for letting you go to Paris." His anger turned to anguish and guilt that twisted his handsome face into a grimace. "So, no, I couldn't walk away—even if you weren't carrying my baby."

Now the guilt was all hers. When she'd gone into hiding, she hadn't thought that anyone would miss her. Least of all Whitaker Howell.

"I'm sorry," she said. "I never meant for you to feel responsible."

Whit groaned, as if he were in pain. But was it physical or emotional? "I don't like feeling responsible. I don't like feeling…*anything*." He tugged her closer. "You make me feel all kinds of emotions I don't want to feel."

"I'm sorry," she said again, in a breathy whisper as attraction stole away her breath.

He was so close, with such an intense look of desire in his dark eyes. Then he was even closer, as he lowered his head to hers. His lips skimmed across hers, gently, only to return with hunger and passion.

Gabby reeled with the force of emotions so intense that her head grew light and dizzy. She clutched at his shoulders, holding tightly to him as her world spun out of control.

Six months had passed but she wanted him as desperately as she had the night of the ball, the night they'd conceived their child. Maybe she wanted him even more because now she knew what to expect.

Ecstasy.

But he tensed and stepped back from her. There was no desire on his face anymore— just shock and horror.

Then she heard it, too—the sound of engines, revving loudly as vehicles sped toward the compound. It wasn't just the doctor returning. There was more than one vehicle—more than one man.

They had waited too long. They'd been found, and if it were the gunmen from the airport coming, they had put the lives of everyone in the compound at risk.

Chapter Seven

Whit cursed. How had he let himself get so distracted? He would like to blame his gunshot wound. But he knew the real reason was Gabriella and all those feelings she made him feel that he didn't want to.

Like guilt. It pummeled him.

"If the guys from the airport found us, we can't let them hurt the children," Gabby said as she rushed toward that open doorway.

Whit stepped in front of her so she wouldn't run outside. "I won't."

She shook her head. "You can't protect them against all those men. I'll just let them take me. It's the only way to keep everyone safe."

She was serious—and more self-sacrificing than anyone he'd ever met. If he survived this, he might personally track down every paparazzi who'd called her a spoiled princess. A shallow ditz. They had no idea who Gabriella St. Pierre really was.

Whit wrapped his arm around her and rushed her toward the Jeep. He turned the key in the ignition and shifted into Drive. "We'll lead them away from here."

It was the only way to keep the children safe. They wouldn't destroy the compound looking for them—if they saw them leave.

"Hang on tight," he ordered her. If only the damn vehicle had seat belts...

And if only the road between the compound and town was more than a narrow path cut through the jungle...

He'd barely made it down that path when there had been no other vehicles on it. He really had no room to pass the Jeep and truck that were barreling down the track toward the compound. But he barreled ahead, and metal scraped metal, the driver's side of the Jeep scraping along the pickup.

Men filled the truck, inside the cab and standing in the box with long guns slung over their shoulders.

"Get down!" he shouted at Gabby.

"No!" she yelled back—even as bullets pinged against the metal of Whit's side of the vehicle. "They need to see me so that they know I'm not at the orphanage!"

As if to prove her point, she lifted her head higher and peered around him. And the windshield exploded as a bullet struck the glass. It continued into the rearview mirror, cracked the plastic and shattered the mirror.

"Get down!" he shouted again. But instead of waiting for her to comply, he reached across the console and pushed her lower.

Then he focused again on the road—just as a Jeep steered straight toward them. He clutched the wheel in tight fists, holding his own vehicle steady on the trail. And he trusted that the guy driving the other vehicle would give in to impulse—the impulse to jerk the wheel at the last moment.

Whit resisted his impulse even when Gabby lifted her head and screamed. But he didn't turn away. Metal ground against metal again, but the impact was lessened as the other driver twisted his wheel and turned the tires. Whit pressed hard on the accelerator, careening past, as the other vehicle bounced off trees and rolled back onto the trail—on its roof.

Shots rang out, continuing to break glass and glance off metal. Whit wouldn't have looked back even if the rearview mirror hadn't been broken. He kept speeding along the winding trail, widening the distance between him and the men who would have grabbed Gabby had they not escaped in time.

And, because his feelings for her had distracted him, they nearly hadn't escaped. For her sake, he could not succumb to emotion again.

GABBY COULDN'T STOP looking back—at the men who stood on the trail firing at them. And at the compound beyond the men. "Are you sure they won't go to the orphanage?"

"They saw you," he reminded her. "They know you're not there."

"But they might go to the compound," she said, her stomach churning with worry. "They might question Lydia to find out where we're going."

Whit snorted derisively. "They know damn well where we're going."

"The airport?"

"We have no other option," he pointed out. "We can't stay here."

"So once they get the Jeep moved and it is no longer blocking the trail, they'll come after us?" She had to know, had to make certain…

Whit nodded.

She exhaled a breath of relief. "So they won't go back to the compound." That was her most pressing concern—making sure the others were safe from the threat against her.

"Like I said, they know where we're going," Whit repeated. "Once they get that Jeep out of the way, they're going to be hurrying to catch up with us—not going back."

And Lydia would have heard the shots and the vehicles; she would have taken the children to the hiding place they'd built into the ground beneath the floors of one of the schoolrooms. They would be safe.

She wasn't so certain about Whit and her and their unborn child. While they'd lost the men—temporarily—he was driving so fast that it was possible they would crash, too, just as the men had.

"They want you," he continued. "You're the one the king will pay for..."

The king had already done it once—when he'd bought her mother's parental rights. It was no wonder so many others had tried to kidnap her over the years. They knew her father would pay their ransom.

But that was back when she had been blindly obedient. Now that she'd hidden from her father for six months, now that she'd become pregnant with the baby of a man who had nothing to offer him politically or monetarily...would he pay for her release? Or was she completely useless to him?

Whit's brow furrowed as he stared through the shattered windshield. "But if they wanted him to pay a ransom, why did they shoot so closely to you? Why risk it...?"

Her skin tingled with foreboding—the same way it had when she had found that crumpled letter under her pillow six months ago. Maybe they didn't want to kidnap her. Maybe they wanted to kill her as that note had threatened.

She braced one hand against the dashboard again and wrapped her other around the roll bar in the roof. She implored him, "Please, hurry."

Not that she needed to urge him to speed; he was probably already traveling too fast on dangerously curved, narrow roads.

"I'll protect you," he assured her.

She believed he meant it, but she wasn't necessarily convinced that he could. "I thought you were going to kill me when that vehicle was heading straight toward us..." And he hadn't backed down.

That was what his men had said about him; that he had never retreated from a fight—in battle or in the barracks. When he and Aaron Timmer had taken over as royal bodyguards, they had brought in their own men as backup. And she had quizzed all those men about their blond superior.

"I had it under control," he said. "You shouldn't have been scared."

She was afraid but not for herself; she was concerned for the child she carried.

And she was scared for the safety of the baby's father, as well.

SHE SHOULD NOT have trusted him. Whit had had no right to make her promises or offer her assurances that he had no idea if he would be able to carry out.

But he hated that her usually honey-toned complexion had gone pale with fear, her voice trembling with it. Her earlier scream echoed yet inside his head.

He didn't want her scared but he wanted her hurt even less. He had to protect her.

How? By taking her back to St. Pierre? He'd also promised that he wouldn't do that. But did he have a choice?

His shoulder was throbbing. His gun was out of bullets. He needed backup—backup he could trust: Aaron or Charlotte or any of the ex-military security guards he'd brought on board at the palace.

What had those armed men wanted with her? Were they working for Prince Linus's dad, or whoever the corrupt U.S. Marshal had been working for who had tried to find out where Josie was?

Were they intent on carrying out a kidnapping for ransom or a murder for hire?

Finally they neared the airport, and he slowed down to pull the Jeep off the road. Gabby reached across the console and grasped his arm. "Where are we going?"

Whit needed backup. But he didn't want her at the mercy of her father's royal commands. "We'll figure it out when we get inside. We're getting on whatever plane is taking off first."

He didn't give a damn where it was going. He just needed to get them the hell out of this place. After the earlier shooting, the airport should have been swarming with police. But he noticed no marked cars. No yellow caution tape…

Why hadn't the police come? Had they been called? Was there even a police force or military presence in this primitive country?

Gabby had a question of her own. "What about the royal jet?"

"We're not getting on it."

But the moment they stepped from the Jeep, men surrounded them. They weren't dressed in police or military uniforms but expensive suits. And like the men who'd stormed the compound, these guys, with jackets bulging over shoulder holsters, were armed.

And vaguely familiar. They had been royal

bodyguards. But he and Aaron had relegated them to perimeter palace guards when they'd taken over as co-heads of security for the king.

"Hey, Bruno. Cosmo," he awkwardly greeted the couple of guys whose names he hoped he correctly remembered. These men had been loyal to the king and to the former head of security, Zeke Rogers. Whit hadn't trusted that they would be as loyal to him and Aaron. It had actually been his call to move them out of the palace. Did they know that? Did they hold a grudge because of it?

"You kept us waiting," the one named Bruno remarked, his beady eyes narrowed even more with suspicion—especially as he studied the princess.

Did he suspect she was an imposter? Charlotte?

Or was he just as stunned as Whit had been to find her not only alive but pregnant?

"You should have given up on us and returned to St. Pierre," Whit advised them.

But no matter that Zeke was no longer their boss, they would remain loyal to the king and their country—probably out of respect and fear.

"We have orders," Cosmo added.

"Plans have changed," Whit said with the tone he used for giving orders in the field and on the job. And for the past several months, he had been giving these men their orders. To guard the gates of the palace. "It's too dangerous to take the princess back to St. Pierre."

Bruno pushed back his jacket and showed the Glock he carried inside the holster. "We have protection."

Whit didn't, and a strong foreboding warned him that he needed it. These men weren't acting like they did on St. Pierre. They weren't acting like he was their superior anymore. Had he been demoted? Zeke had been temporarily reinstated when he'd followed Aaron to Michigan to rescue Charlotte. But that reinstatement was only to have been temporary.

"Did you not hear me?" he asked, in his best no-nonsense boss tone. "I said that plans have changed. We are not going back to St. Pierre."

"We don't have to listen to you anymore," Cosmo said. "We take our orders from someone else now."

Damn. He had been demoted. Or fired.

They had protection, obviously. But he felt like he was the one who needed it now. Could he bluff them into thinking the gun he carried was loaded yet?

As Cosmo grabbed it from him, he realized it was too late. He shouldn't have trusted these men; he shouldn't have trusted anyone—just like Gabriella shouldn't have trusted him.

He couldn't keep any of his promises to her.

AARON'S HEART POUNDED slowly and heavily with dread. "Who did you send as Whit's backup?" he asked the king.

Rafael St. Pierre sat behind his desk in the darkly paneled den in his private wing of the palace. The past six months had added lines to the man's face and liberal streaks of gray to his thick hair. St. Pierre shrugged shoulders that had once been broad enough to carry the weight of his country, but in recent months they had begun to stoop with a burden too heavy—concern for his daughters' lives and safety. "I do not know the names of the men who went."

Neither did Aaron. And that worried him. "The men that Whit and I brought on are all still here in St. Pierre. They were told that Whit did not want them as backup."

"Then that is why they were not sent," the king replied.

Aaron shook his head. "Whit didn't know you were sending that jet after him. If he had known, he would have requested the men that he and I brought on to the security team."

"Are you certain?" the king asked. "I do not

believe Whitaker Howell is as loyal as you believe he is."

Just a week ago, Aaron would have agreed with the king. He'd thought Whit had betrayed him when he'd let Aaron believe that they had failed to protect their last client. Whit had actually helped Charlotte, in her previous position as a U.S. Marshal, fake the woman's death and relocate her. Neither of them had thought Aaron would be able to stand the client's dad's suffering as he mourned her; they'd worried that Aaron would give up the secret.

Maybe they had been right to worry. Because the secret he had now was on his lips, threatening to slip out. The king should be warned that Princess Gabriella was pregnant.

"If Whitaker Howell was loyal, he would not have gotten my daughter pregnant while she's engaged to another man!" the king shouted, anger exploding with his fist slamming against his desk.

Aaron didn't have much room to talk; he had gotten the king's other daughter pregnant. Charlotte hadn't been engaged, though.

"How—how did you hear that?" Aaron wondered. Charlotte hadn't told her father yet, and Aaron had managed to keep the secret until now. "Who—who told you?"

"A man who is actually loyal to me," King St. Pierre replied. Coldly.

He obviously wasn't too happy that Aaron had claimed Charlotte—as his fiancée—before the king had even claimed her as his illegitimate daughter and heir.

Aaron's head began to pound as realization dawned. "This isn't good…"

"No, it's not," the king agreed. "I trusted you and your partner. I believed the recommendations that Charlotte had given you both as exemplary chiefs of security. Yet you two were barely on the job a couple of months before my daughters both went missing."

"They were not hired to protect me and Gabby," Charlotte said as she joined them in the king's den. The guard at the door would have not dared to deny her admittance—even if it wasn't now common knowledge that she, too, was royalty, she could have easily overpowered the man.

She was that good. And Aaron was so proud that she was his.

"You're supposed to be resting," Aaron reminded her. For six months he had been so worried about her, but finding her hadn't changed his concern for her. If anything, given what she had endured and the baby she was carrying, he worried more.

She shook her head. "I spent nearly six months in bed. That's more rest than I can handle and retain my sanity."

The king rose from his chair, all concern now. "But you've been through a horrible ordeal—"

"That was not Aaron and Whit's fault," she said. "They were hired to protect *you*. I was supposed to protect Gabby and myself." Her voice cracked with fear and regret. "I am the one who failed."

Aaron reached for her, sliding his arm around her shoulders. She was the strongest woman he'd ever met—physically and emotionally. But she was hurting now—for her sister.

"What's not good?" she asked him.

And, just as they had all thought of him, Aaron couldn't lie. "Somehow King St. Pierre learned that Gabriella's pregnant."

She shook her head. "That's not possible. I didn't learn that until after I talked to Aunt Lydia, and I haven't told anyone but you."

"And I only told Whit," he assured her. "But the man who was shooting at her—he would have realized she was pregnant…"

The king slammed his fist into his desk again. "Are you saying that members of my own security team are trying to kill my daughter?"

Charlotte cursed with the vulgarity of a sailor rather than a princess. But then she had only just been identified as royalty. "This is why I wanted you to hire Whit and Aaron," she said. "Because all of your other security staff were mercenaries."

The king shrugged. "What is wrong with that? They are ex-soldiers, like Aaron and Whit."

"Mercenaries are not ex-soldiers," Aaron said. Because no one was ever really an exsoldier. "They are still fighting but only now instead of fighting for their country or their honor, they fight for money."

"So they are easily bought," Charlotte explained. "And they are only loyal to the person who's paying them the most."

The king cursed now and dropped back into his chair as if he weighed far more than he did. His burden of concern and guilt was back—maybe even heavier than before.

"We need to call Whit," Charlotte said, "and warn him."

Aaron shook his head and lifted the phone he'd had clamped in his hand. "I've been trying. I can't get a call through to him."

"Call Lydia at the orphanage," Charlotte said. "Maybe they're still there."

"She won't pick up, either," Aaron said.

Both of the royals sucked in little gasps of air and fear.

"But remember the reception is bad down there," Aaron said, trying to offer them both comfort and hope even as his own heart continued to beat slowly and heavily with dread. "It doesn't mean that anything has happened."

Yet.

Would Whit realize before it was too late that the men who'd been sent as his backup were actually his greatest threat?

Chapter Eight

Gabby's heart pounded fast with fear—faster than it had even when Whit had been playing chicken with that other vehicle.

He was playing chicken again—resisting the armed men as they tried directing them through the airport toward the waiting plane. They pushed at him—with the gun barrel, and their hands, shoving him forward. He flinched as one of them slammed his palm into his shoulder.

Gabby bit her lip, so she wouldn't cry out with pain for him. He had already been hurting from earlier, and these men were using that weakness—exploiting his pain. She was too familiar with that cruel treatment—from the queen and her father.

"You kept us waiting long enough," Bruno remarked bitterly. "We have to go."

Gabby needed to leave now, too. With the men focused on Whit, she might have been able to escape. She could try to run back to the Jeep. And take it where? Leaving Whit behind?

Before she could make the decision, she was grabbed. A strong hand wrapped tightly around her arm, the pudgy fingers pinching her flesh. This time she cried out loud, more in surprise and protest than fear, though.

"Let her go!" Whit yelled, his voice so loud it went hoarse. He began to fight. Forgetting or ignoring his injury, he swung his fist into one man's jaw—knocking him out as easily as he had the one she'd shot earlier that day.

He had saved her then. But there were too many of them for him to be able to save her now. A gun barrel was pressed tight to his back, between his shoulder blades.

It was almost as if Gabby could feel it, too. The bite of steel, the fear of taking a breath since it might be her last. Or Whit's last. She didn't want him to move, but he continued to struggle.

"Don't," she whispered, imploring him with her eyes to stop fighting. These men had claimed they no longer took orders from Whit. Had her father fired him? Or were they actually working for someone else?

"I will shoot you," Cosmo warned him.

"Is that one of your orders?" Whit asked. "Did the king tell you to shoot me?"

Gabby took that breath now—in a gasp of shock. She had long ago realized that her father was not the nicest man. He was selfish and manipulative. But was he a killer? Would he have Whit murdered?

She wouldn't put it past him—if he'd learned that his bodyguard had impregnated his daughter and potentially foiled his plans for a royal merger. He would never approve of her being with a man who offered *him* nothing— no money or political influence.

"Stop!" she said, shouting even though she barely raised her voice. Instead she used her father's imperious tone—the one with which he issued commands that no one dared to disobey.

And the men actually stopped pushing them forward—toward that damn plane. It was a royal jet sitting on the primitive tarmac, but it wasn't her father's personal, far more luxurious jet. So he had not made the trip to retrieve her himself. Had he missed her at all the past six months?

"As Princess of St. Pierre, I am ordering you to release Mr. Howell," she commanded. Relieved that she had kept her nerves and adrenaline from cracking her voice, she expelled a soft sigh.

Whit jerked free of Cosmo while two other men helped up the one he'd knocked to the ground. Bruno groaned, too disoriented to avenge himself on the man who'd struck him. Taking advantage of Bruno's weakness, Whit reached for the man's weapon.

But before he could grab it, a shot was fired—into the ceiling, like she had fired earlier. The bullet ricocheted off the metal and sent people running for safety, screaming.

Gabriella covered her stomach with her palms even though she knew her hands weren't enough to protect her child. She had to use her brains instead.

"Stop!" she yelled again. This time her voice did crack—with a show of weakness and fear. And men like these, men like her father, always took advantage of fear and weakness to assume control.

But perhaps she was the only one who'd noticed her vulnerability because the men again paused in their scuffle. Even Whit this time… as if he was afraid she might be caught in the crossfire or the ricochet if more bullets were fired.

"I will not be using the royal jet today," she

imperiously told them, "so you need to take it back to St. Pierre."

The other men turned toward Cosmo, as if to verify her claim. He shook his head. "We have orders that supersede yours, Your Majesty."

Damn her father! The king was the only one whose orders would supersede the orders of the princess of St. Pierre. Was he so desperate to force her into marriage with a stranger that he would risk her safety? That he would authorize the violent treatment of Whit?

Her stomach lurched, and so did her baby, with the fear that her father had learned of her pregnancy. And his anger had overwhelmed whatever capacity he'd had for human kindness.

With a quick glance at his watch, Cosmo said, "We need to board the plane now."

Her father must have been keeping them to a tight timetable. And if she kept them waiting any longer, they would get more impatient and probably violent.

For fear that Whit or someone else might be struck if more shots were fired in the airport, she allowed herself to be ushered outside to the waiting plane. Whit fell into step beside her, occasionally lurching ahead of her as one of the men pushed him.

She wanted to yell again, but he gave a barely perceptible shake of his head. He must have already decided not to fight her father's orders. He had decided the same thing six months ago when he'd waved her off to meet with a designer for the gown in which she would marry another man. Even though she hadn't really gone to meet that designer and she'd had no intention of buying a wedding gown, Whit had not known that. He just hadn't cared…

She'd been foolish to think that he ever might be jealous of her. It didn't matter to him that she was carrying his child. That had not changed the fact that he had no feelings for her—despite what he'd said back at the hut about her making him feel.

And that kiss…

Her lips still tingled with the sensation of his mouth pressed to hers. And that kiss brought back memories of how they'd made their baby—of how those kisses had led to caresses and making love.

No. She'd been the only one making love. She was beginning to think, as those who knew Whitaker Howell best had warned her, that he wasn't capable of feeling anything. They had been referring to his seeming inability to feel fear no matter how dangerous the situation. But if a man couldn't feel fear, then he probably couldn't feel love, either. She should have realized that then, but she'd been so hopeful and naive.

What a difference six months had made in her life. Back then she'd been a silly girl building foolish fantasies around a man who would never be hers. Who would probably never be anybody's...

And now she was a woman about to become a mother, being forced to return to a life she'd never wanted and over which she had no control. Her father was a difficult and selfish man, but was he really so intent on getting his own way that he would risk Whit's life and hers?

At the bottom of the steps up into the plane, she hesitated. If she ran now, would they shoot her? Or just chase her down and force her onto the plane?

And what would become of Whit if he tried to help her? Would he even try?

WHIT'S GUTS TWISTED into a tight knot of anger and frustration as he stared down into Gabriella's beautiful face. Her skin was pale, her eyes wide and dark with fear. She stared up at him expectantly, as if waiting for him to save her.

He had to help her. He shouldn't have made those promises—to protect her and to not bring her back to St. Pierre, but he had. And he needed to figure out how to keep them.

But he was outgunned and outmanned. And if he struggled again, the men might leave him behind—alive or dead.

And then Gabriella would be alone with them.

He lifted his chin to break free of the hold of her gaze. And he turned away from her, heading up the stairs first. He wanted to be aboard—needed to get on that damn flight with her. He couldn't let her go back to St. Pierre alone.

He glanced over his shoulder. A couple of the men flanked her, each grabbing an arm to guide her—hell, to nearly lift her—up the stairs to the plane. He clamped his arms to his sides, so that he wouldn't reach back—so that he wouldn't pull her from their grasp. They better not be squeezing her arms, better not be pinching or bruising her.

He hated them touching her. Hated more that they might be hurting her.

He turned away to step through the door to the plane. As he was shoved down the aisle, he passed a man already sprawled in one of the seats. The guy's shoulder was bandaged, and his arm was in a sling. A big bruise was turning from red to purple along his swollen jaw.

This was the man who had tried to abduct Gabby earlier—when she'd been alone. He must have arrived at the airport the same time Whit had. Hell, maybe he'd even beaten him there. Gabby had figured that the man being there was just a coincidence—that he had seen her alone and unprotected and decided to take advantage of the opportunity. Whit didn't believe in coincidence. He'd figured the man might have followed him from Michigan.

But what if this man had already known where Whit was going? Where Gabby was?

The guy was obviously affiliated with the top guards from the previous royal security regime. As an independent security contractor or a mercenary? He could have been working for anyone. The person who'd left her the threatening note. Or Prince Linus's father. Or whoever wanted to find Gabby's new friend, JJ…

Behind him he heard Gabby's gasp as she, too, recognized the man. Then her gasp turned to a moan. Whit whirled back just in time to see her crumple into a heap in the aisle. He tried to rush toward her, but the guys holding him pushed him down into a seat.

"Princess!" yelled one of the men, as if his shout would bring her back around.

But she wasn't unconscious. Instead she

was clutching her stomach. "I'm going to be sick," she warned them. "I need to use the bathroom."

Cosmo helped her to her feet. Then he guided her down the aisle toward the restroom in the back. As she passed Whit, he fisted his hand at his side, so that he wouldn't reach for her. But he didn't need to touch her to assure himself she was all right.

She shot him a pointed glance. She knew they were in danger, and she was working on a way to get herself and their child the hell out of it. The media couldn't have been more wrong about her.

But no matter how smart she was, she was six months pregnant and as outnumbered and weaponless as he was. Whit had to help her and not just because it was his duty. And not just because it was his baby she carried…

"I need to call the king," he said, slowly reaching for his phone. But his fingers no more than closed around it before one of the men knocked it from his hand. As soon as it hit the aisle, the man slammed his foot down onto it. "I need to tell him that the princess is too sick to travel."

As if on cue—and maybe his words had been exactly that—retching sounds drifted down the aisle from the restroom. This wasn't the king's royal jet; this was another in the fleet, used more for cargo than for passengers. The seats were not as luxurious nor the bathroom as large. She had to be uncomfortable in the tiny space. Hopefully she wasn't really sick; hopefully she was just faking in order to keep the plane on the ground.

"She is too far along in her pregnancy to fly," Whit said, as he stood up. "We can't take off."

"We have orders," Cosmo said. He moved away from the bathroom door—as if unable to tolerate the noises Gabriella was making inside the tiny room. He walked up to Whit, clasped his wounded shoulder and shoved him back down into the seat. "We're taking off…"

Whit ignored the pain coursing down his arm and fisted his tingling fingers. "You can't—"

They weren't listening to him or Gabby. One of the men sealed the outside door shut and then knocked on the cockpit door.

"…now," Cosmo finished with a triumphant grin. "We're taking off *now*."

"If the king knew she was sick," Whit persisted, "he wouldn't want her flying."

The engines fired up, causing the plane to vibrate. Then it moved as it began to taxi down the runway. "You can't take off now!" Whit shouted. "She's not even buckled in."

She would be tossed around in that tiny space—with no seat belt and nothing to protect her and her baby from getting hurt. It would be even worse than her ride in the Jeep because it would be thousands of feet in the air with the risk of turbulence.

He tried to rise up again, but another man shoved him into the seat. Whit couldn't reach her—couldn't help her.

Cosmo snorted. "If she's going to get sick, better she be sick in there than out here." He shuddered, and his throat moved, as if he were struggling with sickness of his own.

"She could be hurt," Whit said. "The king will not approve of that."

Emotionally hurting his daughter hadn't bothered the king. But when the man had seen that trashed hotel suite in Paris and he'd thought she might be physically hurt, Rafael St. Pierre had been distraught. He hadn't feigned his worry for her during the six months she'd been missing.

"So what's he going to do?" Cosmo asked. "Fire us again?"

"He didn't fire you," Whit replied. "You were just reassigned." But maybe he shouldn't remind them that he was the one responsible for their demotion. Then again, maybe goading them would make them rethink their loyalty to the king. "You were assigned to the same job a trained guard dog can do."

As a fist slammed into his jaw, he regretted his words. Bruno shook his hand and cursed. Then he grabbed at the seats around him as the plane's tires lifted from the airstrip.

Whit's back pressed against the seat they'd pushed him into, but he tried to stand up again. He had to get to Gabby—had to make sure she was all right. "If she gets hurt, the king might do more than fire you. He wouldn't have ordered his own daughter harmed!"

"No, he wouldn't have," Cosmo agreed. "You keep making the mistake of assuming our orders are coming from the king."

Oh, God! The royal security force had been compromised and the royal jet hijacked.

Whit doubted he had to worry about their bringing them back to St. Pierre. He had to worry about their bringing them anywhere.

Alive.

GABRIELLA'S HEART POUNDED fast and furiously, and it wasn't just because she was a somewhat nervous flyer. She had her hands braced against opposite walls of the tiny bathroom.

And her ear pressed to the door, she heard everything being said between the men.

They weren't acting on her father's orders. She figured that might have been the case when she'd boarded and recognized the man she had shot. The fact that he'd already been aboard the plane meant that he was working with the men from her father's old security team. And she doubted her father would have approved that man nearly shooting her. Because he would have if not for Whit knocking him out.

She had suspected then how much danger she and Whit and their baby were in. So she had feigned the fainting and sickness to get away from them.

Having her suspicions confirmed actually produced a flash of relief before panic overwhelmed her. These men didn't work for her father.

So who did they work for?

The person who'd left that note threatening her life? Or Linus's father, determined to carry out his creepy plot? Or were they working for themselves, having come up with their own retirement plan: ransom?

If that was their plan, they might let her live—at least until they got money from her father. But what about Whit? They had no reason to keep him alive.

She had been waiting for the royal bodyguard to help her. But he was the one who needed her help. She had only just realized that when she heard him goad the men.

"You can't fire those guns on a plane. One stray bullet and you could bring it down."

Were they already going to execute him?

She eased open the door slightly and peered through the crack. Whit was in the aisle, pushing against the men standing between him and the cockpit.

"Then we'll make sure all of them hit you," Bruno replied, lifting his weapon to point the barrel right at Whit's chest.

The men were so focused on him that they didn't notice as Gabby eased out the door. She stepped into the aisle and snuck toward the back of the plane—to the cargo hold.

Assess the situation...

Charlotte's words echoed inside Gabby's head. Her former bodyguard had used this very scenario as an example in order to teach Gabriella how to protect herself during a plane hijacking.

Gabby remembered giggling at the time, totally amused that her bodyguard had been so paranoid that she'd thought something that farfetched could happen aboard the St. Pierre royal jet. But now that the scenario had become a reality, Gabriella was frantically trying to recall the advice Charlotte had offered. She wanted that voice inside her head, but all she could hear was Whit's.

"Bullets have a tendency to go right through me," he cockily replied and rolled his wounded shoulder as if to prove his point.

Damn him and his macho bravado...

If he got the renegade guards to fire, he would not only die but he would risk the whole plane going down. Gabby needed to find a parachute. Because sometimes the most effective mode of self-preservation was escape...

She pushed open the door to the cargo hold, hoping she would find at least a parachute— hopefully more. But as she slipped into the hold, a commotion erupted inside the plane. Flesh connected with flesh as men threw punches and kicks.

Gabby flinched with every grunt and groan— as if the blows were hitting her. And inside her belly, the baby flipped and kicked. Whit wasn't the only fighter. Gabby could fight, too, and not just how Charlotte had taught her. She could fight now as a mother fighting to protect her child.

And her child's father.

She only hoped she found something to help Whit before it was too late and the men had already killed him.

Chapter Nine

Pain radiated from Whit's shoulder through-out his body—to every place a blow had con-nected. But he had landed more blows than he'd received. He had even knocked out a cou-ple of the men.

But then Bruno lifted his gun again, this time swinging the handle toward Whit's head. He ducked and the blow glanced off his wounded shoulder.

He groaned so loudly that his throat burned from the force of it. Pain coursed through him, but rage followed it, chasing away the pain. Blind with anger, Whit reached out and jerked the weapon from Bruno's beefy hand.

Before he could slide his finger onto the trigger, barrels pointed at him and triggers cocked with ominous clicks.

"Drop it!" Cosmo ordered.

Whit shook his head. "You're not the one giving orders here. Who is?"

"You're not going to find out," Cosmo said. "You're going to be dead long before we land."

Even though he'd grabbed a weapon, there were still too many fighting him. He might not make it off this plane, but he had to know about Gabby. "What about the princess? Does the person giving orders want her alive or dead?"

"What does it matter to you?" Cosmo asked. His eyes narrowed and he nodded. "Ever since you started at the palace, she was always asking everybody about you and following you around, mooning over you. So is that baby she's carrying yours?"

Whit clenched his jaw, grinding his teeth together with frustration that he couldn't claim his baby. Doing so might risk the child's safety and Gabby's. The last man who had thought he'd kidnapped her, but had abducted Charlotte instead, had wanted to get her pregnant with his own child. Even though Prince Linus was in custody, he was still a wealthy man; he or his father could have paid these guys to abduct the right woman this time.

Cosmo took Whit's silence as affirmation and shook his head in mock sympathy. "Too bad you'll never get to see it being born."

Because they were going to kill Whit or because they were going to kill Gabby, too?

"Shoot the damn gun!" The order echoed inside the cabin, but it was a female voice that uttered it. A sweet, strong voice—Gabby's. She stood near the entrance to the cargo hold.

When he'd heard her stop her fake retching, he'd figured she was going to sneak out of the bathroom soon. So he'd provided a distraction for her. That was why he'd started swinging despite being outmatched. He had wanted to distract the other men, so they wouldn't notice her. Apparently she'd gone from the bathroom to the cargo hold. Looking for an escape or a weapon?

"Whit," she said, making it clear her order was for him, "trust me—shoot the gun!"

"What the hell?" Cosmo whirled toward her with his gun drawn.

And Whit couldn't trust that the other man wouldn't fire. So he did. He lifted his gun and fired a bullet through the roof of the cabin.

The other men cursed as the plane dropped, losing altitude fast. Whit leapt over them, heading toward Gabby. He had fired the gun because he'd figured out her plan; he only hoped it wouldn't get them killed.

"YOU TRUSTED me," she said, surprised that he had actually fired. And afraid that he had. She swung a parachute pack toward him.

But the plane lurched and Whit nearly missed it. And he narrowly missed the hands reaching for him as he grabbed up the pack and ran into the cargo hold with her. He shoved the door shut and jammed something against it. "There better be another way out," he said. "And fast…"

She pointed toward the parachute and turned her back toward him to show she'd already put on hers. His hands caught the straps, pulling them tight, as he double-checked all the lines and cords.

"Are you sure parachuting will be safe for the baby?" he asked.

"Getting shot will be a hell of a lot less safe," she pointed out, as the men fired now, shooting their guns into the hold.

Whit pulled his pack on and adjusted the straps, pulling them taut. His shoulder wound was again oozing blood, which trickled down his arm in rivulets. The parachute straps were going to stress the wound even more. She should have considered that, should have thought of something else. But he agreed, "We have no other option now."

"Is the plane going down?" she asked, as it continued to lose altitude.

"Probably crash landing. We have to get out soon." He hurried over to the luggage door to the outside and struggled with its latch. "I think I can get it open…"

She hadn't thought out any of her plan. Maybe Whit shouldn't have trusted her. Maybe he shouldn't have fired. But if he hadn't, he would probably already be dead. While she hadn't been with him these past six months, at least he had been alive. At least she'd had hope that he might one day become the man her naive heart had believed he was. But if he was dead…

Then Gabby had no hope.

"Come here." He held out his hand. "We have to be ready to jump when I open this luggage hatch."

She'd faked getting sick earlier but her stomach lurched now, threatening to revolt for real. She hadn't thought this plan out well—hadn't considered all the consequences. She had parachuted before—with Charlotte, who had set up a scenario eerily similar to this so that Gabby would be prepared if her plane were ever hijacked.

Gabriella had loved the freedom of parachuting, the weightlessness of floating on air. But she hadn't been pregnant then. She'd had no one else to worry about except herself.

The door to the cabin vibrated as if one

of the men were kicking it or slamming his shoulder into it.

"We have to do this now," Whit said. "We're dead for sure if we don't."

And possibly dead if they did...

He opened the door to the outside, causing the plane to buck as if they were trying to ride a crazed bull. Whit grabbed her hand and tugged her out with him—sending them both hurtling through air.

If only there had been time to tell him...

Tell him what?

That she loved him? Six months ago she'd thought she was falling for him, but she hadn't even known him. She'd been attracted to his masculine beauty and his aura of strength and mystery. And the fact that he hadn't seemed to give a damn about anything or anyone...

She'd wished she could have been like that—that the queen's rejections and cruelty hadn't mattered to her. But she'd thought the woman was her mother, so she'd been devastated and desperate to please—so desperate that she'd let her father bully her.

And she'd let people lie to her—because she'd felt the secrets and hadn't probed deeper. She hadn't demanded the truth because she'd been afraid to hear it. She hadn't thought herself strong enough to handle it.

But she was a hell of a lot stronger than she'd realized. She was strong enough to jump out of a crashing plane.

But she wasn't strong enough to tell Whit that she had nearly fallen for him...before she'd begun to fall with him...

All she could do was hold tightly to his hand and hope she didn't lose him—hope that she didn't lose her baby or her life.

HE WAS LOSING her. His arms ached, his shoulder burning, as he struggled against the straps, tugging off the chutes before they pulled them both under water. Part of the chute, the part they'd slipped on with the straps, was a life jacket. But it was thin and barely enough to keep them above the surface of the choppy water. They had landed in the ocean—with no land in sight.

And only God knew what waiting, beneath the surface, to devour them...

After the struggle on the plane, his wound had re-opened. Was his blood baiting the water? Maybe he should leave her before he drew sharks to them. He tried to peer beneath the surface but the setting sun reflected off the water, blinding him. Making the water look as if it were all blood...

"Gabby!"

She squeezed his fingers. She had been clinging to his hand since they'd leaped out of the dropping plane. "I'm here…" But she sounded sleepy, groggy, as if she were so exhausted that she was about to pass out.

Whit recognized the signs in her voice because he felt them in his own body. He pushed his legs to kick, to keep them above the waves that kept lifting them only to drop them again. Water slapped his face, as if trying to keep him awake. He needed that because the life jacket wasn't enough to keep his head above water, but only enough to keep them from dropping to the bottom of the sea. It would make their bodies easier to find when they were dead…

"Are you all right?" he asked.

"Yes," she replied.

"And the baby?"

She smiled. "He's fine. Kicking as if he's trying to swim, too."

"He? You keep calling the baby a boy," he realized. "Do you know…?"

She shook her head now, her wet hair slapping across the surface of the sea. "I don't know for certain. It's just a feeling I have."

A gut instinct. Whit understood that, but unfortunately the gut instinct he had now was bad. If only he'd had more time before they'd jumped, he could have tried to find supplies to take along. But he might have lost them any-way, like he had the gun he'd shoved into the back of his jeans. It had fallen out when they'd hit the water and sunk like a rock.

"I can't believe," she said, "that we sur-vived…"

His gut tightened with dread as he worried that she spoke too soon. "We survived the plane crash," he agreed.

But would they survive a night in the sea?

"Did it crash?" she asked, leaning back to stare up at the sky. It was nearly black now, the last of the light glowing on the surface of the water. There were no lights in the sky.

"Not near us…" He had worried that it might go down as they were jumping and take them both out as it crashed. While he and Gabby had been drifting on air, he'd caught glimpses of the plane as it spiraled forward and down-ward. With its speed, it had gone a good dis-tance ahead of where they landed in the water.

But given the waves and tides, some of the wreckage could drift back toward them.

"But you think it crashed?" she persisted. Maybe she was so concerned because she needed a distraction, or needed to make sure that the men weren't going to come after them again. But knowing her, she was prob-ably worried about the well-being of the men who would have killed them with no hesitation or remorse.

"I don't know." And truthfully he didn't. He'd been in worse situations and had had pilots pull up the throttle and safely land the aircraft. "I don't know who the pilot was. The king's pilot could have handled the changes in cabin pressure. He could have kept it in the air and landed somewhere." But he knew it hadn't been that pilot, or the plane wouldn't have been waiting at the airport as long as the men had complained they'd been waiting.

She expelled a breath of relief. "Yes, they might be okay, then..."

She really was too good—too perfect—to be real. He must have conjured her up from those old, half-forgotten fairy tales. He wasn't as perfect as she was. Hell, he wasn't even close to perfect or forgiving or caring. So he had to ask for clarification, "You're worried about men who would have had no qualms over killing us?"

He tensed as he glimpsed something dark in the water, moving just beneath the surface. Beneath them. Had the sharks begun to circle? They, too, would have no qualms over killing them.

"When I told you to shoot," she said, in a voice hoarse with remembered panic and with regret and probably dehydration, too, "I—I didn't realize that the plane might crash…"

"It doesn't matter if it did," Whit said. "You were in danger." And still was, with no land in sight, and the waves getting rougher. Their bodies bobbed as the waves lifted and then dropped them—almost as if the water toyed with them, giving them hope only to dash it away. He held more tightly to her hand, his own going numb with cold and the effort to keep hanging on. "You had to save yourself."

"I—I don't know for certain that they would have killed me," she said, her teeth chattering slightly.

With the sun no longer warming the water, it had quickly gone cold. Flesh-numbingly cold.

"You think they only intended to kidnap you?" They hadn't seemed concerned enough about her safety, and they knew the king well enough to know that he would have paid no money without proof of life.

"I don't know what they intended to do with me," she said with a shaky sigh. "But I do know what they intended to do with you. They were definitely going to kill you, Whit."

He shivered but not just with the cold. He'd had close scrapes over the years, probably more than his share even for a marine and a bodyguard. But he'd always managed to figure his own way out. Until now...

"So you weren't worried about yourself," he said. "You were worried about me." He wasn't used to people worrying about him. His mother certainly hadn't when she'd packed up her stuff and left him with his father. Back when they'd been friends and partners Aaron had worried, but then Aaron worried about everyone.

"They had no reason to keep you alive," she said, "and more reasons to want you dead."

"With a bum shoulder and no weapon, I didn't pose much of a threat to them," he pointed out.

She chuckled. "But you're Whitaker Howell. You're a legend for the feats you've pulled off in battle, for the people you've protected as a bodyguard. They would see you as quite the threat."

"Or quite the pain in the ass," he said. "And it probably didn't help that I brought in my own men to take their jobs when Aaron and I were hired as co-chiefs of royal security."

She must have shaken her head because a wet piece of her hair slapped against his arm. Her hair and her skin was so cold. He wanted to put his arms around her and warm her up. But then he risked them both slipping under water.

"So you parachuted out of a plane to save me," he mused. "And here I was the one who promised to protect you." A promise he was still struggling to keep, as he tried to keep them both afloat.

Water splashed her face, and she sucked in a breath and coughed. And as she panicked, her head slipped beneath the choppy surface. Whit panicked, too, but he didn't let go of her hand. And with his other arm, his injured arm, he dragged her back up. She sputtered and coughed again, expelling salty water from her constricted lungs.

"Are you all right?" he asked.

"Y-yes," she stammered. "And you are my protector."

With the right resources, he was a damn good bodyguard. He could protect anyone from armed gunmen, from bombs, from fires...

But he had no idea the threats that lurked beneath the surface of the water. And no way of protecting her from them. Or from the water itself as it chilled their skin and blood, threatening hypothermia.

He'd been told it was a peaceful death. It was how his father had gone, too drunk to get the key in the door—he'd died on his front porch during the dead of winter—while Whit had been in the sweltering heat in a desert on the other side of the world. He wasn't going out like his old man. "We need to stay awake," he said. "We need to stay alert…"

"To what?"

He wouldn't tell her his fear that there was something circling them. He focused instead on offering her hope. "If the plane did go down, someone would have noticed it on radar. They might send out boats or helicopters to search for survivors."

Given that he'd seen no sign of land when they'd dropped into the sea, a search party was their only chance.

"You think help's coming?" she asked.

"Yes, if not strangers—then Aaron and Charlotte will send someone or come themselves."

"But how will they know where to look for us?" she asked. "How will they know to look for us—that we're still alive?"

"Aaron will know," Whit said. "Just like he knew that Charlotte was alive." But that was because he loved the woman, because he had a bond with her. Or it was because the man always looked for the best in a situation.

Whit should have known that Gabriella was

alive the past six months. But he'd never been as hopeful or optimistic as Aaron. He always expected the worst; there was less risk of getting disappointed that way.

"He loves her?" Gabby asked.

"Yes."

She fell silent, just floating in the dark. So he prodded her, "We need to keep talking…"

"About—about what?"

He chuckled. "Your nickname is Gabby. You can't think of anything to talk about?"

"I—I only chatter when I'm nervous."

If there was ever a time to be nervous, it was now—adrift at sea at night. "Tell me about the orphans," he said.

She wasn't gabby. She was eloquent, as she told him beautiful stories of the children's triumph over all the tragedies of their lives. She talked until her teeth chattered too much for her to get the words out. "Your turn," she told him.

"I'd rather hear you…" And he would. He loved the sound of her voice, the way it slipped into his ear and into his heart.

"If you want to distract me from how cold I am," she said, "I'm better at listening." Something else about her the paparazzi had gotten completely wrong.

"You're going to make a great mom," he said. If he could keep her and their baby alive...

She sniffled, either from the cold or from emotion. "I don't know about that. I didn't exactly have a loving mother growing up. Or biologically. What kind of mother gives up her baby for money?"

"At least she had a reason," he said. And he talked. He told her about his mom and his dad. Maybe he told her the stories to warn her that he wouldn't be a good husband or father. Or maybe he just told her to keep her awake.

But her grasp on his hand loosened, and her fingers slipped free of his. He couldn't lose her now—he couldn't lose her and the child she carried. Since he was a kid, he had sworn he would never have a family—that he wouldn't put himself through the risk of disappointment and pain.

But now his greater fear was that he was going to lose the chance at having one. Even if a search party was dispatched, the wreckage of the plane was nowhere near them. They would probably be presumed dead. And soon that might be true...

THE KING'S DEN WAS FULL of people now. Because she was so beloved, nearly every member of the household staff had gathered to hear word of Gabriella's well-being. Her fiancé was also there, along with his ex-fiancée, who claimed she had come out of friendship to him and relation to Gabby. She was the queen's cousin, which made her no relation to Gabby. But Charlotte wasn't about to explain that situation—or even talk to her.

Nor was she going to talk to the father and brother of Gabby's ex-fiancé, who claimed they had also come out of concern. She was surprised they'd had the audacity to show, after what Prince Linus Demetrios had done. But maybe they wanted to watch King St. Pierre suffer, as they were bound to suffer with the prince in prison now. They probably blamed the whole thing on the king, for breaking that engagement in the first place.

Charlotte suspected that he was blaming himself, too. Even with all the people gathered around, he looked so alone, removed from the others as he sat behind his ornate desk on a chair that was too modern to resemble a throne. But it was still one regardless of the design.

The man was used to being in control—not just of his own life but of every life in St. Pierre. He was helpless now. Charlotte's heart shifted, as if opening slightly to him. He had made mistakes. So many mistakes…

But so had she.

Would Gabby ever forgive either of them? Or had she died hating them both?

A man strode into the den, and all the chatter in the room ceased. All heads turned to him, as if he were the king about to make a royal decree.

But Charlotte knew him best, so she knew what he was going to say before he even opened his mouth. The anguish and hopelessness was in his blue eyes, dimming the brightness that Charlotte loved so much. The regret was in the tight line of his mouth, and the anger and frustration in the hard set of his strong jaw.

Guilt attacked her first. It was all her fault—her stupid plan that had put them all at risk. But even before the plan, she had hurt Aaron. She'd cost him his friendship with the man who'd been as close to him as a brother. While she'd spent the past three years getting to know her sister, he had lost those three years of friendship; he and Whit had been estranged. Because of her…

They had only just repaired that friendship to lose it again. Forever, this time…

Aaron cleared his throat, as if choking back emotion. But it was clear and steady as he spoke, "The plane went down. A search party went out to the wreckage, but there were no survivors."

Now the grief hit her. Hard. Grabbing her heart and squeezing it in a tight fist.

"She's dead," a woman's voice murmured into the eerie silence after Aaron's pronouncement.

"We don't know that," he corrected her. "Her body wasn't found."

"But you said no survivors…" The woman was Honora Del Cachon, the ex-fiancée of Prince Malamatos.

"From the wreckage of the plane," Aaron said. He looked at Charlotte now, his gaze holding hers. His eyes had brightened again—not as much as they usually were when he looked at her. But he wasn't entirely without hope. "But I'm not sure Princess Gabriella went down with the plane."

"Why not?" Charlotte asked the question now. She had to know if he was only trying to make her feel better or if she had a real reason to hope.

"Because Whit's body wasn't found either…"

She wanted to be as optimistic as the man she loved. But she wasn't like him and Gabriella—who always found the good in everything. She was more like Whitaker Howell, more realist than idealist. "But if they parachuted out before the plane crashed…"

She had an idea of where it had gone down because she'd been with Aaron and the king when they'd been told it had gone off radar. Aaron had gone out to the area where it had crashed, to look for survivors and verify that it had been one of the royal jets. She'd wanted to go along, but he'd insisted she stay behind— probably because he'd worried that she might lose the baby if she had proof that her sister was dead.

That was probably why he was offering false hope now. She couldn't take it.

"…they landed in the middle of the sea," she said, "with no land in sight. No help…"

The only boats to pass through the area, where they would have had to jump to escape before the plane crashed, were drug runners, arms dealers and other pirates.

"And they would have been in the water all night," she added. "With as cold as it gets when the sun goes down, there is no way they could have survived."

She hated that the brightness dimmed again in her fiancé's eyes. But she couldn't cling to a lie. She had to face the reality that her sister and Whit were gone.

Forever…

Chapter Ten

"Stop!" she ordered him. "Put me down."

But Whit ignored her protest and tightened his arms around her. The waves slapped at his legs as he fought his way from the surf to the beach. He staggered onto the sand.

"I can walk," she said, but she wasn't certain if she spoke the truth. After hours in the water, her legs were so heavy and weak that they had folded beneath her when she'd tried to stand in the shallows.

That was when Whit had grabbed her up his arms, arms that had strained against the waves to swim them to shore. Land. They had reached land.

Or was it just a mirage on the endless water? Or a dream? She had nearly fallen asleep several times. Her life jacket had been fairly useless, so her head would have slipped beneath the surface if not for Whit holding her above water.

How had he stayed so strong? So alert? Amazed by the man's power, she stared up into his handsome face.

Despite the cold they'd endured all night, sweat beaded on his forehead and above his tense mouth. His arms shook from exertion. He was more than exhausted. He was wounded, blood streaking down his arm from his shoulder. It was a miracle the blood hadn't drawn sharks to attack them.

"Put me down," she ordered again.

He stumbled as his feet sank in the sand, but he didn't drop her. That promise he'd made to protect her was one he obviously intended to keep—no matter what it cost him. His health. His strength. His life.

He trudged across the sand, which gave way to a slate patio and stairs leading up from the beach to a glass-and-stone house perched on a hill high above the water. "This island is inhabited," he said.

When they'd first noticed it, it had seemed little more than a clump of trees in the distance. As they'd swum toward it, the island had gotten bigger but not much. It was just a small stretch of sand, a rocky cliff and a clump of trees. They'd worried that it would be uninhabited. But maybe this was just a tiny peninsula of a bigger island.

"You're not going to carry me up all those steps." Gabby fought harder, so that she finally wriggled free of his grasp and slid down his body. Her legs, numb with cold and exhaustion, trembled and threatened to cave again before finally holding her weight.

Fortunately there was a railing beside the stairs, which Gabby climbed like a rope to help her to the top of the steep hill. She gasped at the view at the summit. It was just the hill and the house and the beach below that. The other side dropped off even more steeply to rocks and water. It was no peninsula of a larger island or continent.

"This is someone's private retreat," she said as Whit joined her at the top.

He was battered and bruised from his battle with the men aboard the plane. And his skin was flushed either from the sun or with a fever.

After those interminable hours in the darkness, she welcomed the warmth of the sun. But maybe the shock of going from the frigid water to the sunlight was too much for Whit. Could his body handle any more trauma?

He nodded. "There's a helicopter pad over there." He gestured with a jerk of his chin as if his arms were too tired to lift.

She followed his gesture to where the trees

had been cleared on the other side of the hill from the house. "No helicopter. So nobody's home?"

Whit walked around—or more accurately—staggered and peered between the trees down all sides of the hill. "There's a dock on this side of the island." This time he managed to point but not with the arm of which the shoulder was wounded. "But no boat."

Panic struck Gabby. She'd been so hopeful that this place would prove their salvation. But with no means of escaping if someone were to follow them here, they were trapped.

"So there's nothing but the house?" she asked.

It was one hell of a house. Nowhere near as grand as the palace, of course, but Whit preferred its simple lines. Made of glass and stone, it became part of the landscape, bringing the outside in as sunshine poured through the windows, warming the slate floor beneath their feet.

The door hadn't been locked. There would have been no point—probably nobody knew where the place was but the owner. Maybe that was a good thing; maybe a bad thing...

It depended on who owned the place and for what reason he required such seclusion. This part of the world wasn't known for its tourism, more for its guns and drugs and lawlessness.

Whit had checked every room to make sure the place was empty before he'd left Gabby inside alone. Even though he'd only been gone minutes, he expected to find her asleep when he stepped back inside, but she was in the kitchen, flitting around like a bedraggled butterfly.

"You got the power on," she said with a sigh of relief. "There must be a generator?"

He nodded as he took a seat on one of the stools at the granite kitchen island. Like the rest of the house, the kitchen was all slate and glass. "And enough gas to keep it running for a while."

"There's a lot of food, too," she said. "Dry goods and canned fruit and vegetables and juices. We'll have enough to eat until someone finds us."

Whit nodded, hoping that the right people would find them and not the ones they'd just jumped out of a plane to escape. Or worse yet, the person who had given those men their orders. And what exactly had those orders been? To kidnap the princess? Or kill her?

"Nobody will look for us here," she said, as if she'd read his mind and wanted to set it at ease. "They probably think we're dead."

"Maybe they're right." His head pounded

and his shoulder throbbed. And his stomach rumbled with a hunger more intense than he ever remembered, even when he'd been a kid and his dad had forgotten to buy groceries. Or he'd spent the money on liquor instead of food. "I feel like hell."

She pushed a plate of food at him. She'd done something with canned chicken and pineapple, and as he ate it, he became certain he wasn't dead. Because this felt too much like heaven, with her as an angel, and he'd never imagined he'd wind up *there*.

As soon as he finished eating, she was at his side, helping him up from the stool. His legs shook from the effort. God, he was so damned tired. He'd never been so tired—not even during his first deployment with those bombs exploding all night every night...

"You need to rest," she said, guiding him down the hall toward the bedrooms.

He shook his head. "I have to keep watch. Make certain no one takes us by surprise..."

She chuckled and assured him, "We'll hear them coming..."

He listened and could hear nothing but the waves crashing against the shore below. He never wanted to hear water again—never wanted to be near it—not after all those endless hours they'd spent drifting in it.

"Go to sleep," she said, gently pushing him down onto the bed.

He caught her hand, needing to keep track of her. He couldn't lose her again—not like he had six months ago—when he'd thought he'd lost her forever—not like when she'd slipped away from him at sea.

"Don't go," he said. "Don't leave…"

The words brought him back to his childhood—to what he'd said when his mother had packed her bags and walked out with them—leaving him behind. She hadn't paid any attention to what he'd said, to what he'd wanted or needed.

But Gabby settled onto the bed beside him. And her cool hand stroked across his brow. "You're so hot. I wish Dominic was here."

Jealousy flashed through him that she wanted another man…when he wanted only her.

"You need a doctor," she said.

He shook his head. "No. I only need you…"

I ONLY NEED *YOU*.

He'd been delirious with a fever when he'd said those words. He probably hadn't even known who she was. But still she couldn't get that line out of her head. And when she slept… she dreamed it was true.

That he really needed her. That he loved her as she had never been loved. Now she was back to being the young girl weaving foolish fantasies.

It was time to wake up. The sun was beating hard through the windows, warming the room and her body. She squinted even before she opened her eyes. But the sun wasn't shining in her face.

A shadow covered her—the broad-shouldered shadow of a man. Backlit by sunshine, she couldn't see more than the shadow at first. So she screamed.

He leaned back, and the sun bathed his face and glinted in his golden hair. "It's all right," he said. "You're safe. It's just me."

Then she wasn't safe at all. Not emotionally. He'd gotten to her again—gotten into her heart. The night they'd spent on the water, endlessly talking, she'd learned more about him than any of his friends could have told her. She wondered if even Aaron knew exactly how Whit had grown up. Alone.

He had probably thought they were going to die. That had to be the reason why he'd told her all that he had. All his pain and disappointments...

Or he'd hoped that if they lived, she would know better than to expect a happily-ever-after from him. He didn't believe they existed. And with good reason.

She shouldn't believe in them, either. But even though she hadn't experienced them personally, she'd seen them—when she'd visited boarding school friends who had found happiness with men who loved them.

But maybe Whit couldn't love—because he didn't know how. And she wasn't certain that was something that could be taught. No one had taught her to love, but it hadn't stopped her from falling for this man. With resignation and wonder, she murmured, "It's just you…"

His lips twitched into a slight grin at her remark. His hair was damp and water glistened on his bare shoulders and chest.

"You took a shower," she said, around the lump of desire that had risen up to choke her. A droplet trickled down his chest, and she had to fight to resist the urge to lick it away.

"I needed to—to wake up," he said. "Looks like you did, too. Your hair's still damp." He put his hand in it, running his fingers through her hair—which was probably still tangled despite her efforts to comb through the thick mess.

Grateful for the generator running the pump, she'd taken a shower and put her clothes in the mini–washing machine she'd found. But she hadn't found any clothes to wear while she slept. So the only thing between her and him was a thin sheet and the towel draped low around his lean hips.

"How long was I asleep?" he asked. "Days?"

He touched his jaw—which was clean-shaven now. He must have found a razor because when she'd checked on him last he'd had a lot of dark blond beard growing on his jaw. Even asleep, he'd been tense—his jaw clenched. "Weeks?"

She had lost track of time, thinking of him. Dreaming of him. But since her hair was still damp, she hadn't been asleep that long.

"A day and a half," she said. "And you probably still need more rest."

"No." He shook his head and leaned close again. His dark eyes were intense as he met her gaze. "That's not what I need."

Her pulse started racing, her blood pumping fast and hard through her veins. She had to ask, "What do you need?"

"You," he said. "Only you…"

She must have been sleeping yet—caught so deeply in the dream that it felt real. Like his lips skimming across hers, she could feel the warm soft brush. And then his tongue slid inside her mouth—in and out. Her skin tingled with desire and then with his touch, as his hands skimmed over her naked shoulders. He moved his lips across her cheek, to her neck.

She shivered now.

"Are you cold?" he asked.

She shook her head. Her skin was catching fire with the intensity of the passion she felt for him. That desire chased away the last chill from their night in the cold sea. "No…"

He kissed one of her shoulders and then her collarbone and the slope of her breast. Then he pushed down the sheet, skimming his hands over her breasts. But he stopped with his palms on her belly. "Can we do this?" he asked.

"We jumped out of an airplane," she reminded him. And during the whole parachute trip down to the water, the baby had kicked— as if with excitement. He was probably already as fearless as his father. Panic flickered at the thought, at how she would have to worry about him, like she worried about Whit.

"I doubt a doctor would have recommended that." Whit tensed, his eyes widening with shock.

"Are you all right?" she asked. "Are you hurt?"

She knew he had needed more rest and a doctor to examine his wound. But it looked better now, the edges of skin melding together around the puckered hole where the bullet had entered his body.

"I—I'm fine," he said. "And so's he. He's kicking." He stared down at her belly, obviously awed that there was life inside her. "He feels strong."

She smiled at the fatherly pride he was already showing. "He is."

"You really think the baby's a boy?" he asked, almost hopefully.

Did all men want sons? She knew her father certainly had. Perhaps that was why he hadn't claimed Charlotte because she hadn't been the male heir he'd really wanted. And then by the time Gabriella had come along, he'd wanted an heir so desperately that he'd taken what he'd gotten despite his disappointment. Now he intended to barter her for a man, for a son-in-law, to help him rule his country.

No matter how much she had fallen for Whit, her father would never approve him as her husband. He had no family. No country. Nothing her father could take in trade. Gabriella only wanted one thing—from both men. Love.

If she couldn't get it for herself, perhaps she could for her child. "I don't know for certain he's a boy. The orphanage had no access to an ultrasound to prove it."

"What about other prenatal care?" he asked.

"Dominic took care of me."

That muscle twitched in his cheek again. "You should have found me, should have told me, and given me the chance to take care of you."

"I didn't know that you'd want to," she admitted. "In fact I was pretty convinced that you wouldn't want to."

He uttered a ragged sigh. "If you had asked me if I wanted to become a father, I would have told you no."

She flinched as his brutal honesty struck her hard. "I'm sorry…"

"But now that it's going to happen," he said, "I'll deal with it. I'll figure out how to be a good parent."

"Figure out?"

He shrugged. "I told you—that night on the water—I didn't have good examples."

"I know," she murmured. The stories had been more about warning her than sharing with her.

"My mom took off when I was little," he reminded her, "and my dad cared more about drinking than raising a kid."

As it had when he had first told her about his upbringing, sympathy for him clutched her heart. "I'm sorry…"

"You didn't have any better examples," he reminded her—again with the brutal honesty. "Aren't you scared?"

"Terrified," she admitted.

"You don't need to be," he assured her, stroking a fingertip along her cheek. "You will be a wonderful mother."

He had told her that before—on the water. And she hadn't asked then what she should have. "How do you know?"

"Because you care about people," he said. "You're not selfish…"

"Like my father?" Would she be as controlling with her kid as he'd been with her?

"He wasn't responsible for those men on the plane," Whit said in his defense. "They weren't following *his* orders."

So he wasn't a monster, just a bully. "I know," she said. "That's why I figured out we needed to jump."

"You took a huge risk…"

Her heart flipped with fear even just remembering. So many things could have gone wrong.

"Take a risk on me," he said, lowering his head to hers. He kissed her again—with passion and desire.

He had to be real. This couldn't be a dream.

But what did Whit want her to take a risk on? Loving him?

It was too late. She'd already fallen in love with him. Six months ago. And so many things had gone wrong…

Except for conceiving their child. And except for making love with him. That hadn't felt wrong. That had felt as right as what he was doing to her now.

He made love to her mouth and then he made love to her body, kissing every inch of her. He teased her breasts with his tongue, tracing a nipple with his tongue before tugging the taut point between his lips.

She cried out as pressure built inside her body. She arched her hips up, silently begging for the release she knew he could give her. And he teased her with his fingers, sliding them gently in and out of her. Then he pressed his finger against the point where the pressure had built. And she came, screaming his name.

He moved away, dropping onto the mattress next to her. Sweat beaded on his brow and his upper lip, and the muscle twitched in his cheek.

"Are you all right?" she asked, concern chasing away the pleasure afterglow.

He groaned. "I will be. I just need a minute."

His body betrayed him. He'd lost his towel, so she saw the evidence of his desire.

"Make love to me," she urged him.

"I don't want to hurt you," he said, and he pressed a hand to her stomach. "Or him…"

"We're fine," she assured him. But she wasn't completely fine because the pressure was building again. "But I need you. I need to feel you inside me." And because she was afraid that he would hold back, she took the initiative.

She straddled his lean hips and eased herself down onto his pulsing erection. She moaned as he sank deeper and deeper.

He clutched her hips and lifted her up. But instead of pulling her off, he slid her back down. Up and down. He thrust inside her. And as he thrust, he arched up from the mattress. He kissed her, imitating with his tongue what he was doing to her body.

The intensity of the pressure built and built…until he reached between them. He pushed against her with his thumb, and she came again.

He thrust once more and uttered a guttural groan, as he filled her with his pleasure.

Tears stung her eyes from the intimacy of their joined bodies and mutual ecstasy. Her heart swelled with emotion, with love. She had never felt anything as intense until she'd felt her baby's first little flutter of movement.

She loved Whit with the same intensity that she loved their baby. And she wanted to share that love with him.

But when she opened her mouth to speak, he pressed his fingers against her lips. "Listen," he said.

And she waited for him to speak, hoping that he was going to declare his feelings. Hoping that he loved her, too.

But he said nothing. Instead he cocked his head and narrowed his eyes. Then he asked, "Do you hear that?"

"What?"

"I think it's a helicopter."

"You think the owner is coming back?" Heat rushed to her face over the embarrassment of the homeowner finding them naked in his bed.

"I hope so," Whit said, but his body had tensed again. And that muscle was twitching in his cheek.

"But you don't think it is?"

He shrugged. "It could be. But my gut's telling me that it's not."

"You think they found us?" She had almost

hoped they would believe she was dead again and not look for her.

"I think we're about to find out."

Chapter Eleven

Earlier, when he'd awakened from his long sleep, Whit had checked out the house again. Instead of just searching rooms, he'd searched every drawer and cupboard. And he'd found something the owner had left behind that he'd worried might prove useful.

A Glock.

He pressed it into Gabby's hand. "You take this," he insisted. "And stay out of sight."

They had dressed quickly, in clothes that were still damp from the washer, and Whit had retrieved the gun, before they'd slipped out of one of the many sliding doors of the house. That first day, he had found a little storm shelter close to the outbuilding that held the generator. But the cavelike hole was so small that they both barely fit inside its stone walls. That didn't matter, though, since Whit wasn't staying. He moved toward the cement steps that led back to the trapdoor like entrance.

Gabby clutched at his arm with fingers that trembled. "Don't leave."

"You'll be safe here," he assured her.

"Then you will be, too," she said. "Stay here. Stay out of sight with me."

He shook his head. "That might be help arriving on that helicopter." It had probably already landed, but the generator was too close to the shelter and too loud for them to hear over the droning engine. "It could be Aaron and Charlotte."

He doubted it, though. If the plane had crashed, there probably would have been no survivors—no one to share the news that they'd parachuted out. But before the plane had gone down, one of them might have called his boss—the one really giving the orders. That person might be aware that they'd gotten off before the crash.

And he might have launched a search party to make sure they hadn't—or wouldn't—survive.

"I'll go with you," Gabby said, anxious to see her sister now. How like Gabby it was to have already forgiven Charlotte for the secrets she'd kept...

"We don't know for sure who it is," he pointed out. Even if it was the homeowner, Whit wanted to meet him alone first and gauge the person's trustworthiness before he revealed the princess of St. Pierre. "So I need to check it out first."

"Then take the gun with you," she said, pressing the Glock back into his hand, "in case it isn't help arriving."

"If it isn't, you may need the gun," he said. "It didn't take me long to find the shelter—they could find it, too." He intended to cover that door in the ground, though, with branches and leaves.

"You'll need the gun more than I will, then," she argued, "since you'll be encountering them first."

The woman was infuriating and beautiful and generous and loving. And Whit should tell her all those things. He had wanted to tell her earlier. Those words and so many others had been on the tip of his tongue, but then he'd heard the helicopter in the distance. And he had known that this was neither the time nor the place for him to share his feelings.

And if that wasn't help arriving, there may never be a time and place for him to tell her that he was falling in love with her.

"You need the gun," he said, "to protect yourself and our baby."

She drew in a shuddery breath and finally stopped trying to push the gun on him. He knew that she wouldn't have kept it for herself, but she wanted to protect their baby.

So did Whit. He would make sure that she wouldn't need to use that gun. He would protect her and their baby no matter the cost—even if he had to give up his life for theirs.

GABBY FLINCHED AS the baby kicked her ribs—hard. He was kicking her, too, like she was kicking herself for keeping the gun. She should have insisted Whit take it with him. She shouldn't have let him leave the shelter with no protection.

Maybe she should sneak out and see who had arrived, see if Whit would need the gun. She climbed the stairs toward the trapdoor, and standing beneath it, she listened intently. But all she could hear was the generator and the sound of her own furiously beating heart.

The baby kicked again, and she pressed her free hand against her belly—trying to soothe him even as her own nerves frayed. If she really was safe where she was, why hadn't Whit taken the gun?

Could she risk her child's life to save his father?

Whit would never forgive her if she ignored his wishes and risked her own safety and their baby's. But perhaps even being where she was would endanger them. If someone found them, inside the shelter, they would be trapped. She could get off a few shots, might hit one or two of them. But what if there were more than a couple of them?

No. She couldn't stay in the shelter. It wouldn't be safe if she were to be discovered hiding in the cavelike hole because there was only one way out—through the trapdoor. She tried to lift it now, but it was heavy.

She managed to raise it an inch and dirt and grass rushed in through the narrow space. Choking on dust, she dropped it back down. Whit had covered it, had tried to camouflage it.

His friends claimed that his instincts were legendary and had saved more than one life during their deployments. For him to hide her as he had, his instincts must have been telling him that it wasn't help arriving.

They'd jumped out of a plane that had probably crashed. Why would anyone suspect they lived? Charlotte and Aaron were too realistic to believe in miracles. The only person who might know they'd survived was the one who'd hired the men, if the pilot or one of them had called him before the crash.

And if it was one of them, then Whit was disposable. He was only in the way of whatever plan that person had for her. Kidnapping or killing…

Whit, no doubt, had a plan to protect her and their baby. Like covering the hole to the shelter so no one would find her. But she worried that in order to carry out his plan he would have to sacrifice too much.

Perhaps his life…

WHIT HAD WALKED BACK through the living-room slider before passing through the house to the front door. That way, hopefully, the person wouldn't realize he had been outside.

He drew in a deep breath and opened it to a man he wasn't surprised to see. The guy was bald with heavy black brows and more scars than Whit and far fewer morals. Zeke Rogers had accepted his demotion with even less grace than the other men. He had to be the one who'd been giving them orders—since that had been his job before Whit and Aaron had taken it from him.

Whit was glad that he'd given Gabby the gun because Zeke was smart. He would find her eventually—unless Whit could outsmart him.

"You're like a cat with nine lives, huh?" Zeke remarked almost idly. He obviously wasn't surprised to see Whit either, or to find him alive and on this island. "You just keep coming back from the dead."

"I haven't died once," Whit corrected him. Yet. He had a feeling this man intended to change that.

"I heard about the bullet you took in Michigan," Zeke said. "That's why the king had me resume my duties at the palace, as his royal guard."

"We agreed that would be best," Whit admitted, "while Aaron and I concentrated our efforts on finding Charlotte and Princess Gabriella. But Charlotte has been found." And Aaron should have resumed his duties as chief of security, dismissing Zeke again.

"The princess has been, too," Zeke claimed.

Whit's stomach muscles tightened as if he'd taken a blow. But he resisted the urge to glance toward the shelter and make sure Gabby wasn't being dragged from her hiding place. Zeke could have other men searching the island. One of them could have found her.

But she was a fighter. He doubted she would have been taken without firing at least one shot, which he would have heard even over the drone of the generator engine.

Denying Zeke's claim, Whit shook his head. "She's gone…"

"The king sent you to retrieve her from

Charlotte's aunt's orphanage." The man had obviously been briefed—either by the king or by someone else. "You had her. You two were on the royal jet together before it went down."

"It went down?"

Zeke nodded, but his face displayed no emotion. He didn't give a damn that men he'd worked with had probably lost their lives. Probably while they'd been trying to carry out his orders...

"Were there any survivors?" Whit wondered.

Zeke shook his head now. "Just you and the princess."

So he had been in contact with the men on the plane—obviously right up until the moment it went down. "Why would you think that?" Whit asked, trying to get the man to make the admission. Not that it mattered if he confessed...

Whit was convinced Zeke Rogers wasn't there to help him or Gabby.

"Well, obviously you're alive."

Whit nodded. "Obviously."

"You and the princess parachuted out of the plane."

There was no point in denying what Zeke had apparently been told. "That's true."

"You weren't easy to track down," Zeke

said, resentment flashing in his beady eyes. "I had to talk to some parachuting experts and some experts on ocean currents to figure out where the hell you might have washed up."

Whit had a feeling the man had been hoping to find bodies rather than survivors. "It really was nice of you to go to all the trouble to rescue me."

"I'm not here to rescue you," the man ominously corrected him.

Whit lifted his arms, ignoring the twinge in his shoulder, and gestured around the empty house. "Well, I'm the only one here."

Zeke chuckled. "Where are you hiding the princess?"

Whit forced a ragged sigh of regret and resignation. "She didn't make it."

"She wasn't on that plane when it went down," Zeke insisted. "She parachuted off with you."

"Yes, but that was much too dangerous in her condition. There were complications…" He paused, as if choked up.

"With her pregnancy?" Zeke asked.

He was too superstitious to lie about that, not wanting to tempt fate. So he just shook his head. "She was weak and the water was just too damn cold. We were in the sea overnight." He shuddered, for real, as he remembered the frigid water and how it had numbed his muscles and burned his skin. How the hell had they survived?

He shuddered again. "She didn't make it…"

Zeke narrowed his eyes. His voice terse with skepticism, he asked, "You just let her die?"

"I couldn't do anything to help her." He really hadn't. She'd fought for herself and for their child.

Zeke snorted, derisively. "So you're not the hero everyone thinks you are."

Whit shrugged. "I never claimed I was a hero."

"You haven't needed to—all those men you hired that you served with—they make the claims for you. That's why the king made you his right-hand man." Along with the resentment, there was hatred.

"You'll probably get that job back now," Whit said, "since I failed to protect what matters most to the king." No matter how callously he'd treated his daughter, the man did love her. He had been so genuinely distraught over her disappearance that he had to care. And as Whit had learned for himself, the woman was damn hard not to love. He'd fought his feelings, but it was one of the first battles he'd ever lost.

"I thought she mattered to you, too," Zeke remarked.

"Why would you think that?"

"Heard she was following you around like a puppy before she disappeared," he said. And now there was jealousy. He was too old for Gabby. But hell, at thirty, with the life he'd lived, so was Whit. "And nobody missed the way you looked at her, too."

"She's a beautiful woman."

Zeke arched one of those creepily bushy brows.

"Was," he corrected himself, silently cursing the slip. "She was a beautiful woman."

"She was pregnant, too," Zeke said.

"Did you have a bug on that plane?" he wondered. The men wouldn't have had much time to tell him everything. But the first man, the one Gabby had shot, would have had time to inform him of the princess's pregnancy.

"I'm just thorough," Zeke said. "I believe in doing a job well."

Whit couldn't argue with him. While Zeke had protected the king, the monarch had not been harmed. But Charlotte hadn't trusted the former mercenary. She had suspected that his loyalty was for sale to the highest bidder, and that if someone paid him more than the king, that Zeke Rogers would do whatever they wanted. The man had no morals, no principles and no conscience. Obviously Charlotte had been right.

"Maybe you should have been sent to retrieve the princess then," Whit said.

"I have been," Zeke retorted. "Now."

The skin on the nape of Whit's neck tingled with foreboding. "It's too bad that you're too late."

"It would be if I actually believed you." The man pushed past Whit and strode purposely through the house, searching every room.

Feigning shock and offense, he asked, "You don't take me at my word?"

Zeke snorted in reply and just continued to search.

Whit followed, breathing a sigh of relief that he'd stripped the bed in the room in which he'd awakened. It didn't look as though anyone had slept in it. It didn't look as though anyone had slept in Gabby's bed, either. The sheets were tangled and damp.

But Zeke didn't seem to notice. He checked under the bed and the closet and continued through the house.

"Satisfied?" Whit asked. "She's not here."

"I won't believe Princess Gabby is gone,"

Zeke replied, "until I see her dead body." And if her body wasn't dead, did he intend to make it that way?

"You're not going to find it in the house." Whit managed to furrow his brow with feigned confusion. "I've been checking the beach..."

"Waiting for her to wash up?"

He flinched at the agonizing thought.

"Give up trying to sell me on this line of bullshit, Howell," Zeke said. "There's no way in hell you lost her in the ocean."

He nearly had—when her hand had slipped out of his. But he'd caught her before she'd slipped beneath the water.

"We didn't land near each other," Whit lied. "By the time I swam toward where she'd landed, the chute lines had pulled her under. She was gone..."

Zeke pulled his gun from the holster beneath his jacket. "You better hope you're telling the truth, Howell, because if I find her..."

"You're going to kill her?"

Those bushy brows arched in question. "Why would that matter to you—if she's really already dead?"

"Just didn't think the king would order his daughter killed," Whit said. "So who are you working for now?" He knew Zeke didn't intend to let him live, so he might actually tell him the truth.

"Someone who wants the princess to never return to St. Pierre."

"Who?" Whit persisted.

Zeke taunted him, "If she's really dead, what does it matter?"

Whit couldn't say it—couldn't bring himself to utter the lie. Before today he had never been superstitious, but he couldn't risk it now—that saying she was dead wouldn't somehow make it come true.

"I want to know who you're working for," Whit persisted.

"Why?" Zeke asked. "It's not like you're going to need a job anytime soon."

Whit shrugged. "You don't know that. The king is not going to be happy with me for not bringing the princess home."

"The king won't fire you," Zeke assured him. "Because he won't need to. I'll fire you for him." And he lifted the gun and pulled the trigger.

Chapter Twelve

The sound of the gunshot echoed off the hill-top. Gabby felt the vibration of it in the sliding door against which she leaned, trying to see inside. But Whit had pulled the drapes across it, blinding her to what was going on inside the house.

Who had gotten off the helicopter? And had Whit just calmly let them inside the house to shoot him?

Her heart pounded furiously and so loudly she could hear it ringing in her ears. Or was that just the echo of the shot yet?

The wind picked up, whipping her hair around her face. And she realized what the noise really was: the sound of another helicopter.

Was it backup for the first? More of the men from the plane?

She clutched the gun she held. Should she storm inside the house? Or should she run to the helicopter in the hopes that it might actually be someone to help? Her head pounded with indecision and fear. Her instincts had her wanting to storm inside the house—wanting to protect Whit.

So she followed her instincts and pushed open the patio door. She listened but heard no voices, no sound above the pounding of the helicopter blades as it approached that small pad on the other side of the house. She drew in a deep breath and lifted the gun before stepping inside.

Glass crunched beneath her feet as she crept across the living room. The coffee table top had shattered, leaving only the brass frame. And that had been twisted. Chairs had toppled onto the slate flooring.

There had been a struggle. But there was no body left behind to tell her who had won or who had lost. Where was Whit? And with whom had he struggled?

He had rested for a day, but he hadn't completely recovered from their overnight in the sea or his gunshot wound. As she studied the mess, she noticed the dark liquid spattered across the glass fragments and the slate. She crouched down, as far as her burgeoning belly allowed, and reached a trembling finger toward the spill. Then she lifted her hand and analyzed the stain smeared across her fingertip. A bright red stain.

Had Whit's wound re-opened or did he have a new one?

Tears stung her eyes. Tears of regret and guilt and anguish. She shouldn't have waited so long before coming out of the shelter. She should have followed him right back inside the house. What kind of mother was she going to be for her baby if she'd done nothing while his father had been harmed?

Where was Whit? How badly was he hurt?

She wasn't just concerned that her baby might have lost her father. She was concerned that she might have lost the man she loved... and before she'd even had a chance to tell him how she felt.

WHIT HAD HAD to get Zeke outside—because he'd noticed the shadow outside the slider. And he'd known that Gabby had been too worried to stay where he'd put her. She'd been worried about him—when she should have been more concerned about herself and their child.

She'd done the same thing at the orphanage—making sure the men had seen her, so that they would leave her aunt and the kids alone. She had used herself as bait to lure the danger away from the others.

She cared so much about everyone…but herself.

"It took two of you to replace one of me," Zeke taunted him as he pushed Whit forward with the barrel of the gun buried between his shoulder blades. "You really think you alone are any match for me?"

"Are *you* alone?" Whit asked. He had seen no other men with the guard. And Zeke had been a helicopter pilot when he'd served his country and later when he'd served whatever country had paid him the most.

Zeke snorted. "More alone than you are. Where is she?"

"I told you. She's dead." He hated saying it; hated how the words felt in his mouth. Bitter and sickening. And he hoped like hell his superstition wouldn't be proved a reality. Ever.

"The next time I shoot, it won't be a coffee table," Zeke warned him. "And the only one who's going to be dead is you."

Whit chuckled and reminded Zeke, "But you're the one who's bleeding."

When the guard had shot the coffee table, Whit had struck him hard—trying to knock him out. But the man had an iron jaw. All Whit had done was broken his skin and drawn blood.

And rage.

Zeke had swung the gun toward Whit then. But he'd kept him from firing by saying that her body had washed up on the beach. And so he'd drawn Zeke outside to the steepest edge of the hilltop.

The wind picked up, and the pounding of helicopter blades alerted them to the arrival of another aircraft. Backup for Zeke?

But all his men must have been gone because he lifted his gun and aimed it at the helicopter. As it flew over them, Whit recognized the royal seal of St. Pierre. Maybe Aaron was inside—maybe he and Charlotte had figured out Zeke's duplicity and followed him here.

Zeke must have come to the same conclusion because he squeezed the trigger, getting off one shot before Whit struck him. Instead of swinging toward the man's iron jaw, though, he slammed his fist into Zeke's arm—with enough force to knock the weapon for his grasp.

The Glock flew from the man's hand, dropping over the cliff. While Zeke turned toward where it had fallen, Whit pushed—sending the man tumbling over the side.

But Zeke's arms thrashed. And as he reached

out, he caught Whit's shoulder and pulled him over the edge, too. He felt the weightlessness that he had when he and Gabby had jumped from the plane. But this time he had no parachute strapped to his back—nothing to break his fall on the rocks.

AARON'S HEART LURCHED as the helicopter took the hit. His gaze flew to the pilot, who grappled with the controls as the aircraft shuddered and shook. "This is why I wanted you to stay at the palace," he told his fiancée.

"And let you take on Zeke Rogers alone?" Charlotte asked, shaking her head at the thought.

"I would have brought some of the men Whit and I trust," he said.

She passed over the island, struggling to bring the helicopter under control again. Over open water, the engine sputtered once. Twice.

"We can't trust anyone," she said. "But each other…"

He trusted her. He trusted that if anyone could save them right now—it was her.

But what about Whit? Were they already too late to save him and Princess Gabriella? Were they on this island—as the parachuting and ocean current experts had told first Zeke and then them?

Or had they been lost at sea as Charlotte had been so convinced? She wouldn't let herself hope. Instead she'd been intent on tracking down who was responsible for the attempted kidnapping that had gone so very wrong...

And when they'd gotten on Zeke's trail, it had led them here. To this private island getaway. Or rather, hideaway, given that the man who owned it had used questionable methods accruing the wealth to acquire the island.

He could have been the one shooting at them. Whit wouldn't have been. He would have recognized the royal seal and waited to see who landed. Then he might have started firing if he'd realized Zeke Rogers had sold himself to a higher bidder.

Why had it taken the king so long to realize that Charlotte had been right not to trust the man? Why had he?

It was a mistake that had cost him. He'd aged another ten years with the realization that he had been the one who'd put his daughter at risk. Not Charlotte. Not Whit.

And what about Whit?

No bodyguard had ever taken an assignment as literally as Whit. He would do whatever was necessary to protect a client—even give up his own life for theirs. Aaron suspected that was never truer than now, with Princess Gabriella carrying Whit's child. The guy had always claimed that he would never get married, never be a father. Aaron didn't know his reasons why, but he doubted one of them had been death.

A dead man couldn't become a husband or father...

Aaron should have married Charlotte before they'd ever left Michigan. He shouldn't have let him talk her into making sure Gabby was safe first.

"That's definitely the helicopter Zeke took," Charlotte said. The royal seal was on the bottom of it but it was the same royal blue and bright magenta of the one she flew. Or tried to fly.

The engine sputtered again. They needed to land. But Zeke had planted his helicopter in the center of the small cement pad. The island wasn't big enough to have a clearing where they could land. There was only the house and then the hill dropped steeply off to the rocky beach below.

He trusted Charlotte. But there was only so much she could do. The helicopter was going down whether or not she found a place to land safely.

GABBY'S THROAT BURNED yet from the scream she'd uttered when she had watched the two men tumble over the cliff on the other side of the helicopter pad. She'd checked out the island earlier—when Whit was asleep. She knew this side had no stairs leading to a beach. It had no sand—only jagged rocks from the top of the hill to the water below.

Dread kept her legs locked in place—unable to move forward, to run toward the edge of that cliff. She had a horrible feeling that she knew what she would see when she looked over the edge.

Like a bird of prey, the helicopter circled back again. It was the colors of her country. But that offered Gabriella more fear than comfort. The only one she could trust who worked for St. Pierre was Whit.

And he was gone.

The helicopter engine sputtered. The metal screeched, trees scraping it, as the helicopter made its crash landing. It landed in a tiny clearing behind her, between her and the house. Leaving her an unobstructed view of that cliff.

She kept watching it. But Whit didn't pull himself up it. Neither did the man he'd pushed over the side. No one came back up.

Finally she forced herself to move toward where they had fallen. But her legs trembled so badly that she had no balance. She stumbled and pitched forward. To protect her baby, she put out her hands—and dropped the gun Whit had left her for protection into the thick grass.

Behind her the helicopter engine whined down to silence. It was eerily silent. So quiet that she heard the footsteps on the grass.

Panic overwhelmed her, sending her scrambling for the gun. She delved her hands into the grass. But it was so thick and long that she couldn't find the weapon.

She had nothing to protect her. No gun. No Whit. Tears of loss and fear and frustration stung her eyes, so that they watered. And her throat filled with emotion. She couldn't even scream.

But what did it matter? Who would hear her? Anyone who cared was gone.

Strong hands grasped her arms and pulled her to her feet. She drew in a shuddery breath, trying to summon the strength and courage to fight.

Whit might have been gone. But she still had her baby. She had to fight for him—to protect him and herself from whoever had come for her.

So when she turned, she lifted her leg and kicked out with her all might—hoping to knock her attacker's legs from beneath him—

hoping to knock him off balance enough that she could escape.

But there was more than one.

Chapter Thirteen

Aaron caught Charlotte, stopping her fall. Gabby gasped in shock over seeing her sister and realizing that she'd nearly knocked down the woman—the very pregnant woman.

"Oh, my God!" she exclaimed. "Are you all right?"

Charlotte nodded. "Are you?"

The tears she'd momentarily blinked away rushed back, filling her eyes and her throat, so she barely got out her, "Yes."

It had been Charlotte and Aaron on the helicopter. Charlotte and Aaron who had nearly crashed. She'd nearly lost them, too.

"Where's Whit?" Aaron asked anxiously, his blue eyes bright with fear for his friend's safety.

Hysteria threatened, but Gabby pushed it back to reply, "Whit's gone…"

"Where's Whit?" Aaron asked, glancing

around the small area. "Did Zeke take him somewhere?"

Zeke Rogers. That was who had landed in the first helicopter. That was who had fired those shots. That was whom Whit had been fighting when he went over.

"Come quick," Gabby ordered. She hadn't believed help would come, but it had. So maybe she needed to believe again—in Whit. To hope…

"They were fighting," she said, gesturing ahead of her at the cliff as she struggled to run through the tall grass, "and they fell."

She ran but Aaron wasn't pregnant, so he was faster. He beat the women to the cliff, stopping only at the edge. His jaw clenched as he stared over the side.

When Gabby rushed up, he turned around and stopped her with his arms on her shoulders. "Don't look!"

That had been her first instinct, too, not to look when she was so certain of what she would find. Utter despair and loss. But she hadn't thought there would be help, either. She hadn't really believed that anyone would ever find her and Whit. So she had to look. Had to know for certain…

She tugged free of Aaron's grasp and looked around him. Her gaze was immediately drawn to the edge of the water below, to the body so busted up on the rocks so that it looked like a broken marionette.

"That's not Whit," she said with horror. It couldn't be Whit. He couldn't be gone.

But they wouldn't be able to confirm or disprove the identity of the body because waves tugged at it, pulling it from the rocks to disappear into the ocean.

She screamed.

WHIT'S ARMS BURNED with his effort to hang on, his hands wrapped around a rock jutting from the cliff. The rock was damp, and his grip began to slip. He didn't want to wind up like Zeke, who'd crashed onto the rocks below. His eyes had been wide open, staring up at Whit in death. But now he was gone.

And Whit heard Gabby's scream. It chilled his blood with fear—for her safety more than his.

"Gabby!" he yelled back. "I'm coming. I'm coming!"

He wouldn't leave her—not like this. Not any way. As one hand slipped off a wet rock, he lurched up, reached out blindly with his free arm and somehow managed to clasp another rock while not letting go of the one he held. The rough edges cut into his palm, and his shoulder strained with the movement. But he didn't care. His own discomfort was nothing in comparison to the fear and anguish he'd just heard in Gabby's scream.

She screamed again—his name. But now her voice was full of hope and relief. "Whit!"

He stared up at the hilltop and found her leaning over the edge. A rock beneath her foot slipped loose and tumbled down the cliff. And she slipped, too.

"Gabby!"

But strong hands grasped her arms and pulled her back. He couldn't see her—couldn't see who had her or if she was really safe.

"Gabby!"

Now someone else stood on the edge, staring down. "Son of a bitch," a deep voice shouted. "What the hell…"

"Aaron!" Relief that Gabby was safe flooded Whit. His friend would protect her, like Whit had tried, with his life if necessary.

"How the hell am I supposed to reach you?" Aaron asked with frustration, as if he were trying to figure out a particularly vexing puzzle.

Whit's grip, on one rock, slipped again. But once again he held tight with the hand that had a hold on a rock and swung his free arm. He managed to catch the edge of another rock—higher up. "I'm coming," he assured them.

Aaron must have taken him at his word because he disappeared from sight. Disappointment and panic flashed through Whit. They had only just regained their friendship and their trust. So he suffered a moment's doubt—wondering if his old friend was really going to help him.

That panic had him swinging his arm again, trying to reach a higher rock. But his fingertips slipped off, and his arm swung back—nearly making him lose the grip he had with his other hand. He kicked out, trying to find a toe hold.

And beneath him the waves crashed against the rocks, as if getting ready to carry his broken body out to sea, too.

But he wasn't giving up. Not yet. Not ever. He swung his arm toward the wall of rocks again—trying to catch hold. And his fingers touched something else—rough fibers. A rope dangled over the edge.

"Grab it!" Aaron shouted.

Whit grasped the rope in a tight fist. But he didn't let go of the rock with his other hand. And finally he got a hold with his foot.

"I got you," Aaron said. "I can pull you up."

Maybe he could. While not as big as Whit, Aaron was a strong guy. But still Whit couldn't completely give up control or trust. Instead of just holding on and letting Aaron pull him up, he used the rope as a railing to make the climb himself.

He was climbing up to Gabby—to make sure she was safe. Even though Zeke was gone, it wasn't over. If Zeke had been working for someone, that person could hire another mercenary to finish the job. But even if they figured out whom Zeke had been working for, Gabby would always be in danger; her life and her safety always at risk because of who she was. Princess Gabriella St. Pierre.

And he was just a royal bodyguard…with nothing to offer her but his protection. And he hadn't done a very damn good job of protecting her yet.

She would be safer with Charlotte. And happier with a prince. So when he stepped foot on the topside of the hill, he resisted the urge to grab her up in his arms and hold her close. And when she reached for him, he caught her hands and stopped her from embracing him. Because if he gave in to temptation and hugged her, he would never let her go again.

"Are you all right?" she asked, her beautiful face stained with tears she'd shed over him.

She was too good for him. Too good for anyone...

"What the hell happened?" Aaron asked.

Whit nodded. "I'm fine. It was Zeke who hit the rocks."

Charlotte nodded. "We figured it was Zeke."

"Acting out of revenge," Aaron said, "for us getting him fired."

Whit shook his head. "It was about money."

"Was he going to kidnap me to get my father to pay him a ransom?" Gabby asked. She tugged her hands free of Whit's, as if self-conscious that she'd reached for him and he'd held her off. She slid her palms over her stomach, as if to soothe their baby.

He could walk away from her—to keep her safe. But could he walk away from his son? Hell, the child—heir to a country—would probably be in even more danger than Gabriella had been.

"I think it was about money," Whit agreed. "But I think someone was paying him..."

Gabby flinched, as if in pain. And he couldn't add to that—couldn't tell her what Zeke had been paid to do: kill her.

"You're not feeling well," he said.

She glanced up at his face, as if dazed. And she began to tremble. "I'm fine," she said. But she had to be lying.

"Aaron, get them back to St. Pierre," he ordered.

"What about you?" Aaron asked. "Aren't you coming with us?"

"I need to clean up around here—make sure Zeke was alone." And that the man was dead. He intended to go down to the beach below.

And Charlotte and Aaron must have read his intentions. "Aaron can stay with you. I'll take her," the former U.S. Marshal said. "We have a pilot with us."

"But your helicopter was hit."

"The bullet did no structural damage."

"Is the pilot someone we can trust?" Whit asked. Before they could answer, he shook his head. "You better fly them, Aaron." Because somewhere out there, someone still wanted Gabriella dead.

"I'm the one who flew us here," Charlotte said. And then she was the one who'd landed the helicopter after it had been hit. "I've had my pilot's license for years."

"Of course you have," Gabby murmured—with a flash of bitterness.

And Whit remembered that the women had unfinished business between them. Charlotte had kept secrets from Gabby that she'd had no right to keep even though she'd had her reasons. Maybe sending the two of them off alone together wasn't the greatest idea.

"So let's go," Gabby said, and she left him without a backward glance—as if she'd dismissed him after he'd done his job. Was that all he was to her? An employee? While she walked away, Charlotte and Aaron embraced—as if the thought of spending just mere hours apart was intolerable to them.

"Be safe," Aaron implored his fiancée.

"Always."

"I love you."

"I love you more," she said and pressed a hand to her own swollen belly. "Because I love you for the both of us." With another quick kiss for her baby's father, she followed Gabby to the helicopter pad.

Both men stood until the helicopter lifted off and flew away—its engine loud and strong and its course straight.

"No smart remarks?" Aaron asked.

"About what?" He knew, though. He'd teased Aaron in the past about his public displays of affection. The man always fell easily and hard. But he'd never fallen as hard as he had for Charlotte Green, and those feelings were so much stronger because they were reciprocated. Whit couldn't tease him about that—not when he was envious as hell of what his friend had found.

Aaron narrowed his eyes, which were an eerie pale blue, and studied Whit's face. "Are you really okay? You didn't hit your head when you went over the cliff?"

Whit shook his head. "There are steps over here leading down. We need to check down there—"

"He's gone," Aaron said. "There's no way he survived that fall." He shuddered. "I can't believe that you did—that you caught yourself. You are so damn lucky—like a cat with nine lives."

Whit nearly shuddered, too, at Aaron making the same comparison the mercenary had.

"But knowing you like I do, you probably used up the last of those nine lives today," Aaron continued. "So we shouldn't risk going down that cliff."

"Maybe Zeke lost his phone," Like he'd lost his life, on the rocks, "when he fell. If we can find that and figure out who he was talking to, maybe we can figure out who hired him."

"You think Gabby's still in danger?" Aaron asked, with a glance toward the sky—obviously concerned about both women. But the helicopter was long gone.

"I know she is." And even after they found whoever had hired Zeke, she would still be in danger—still have people trying to kidnap her for her father's fortune.

"What else do you know about her?" Aaron asked. "Who the father of her baby is?" The question was obviously rhetorical; his friend was pretty damn sure it was his.

Whit clenched his jaw.

And Aaron whistled. "I can't believe it—after everything you've said about never getting married—"

"That hasn't changed," Whit said. There was no way in hell a princess would ever consider marrying him. And even if she did take the chance on him, her father would never approve their marriage.

"And the fact that we have a job to do hasn't changed, either," he continued. "We need to protect her."

"From whom, do you think?" Aaron asked.

Whit shrugged. "I don't know. We thought it might be Prince Linus's father. She doesn't think her ex-fiancé could have concocted that elaborate a plot on his own."

Aaron gasped. "King Demetrios and his younger son are at the palace. They said they were concerned about her. Why would they want to hurt the princess?"

Whit shook his head. He couldn't fathom why anyone would want to hurt Gabby. "I don't know if they're involved. All we know for certain is that someone wanted her to *never* return to St. Pierre."

And Gabriella was already on her way…

"I DON'T NEED to ask who the father of your baby is," Charlotte remarked, once she and Gabby walked into their private suite of rooms in the palace.

They hadn't talked at all on the helicopter. Gabby hadn't been ready to deal with the woman she now knew was her sister. Nor had she been able to deal with her disappointment over how Whit had treated her. It was like their making love had been just her dreaming.

Because he had acted like it had never happened. He had acted like they had never been intimate enough to have conceived the child she carried. His child.

"You don't?" Gabriella wondered. Because Whit had certainly not betrayed their relationship. But Charlotte had always been able to read her—even while she, herself, had been keeping so much from Gabby.

"You love Whit," Charlotte said, her voice soft with sympathy. From the way he'd acted, she had undoubtedly been able to tell that Gabby's feelings were not reciprocated. "You were falling for him six months ago, but now you love him."

Gabriella shrugged. It didn't matter how she felt since her feelings were not returned. He'd asked her to take a risk on him...

A risk that he would figure out how to love? That risk had obviously not paid off.

"I don't need to ask who the father of your baby is, either," Gabby said, her heart warming as she studied Charlotte's face—so like her own except for the happiness that illuminated it from within—making her breathtakingly beautiful.

"I got pregnant the night of the ball," Charlotte said, pressing her palms to her belly as Gabby always did. "The same night I assume you must have since we both left the next day." Her light of happiness dimmed. "I'm sorry. I'm sorry that my plan went so wrong."

"You were the one who was kidnapped," Gabby reminded her. "I'm sorry..."

Charlotte shook her head. "It wasn't your fault. None of it was. Aaron found me." The light inside her brightened again. "He rescued me."

"He loves you."

Charlotte smiled. "Yes. He asked me to marry him, and I accepted. I love him."

Gabby flinched with jealousy and then was angry with herself for being so petty as to envy someone else's happiness.

Charlotte reached out, pulling Gabriella into a close embrace—or as close as their pregnant bellies allowed. "And I love you," Charlotte said. "That's why I couldn't tell you that I'm your sister. I couldn't tell you about our mother."

"But you knew how the queen hated me," Gabby said, pulling free of her. "You knew how that bothered me." Even after the woman had died. "You could have told me she wasn't really my mother."

Charlotte shook her head. "If I told you the truth, I would have been fired. It killed me to keep it from you, but it was better to keep the secrets and keep you safe."

Whit had been right about her reasons. Tears stung Gabby's eyes. "You—you wanted to tell me?"

Charlotte nodded, and the gesture had tears spilling from her eyes to trail down her face. "As soon as I found out I had a sister, I wanted a relationship with you. That's why, when I found the letter in the things my mom left behind when she died, I quit the U.S. Marshals."

"I thought you quit because of what happened with Josie and Aaron and Whit."

Charlotte had had Whit help her fake Josie's death so that she could relocate her. Making Whit keep the secret from Aaron had destroyed their business partnership and their friendship.

"Making Whit keep that secret…" Charlotte let out a shuddery breath. "I understood what it cost him…when I had to keep secrets from you."

"It won't cost you what it cost Whit," Gabby assured her. "You won't lose me." She hugged Charlotte tightly. So tightly that their babies kicked in unison.

Charlotte laughed. "They're already getting to know each other."

"They're going to be close," Gabby said.

"And so are we now that we have no secrets." Charlotte squeezed her. "Thank you for forgiving me."

"It wasn't your fault," Gabby said. "It was his…" Her stomach churned as she thought of him and how little he'd really thought of her.

"He apologized to me," Charlotte said. "He wants to treat me as a daughter now. Not an employee. Aaron will continue to work for him and protect us all."

What about Whit? But only Whit could answer that.

"He wants to make up the past to me," Charlotte said. "And I'm going to stay here and give him the chance."

Her sister was more forgiving than she was.

"He wants to see you," Charlotte said.

To control and manipulate her, no doubt.

She shook her head, wanting to put off the moment when she had to face her father, and all his disappointment. "I need to get ready first."

"Sure, clean up."

She didn't need a shower. She needed to gather all her courage and resentment and tell her father that she was not one of his loyal subjects. She was his daughter, and he was finally going to treat her and her wishes with respect.

"Don't keep him waiting too long," Charlotte said. "He's been through a lot these past six months. Thinking you were dead…" Her voice cracked with emotion as she added, "…and that I was dead, really changed him."

"He's not going to fire you over my finding out that you're my sister?"

Charlotte shook her head. "No. He acknowledged me as his daughter."

Maybe that was because he was about to disown Gabriella for letting him worry for six months and for getting pregnant with the baby of a man who wasn't royalty—except for being a royal bodyguard.

Whit had risked his own life to protect Gabby. But before she could romanticize his actions, she had to remind herself that he'd only been doing his job. She meant nothing to him.

"I'm glad I'm not the only princess now," Gabriella said. "But be careful that he doesn't try to run your life as he has mine."

"Talk to him," Charlotte urged.

Was it possible to talk to someone who had never listened to her? She nodded, acknowledging that she had to at least try.

Charlotte smiled as she headed for the door. "I'll let him know that you'll be meeting with him soon."

As soon as she could gather her courage and control her anger over all the secrets he'd kept from her. To splash some water on her face, Gabby stepped into her bathroom and gasped in shock.

Scrawled across her mirror in scarlet red lipstick was a note even more ominous than the letter left under her pillow. "You should have stayed dead!"

Chapter Fourteen

"I want to see her now!" Prince Tonio Malamatos commanded Whit as he paced the front salon of the palace. It was the most public parlor, the one farthest from the royal quarters and the royals.

Whit's head was still pounding from his struggle with Zeke Rogers. But he wasn't above fighting another man, and this tall thin man would be easily beaten. If only Whit had that right...

Gabby carrying his child wasn't enough—not when she was still engaged to this man. An engagement he apparently had every intention of seeing through to his wedding day—even though his ex-fiancée had arrived at the palace with him. Damn Aaron for hurrying off to find Charlotte as soon as they arrived, leaving Whit alone to deal with this royal pain in the ass.

He wasn't the only one demanding to see

her. King Demetrios had also requested an audience with her, to extend his apologies for the behavior of his son, and, Whit suspected, to introduce her to his other son. The young man followed his father like a puppy, like the ex-fiancée followed Prince Malamatos. Whit had had other men follow them back to their rooms. Men he trusted stood guard to make sure they wouldn't leave their rooms undetected.

"She needs to rest and recover," Whit told the prince. "She's been through a lot."

King Demetrios had accepted that excuse the first time Whit had offered it, and he and his son had retired to the guest rooms King St. Pierre had offered them. Prince Malamatos was much more stubborn.

"Whose fault is that?" the woman asked, her tone as waspish as her thin face. Honora Del Cachon, with her pale face framed with thin, dark hair, was a brittle and bitter woman—some distant relative of the queen. The queen had already been dead when Whit started working for the king, so he'd never met her. But meeting this woman gave him some indication of what Gabby had dealt with, and how she'd grown up with disapproval and resentment and cruelty.

Whit was hurting too much and too tired

to worry about protocol. Hell, he didn't remember what she was anyways—a princess?
A duchess? He figured she was just a royal
bitch. "I could give you a list of names of men
who were trying to hurt her."

But still one name eluded him. He and
Aaron had found nothing of Zeke's—not even
his body. While they'd been searching the island, they had had the guards they trusted
searching Zeke's apartment. They had found
nothing there to indicate who had hired him—
if anyone even had. There had been nothing to
link him to anyone else. Maybe he had been
acting on his own—out of vengeance.

"You are not going to take any responsibility for the princess's condition?" the woman
demanded, her tone as imperious as the king's.

She was not a queen; Whit knew that much
about her. Obviously she did not realize that
herself. And how the hell did she know that
Gabby was pregnant?

Aaron had said that only he, Charlotte and,
damn it, the king knew.

"What do you mean?" he asked her.

"Are you not a royal guard?" the woman
said. "Is it not your duty to protect her?"

"I am her fiancé," Prince Malamatos declared. "I will protect her from now on."

"She's been hiding for six months," the

woman said, turning now on the man to whom she'd been engaged. "She does not want to marry you."

"She was frightened," the prince stubbornly defended Gabriella. "I will hire many royal guards, men who can be trusted, and she will feel safe in my palace."

"She is pregnant," the woman said, betraying that she did know a secret.

Prince Malamatos didn't react to her news; obviously it wasn't news to him. Who had already told him? This woman or Zeke Rogers?

"How do you know?" Whit asked her.

The woman's shoulders lifted in slight shrug. "I saw her and the one who looks just like her as they arrived," the woman explained. She leaned closer to Whit, as if ashamed that she was about to gossip. "They are both the king's daughters, you know. The queen, my dear cousin, revealed to me on her deathbed that they are both his children by a former mistress. He bought her Gabriella like one would buy a doll or a puppy."

The prince betrayed no surprise. Obviously he already knew that, too.

"Why are you really here?" he found himself asking the man. Did he want to marry Gabby or punish her for betraying him during their engagement? St. Pierre wasn't that far away in geography or culture from the places that practiced honor killings. Was Prince Malamatos's country such a place?

"That's impertinent of you," the prince replied. "But as I told you, I want to see my fiancée. I want to set a date for our wedding."

"You still want to marry her?" the woman asked. "Even though she is pregnant with another man's child." From the arch glance she cast at Whit, it was apparent she knew which man.

The prince shrugged. "To merge my country with the resources of St. Pierre, I will claim the royal bastard as my own. After all, I will be marrying a royal bastard."

Whit wasn't tired enough to ignore what the man said. Or maybe he was too tired to summon the control it would have taken him to ignore that comment. For he swung and smashed his fist into the prince's weak jaw.

The man crumpled to the ground, the woman screaming and hovering over him.

"Whit!" Aaron yelled as he walked back into the salon. "What the hell!"

"Did you hear what he said about the princess?" Whit demanded.

"It was all true," the woman replied. "You are a barbarian."

He was a man in love. But all he could offer

Gabriella was his protection, of her life and her reputation…

"The king wants to see you," Aaron told Whit.

Whit's stomach knotted with dread at the look on his friend's face. He couldn't meet his gaze. Obviously the king was furious with him. Someone must have told him about the baby.

"He's going to fire you for your impudence," the woman said.

If he was going to get fired for it, he might as well tell the king exactly what he thought of him and the way he'd treated the sweetest woman Whit had ever known. He stormed past Aaron, heading toward the king's private rooms.

GABBY ROSE UP on tiptoe and tried to scrub at the mirror with a tissue. She scrubbed so hard that the mirror actually cracked from the pressure she applied—and probably from age, as well. It was an antique with a gilded frame.

Perhaps she should have called Charlotte back and shown her the message on the mirror. But Gabriella had chosen to ignore it—at first. She'd showered and changed into a gown. Since it was evening, formal dress was protocol even if there hadn't been guests in the palace. Fortunately she'd found a dress with an empire waist and a skirt billowy enough for her pregnant belly. Wearing a tiara was also protocol, so she'd turned to the mirror in order to see where to pin the diamond-encrusted jewelry into her hair.

And she hadn't been able to ignore the message any longer. Because the shower steam had smeared the lipstick and sent it running down the glass in rivulets, Gabby couldn't see beyond it.

And she wasn't certain she wanted Charlotte to see it. The last time she'd shown her a threat, her bodyguard had whisked her away and they'd both disappeared for six months. Gabby wouldn't have minded going back to the orphanage, but she couldn't now that people knew she'd been there.

Was there any place for her to be safe? She thought of Whit's arms, wrapped tight around her, her head on his chest with his heart beating strong and steady beneath her ear. She would be safe with him—only with him.

The door creaked open, and she lifted her gaze to the mirror to see who'd come up behind her. Her heart filled with hope that it was Whit—that he was back and had come to see her the moment they had landed.

It was probably Charlotte though, prodding

her because she'd kept the king waiting too long. Keeping him waiting was never wise. But then she peered around the lipstick blocking the image in the mirror and realized that he would probably be waiting longer.

"Hello, Honora…" She turned to greet the woman holding a gun on her.

"You are not surprised to see me."

She gestured behind herself at the mirror. "I figured out that was your shade. It certainly isn't mine."

"Of course not," Honora snapped. "You wouldn't wear something so stylish."

"I was thinking…" Garish. But it wasn't wise to provoke the lunatic holding a gun on her. "…exactly that."

"You've always envied me," Honora said.

"I have…" Given her very little thought over the years. The queen's cousin had always been unpleasant to Gabby—even when they were children.

"You've always wanted what I have."

A nasty disposition? Dissatisfaction with everything in life? Hardly.

"That's why," Honora continued, "you had your father arrange your engagement to my fiancé. You have to have everything I have."

For years Gabriella had just thought her cousin was nasty; she hadn't realized that the woman was actually delusional and paranoid and possibly mentally ill. "I'm sorry…"

"You should be—you will be—for trying to ruin my life!" Honora raised the gun so that the barrel pointed at Gabby's heart.

"I'm sorry that my father manipulated all of us," Gabby said. "It was him. Not me. I didn't ask him to break my engagement to Prince Linus."

"You would have married that psychopath?"

She shouldn't throw stones, but Gabby wasn't about to offer her that advice. "I had no idea my father was going to arrange an engagement with Prince Malamatos."

"Of course you did," Honora scoffed. "Of course you put him up to it. And of course your father will give you whatever you want. He has spoiled you rotten, just as my cousin the queen complained."

Gabriella snorted in disgust. "The queen constantly complained."

"Do you blame her?" Honora asked, obviously outraged on her dead relative's behalf. "She was forced to raise her husband's bastard as her own. That was cruel."

No, how the queen had treated Gabriella had been cruel. She hadn't cared that she'd been an innocent child, unaware of her parents' duplicity.

"As cruel as it will be if you were to try to force Tonio to raise your bastard as his own."

"I wouldn't do that," Gabriella insisted.

"You won't have to," Honora said. "Tonio is an honorable man. He intends to claim your bastard, which is more than I can say for that barbarian that actually fathered your kid."

"Barbarian?"

"The American," she said, her lip nearly curling with disdain. "The golden-haired one. I can understand why you would bed him…" She gave a lusty sigh. "But you should have been more careful than to become pregnant with his child. But then, of course, your father was careless too when he got his mistress pregnant with first your sister and then you."

Apparently Gabriella had been the only one not privy to the secrets of her family. She pressed her palms to her belly in which her child moved restlessly. "I don't regret this baby."

"I regret you," Honora said. "I wished you had never been born. So I will fix that now." Her finger twitched along the trigger.

"You don't want to kill me," Gabby bluffed. "You just don't want me to marry Prince Tonio. And since I have no intention of doing that, there is no reason to hurt me." Or her child.

Honora chuckled bitterly. "You would be a

fool to break that engagement. Not only is he a handsome, powerful man but he is the only one who'd be willing to marry a woman carrying someone else's bastard."

"I don't want to marry anyone," Gabby insisted. She wanted to punch this woman in the face for the horrible name she kept calling her baby. She drew in a deep breath and reminded herself that Honora was sick.

"You're lying!"

She expelled the shuddery breath she'd just drawn. "Yes. I am."

The gun trembled in Honora's hand. "I knew you were lying. I knew you wanted Tonio— because he's mine!"

"He is yours—all yours," Gabby assured the deranged woman. "I don't want to marry *him*. But I do want to marry someone."

The woman stared at her through eyes narrowed with skepticism and faint curiosity. "Who do you want to marry?"

Gabby stroked her hands over her belly, and she couldn't stop her lips from curving into a wistful smile. "The father of my baby."

But Whit marrying her was about as likely as Gabriella being able to talk Honora out of shooting her. She had to try…getting through to Honora. She'd given up on Whit. He'd faced death dangling from a cliff, and even that close scrape hadn't lowered his guard enough for him to let his feelings out. Maybe he really didn't have any feelings—for her or anyone else.

"THAT BARBARIAN?" Honora scoffed. "He has nothing to offer you."

Whit couldn't argue with her—even if he dared let his presence be known to either woman.

He had been on his way to see Gabriella and say goodbye when he'd noticed that royal bitch slipping into Gabby's private rooms. His first thought had been to turn around and leave without saying goodbye. But then he'd noticed the glint of light off the metal object Honora gripped in her hand.

A knife? A gun?

She wasn't sneaking into Gabby's room for girl talk. For revenge for her broken engagement? Was she the one who'd paid Zeke to make sure Gabriella never returned to St. Pierre?

He slipped into the room behind her. But before he could grab her, she'd pulled the gun. If only it had been a knife…

He could have pulled his trigger and killed her before she got close to Gabby. But with the gun, even if he shot her, she might reflexively pull the trigger. She might kill Gabby—or the baby—even as she was dying.

"Whitaker Howell," Gabriella saying his name drew his attention back to her, "is twice the man that Tonio Malamatos is. I don't want your prince, Honora."

The woman gasped in shock and horror. "Do you really expect me to believe that you would prefer a bodyguard over a man who will soon rule his own country and, according to the deal he made with your father, this country, as well?"

If Malamatos thought King St. Pierre was about to step down as ruler of the country named for him, he had gravely misunderstood their deal. Or was that just the reason he'd given his crazy fiancée for breaking their engagement?

Maybe old Tonio had been afraid of telling the woman the truth—that he just didn't want to marry her. Whit opened his mouth to draw the woman's attention to him and away from Gabriella.

But then Gabby was speaking again. "Whit Howell is a hero," she said. "He was a hero during his deployments with the U.S. Marines, and he was a hero protecting his clients. And he saved my life more than once."

"Zeke Rogers assured me that no one would,"

Honora said. "I paid him a lot of money to make sure you would never return to St. Pierre."

"He died trying to do the job you hired him to do," Gabby said—with apparent sympathy for a man who'd intended to kill her.

How could she be that selfless? That good? Especially given how no one had ever given her the love and concern that she freely offered to everyone else. She was just innately good. More people like her were needed in the world—not fewer.

Honora shrugged off any responsibility. "Your barbarian killed him."

Zeke's death had been an accident. Whit had wanted him alive, so that he would be able to tell them who had hired him. But he'd pushed him too hard...

"Whit is not a barbarian," Gabriella said. "He's a good man."

How could she say that about him? How could she see in him what he had only seen in her?

"You really are in love with a bodyguard," Honora remarked as if horrified.

"Yes," Gabriella said—as if proud of the declaration.

Could she actually love him?

No. She was probably just trying to convince the crazy lady that she was no threat to her relationship with the prince. Gabriella St. Pierre was far smarter than anyone had given her credit for being—including this jilted fiancée.

"Then you're stupider than people think," the woman replied. "Your father will never approve. In fact he just fired the man."

Gabby gasped now. "He fired Whit?"

The woman uttered a cackle of pure glee. "Guess he didn't approve of the hired help getting his daughter pregnant."

King St. Pierre hadn't actually explained his reasons for terminating Whit's employment. He'd just bellowed that he was done here and had only hours to leave the palace and St. Pierre.

Honora was probably right that the man had wanted better for his daughter than a bodyguard. And he wasn't wrong. Her other fiancés had been able to offer her palaces and countries. Whit didn't even have a home to call his own.

Never had...

That was why he hadn't argued with King St. Pierre. He'd only nodded in acceptance and walked out. He'd figured it was for the best—for Gabriella and for their baby.

Whit couldn't give them what the prince

could. But he could give them what the prince couldn't: his protection. He lifted his gun.

But he had to get Gabriella's attention to let her know that she would need to get out of the way when bullets started flying. She needed to drop to the marble floor or jump into the marble tub. He had to make sure that neither she nor their baby was hit.

But Honora was still talking, still taunting Gabby with knowledge she must have gained from spreading money around to servants or from listening at doors herself. "And Howell packed his bags and left without ever bothering to come say goodbye."

"That's not true," he corrected the woman. "I came to say goodbye. But you first, Honora…" Hoping that the woman turned toward him, with her weapon, his finger twitched on the trigger.

He had to make this shot count. Had to kill her before she killed Gabby. And he had to make damn sure he didn't miss and kill the woman he loved himself.

Chapter Fifteen

"Stop!" Gabriella yelled but not at the woman who held the gun on her. "Don't shoot her!"

She had only just noticed Whit when, with his gun drawn, he'd stepped through her bathroom doorway. So she had no idea how long he had been standing there.

Long enough to realize that Honora was mentally ill?

Long enough to learn that Gabriella was hopelessly in love with him?

Whit held his fire—probably out of instinct more than his actually caring what she'd said. "You tell me to shoot on an airplane but not in your bathroom. Afraid I'll break the mirror and get seven years of bad luck?"

The mirror was already broken—the bad luck all hers. Or maybe not.

Honora swung toward him with her gun drawn.

"Don't shoot him, either," Gabriella said. "You don't want to kill him."

"Because you love him?"

"Yes," Gabriella said. "And because he's an amazing shot. He will kill you, and then you will never have a future with Prince Tonio."

"I have no future with him now!" Honora trembled with rage. But instead of firing at Whit, she turned back to Gabby. "Because of you!"

Gabby shook her head—as a signal for Whit, and Charlotte and Aaron who'd snuck into the room behind him, not to shoot Honora. "I don't want to marry your fiancé," she reiterated. "The only man I will ever marry is the man I love."

And that was what she had intended to tell her father when she met with him. Now she may never get the chance to talk to him.

"All I want is to marry the man I love," Honora said. The facade on her thin face cracked like the mirror behind Gabriella. "But he doesn't love me…" She lifted the gun again, but this time she pressed the barrel of it to her own temple.

"Don't!" Gabriella said. "Don't do it!"

Honora's finger trembled against the trigger as her whole body shook. "Why not? I have nothing to live for."

"What you feel isn't real love—real love is reciprocated."

Gabby needed to remind herself of that—

that what she felt for Whit wasn't real. It wasn't what Aaron and Charlotte had. She may have gotten pregnant the same night Charlotte had, but that was all their situations had in common.

While the woman appeared to contemplate Gabby's declaration, she was distracted enough that Whit reached out and snapped the gun out of her hand.

"Noooo…" Honora cried, and she crumpled into a ball on the floor.

Gabriella reached out and touched her hair; it was as brittle as the woman herself. "You'll be okay," she said. "We'll get you some help. It'll get better."

"I'm sorry," she said, her voice breaking with sobs. "So sorry…"

"Get her help," Gabby told the others.

"I'm not leaving you alone with her," Whit said, stepping closer as if he intended to step between them.

But Honora was no threat. With her arms wrapped tight around herself, she was barely holding herself together.

Outwardly Gabriella probably appeared calm. But inside, she was shaking as badly as her would-be killer. She realized she'd taken a risk in not letting Whit just shoot the woman.

But too many people had already died. She hadn't wanted anyone else to lose their life.

And although she and her baby had escaped harm, she was shaken at how close a call she'd had.

"I'll stay while you get help," Charlotte offered. "I'll make sure they're both okay." She looked at Gabby as if she knew that nerves and emotions swirled tempestuously beneath the surface. And she knew that Gabby needed Whit gone so that she wouldn't fall apart and fall at his feet, begging him to love her back.

"You need to talk to the king anyway," Aaron told Whit.

Had Honora been telling the truth? Had he been fired? And was he going to just leave without saying whatever he must have come here to say to her?

He walked out without a backward glance. And Gabriella's heart cracked like the mirror.

"I FIRED YOU," King St. Pierre reminded Whit of their conversation only an hour ago. "Then I told Aaron to make sure you had left my property. Instead he found you saving my daughter's life."

"She saved her own life." Because if he'd shot Honora as he nearly had, she might have fired, too. And if a bullet had struck Gabby or the baby...

The king's brow furrowed, as if he tried to fathom how the princess could have protected herself. "Did she use the maneuvers her sister taught her?"

So he really was claiming his oldest as his daughter, too, now.

"No, Gabby used her innate talent—the one no one taught her," Whit said and with a pointed stare at the king added, "and the one no one managed to destroy."

Anger flashed in Rafael St. Pierre's dark eyes. "What do you mean?"

"No matter how cruel your wife was to her or how disinterested you were, she never grew bitter or selfish," Whit said, amazed at the strength that had taken Gabriella, even as a child, to remain true to herself. "She stayed sweet and caring, and it was those qualities that saved her life. She talked Honora out of hurting her and out of hurting herself."

The king sucked in a breath of surprise. "Gabriella did that—on her own?"

Whit nodded. "Despite my interference, she calmed Honora down." He flinched as he remembered how the woman had reacted to his presence. Maybe if he'd stayed quiet, if he'd trusted Gabby to take care of herself, she would have reached the woman even sooner.

The king uttered a heavy sigh of regret. "Are you sure it was Honora who paid Zeke Rogers to kill Gabriella?"

"She confessed to all of it." Actually she had bragged about it, but he suspected now that that bravado was part of her illness.

Gabby had been right to save her. The woman could be helped, and he knew his sweet princess would make sure she got help.

The king stared at Whit. "You may need to testify to what you heard."

He nodded. "Fine." He wanted the woman put someplace where she couldn't hurt herself or anyone else again.

"So you will need to remain on St. Pierre until her trial."

"I thought you wanted me out of your country," Whit reminded him now.

"Perhaps I reacted before I had time to understand the situation."

The fact that Whit had gotten his daughter pregnant while she was engaged to another man, a man who was now really free and ready to commit to someone else—was that the situation the king had needed time to understand?

Whit needed more time because he still

didn't understand it, had no idea why Gabriella would even look at him much less let him touch her. Make love to her...

He had nothing to offer her. Nothing like her other fiancés. But maybe he had something...

Maybe he had the one thing no one else had ever given her...

"You have my permission to explain yourself," the king said, as if issuing a royal decree.

"You're not the one I need to explain myself to," Whit said, only just realizing himself what he had to say and to whom.

The king's face flushed with fury as he slammed his fist onto his desk. "If you intend to continue in my employ, you will damn well answer to me."

The fist pounding didn't intimidate Whit in the least. In fact it amused him how a grown man could act so like a spoiled child. "You already fired me."

"That was precipitous of me. If you explain yourself, I will reinstate you," the king said, offering another royal decree.

And Whit chose to ignore this one, too. "I'm not going to tell you what you want to hear," he said, "so you might as well fire me again. Or still."

"Young man—"

"You know what—it doesn't matter if you've fired me or not," he said. "I can't work for you any longer. I quit."

"What the hell are you doing?" Aaron asked the minute Whit slammed open the door and stalked into the hall. He must have nearly knocked his old friend over with the door, for Aaron had jumped back. "You can't just walk away from this job."

"I can't work for him." It didn't matter what King St. Pierre thought of Whit and what he had to offer his daughter. It mattered more to Whit what the king had never offered Gabby— his love or respect. And he couldn't work for a man so stupid and cruel.

"Why not?" Aaron asked. "You two are awfully alike. And I do mean awfully."

If he wasn't so damn tired—physically and emotionally—Whit might have swung his fist into the other man's face for uttering such an insult. "I am nothing like that man."

"You're both stubborn and selfish and think you're always right and you appoint yourself to decide what's right for other people."

Whit flinched at the anger and resentment in his friend's voice. Aaron might as well have physically struck him because the hit was that direct. And probably that accurate.

Maybe he'd been a fool to think that Aaron

could ever forgive him, that their friendship could ever be repaired after Whit had betrayed him.

"I thought you were done being mad at me."

"I am," Aaron said. "But if you leave here, *she* will never get over being mad at you."

"Gabriella?" Whit chuckled. "She just forgave the woman who tried to have her killed."

"Honora may have threatened her, but she never really hurt her," Aaron explained. "You've hurt her. I saw it on that cliff—when you wouldn't let her hug you. And I saw it in her rooms when you turned and walked away—like you're walking now."

He was actually tempted to run as he headed toward his room in the employee's wing. This time he would finally pack up his things. There was nothing for him here.

"I can't believe you're being so stupid," Aaron said, following him like a dog nipping at his heels. "You already know how hard it was to find a job like this but you just willingly gave it up."

"There are other jobs," he said. "Hell, I could re-enlist if I can't find anything else."

Aaron sucked in a breath of shock. "You'd go back to active duty?"

"Why not?"

"I can give you two reasons—Gabby and your baby," Aaron said. "You might be able to find another job, but you'll never find another woman who loves you like she does."

He had never found anyone who loved him at all—let alone like Gabby had claimed to love him. "She was just saying those things to Honora," he insisted, "to make the woman think she was no threat. To make her think she has no intention of marrying Prince Malamatos."

"You think she does intend to marry him?" Aaron asked.

He shrugged. "As his ex-fiancée said, the man's quite a catch. A real prince of a guy."

"She's crazy," Aaron reminded him, "and so are you if you walk away from a woman like Gabriella."

"You've thought me crazy before," Whit said with a shrug, as if his friend's opinion didn't matter. But it mattered a lot—especially that Aaron believed she loved him.

But then Aaron had never been the best judge of character—because, like Gabby, he always saw the best in everyone. Even Whit.

Conversely, Whit always saw the worst in everyone—even himself. Except for Gabby—because there was only good in her.

And if he was the man she and Aaron thought he was, he would walk away and give her a chance at the life she deserved—that she had been born to live.

"YOU FIRED the man who saved my life!" Gabby accused her father the moment she stepped inside his rooms.

His shoulders drooping, he sat behind the desk in his darkly paneled den. His hands cradled his head, as if he had a headache or was trying hard to figure something out. Veins popped on the back of his hands and stood out on his forehead. He looked stressed and weary, as if he'd aged years in the six months she and Charlotte had been gone.

Despite her anger and resentment with him, affection warmed her heart. No matter how he had treated her and those she cared about, he was her father and she loved him. She nearly opened her mouth to tell him so, but then he lifted his gaze.

Instead of looking at her face, he looked at her belly—at the child she carried. And she thought she glimpsed disappointment on his face.

That was all she had ever done with him and the queen. Disappoint them.

"Whitaker Howell quit," her father corrected her.

She shook her head. "I heard that you fired him."

"Perhaps," he admitted with a slight nod of acquiescence, "but then I gave him the chance to stay, and he chose to leave."

Of course he chose to leave. Now that she was safe, he had no reason to stay. He had done his job. And that was all she must have been to him.

She blew out a ragged breath of pain and regret that he hadn't tried to stay, that he hadn't at least tried to love her and their baby.

Take a risk on me...

She had risked everything—her heart, her future, her baby's future. And she'd lost him.

"But Prince Malamatos is here," the king continued. "He refuses to leave until he sees you and makes certain you have survived your ordeal."

"Ordeal?" she asked. "I hope you're talking about recent events and not the six most useful and productive months of my life."

"At the orphanage?" he asked, with a brow raised in skepticism. "I can't believe Charlotte sent you there to hide."

"I'm glad she did," Gabby said. "Otherwise I might have never learned the truth."

The king's mouth drew into a tight line of disapproval. Had he never intended to tell her the truth?

"I was referring to the country she sent you to," he clarified, "and how dangerous it is."

"Yet I was in no danger until everyone learned where I was." And then because she had to know, she asked him, "Would you have ever told me?"

"About your mother?" he asked and then uttered a heavy sigh. "I promised the queen that I would never..."

Because then Gabriella might have realized that it hadn't been her fault the woman hadn't loved her... The woman had been cruel right up until the end. "After she died, you could have told me."

He sighed again. "But your biological mother had already died, so there seemed no point in dredging up ancient history."

And probably his embarrassment over his affair with a con artist.

"No point in my getting to know my sister and my aunt?" Perhaps he hadn't wanted her to get to know and emulate two of the strongest women she had ever met—because then she wouldn't blindly obey him. His efforts to keep her ignorant had been futile. It didn't matter how short a time Gabriella had known them;

she was still going to emulate them. He was done controlling her life.

"We will discuss this another time," the king imperiously announced—which meant that he never intended to discuss it.

Because he had been wrong and would not admit it. And he compounded that arrogance when he continued, "You have kept your fiancé waiting long enough."

She shook her head. "Prince Malamatos is not my fiancé. He's yours. You chose him. You can marry him. I'm not."

"Gabriella!" The king shot up from his chair, anger turning his face a mottled red. "You are impudent."

"No," she said. "But I should have been before now. I should have made it clear to you that while you rule this country, you do not rule my life. I will make my own decisions from now on."

He pointed to her belly. "Being a single mother is what you choose?"

No. But she couldn't force the baby's father to love her. Too weary to deal with her father, she turned toward the door.

"Prince Malamatos will claim the baby."

"Like the queen claimed me?" she asked. "I won't take the risk of his treating my baby the way I was." She wanted to give this child two parents who loved him. And Honora had already shared Tonio's opinion of Gabby's baby; it was an inconvenience but he would adjust to include it in his plan of ruling two countries.

"You need to talk to your fiancé," he persisted, "and let him discuss your future."

Another man telling her what to do? Disrespecting what she wanted?

She shook her head. "No one talked to me about this engagement. You didn't. Tonio didn't. I don't even know the man. Why would I even consider marrying him?"

"You have always been so naive and idealistic, Gabriella, believing in fairy tales of love and happily-ever-after," her father said with a snort of disdain. "That is why I have had to make your decisions for you."

She turned back to him and met his gaze and decided to share with him the real struggle between them. "I want to hate you, Father."

He sucked in a breath, as if she had struck him in the stomach. Or perhaps the heart…

"But I can't," she assured him. "I feel too sorry for you."

Pride lifted his chin. "You feel sorry for *me?*"

She gave him a slight smile, one full of pity for all he had missed experiencing. "Because you have never been in love."

"What makes you think that?" he asked, but he didn't rush to deny her allegation either.

"Because if you had ever felt love—true love—yourself," she explained, "you would not try to force me to marry someone I don't love…"

He studied her face as if he were truly seeing her, as if he had really heard what she'd told him. Perhaps it was a first for them. Then he cleared his throat and asked, "You love Whitaker Howell?"

"Yes."

He dropped heavily back into his chair. "He did not stay," he said, as if warning her. "He did not fight for your hand in marriage."

She flinched as if he'd struck her now. And he had aimed directly for her heart. "It doesn't matter whether he stays or goes." It did not change the fact that she loved him. That her heart would belong to him and no other—certainly not any fiancé her father found her.

The king chuckled. "You were never able to lie. I could always tell whenever you tried to be less than truthful with me."

"If only I had been able to tell the same," she murmured. It would have saved her from all the years she'd spent in the dark, oblivious to all his secrets and lies.

He heard her. His skin flushed again. But he

ignored her comment and continued, "You are lying now. Whether Whitaker Howell stays or leaves, it matters to you. Greatly."

She shrugged. "But *I* don't matter to him. Even you said that he wouldn't fight for me."

"He fought for you," the king reminded her. "He fought to save your life. He fought to find you these past six months."

"He was just doing his job," she told him, as she'd kept telling herself.

The king shook his head. "Not just his job. He cannot say enough good things about your caring and your selflessness."

"He can't?" Hope flickered, warming her heart.

The king grinned and nodded. "He loves you."

Gabby's head pounded with confusion. "Then why would he leave?"

"Because you are a princess and he is a bodyguard. He thinks he has nothing to offer you." The king's brief grin faded. "And he's right."

"If he loves me," she corrected her father, "he has *everything* to offer me." Because love was all she had ever wanted...

She turned toward the door. But her father made a sound, something akin to a sniffle, that had her turning back to him. He lifted his gaze to hers, and his eyes were wet with emotion. "I have loved you," he said, as if he'd read her mind, "I have always loved you."

She had waited her entire life for her father to declare his feelings for her. But suddenly how he felt didn't matter so much to her anymore. "I have always loved you, too," she said. It was why she had always tried so hard to please him. But now she wanted to please herself. So she headed for the door.

"He's probably already gone," her father warned her.

Probably. But she would not be deterred now. "Then I will find him."

"It took us six months to find you," he said. "It'll take you much longer to find Whitaker Howell if he doesn't want to be found."

Chapter Sixteen

"Stop!"

The shout reverberated off the walls of the corridor leading away from the wing of employees' rooms. Just as he had earlier, Whit automatically obeyed. He froze in place, his suitcase clutched in his hand.

"That's the second time today that you've told me to stop," he said, turning toward her.

Gabriella's eyes were bright with anger—an anger so intense that she trembled with it. She wasn't the only angry one.

He kept flashing back to what had happened with Honora, and in his head, it ended differently—it ended badly, with Gabriella bleeding on the floor. "You could have gotten yourself killed the first time."

"She wasn't going to hurt me," Gabby insisted.

He dropped the suitcase, so he could reach out and shake some sense into her. But he only closed his hands around her bare shoulders. Then he had to fight the urge to pull her closer. And never let her go...

But first he had to deal with other emotions—with the helplessness and fear that had raged through him when he'd stood in the doorway watching that madwoman threaten the mother of his unborn baby—the woman he loved.

"She hired Zeke and those other men to kill you," he reminded her. "She didn't intend to just hurt you—she intended to kill you!"

"She intended for them to kill me," she agreed—maddeningly. "Them—not her. She isn't capable of personally killing someone—it made it real for her. And she realized that it was wrong."

He tightened his grip on her shoulders, tempted again to shake her. She was so sweet and innocent, so hopeful that there was goodness in everyone. "Murder is wrong no matter if you do it yourself or hire someone else to do it for you."

"She's not well," Gabby defended the woman who'd nearly killed her.

"And neither are you," he said, "for taking the risk you did with yourself and our baby."

"Our baby?" she asked, her eyes widening with shock. "You're claiming him now?"

He narrowed his eyes at her. "I already have. I never doubted that he was mine."

She narrowed her eyes back at him. "Not for a moment? Not even when you met Dr. Dominic?"

"I hate that guy," he admitted, barely resisting the urge to grind his teeth with the jealousy that shot through him. He had never been jealous before—had never cared enough to be jealous of anyone else.

Her lips curved into a slight smile. "Of course," she agreed. "He moved to a third-world country to offer his services free to take care of orphaned children. He's a horrible, horrible person."

A grin tugged at Whit's lips, but he fought it. He knew how ridiculous he was being. "Yes, a horrible person."

"And ugly, too," Gabby said, her brown eyes warming and twinkling as she teased him back.

His heart pounded harder with excitement; the woman attracted him more strongly than any other woman ever had.

"I'm glad you see that, too," he said.

"I always thought he was hideous," she said with a girlish giggle.

"A regular Dr. Jekyll and Mr. Hyde," Whit added.

Her amused smile faded. "No. That would be you."

He chuckled at the illogical insult. "How's that?"

"One minute you're this sweet, funny guy and the next you're acting like my father," she accused him, "bossing me around and unilaterally making decisions that affect both of us."

"What decisions have I made?" he asked. She and Aaron had both really read him wrong. But then it wasn't their fault when he'd been afraid to make himself clear before now.

She pointed a trembling finger at the suitcase. "You decided to quit. To just take off and leave me and your baby behind without another thought."

He chuckled at how wrong she was. "You're more like your father than I am," he argued. "You're the one who keeps shouting out orders at me."

"Is that why you quit?" she asked. "You're sick of getting bossed around?"

Aaron had already told him he was a damn

fool for quitting. But Whit didn't want to do this as her father's bodyguard—as a member of the staff or even as the baby's father.

"By your father, yes," Whit agreed. "But I think I'm getting used to your bossing me around."

He slid his hands from her shoulders, down her bare arms to grasp her hands. Once their fingers were entwined, he dropped to his knees. "And just so you know...I could never not think about you. For the past six months every thought I had was about you."

She sucked in a sharp breath, pulled her hands free of his, and touched her belly.

"Are you okay?" he asked. "You're not having contractions or anything?"

She bit her lip.

He pressed his hands over hers on their baby. "Gabby, are you all right?"

She nodded. "I just..." Her voice cracked with the tears that pooled in her eyes. "I can't believe this... I thought you were leaving. Or that you might already be gone. And I didn't know if I could find you...if my father was right and you didn't want to be found..."

She was chattering as nervously as she did for reporters until Whit reached up and pressed a finger across her lips. "Shhh..."

She stared down at him, her eyes so wide with fear and hopefulness.

"I had no intention of leaving without you," he said, still on his knees. "I know you never wanted to come back here. That's why I quit. I didn't want to force you to live where you've never been happy."

Now the tears fell with such intensity she trembled as uncontrollably as she had when they'd been freezing in the sea. "I will be happy wherever you are."

"So you'll marry me?"

She threw her arms around his neck and clung to him, too choked with sobs to answer him.

Was she saying yes? Or sorry? He couldn't understand her. "Gabriella?"

She loved him; he knew it. But was love enough to overcome their differences?

"You haven't answered me," Whit said, his voice gruff with impatience as he closed the door to her suite behind them.

"I will answer your question," she said, "after you answer mine."

"What question can you have?" he asked. "I thought my proposing said everything."

Of course he did. He was a man. He didn't

understand that she needed more of an explanation. That she needed more...

"Why did you propose?" she asked, her heart beating frantically with equal parts hope and dread. "You haven't told me yet *why* you proposed." But she had a horrible suspicion she knew the reason, that she carried it in her belly.

His brow furrowed with confusion. "I thought my reason was obvious."

She touched her belly. The baby moved restlessly inside her. "I hope it isn't..."

His mouth dropped open with shock, and then his jaw tightened and a muscle twitched in his cheek. He was obviously offended and angry. "You think the only reason I want to marry you is because you're pregnant?"

That was her fear—that he only wanted her for what she was—the mother of his child—and not for who she was.

Too choked with fear to answer him, she simply nodded.

He chuckled. "You and I are quite the pair, aren't we?"

"What do you mean?"

"I would have told you how I felt earlier," he said, "but I didn't think you could love me."

Shock and sympathy for the pain that flashed

across his handsome face had her gasping. "Why not?"

His broad shoulders lifted and dropped in a heavy shrug. "I didn't think I had anything to offer you."

"Didn't you hear what I told Honora about you?" she asked, pretty certain that he had been there at least long enough to have over-heard some of what she'd told the deranged woman. "About all the reasons I love you?"

He nodded. "I heard, but I thought you were lying—that you were tricking her into think-ing that you didn't want her fiancé."

"You thought it was all a ploy? Everything I said to her?" Was it that he thought that lit-tle of himself or that much of her? "You think I'm that smart?"

"I know you're that smart," he said. "And you're loving and caring and forgiving. You're so damn beautiful inside and out that I couldn't even believe you were real. I thought you were just some fairy-tale princess until that night…"

Her face got hot with embarrassment. She had been unbelievably bold that night. He had tried to be all business—just a royal body-guard. But she had undressed in front of him…

"I'm talking about earlier that night," he said, as if he'd read her mind. Maybe he had noticed that all her skin had flushed with desire and her pulse was leaping in her throat. "About when you got so angry you actually pounded on me."

She laughed. "You like abuse?"

"I like everything about you. Your sweetness and your fire. Your patience and your passion..."

"Like?" she asked. "I need more to say yes." She needed love.

"I love you with all my heart," he said. "That's the only reason I want to marry you." He laid his hand on her belly. "This baby is just a bonus—like the prize in a box of Cracker Jack."

"Cracker Jack?"

"I forget that you're not American," he said. "Cracker Jacks are—"

"I know what Cracker Jacks are." She wrinkled her nose at his less than romantic compliment. "Sticky popcorn."

"Sweet." He leaned down and brushed his mouth across hers. "And I love sweets..."

"And I love you," she said. She lifted his hand from her stomach to her arm and then she squeezed his fingers together. "Pinch me to prove this isn't just a dream."

He moved his hand from her arm to her butt and pinched.

She squealed—with shock and delight. Then she reached around and pinched his butt.

He laughed out loud. "I can't believe this is real, either," he said. "You make me happier than I thought it was possible to feel. You make me *feel*."

And so many people had warned her that he couldn't—that the man didn't have a heart. But as his arms closed around her, she laid her head on his chest and heard his heart beating strong and fast. For her...

His hands cupped her face and tipped it up for his kiss. His lips brushed across hers. But then he deepened the kiss. His tongue slid inside her mouth, tasting and teasing her.

Gabby didn't want to be teased anymore. She wanted to make love to the man she loved. So she unbuttoned his shirt and unclasped his belt. Whit helped her discard his clothes. Then he reached for her and the zipper at the back of her gown. He fumbled with the tab before tugging it down. Her dress slid down her body—leaving her naked but for a bra that barely covered her full breasts and a thin strip of satin.

He did away with her underwear, too, and then—despite her extra weight, he easily lifted and carried her to the bed. "You are even more beautiful now than you were that night," he said, his hands stroking over her more generous curves.

"I'm huge," she said, pursing her lips into a pout.

He kissed her mouth. "You're beautiful." He kissed her cheek. "Breathtaking…" He kissed her neck.

She moaned as desire quickened her pulse so that it raced. And her skin tingled.

"You're beautiful," she said.

With his shock of blond hair and dark eyes, he was beautiful—and strong with muscles rippling in his arms and chest. And his back.

She dug her fingers in, clutching him close. "I am so in love with you." She had fallen for him at first sight and then she had fallen harder and deeper the more she'd gotten to know him. "You are an amazing man."

He touched her intimately, stroking her until she writhed beneath him. Pressure wound tightly inside her, making her body beg for release.

He lowered his head and kissed her breasts, tugging one nipple between his lips. He nipped gently at it.

And she came, screaming his name.

The man gave her pleasure so easily—so generously. She pushed him back onto the mattress and reciprocated. Her lips moved from his mouth, down his throat, over his chest. And lower. She loved him with her mouth, until he tangled his fingers in her hair and gently pulled her away.

"You're killing me," he said, his chest rising and falling as he struggled to catch his breath. "I can't take any more."

"You're going to have to get used to it," she warned him. Because she intended to spend the rest of her life loving him.

Whit couldn't believe how happy he was—how happy Gabriella made him. He wrapped his arms around her, holding her close as he rolled her onto her back.

She arched her hips. "Make love to me," she said, bossing him again.

And he loved it.

He groaned, his arms shaking as he braced himself on the bed and gently pushed himself inside her. But she tensed and gripped his shoulders.

"Stop!"

Sweat beaded on his upper lip, as he struggled for control. It reminded him of that night they had first made love—when he had discovered that she had never made love to another man before him. She hadn't told him to stop that night, though. She'd begged him to continue—to make love to her. And then she'd moved beneath him, taking him deep inside her.

"Why do I have to stop now?" he asked, gritting his teeth with the effort to control his desires. "Is the baby all right?"

"The baby is fine," she assured him. "But you shouldn't be."

"I'm damn well not fine," he said. "I want to make love to my fiancée."

"I am not your fiancée yet. I didn't answer your question," she reminded him. "I asked you why you asked. But I never answered you."

He tensed. "You told me you loved me, too." But she had never told him yes.

"But I haven't accepted."

"Why not?" Had she changed her mind? Did she think that love wasn't enough to overcome their different upbringings?

"I didn't have the chance yet," she said with a teasing smile.

The woman infuriated him and fascinated and captivated him.

"So what is your answer to my proposal?" he asked. "Will you marry me?"

"Of course I will marry you," she said, as if he'd been silly to worry. "I can't wait to be your wife."

He breathed a ragged sigh of relief. "And I can't wait to be your husband."

"Now," she said, "make love to your fiancée."

He chuckled. "You are getting really comfortable bossing me around."

She smiled. "Do you mind?"

He thrust gently inside her. "We want the same things," he said.

"Each other..." She moaned and arched, taking him deep inside her, as she raked her nails lightly down his back. She met his every thrust, moving in perfect rhythm with him.

She came, her body squeezing him tightly as pleasure rippled through her. And her pleasure begot his. The pressure that had built inside him exploded as he came.

"Gabriella!" His throat burned from shouting her name. He dropped onto his back next to her and wrapped his arm around her, holding her close to his side. "Now that I've made love to my fiancée, I can't wait to make love to my wife. We need to get married as soon as possible."

Then he needed to find a job and a house—someplace safe enough for him to protect a princess and a royal heir.

"I want to get married here," she said.

He sighed, hating that he was already unable to give her what she wanted. "I don't think your father will agree to that."

"I think he will," she said, "and I think he'd like you back working for him."

"I don't care what he wants," Whit said. After the way he'd treated his daughter, the man deserved little consideration for his feelings. But then Whit remembered how much the man had emotionally and physically suffered the past six months. "I care what you want. And you don't want to live here. You didn't even want to come back here."

"I didn't want to come back and marry a strange prince," she explained. "But I don't mind living here. No matter how much time I spent in boarding schools growing up, this was still my home."

"I never had a real home," he admitted.

"You do," she said. "With me and our baby."

"We're a family," he said. "But we need a home—one where I can keep you both safe."

"I think that home should be here," she said, "with Aaron and Charlotte and even my father…" She looked up at him, as if she held her breath waiting for his decision.

He could keep his wife and child safe here—especially with Aaron and Charlotte's help. "Are you sure this is what you want?"

She smiled. "Our baby growing up with Aaron and Charlotte's?"

"They're staying here?"

"Charlotte wants to get to know the king as her father. He asked her to stay—not as employee but as his daughter. I want to live with my sister. I want my baby to know his aunt and cousin."

She painted a pretty picture for Whit—not just of a home but of an extended family, as well.

"They say it takes a village to raise a child," he remarked.

"We have a country."

He grinned. "We have more than I ever believed I would have…because of you."

"We have happily-ever-after," she said. "Like a real fairy tale."

"And I have my real fairy-tale princess."

It was a dream—one he never would have dared to dream—but it came true anyway. And his happy present and future made him think of his past and someone who'd had to give up her home and her family or lose her life.

He hoped she'd found a new home. A new family and the happiness he had.

CHARLOTTE WAS HAPPY—happier than she'd thought possible as she lay in her fiancé's arms, listening to his heart beat strong and steady beneath her cheek.

But one thing marred her happiness and kept her from sleeping peacefully…

A man had killed trying to find out where a witness was. Like Zeke Rogers, he'd been paid. They had found out who'd hired Zeke, but she had yet to find out who had hired her former partner to locate Josie Jessup.

No one but she, Aaron, Whit and Gabriella knew where JJ was. But it worried her that someone else out there knew the woman was alive and was determined to find her. And Charlotte didn't even dare try to contact Josie to warn her. Because whoever wanted to find her knew that Charlotte was the one who'd hidden her. They were undoubtedly waiting for her to lead them right to Josie.

And only the devil knew what they intended to do when they found her. Kill her?

* * * * *

LET'S TALK
Romance

For exclusive extracts, competitions
and special offers, find us online:

- 📘 facebook.com/millsandboon
- 🐦 @MillsandBoon
- 📷 @MillsandBoonUK

Get in touch on 01413 063232

For all the latest titles coming soon, visit
millsandboon.co.uk/nextmonth